Angry Night Flower
Press

CONTENT WARNING

This book contains graphic violence including people being burnt alive, coarse language, sexual assault, human sacrifice with depictions of hangings and torture, parental death, sexual content, scenes of domestic violence, and mentions of rape, past trauma and suicide.

Some contents within this book may be triggering or disturbing for some readers.
Reader discretion is strongly advised.

All characters depicted herein are over 18 years of age.

To everyone stuck in the dark, remember,
at the edge of darkness there is light.

CHAPTER ONE
ELIANA

No sane person would be caught dead out after dark in Datura unless they had a death wish. That's what lurks in the shadows of this small town: a slow and painful death.

Yet here I am, heading down the labyrinth of alleyways that snake around the town, waiting to lure their next victim into their meandering and senseless turns. My heart is practically vibrating, trying to rid itself from my chest as I walk down the dimly lit streets. The air feels damp and foreboding, as if trying to warn people of the dangers lurking around the town. Everyone has already locked themselves inside their homes.

It's late. Too late.

The sun has dropped behind the buildings, beckoning the darkness. The fiery orange and deep magenta remnants of light mockingly dance off in the distance, safety slipping away with each step I take. I try to keep my breathing as steady as possible, but I can feel the drum of my heart in every inch of my body. The flickering street lights that jut out from the buildings over the alleyways send an ominous shiver down my spine as I try to get home quickly.

The chilly air sweeps around me, whipping my short blonde hair into my face. My nails scrape against my skull, pushing my hair out of my eyes, and the bottles clang together in the bag resting in the crook of my elbow. I wrap my arms tighter around my body, hugging the bottles closer to my chest through the plastic and quickening my pace. It's unseasonably cold for this time of the year.

The beautiful, old buildings surrounding me showcase artisanal craftsmanship that would be lost in a modern world where ease and efficiency are prioritised over art. These structures are rich with history, from the arching windows clad with delicate iron to the deep, burnt clay brick facades with imposing transom windows above the doorways adorned with protective runes. If only they could speak and share the secrets they hold within. I'm quietly glad our government hasn't bothered expanding the town. I often wonder if they would keep the same beautiful architecture of their forefathers or if they would opt for something more modern—modern meaning boring, quick and cost-effective to build. Even if the lack of expansions results in the citizens of Datura living on top of one another and a town that sometimes feels like it's ready to burst at the seams.

As the darkness engulfs everything in its path, that beauty and wonder turn menacingly dark. The arch windows are black and reflective, giving the impression that someone—or, more likely, some*thing*—is following you.

And that something following you is hunting you.

The thought sends my heart spiralling, every nerve in my body going on high alert. I silently send a prayer to

Achel and Vid, the gods of life and death. Their temple sits primarily empty in the centre of town—except for those few devoted worshipers who still believe the merciless gods watch over them and will keep them safe. I have long since stopped believing in such higher powers. After all, they have never answered my prayers in the past. Yet here I am, sending them a silent prayer to protect me.

My reflection catches my attention in the window. High-waisted jeans that hug the curves of my body and a black crop top expose a sliver of my midriff. This morning, I felt sexy and confident as I dressed for my job interview at a trendy department store, just another in the long line of meaningless jobs I've had in the last three years.

But now that bit of extra skin makes me feel naked, my mind hyper-focused on every inch of exposed flesh, of the wind, gently licking at it and taking my scent away. Sucking in a lungful of damp air, I try to calm my breathing, but it comes out rough and short. Anxiety grips tightly around my lungs, squeezing out all the air. I try to shake the feeling and continue down the meandering curve of alleyways that snake around Datura, all of which double back on themselves, ready to trap and confuse someone off their guard.

I should have grabbed a jumper, I think with a shudder. But when I left the house this morning, it was sunny and warm. Plus, I didn't intend to be out after dark. No one ever intends to be out after dark. The light over me flickers ominously; if I were a superstitious woman, I would take it as a sign. However, I know our town is old, and maintenance isn't high on the government's list.

The alleyways always seem to flood in the evening, and the lights overhead flicker with an ominous sense, some barely alive, others completely burnt out. Not that it matters too much to anyone else because they're all safe in their homes, and not one of them would notice or care.

Besides, witches, vampires and werewolves are only stories meant to scare children. Nothing terrible will happen if you walk under a ladder or pass a black cat. Throwing salt over your shoulder just creates a mess to clean up later.

Though, I would much rather run into a fictitious vampire or werewolf in these dark alleyways than the very real monsters lurking after dark.

Flesh-Hunters.

Don't think about it. Don't think about it. I shake my head aggressively, trying to rid myself of the thought before it can embed itself in my mind. As the sun sets over our town every night, the Flesh-Hunters crawl out of whatever hole they live in to hunt for their prey. But there are far worse monsters out there, and not just those living in the forest surrounding our town like an inescapable ring of fire. So, although we're completely locked away from the rest of the world, the woods surrounding our town filled with deadly creatures straight from your nightmares, we're doing alright. We've got electricity to light our homes and power our TVs, to which creative hands animate movies and TV programs for entertainment, but most importantly, we've got gin and waffles.

I try to think of something else—anything else—as I hold my bag of liquid gold closer to my chest. But the idea of being hunted by a Flesh-Hunter has already invaded my thoughts. Memories I've tried to suppress threaten to paralyse my body. I've encountered a Flesh-Hunter on two separate occasions, and I have tried very hard to block those traumatic nights of witnessing my loved ones die at those monsters' knife-like arms and razor-sharp teeth. I was lucky to escape with my life, and since then, I have been painstakingly cautious about not being caught out after dark.

If it were not for the ravenous dreams that claw at my subconscious, demanding to be seen and heard, I would not need to reach for the bottle of gin night after night. Those memories that replay in my dreams eat away at any scrap of happiness I have left.

After my spectacularly horrible job interview—which I am sure I won't get because I stumbled over most of the questions—I decided to replenish my stock at The Bottle-O. I would have made it home with plenty of time too. However, between the dramatically embarrassing interview and one of those insatiable memories still clawing at the back of my skull, I needed the numbness of the liquor too much to wait until I got home. So, I sat in one of the littered gutters, drowning in self-pity and staring at a wall covered with missing person posters from families and loved ones who still carry too much hope that those lost will return safe and whole.

I greeted the gin's burn and the rush it sent to my head, driving away those memories. Still, when the alcohol hit my empty stomach, the buzz turned my sense of direction into a mess.

Usually, I can navigate the winding alleyways, but tonight I feel so lost as if someone has spun the buildings around me, and now they're all out of order like I am stuck in a labyrinth. My stomach tightens at the thought of being alone in the dark, and the lump in my throat forces my breathing to come in quick gasps.

A structure in front of me splits the road in two separate directions. The graffitied building is littered with photos of missing people and prayers to Achel and Vid for their safe returns. The buzz in my brain has me second-guessing which path I need to take.

Left.

I am confident in my decision as I inspect the two options. I let out a deep sigh and take another swig straight from the bottle. There is little to enjoy in this godsforsaken town, but at least they know how to make good gin. As I start towards the road, a rasping voice catches my attention, so quiet that I brush it off as just the wind blowing through the buildings.

But the night is still.

I frown down at the bottle. *How much have I drunk?* Rubbing my eyes with the back of my hand, surely smudging my mascara, I hear that voice whisper again. "*Run,*" it breathes.

I look over my shoulder, trying to figure out where it is coming from. But I am alone. I haven't gotten far, still within the town's business district, but I am the only fool left wandering the streets. All the surrounding buildings are locked up for the night, and the darkness has consumed them.

"*Run,*" the voice pleads again. And again. And again. The sound circles my head like a buzzard tormenting its prey, getting louder and louder with each imploring call. It cannot be the wind, not with the way its voice grows more desperate as it reverberates around me. Not to mention that there isn't even a wisp of breeze, as if the air itself is holding its breath.

Spinning on my heel to find the source of the voice, I stumble over my feet, falling into the hard wall. The grit of the bricks digs into my arm, grazing my skin. The bottles clink against each other in the bag as I press my hands over my ears. *It's all in your head.*

My heart stutters, my breath hitches and my back seizes up with a familiar, inescapable fear taking over. I drop into a squat, discarding the empty bottle of gin. The glass clinks across the cobblestone and echoes around me. Cracking open a fresh bottle and taking a large swig, the liquor burns down my throat, warming my belly, and I bite back the bile that threatens to come back up because of too much alcohol and not enough food.

The bottle freezes mid-air. My arm refuses to lift it an inch further, the rim resting on my bottom lip as a guttural clicking sound echoes down the deserted alleyway.

My blood turns cold, and my palms sweat, the bottle shaking against my lips. An unnaturally tall, slender body stalks slowly out of the darkness. Its attention is fixated on me, its dark, lifeless face propped on a spindly, spine-like neck. Two slits for a nose and a harsh line for a mouth, stretching from where one ear would be to the other. My eyes zero in on its arms, long and slender, ending in lethal blades rather than hands.

A Flesh-Hunter.

One of the very real nocturnal monsters that lurk in the shadows and will kill anything it comes across.

CHAPTER TWO
ELIANA

I can't move. My heart is pounding so wildly that I am sure the Flesh-Hunter can sense exactly where I am, but I can't move. Fear has my feet frozen in place.

This is where I am going to die.

If only it would be a quick and painless death. But no, Flesh-Hunters pin down their prey with their large bodies and, using their incredibly sharp-bladed arms, slowly slice off the skin one piece at a time, devouring each portion before going for the next. You're still alive, feeling every slice of your skin as it's peeled off, hearing the sickeningly wet sound of being consumed.

The rotten stench of putrefaction and decay fills my lungs as the monster takes a tentative step forward. Memories flash before me, mixing with the liquor in my stomach. *I'm going to be sick. I'm going to pass out. I don't want to be eaten alive!* My brief training as a medic before I realised I was in no way suited or stable enough for that field of work comes crashing back to me.

You must lose about 40 percent of your blood to die from blood loss, I recall. The Flesh-Hunters are methodical in the way they attack. They keep you alive until they have consumed every inch of your flesh, leaving nothing but a bloody-skinned carcass for the rats and other vermin to devour.

Most people who die from Flesh-Hunter attacks are awake, feeling everything until their brain processes the immense pain and starts misfiring electrical impulses, sending the body into shock. If—or when—this happens, the brain can become so overwhelmed that it shuts itself down in self-preservation. Thankfully, the person will then lose consciousness.

Despite their debilitated, skeletal bodies, covered in reddish-brown leathery skin, they are strong and fast when they attack, leaving us no chance to fight them off.

Flesh-Hunters know they are the apex predator. They'll let you run. Make you feel like you've escaped, giving you a sense of safety, making you think you've cheated death. And then, when you're full of hope, they strike—pressing you down on the cold, wet ground, slowly slicing your flesh from your body like a hot knife through butter. Some scholars have theorised the chase, that spark of hope, makes us more appealing and tastes better.

"Run!" the voice hisses again, seemingly coming from directly behind me. I snap my head around to find the culprit, but instead of a person standing behind me, I find nothing but emptiness. I take a deep breath, willing my feet to move, and straighten myself on shaking legs. Keeping my back pressed against the building, I force myself to breathe slowly through my nose as I inch along the wall back the way I came. A shiver runs down my spine, and my anxiety crushes against my chest like a boa constrictor. Another deep, hollow, clicking vocalisation reverberates from behind me. "Fuck," I mutter the word on a shaky breath as

tears prick at my eyes. I clutch the bag of gin bottles to my chest, trying to stop them from rattling in my trembling hands.

I reluctantly turn my attention away from the Flesh-Hunter before me to confirm my worst fear. A tear slips free and down my cheek as another monster starts its languid stalk up the alleyway.

There's no way I am going to get out alive, I think. But I'm stubborn. Aggressively, I wipe the tears away. *I've fought too long and hard to let these monstrosities get an easy dinner. If they want to kill me, they'll have to fucking work for it.* I launch forward, running towards the fork in the road, before darting down the right alleyway. My legs feel heavy as my feet pound against the pavement, and my breath is caught in my chest. *Faster. Must go faster.* The chant replays in my mind repeatedly as I hold the bag close to my chest. Willing my legs to move, I squeeze my eyes shut and force lungful after lungful of air down my throat. I need to remain calm to think clearly, but the adrenaline and the buzz from the gin have me in a spin. My legs ache, and a stitch pains my stomach and chest before my vision blurs. I whip my head around. I know it's foolish to think I've outrun them, but there's a sliver of hope when I see I am once again all alone. Rounding the corner into another—thankfully empty— alleyway, each step fills me with more and more promise. Maybe the third time is the charm. I might get out of this gut-wrenching situation alive ... again.

How much luck can one person possess? I wonder as I press my body against the cool brick wall, trying to catch my breath. The bag hanging by the crook of my arm clinks loudly against the wall, but I barely hear it over the beating of my heart.

I shouldn't stop. The Flesh-Hunter will already be

closing in. I can hear their stagnant footsteps on the damp ground. *They've tracked my scent or the rapid beating of my heart.* I push the thought from my mind. *I've got to keep moving.* Pressing my palms against the brick, I push off running. I look around, trying to figure out where I am, and realise I'm heading back towards the town centre.

At the heart of Datura is a singular oak tree. The buildings were constructed in concentric circles around that tree. The structures in those smaller rings are for commercial and government use, all indubitably locked by now—their big, heavy wooden doors barred to those outside. The exits are surrounded with ancient markings; legend has it that when the town was built, a magician carved the runes into each doorframe to ward off the Flesh-Hunters from entering the buildings. My father, a logical man, told me it was all a load of shit and that the Flesh-Hunters couldn't enter the buildings because they didn't have hands. Bullshit or not, the ancient runes always made me feel safer when locked behind those large wooden doors, and I am sure the rest of Datura's population feels the same.

The temple may be unlocked. I can hide in there until morning.

That wishful thinking gets the adrenaline pumping again, and I push myself to go faster still. The temple of Achel, the God of Life, and Vid, the God of Death, is presumably my best chance of survival. However, I have made a conscious effort not to step foot in that godsdamned place when neither god has ever answered a single prayer of mine. *If I made it to their temple, would the runes inscribed into the doorframe protect me? Or would the gods see I am not worthy of the protection the markings offer and instead watch as the Flesh-Hunters feast on my body on their temple floors?*

There is a break in the buildings up ahead, and I can see

the well-lit circular centre of Datura. The many winding, narrow alleyways spread out from the centre like the kilometres of blood vessels in the body, all intertwined, and will eventually lead one back to the centre of Datura and the tree.

The panic in my chest is crippling. My mind spins images of glistening rubies of blood in crisp white snow. I try to push those memories from my mind and think of something more cheerful. In the spring, twinkling lights and pastel silk ribbons run from the buildings towards the tree for the Spring Equinox. It's the only thing that makes living in this godsforsaken town pleasant.

Tears burn my eyes as the clearing of the town centre comes into view. It's almost within my reach when I look over my shoulder. My stomach drops as a fresh wave of nausea washes over me. A Flesh-Hunter is still stalking me —mockingly so, no longer sluggish in its movements but also not moving at its full potential. I let out a string of curses as I turn back towards the clearing. Tears of pure terror sting at my eyes, and a helpless whimper slips between my lips. Another figure is standing between me and my potential safety. With tears blurring my vision and the scent of rotting flesh, I am left gritting my teeth together to avoid vomiting all over the street.

I'm trapped.

I stumble over my feet, falling backwards into the gutter. The sound of glass bottles breaking fills the air—

Shit!

A sharp pain shoots up my left arm as I fall hard on my ass, my palm and wrist scraping against the cobblestones and broken glass. Something sticky and warm seeps from the acute stinging in my arm, and I lift my shaking, bloody hand to see the damage my clumsiness caused. It's not a deep cut, but the blood pouring from it is enough to entice the monster even more. My eyes snap up to it as it sniffs the air. The Flesh-Hunter in front of me makes a deep, grinding sound, reminding me of someone grinding their teeth, before the hard line of its mouth slowly unfurls like someone has pulled it open with a zipper, displaying rows of pencil-sharp teeth gleaming in the light. It screeches in its frenzy before I can push myself to my feet.

The Flesh-Hunter's scream reverberates off the walls and straight through me, finding its way into the deepest, darkest parts of my soul. The animalistic sound is so unnatural, and yet it's almost human-like. It lurches forward, the strongly curved unguals digging into the cobblestoned street and ripping up flecks of stone. *This is it. This is where my luck runs out.* Flinging my bloody arm over my face so I don't have to see what happens next, I brace myself, knowing this will be a drawn-out and gruesome death.

Before I can fully brace myself for the Flesh-Hunter's impact, something grabs me by the back of my shirt and drags me back towards the wall. The force of the pull chokes me, and I grasp at the collar to let air back into my lungs when suddenly, the tension is gone. My body is discarded against the icy wall, and my head hits the bricks with a thud, blurring my vision as the pain skitters down my spine like lightning.

I strain my eyes as the tall figure who just pushed me out of the way now stands where I sat a moment ago—standing between the Flesh-Hunter and me.

My heart stops as my eyes focus on the tall man dressed in black. That figure from before wasn't another Flesh-Hunter at all. It was a man.

A man? It takes my mind a moment to register that there is, in fact, another human standing between the

Flesh-Hunter and me. He's just standing there. I want to scream, but my throat is dry, and I can't find my voice. It is like one of those horrible nightmares where you try to shout, but no matter how hard you try, nothing comes out. But this isn't a dream. We are going to die. As the Flesh-Hunter draws closer, the man reaches behind his head and pulls a sword free.

A sword? What the fuck?

I didn't notice it was strapped to his back before.

Many have tried to kill the Flesh-Hunters. Of course we have tried to kill them. What civilisation hasn't attempted to eradicate a threat to their safety and well-being? But our bullets seem to go straight through them, and anyone who's tried to get to them with a blade hasn't even gotten a swing in before they were pinned down, their weapon tossed from their hand. So we have just learnt to co-exist.

I rub my eyes. Either I have a concussion, or the gin has gone to my head, and I am hallucinating because the blade of this mystery man's sword is glowing! It must be the alcohol because that's impossible. I rub my eyes harder, white spots blurring my vision as I strain to focus on the blade. He spins his sword, preparing for what I know will be a losing battle.

He looks confident—cocky, even—with his nonchalant stance. His shoulders are relaxed, but his muscles are taut, and from the way he swings his sword, it's apparent that he is ready to fight.

The blade is unquestionably glowing lilac in the darkness. The Flesh-Hunter is upon the man, and he gracefully steps to the side and swings his arm in a wide arc. A blood-curdling, animalistic scream rips through the Flesh-Hunter's throat as black liquid sprays onto the ground before me. I pull my legs tight to my body in an attempt not to get any on me. It takes a moment for me to realise this must be its blood. The Flesh-Hunter's screams are so high-pitched I press my hands over my ears to block them out. To my astonishment, the tall, muscular, idiotic man has wounded the beast. *We might actually have a chance of getting out of here alive.* I know I should take this opportunity to run, but I don't know if my feet will support my weight.

A low clicking grumbles from deep within the chest of another Flesh-Hunter, resounding behind us. The man swings his sword again as the monster darts forward. But this time, he doesn't hesitate as it approaches him. My eyes are glued to the scene unfolding in front of me. It's like a building on fire—so tragic, yet I cannot look away. His glowing blade slices through the Flesh-Hunter's neck as seamlessly as before. The putrid stench of rotting flesh fills the space, and there is a sickly crunch and thud as the head smashes into the wall opposite me, peppering me with its blood.

The lifeless body hits the ground.

I push myself forward a little in disbelief. *It's... dead. Who is this guy?* I wonder.

He spins on his heel, gracefully kneeling before me, his firm hand on my shoulder, pressing me back against the brick wall. "Don't move," he growls as he lunges towards the opening of the alleyway. The first Flesh-Hunter has weakly pushed to its feet, abandoning its lifeless arm on the ground. The monster seems to be in so much pain that it can scarcely move. It stands there, swaying from side to side. The Flesh-Hunter looks like it might die where it stands from the trauma alone. Still, the man doesn't take any chances as he advances towards it, swinging his sword and sending specks of black blood flying before raising it to deliver the final blow. Before he can make contact, the Flesh-Hunter turns its sharp-bladed arm around with such speed that it is all but a blur.

Was the creature faking how injured it was to throw the man off his guard? The thought of the Flesh-Hunters manipulating and having a greater consciousness than just killing is devastating. They could pose a greater threat to our survival than we ever thought.

Metal clangs against the cobblestone vibrate through the alleyway and my body, the sound like Vid, the God of Death, announcing his arrival. The Flesh-Hunter's arm presses against the man's throat, propelling him towards the wall opposite me. He digs in his heels, and despite him being powerfully built and about six-foot-something, the Flesh-Hunter pushes him effortlessly. His boots slip and stumble over the wet cobblestone street until his back is pressed against the brick wall.

Muscles straining against his black shirt, the man grunts out curses as he tries to reach up to release himself from the Flesh-Hunter's grip.

The monster—unaware of its prey's feeble attempts to free itself—slowly unzips its mouth. It deliberately showcases every one of its razor-sharp teeth as it slowly brings its face closer to the man while dragging his body up the wall.

"We're going to die," I mutter, my voice hoarse with fear. Every muscle in my body pleads for me to run, to save myself. But something inside me forces me to stay. The faces of those I have lost to the knife-like hands of Flesh-Hunters flash before my eyes. I couldn't save them.

Couldn't or wouldn't? a dark, liquor-induced voice slurs in my mind.

"The sword. Grab the sword," that eerie voice on the

phantom wind calls around us. Again, I search for the source, but no one is there. The Flesh-Hunter has the man preoccupied with not getting his face eaten off. His lips curl back in a silent growl as he pushes against the bladed arm. The siren calls again to grab the sword. The voice is soft, almost feminine. It can't be this man from the two words he growled at me and the string of curses. His voice is definitely the opposite of feminine.

Out of the corner of my eye, the unnerving, lilac-glowing blade catches my attention. Without thought, my body lunges forward. My hand grips the leather-wrapped handle and pulls the sword closer, the rasping sound of metal over the cobblestone echoing amongst the snarls and throaty clicks of the Flesh-Hunter.

I push myself to my feet, my knees shaking with panic, and draw up the sword. I grip the handle with both hands and pull it close to the side of my chest, just as I have seen countless animations do in films. It's warm in my hands, and I am unsure if the heat is from the blade itself or my own sweaty, anxious hands, but the sword is lighter than I expected. It feels as if it was forged from plastic, not steel.

I re-adjust my hands around the leather grip, feeling a strange sense of power flow from the sword into me. I raise the blade, swinging it above my head. With a swift arc, the edge slices through the Flesh-Hunter's neck, hot, sticky blood splashing across my arms, chest and face. It feels almost too easy, decapitating the Flesh-Hunter with this blade.

The head flies off the body towards the centre of town. I watch dumbly as it rolls in a slow circle where it lands. A sound, I assume, is the Flesh-Hunter's body falling to the ground with a loud thump, like someone has dropped a sack of potatoes onto the floor. I cannot suppress the shudder that comes at the sound, but my eyes still haven't left the decapitated head, its mouth lying ajar.

A firm hand gently wraps around mine, bringing my attention away from the carnage I created. *Death follows you,* the dark, drunken voice slurs as I look up at the man, who is covered in a splattering of black blood over his face and is standing incredibly close. I can almost feel his steady heartbeat, unlike mine, which is racing faster than a hummingbird's, my body still filled with adrenaline. But this man is... He is beautiful. And dangerous. His grip tightens around my hand, and I suck in a breath.

"Let go," he whispers in a menacing tone.

His cerulean-coloured eyes bore into me with an intensity like he is trying to read my mind. He cocks a dark eyebrow, and my heart skips a beat. Despite the blood splattered on his face and his grip on my wrist, he's rather handsome. His short, dark hair is messy in the middle, as if he's constantly running his fingers through it, and shorter on the sides. His dark brows shadow over intense eyes and a delicate scattering of facial hair, though I'm sure there's nothing soft about this man. My breath catches at the look of his mouth; full lips with a faint scar slicing through the left side.

He clears his throat, and I realise I have been staring at his lips for too long. My cheeks flush hot under his gaze, and he cocks his eyebrow again, his grip on my wrist tightening a little more. Not yet to the point of pain, but as if he's trying to gain my attention and get me to focus on what he's saying.

"*Please*, let go." His voice is stern, with an edge of acidity in the word *please* as if he doesn't think he should have to ask—a threat that he will take the sword back by force if I do not let go. I release the blade into his care, dropping my hands to my sides, and take a shaky step away. "Good girl," he growls quietly with a curve of his lips, sending a shiver down my spine and making my stomach flip.

I stumble back into the opposite wall, putting as much distance as possible between us. He pulls a handkerchief out of his back pocket and carefully cleans the blade in long strokes before returning it and the bizarrely glowing sword to its sheath along his back. The muscles of his arms flex in the moonlight, almost hypnotically, and I briefly forget the promise I made to myself.

His eyes narrow as he looks me up and down. "Who are you?" he asks, his gaze so intense that it makes me slightly self-conscious.

I wince as I fold my hands tight against myself, my wrists and forearms stinging from the added pressure of the cuts. He strides over to me, closing the distance between us in two movements. My face must be an open book, showing the movement's discomfort because he gently grabs my arms and pulls them apart to examine the wounds.

"Are you okay? Are you hurt anywhere else?" He looks up from my hands as I try to pull away, but his grip holds me firm as he looks over the rest of my body. I shake my head, unable to find my voice. I need to put as much distance between the two of us as possible.

How-how did he—did I just kill...

My mind is racing. "This needs to be cleaned and covered unless you want more Kailadons on our tail." I look up at him, my mind still spinning and confused. He is at least a head taller than me. *On our tail again...* There is no plural pronoun between us. It is him, and then there is— *Wait...*

"I'm sorry, a what-a-don?" I demand.

He lets out a small chuckle. "A Kailadon," he corrects matter-of-factly. "You know"—he gestures to the dead Flesh-Hunter on the ground, and I flinch—"Oh, that's right, your people decided to call them Flesh-Hunters," he continues as if not noticing my reaction. "How original," he says mockingly, with a roll of his eyes. I just stare at him in disbelief. *What the hell is he going on about?* Surely, this is a dream.

"Who are you?" he asks again. I swallow hard, my throat dry as I try to take a step back, his eyes burning into me.

"Eliana. Eliana Nightingale." My voice sounds funny and dissimilar. My knees shake with apprehension. The fog the gin provided has vanished, and my mouth is dry, desperate for more.

This man is intimidating and vicious. He just murdered two Flesh-Hunters in cold blood without even a lick of remorse. He looks down at me; something about how his eyes bore into me makes me feel a little uneasy like I shouldn't have given my name so quickly. Something flashes behind those cerulean eyes, but it is gone in a blink, his expression evening out and going cold again. I straighten up, not that it makes a difference with him towering over me. But confidence is everything, right? I raise my eyebrows and look him up and down, trying to convey some sense of resilience instead of being one step away from freaking the fuck out. I clear my throat, attempting to steady my voice.

"And... you are?" I stumble out, not nearly as intimidating or impressive as I was aiming for. I mentally face-palm myself.

A wicked smile hints at the corners of his mouth. "Mallrie," he says, amused. "Just Mallrie."

I nod absent-mindedly, my brows coming together in a slight frown. There is something about Mallrie that makes me feel anxious.

Probably because he just killed two Flesh-Hunters right in front of you, I think. *Well,* you *killed that second one all by yourself,* adds a bitchy voice from the back of my mind.

There is something more than that. *Why is Mallrie out here killing Flesh-Hunters? What did he mean by their correct name being a Kailadon?* I have never heard anyone call them that before, not even in the history books.

And why hasn't this vigilante been in the news? From how he attacked the Flesh-Hunter, Kailadon or whatever he wants to call them, it's clear this wasn't his first time. Surely someone has seen him before.

"We need to go. I'll escort you home." I look up at him as a small wave of terror rushes through me. *This man, Mallrie, just saved my life, but how do I know I can trust him? After all, no one in their right mind is out after dark, yet here he is.*

Here I am.

CHAPTER THREE
MALLRIE

"The Enkanti Tree," I mutter as we pass the large oak tree in the centre of Datura—loud enough for Eliana to hear but still quiet enough that she would have to question me on it. *I wonder how much she knows and how much she was told...*

The full moon glistens through the twisting branches, casting shadows along the cobblestone and illuminating her blonde hair, making it look like it's spun silver, distracting my thoughts. The sight of her covered in the black blood of the Kailadon she slayed, walking through the moonlight like this, sends my mind into a flurry. She looks like a warrior, strong, powerful and absolutely stunning. And yet she is terrified. *Doesn't she know how powerful she is?*

Her fingers twitch at her sides as if they're seeking something to hold, her shoulders tense up and she quickens her pace, trying to put distance between us.

I have to repress the smile playing on my lips. At least she seems to have some common sense, even if she is wandering the streets of Datura, half-drunk. She should be afraid of me.

Even if I just saved her life.

Eliana looks back and notices me shamelessly watching her every move, like a wolf watching a deer. She rolls her large, doe-like brown eyes and walks as if dismissing my subtle prodding attempt.

"Have you no idea why your town was built around this tree?"

"It's just a tree." She shrugs, matching my tone of arrogance. Eliana may be afraid of me, but she is unwilling to show an inch of it in her tone. "The first settlers probably saw a pretty tree and thought, 'Hey, why not build a town around it?'"

My startled laugh echoes around us as her nonchalant response slightly throws me. Her body shudders at the sound, and she rubs her hands over her arms as if she just got a sudden chill.

Spinning on one foot like an uncoordinated dancer, Eliana glares at me as she defiantly walks backwards. I lose the fight against myself, and a smirk spreads across my face. She almost trips over her feet. *I knew she was clumsy, but really?* Her eyes slip past me to the tree at my back, glazing over as if a memory is flashing before her, and her lips quirk up on one side. *A good memory, then.*

Our eyes meet again, and she quickly turns on her heels, trying to hide the blush creeping across her face before I can notice it. But I did. I see more than she realises.

I sigh, slightly disappointed \ she won't question me and that I will have to explain it all to her like a stubborn child who doesn't want to know the truth. "They named the Enkanti Tree after the witches—"

"There is no such thing as witches," she snaps, cutting me off as she flicks her hair out of her face. I raise an eyebrow at the back of her head, her short blonde hair a little tousled from the altercation in the alleyway.

"The original owners of this land *were* witches," I reply sharply, pretending like she didn't just interrupt me. My eyes are trained on her back, afraid that if I look away, she might just slip into the night like mist on the water.

"Enkanti—the name of the coven, who were the initial owners of this land—means power and protection." I inhale the stale, damp air of Datura. The stench of too many people living on top of each other is suffocating. But, of course, the townsfolk don't know how stale their town smells when it's the only thing they know. "The Enkantians chose this tree as the centre point of their coven because of its magical properties and built their cabins in a circle around it—just like how your town was built. Magic is more powerful in a circle."

I can practically feel Eliana roll her eyes when she scoffs.

"You know certain symbols hold power, don't you?" I ask, quietly wondering if she believes in the runes marked around the doors of Datura.

"Yeah, nah," Eliana scoffs sassily. "The runes protect us from the Flesh-Hunters or whatever." But she doesn't sound convinced. I smile, a little pleased to know she doesn't believe in the fallacious markings used to trick the townsfolk into a sense of security. But, of course, the Kailadons cannot enter the buildings—their brains cannot understand how doors work. To them, it's just a solid wall. "A circle is a powerful symbol," I continue. "Once it is connected, it does not have a beginning or an end, securing whatever magic is performed within."

"Hence, the buildings are in a circle," Eliana mutters. The stench of gin clings to her clothes, and I frown at the back of her head. She needn't find peace at the bottom of a bottle; there are other ways to find the quietude she seeks.

"Hence the buildings," I agree. "The Enkantian witches infused their elemental magic into the oak tree to amplify the Fae magic already within, putting a protection spell on it and all those within their coven."

"Wait—" she blurts, spinning on her heel to face me and tripping over her feet. I grab her around her waist, steadying her, and unintentionally pulling her close. Her hands press against my chest, and I feel their warmth through my shirt. I inhale deeply, a subconscious reaction to her sudden proximity. She smells good. Under the stench of gin and Kailadon blood, she smells of peppermint and the faintest hint of smoke.

"You need to stop doing that," I say. A growl slips past my lips, and I feel her tense in my embrace. "You're going to hurt yourself again, and it's already been a long night."

These last few years have been too long. For so long, I have been waiting, watching...

I settle her back onto her feet, and she looks at me like a doe in headlights. She clears her throat and looks like she could do with another drink, yet her eyes light up. "Did you say Fae? As in fairies?"

That's the part she fixates on? "You're sceptical about this story," I say, already knowing the answer. Every mayor of Datura has been privy to the truth of the past and worked to keep it hidden from its townsfolk.

"Well, yeah, if there really are such things as magic and witches and a protection spell, why are the Flesh-Hunters—"

"Kailadons," I correct.

Clicking her tongue and rolling her brown eyes, she

says with added emphasis, "Why are the *Kailadons* still here then?"

A satisfied smirk spreads across my face at her distrust. Not just about me and my presence here, but about everything I am telling her. But there's a fire in here, a sass, that has my body humming with excitement. There is a part of her that's enraptured by the story. Eliana wants to know what happened. She's got a thirst for knowledge—something that could cause a few problems down the road.

Of course, she shouldn't trust me, I remind myself, releasing her and putting some distance between us.

I continue our walk. We've been standing out in the open for too long. The unseasonably cool air rushes around us and carries our scents away.

The sound of her footsteps quickening to catch up to me is like music to my ears, even though it shouldn't excite me as much as it does.

"Because," I say, taking a deep breath to calm the rage simmering in my blood, "the first settlers, you know, have expunged the truth from the history books. They heard of the Enkanti witches, their magic and the protection spell. They came, demanding the High Witchess grant them protection and sanctuary from the Kailadons. The High Witchess happily agreed. However, the mortals grew jealous of the witches' power and the monthly rituals. They thought"—I cast her a sharp look and watch as she shrinks away. *Clever doe*—"the rituals and magic were fake. They thought the Enkanti witches were doing it as a reminder of their dominance. That this was their land and the mortals were but visitors." I arch an eyebrow in her direction, waiting for her to object, to say something—anything.

She shrugs a shoulder with indifference. "Could you really blame someone for believing the whole magic act was fake? Like, come on." She looks up at me, her face pinched with doubt. "It's far-fetched."

"Just because you can't see something doesn't mean it isn't real. Do you stop believing in the moon when the sun comes up?"

A dry laugh escapes her full lips. "I'm sure many would doubt the sun would rise again when we know what lurks in the dark."

I can't argue with her there. Charleston may have rewritten the past, but by doing so, he had convicted his descendants of living with a fear of the darkness.

"Albert Charleston, the leader of the first settlers—who I am sure you're familiar with—decided he didn't like the High Witchess being in charge. He believed a woman was too emotional to make rational decisions." Eliana scoffs, rolling her eyes—*again*. My eyes roam her body, over her soft, sensual curves and the tiny sliver of pale skin between her shirt and pants. She would have liked the Enkantian witches. Especially the females, with their sharp-witted tongues and fiery souls.

"Charleston demanded that she step down and command her people to obey his orders and cease all witchcraft immediately. The High Witchess kindly explained they were the rightful owners of this land and that without them and their practices, the magic and protection would wear off, leaving them all in danger of the Kailadons and the other creatures that lurked within the forest surrounding them. Charleston wouldn't listen."

"Why?" she asks, her dark brows pressed together. I can see the conflict in her eyes as she fights between wanting to believe this to be another fictitious tale, asking questions and knowing more, or just wanting to walk home in silence as if I am merely a spirit by her side. I can see her curiosity fighting the battle, and a burst of pride warms my chest. "I just mean, why would Charleston demand that the magic *supposedly* protecting everyone against the Kailadons be stopped? It just seems idiotic," she adds quickly.

The corner of my mouth tugs up with a hint of approval at how quickly her brain is piecing together the lies her government has spread. "Idiotic indeed," I agree. "Men like Charleston aren't concerned with logical reasoning, only power and control." I look behind us to the Enkanti Tree, standing in the darkness like a lone sentry, a dark reminder of a promise I made long ago. We have once again stopped walking, too captivated by discussing the dark past of Datura. "He gathered his men and staged a coup against the Enkanti coven. His men overpowered the witches—"

"I'm sorry." Eliana laughs almost doubtfully. "How did a mortal man overpower an entire coven of witches? Sounds a little—"

"Do not underestimate the will of man's selfish desire to gain power," I seethe. My muscles tense, and my hands itch to grab my sword.

Eliana backs up a step, brown eyes wide with something almost like fear. A part of her is fighting with itself, a voice perhaps telling her she can trust me. *Foolish doe.* Her mouth opens to speak, but she wisely closes it once again before whispering, "So how did he do it?"

A part of me wants to spill my guts, telling her everything. I look over my shoulder once again at the tree. "Everyone has a weakness, Eliana." I turn back to her. "Don't be fooled to think that because Charleston was mortal, he didn't figure out how to exploit and manipulate the witches to discover their weaknesses."

"What was the witches' weakness, then?" Eliana prods.

"Why do you care if it's just a bunch of hocus pocus?" I

reply, raising a brow. My eyes take her in once again. Her slightly dishevelled blonde curls have dropped, highlighting the Kailadon's blood splashed across the swell of her breasts.

Silently, I curse, reprimanding myself for my lustful gaze. Now is not the time to lose my focus. All these years, I have been working towards fulfilling the promise I made, and I won't let *her*, of all people, distract me now. Even if the sight of her covered in Kailadon blood and holding my sword has my cock stirring.

Before she can reply, I finish the rest of my story. "Charleston's men killed most of the coven before taking the High Witchess hostage. He tied her to the Enkanti Tree and gathered what was left of the coven. He demanded their loyalty. Those who refused were tied to the tree with the High Witchess. Only a handful stood with Charleston. They stood by and watched their fellow friends, family and their High Witchess burn." My tone is clipped, and the words come out in harsh, short bursts.

A bubble of guilt swells in my chest at the reminder of the past, the promise I made and what needs to be done. I look at *her*. Her plump lips part as if to speak, but she snaps them shut. I take a breath, forcing my tone to soften. "As they perished, those tied to the tree performed one last spell to protect the tree from burning to the ground alongside them. As the High Witchess burnt, her flesh, bones and ashes infused with the tree. And it remained untouched by the inferno. As the High Witchess, she harnessed all five elemental magics—Earth, Fire, Water, Air and Time—and infused all of her power into the tree unbeknown to Charleston. This was done so that, one day, her people could reclaim that magic and be protected from the Kailadons. Of course, Charleston was equally furious and scared shitless when he found out. So, he named it the Enkanti Tree to remind his people of the dangers the native witches possess."

"So, the tree's magic was lost when they burnt the witches?" she asks. Her voice sounds sad, but her face twists with disbelief. I nod solemnly and start walking again.

We start down another alleyway, and an inch of water splashes under our feet in a disjointed rhythm. The streets always flood when the Kailadons make their way to the surface. Eliana wraps her arms around her body, shifting her weight uncomfortably. I look around, trying to see this from her point of view, and I can sense how terrified she must be.

Say something. Anything, a small voice urges me to comfort her. I open my mouth to say I don't even know what when I hear it.

The faintest sound on the wind. Swinging out an arm, I catch Eliana around the waist. Gently squeezing at her soft curves, I lift her off her feet and pull her back against the wall.

Fuck. I've let my guard down too much.

I should have just taken her home and stuck to the plan. But instead, I wanted to stay in her presence and talk to her a little longer, even if she didn't believe a word I was saying.

Her face twists with anger, opening her mouth to snap at me, but I pull her wrists towards me. Whatever she's yapping about, I don't hear as my eyes examine the blood from her fall. The blood has crusted over already, but the smell still lingers.

"Shit," I curse, tugging her elbow and pulling her down into a crouch. *This isn't ideal. How could I have been so stupid? This is how people get killed.* Scooping some water from the gutter into my hand, I scrub the flakes of dried blood from her arms. Her face scrunches up, and she tries to pull away, but I am bigger and stronger and hold her exactly where I need her.

That's when she hears it.

Slow, languid footsteps drag through the water. Eliana's head whips from side to side, trying to determine where the sound is coming from. I roughly pull her to her feet and try to wipe as much blood and water from her arms as possible. The audible wince that escapes her lips is unpleasant and something I don't want to hear again.

The sound of fabric tearing fills the dark alleyway as I rip off the sleeve of my black shirt and bind her arms.

This is not ideal for so many reasons.

Unfortunately, I am fresh out of my usual resources. Suddenly, my mind is overwhelmed with the fear of her not cleaning these grazes properly when she gets home and potentially getting an infection from the dirty water. Her cheeks flush at the sight of my bare arms, and my body notices how she looks at me. Her tongue darts out of her mouth, wetting her lips, and she faintly drags her teeth across her bottom lip. *I've got to get her out of here.*

Holding onto her wrist, I pull her down an alleyway, then another, and another. The labyrinth of Datura makes up a clear image in my mind. Her steps falter as she struggles to keep up, but *time* is running out.

Pulling her arm again, she calls my name out in a breathless plea. "Mallrie." My mind reels with all the ways I could make her say my name like that again, but I push them aside. We've got more significant problems to deal with right now. "Wait." Eliana tugs against my grip on her arm.

We're surrounded.

I stop suddenly, Eliana crashing into my back, her hand reaching out around my waist to steady herself—*Fuck!*

I whirl around and press her against the wall. She looks up at me with those big brown eyes. Our bodies are so close that if I just leant down a little, I could take her mouth with mine. Cursing, I remind myself of my promise and what I must do. Eliana may be a part of that plan, but not like *that*.

A bubble of unease ripples to the surface at what *this* could do to the *Timeline*—the delicate balance of life created by the Fates. To be gifted with the element of time is a gift from the Fates, one only bestowed on a handful of witches. The responsibility that comes with that gift is heavy. Once upon a time, before elemental witches, the Fates were the only ones who could alter the *Timeline* consciously.

Think of the Timeline like a spider's web, my mentor, Avark, told me. *"The centre of it is you—or the person you're focusing on—and each silk that extends from the bridge thread is all the variations the Timeline could take. Most of them inter-connect because even though the end destination might be the same, there are millions of ways to get there."*

And just like a spider's web, the *Timeline* is fragile. I have spent years looking into this particular *Timeline* and making sure that what I need to get done happens in the most efficient way possible. I don't need *her* messing this up.

"Mal—" Eliana's voice cuts through the fog, dragging my attention back to her. My head snaps to hers, her brown eyes searching mine.

"Shh," I cut her off, forcing her down onto her knees. Her breath catches as she looks up at me. *Damn, she looks good on her knees.* She slowly bites her lip again, colour creeping up her neck and flushing her cheeks. *Wicked little doe.* I wrap her arms around her body, trying to keep the scent of her blood concealed by the gin. Then, reaching for the sword secured to my back, I pull it free. The sound of metal scraping through the scabbard is like greeting an old friend. Eliana's eyes track the glow of the blade.

"Stop that," I growl. As much as I enjoy seeing her blush, the sudden rush of blood to her cheeks is still an enticing scent to the Kailadons. Not as intense as an open wound, but enough when they're already tracking us.

"Stop what?" she demands, her features hardening in defiance. As if she doesn't know her body is pumping itself silly with adrenaline or that my presence arouses her.

"Blushing." The word drips from my lips like honey, thick and filled with amusement. Giving me her best doe-like impression, she widens her eyes and bats her eyelashes as if she doesn't know what she is doing to me. I press down the urge to grin at her. *Think of the Timeline. Remember your promise.*

"Sorry," she whispers, lowering her eyes. While her attention is elsewhere, I take the opportunity to sneak away.

A pang of guilt runs through me. Maybe I should have let Eliana know what I am doing, but one way or another, I'll have to learn to deal with this newfound guilt, and she will have to realise there are some things she doesn't need to know. So, silently, I run around the corner.

She'll be fine... for now.

CHAPTER FOUR
ELIANA

*H*e's gone.

I look around, praying to the gods' deaf ears he didn't *actually* abandon me. A sense of desertion should be gripping me in a blind panic, but instead, only fear and anger rush through me.

He left me. He just fucking left me!

The realisation is like a wave threatening to crush me. I curse myself for how I looked at Mallrie, how his muscles bunched up when he drew his sword from its sheath attached to his back and how he held me in his arms.

This is why I don't do the whole feelings thing. I've gone and shot myself in the foot. I let down my guard, and look where that has led me! Alone. *With a Flesh-Hunter stalking me.*

My chest tightens, and I'm starting to hyperventilate. I haven't had a panic attack like this since...

Squeezing my eyes closed, I try to block the memories, but no matter how much air I suck in, it doesn't seem to fill my lungs. Instead, the scent of damp air mixed with the rancid stench of death squeezes my stomach uncomfortably, and I am on the cusp of throwing up all the liquor sitting in my empty stomach.

The sound of someone approaching has my head whipping up from between my knees. My heart goes into a frenzy when I hear feet dragging. But the sound is too sluggish to be Mallrie, even if he was injured.

Please! Oh, gods, please don't let this be happening again.

Squeezing my eyes shut, I pray this is just some horrible dream, my memories twisting into some new form of torture. I open my eyes just in time to see a long, knife-like limb slowly reaching around the corner. "Fuck," I mutter to myself. The Flesh-Hunter lazily pulls itself around into my alleyway.

It freezes. I'm paralysed, crouching in the street with my back against the wall. Looking above me is a weathered, black gooseneck streetlight protruding from the building. The static hum of the electricity coursing through the cables that spread from the rooftops to the underground turbine generators is a comforting sound. Yet, the warm, golden glow cascades over me with a false sense of security. Most streetlights in Datura are flickering or completely burnt out. Still, it's not like a committee is ready to volunteer to check and replace broken lights. They just slowly die out until the darkness engulfs a whole alleyway. It seems somewhat poetic. Like the citizens of Datura are just waiting for their light to be snuffed out by a Flesh-Hunter.

Considering this alleyway is well lit, I wonder if the Flesh-Hunter will venture down here. The monster tilts its head back, and even though there is a reasonable distance between us, I can hear the distinct sound of it sucking in a breath through its slitted nose. One after the other, smelling for something. *Smelling me.* The realisation has me pulling myself in tighter, trying to shrink into the wall. The buzz from the gin has well and truly worn off now, and I wish I had a bottle nearby.

Click, click, click. The Flesh-Hunter makes a sound in the back of its throat that reminds me of teeth grinding, and it sends a shiver down my spine. *Click, click, click*—a predator hunting for its next meal.

The sound has my body trembling. Memories I have tried so hard to forget bubble to the surface, like the bubbles in the gin and tonic I use to drown them in. The Flesh-Hunter's mouth slowly unravels, revealing a sinister smile of needle-sharp teeth. My palms sweat, and an icy shiver works through my body.

My heart stutters as my eyes focus on the glistening red fangs. Fresh blood drips from its thin lips, the remains of someone's flesh stuck between its teeth. My first thought turns to Mallrie.

Surely, it can't be him. He hasn't been gone that long.

But I didn't see which way he went. He could have easily run right into this Flesh-Hunter. *Kailadon,* Mallrie's voice corrects me in my mind.

Whatever!

My stomach feels like a bubbling, viscous mess as my heart aches for someone I've just met. I curse myself for feeling this way. *This is why I keep to myself!* If you're alone, you can't get hurt.

Mallrie... It had to be him. He's gone. No one else would be out after dark. It's just not what we do. We know what is out there.

All attempts of holding in the bile swishing around my stomach break away, and I double over, throwing up gin and the cheap spring roll I bought from Rowan's Haus of Pancakes. The thought of Rowan's experimental dishes has my stomach threatening to empty even more of its contents.

The Kailadon starts forward—an apex predator stalking its pathetic prey. I turn to look the way we've just come. It's empty. I could run—again. But this time, I have a sickening feeling knowing no one will save me. Running won't help. I can't prevent the inevitable.

A slow and painful death.

I turn to look at the tall, skeletal creature stalking towards me, the thin, leathery skin clinging to its ribs, teeth bared in a threatening, silent growl, blood dripping onto the sidewalk. Tears prick behind my eyes, and my throat swells with emotion. I shake my head, forcing the tears back down.

NO!

I press my hands hard into the wall behind me. If there is one thing I'm not, it is someone willing to give up. Even in the most challenging situations, I grit my teeth and push through.

I am a fighter.

Turning away from the monster, I push myself from the wall. My well-worn boots struggle to keep traction with the damp cobblestones, and I trip over my feet, thrusting my hands out before me to prevent myself from kissing the ground. I use my hands to propel myself forward. My nails crack under the pressure of digging into the unforgiving ground, but I don't feel the pain. My heartbeat is deafening, like a doomsday clock ticking down until the end. I race forward as an alleyway comes up on my right. I dash down it.

Colliding into something hard, I fall backwards onto my ass. My arms fling back onto the hard ground, scraping my elbows.

"Fucking hell!" I curse breathlessly, frustration rising that I can't catch a break tonight. I look up, expecting the worst—a Flesh-Hunter looming over me, dropping its weight onto me, pinning me against the cold pavement, slowly severing nerve from nerve as it peels away my flesh...

With an unexpected lightness, my heart flutters in my chest with relief as the lilac glow of a sword splattered with black Kailadon blood stings my eyes.

"Mallrie!" I cry out, my tight muscles loosening at the sight of him. *He's okay!*

His handsome face twists with rage; dark brows pressed together, a small crease forming between them, his black hair tousled. His grip tightens around the sword as he looks down at me, then back up towards the Flesh-Hunter following me. He steps around me, stalking forward—predator versus predator.

A rival of strength.

I am still sprawled out on the ground, unable to push myself to my feet, my whole body aching as I twist to watch the scene unfold behind me.

Mallrie quickens his pace until he is running straight towards the monster, the Flesh-Hunter hurrying to match his speed, raising one of those deadly arms to swing at Mallrie's head. The urge to close my eyes, to not watch the fatal blow, has my body itching, but my eyes are glued to the scene unfolding before me. Sliding on his knees through the inch of water on the ground, sword outstretched, Mallrie slices effortlessly through the skin and bone of the Flesh-Hunter's knees. It falls forward face first into the hard ground, its long arms fumbling to push itself onto the rest of its legs. Using its long arms, it drags itself back towards him.

Mallrie draws himself up to his full height and swings

his sword in a swift arc above his head, plunging it down into the Flesh-Hunter's neck. Thick, black blood squirts around the glowing blade. A gurgling sound escapes the monster's thin lips as it tries to breathe through the blood seeping into its lungs. A twist of the blade pushes it deeper, no doubt severing the spinal cord. Then Mallrie swiftly removes the sword from its neck, blood squirting from the wound, and the sword descends gracefully, beheading the beast. The stench of decaying flesh fills the alleyway.

Kicking the lifeless head out of his way, Mallrie stalks towards me. Before I can push myself off the floor, he is standing before me. He drops the sword to the ground with an echoing clang and reaches out, pulling me to my feet. The previous look of anger has been replaced with concern. His eyes scan my body, looking for any sign of injuries.

"Are you hurt? Did it get you?" He brushes strands of my short hair away from my face. Before I can stop myself, the lump in my throat betrays me, and my eyes sting hot with tears. I try to blink them back, but Mallrie's frown only deepens. "Eliana, are you hurt?" My name rolls off his tongue like silk, and my chest aches.

How dare he! I brush my eyes with the back of my hands. "You left me," I stutter between tears, feeling somewhat childish. "*You fucking left me!*" I repeat louder, tears streaming down my face. I look around Mallrie's powerful body to the lifeless monster on the ground. I shake my head and swallow hard, trying to be rid of the lump in my throat and the feeling of helplessness in my gut. "I thought it got you. I thought you were dead." His rough, calloused hand cups my face, his thumb brushing away the tears.

"So emotional," he whispers.

I punch him in the chest as hard as possible, but it's like

beating a brick wall. I cup my fist before pushing him away, anger rising in me.

Emotional? How fucking dare he! He doesn't even know me! But I don't know him either, yet here I am getting all worked up over thinking a Flesh-Hunter could have killed him. I shake my head, trying to dislodge that thought. I have seen too many lives end by the fate of the monsters of Datura. I don't need any more blood on my hands or tainting my soul. *This* is why I have kept my distance from people these few years. Yet, there is a fire in me, simmering with rage that Mallrie had the audacity to leave me *alone* and expected me to stay put while he gallivanted off for gods know what reason. "*You fucking left me!*" I shout. "You left me to *die!*" I shove at his chest again. *No point trying to hit him,* I think with an internal eye roll. *Damn him and his muscles.* "Then that-that *thing* is here, blood dripping from its—" My mind is racing. I press my hand to my head and breathe. Mallrie opens his mouth, but I don't give him a chance to voice whatever pathetic reason he may come up with. "You're the only other idiot out here." I sigh as if trying to reason why this has me all worked up. I am being emotional, but I won't admit he was right. A ghost of a smile forms at the corners of Mallrie's lips. *Fuck him. He doesn't know me. He should keep those comments to himself!*

"You don't know me. You do not know what I have been through. If you knew, you'd understand why I'm *fucking emotional.*" *Well, there goes "I won't admit he was right" out the window,* I think as I throw his words back in his face. A single dark eyebrow creeps up his face. "*You godsdamned left me to die!* Then I am freaking out thinking—moronically, I can see now—that you're dead." My voice shakes with anger as I turn to walk away. I *have* to walk away. I feel like I might burst into flames if I don't.

"Eliana—"

Something about him makes me want to rethink every decision I have ever made. It is like a string, pulling me towards him, an instinct to trust him. *I don't know him.* He could very well be a murderer, for all I know. He seems to have no issue with killing. I am better off alone. I stalk off into the darkness, secretly hoping—not that I will admit it even to myself—he will follow me in case I run into another Flesh-Hunter. I can hear him sigh and the scrape of metal as he picks up his sword. Stealing a glance over my shoulder, I let out a sound of relief as I watched him clean the blood off his sword. Mallrie's eyes flick up and meet mine briefly before I look away as a smug smile stretches across his lips, softening his features.

Heading down another alleyway, the glow of his blade in my peripheral vision, I turn to find Mallrie at my side, matching my speed, his sword resting lazily over his shoulder.

"Stop following me," I bite. My apartment is just around the next corner, and I don't need his escort anymore.

"I would never just leave you," he says flatly. "I didn't mean—It's just—I didn't want you to get hurt."

I glare up at him. There's a hint of hurt in his eyes. *Good. Maybe he will leave me alone.* "I just want to get home and forget this whole mess," I spit out. His gaze shifts from me to the road straight ahead, expressionless.

"As you wish."

CHAPTER FIVE
ELIANA

My lumpy old mattress shifts under my weight as I prop myself onto my elbows, my hands and wrists aching under the makeshift bandages of Mallrie's torn shirt. I'm filthy. The water wouldn't warm up fast enough last night, so I gave up on waiting and fell in a heap on my bed, shoes and all.

I groan a little as I force myself to get up and start my day, stripping off the sheets with me—there is no way I could ever get another good night's sleep in these sheets again. Not that I've had a good sleep in about four years. The memories of my past may be kept at bay during the day, but like the Flesh-Hunters, they crawl out of the deepest, darkest recesses of my mind and plague my dreams. I pout a little to myself as I force my pillow out of the slip that all my gin got destroyed in last night. My grandmother left me with a decent inheritance, but as much as I will splurge for the good shit, I don't want to spend all my savings on waffles and gin.

As I throw them into my wash basket in my tiny bathroom, I notice the black stain stark against the coffee-coloured sheet.

Blood.

Flesh-Hunter—*Kailadon, whatever!*—blood.

I drop the sheets to the floor and kick them aggressively out of the bathroom, fear bubbling inside me, the heat of tears burning at my eyes. My hands shake as my breathing quickens until I am hyperventilating. I rip my sweat, blood and dirt-covered clothes from my body. Tearing off the makeshift bandages and cursing as one of them catches on the wounds, I pull away the fresh layer of skin already healing. I curse under my breath at the sting of pain and new dots of blood pebbling to the surface, but I've always been a quick healer, so I reassure myself it'll be fine.

I toss the clothes and shoes outside the bathroom and slam the door shut. Sliding down the door, naked, I press my knees to my chest and try to focus on breathing.

Breathe in. Hold... hold... hold. Breathe out. Again.

Breathe in. Hold... hold... hold. Breathe out. Again.

Finally, with my breathing back under control, my hands stop shaking. I step into the small shower and forcefully scrub my entire body, trying to wash away the memories of last night. The hot water feels good against my sore skin. I stay there, under the running water, for a long time, even after being satisfied that I have scrubbed enough of the memories away.

The steam from my shower fills the room, small tendrils lifting from my skin as I wrap a towel around my body and pad over to the fogged-up mirror. A bubble of unease fills my stomach. As I look at my distorted reflection in the mirror, one hand clutching at the towel, I lift my free hand to wipe away the condensation on the glass. The bubble of unease bursts in my stomach, stealing away my breath. In the mirror's reflection, standing right behind me is the skin-tight torso of a Flesh-Hunter. A blood-curdling scream escapes my throat, the sound right out of a slasher film. I stumble backwards, fully expecting to collide with the monster, its arm slicing my throat open. Gasping for air, I see my blood spilling from the wound at my throat. My hands reach up, trying to hold the two slices of flesh together. I stumble backwards, the towel rail digging into my back, knocking the breath out of me as I land on the cold, tiled floor.

Sitting in a heap, still clutching at my throat, it takes a moment for me to realise there isn't any blood spilling from my throat. That it was all in my head. I push myself onto my hands and knees and scurry out of the bathroom, slamming the door behind me. I crawl over the spoiled sheets and clothes to my bed, sitting on the floor naked, wet and shaking, trying to calm myself. I try to recall the breathing exercise the therapist taught me the only time I went.

Breathe in. Hold... hold... hold. Breathe out. Again.

It feels as if the walls of my already too-small apartment are closing in on me. The panic attack has eased, but my breathing still feels shallow.

I cannot stay here.

Quickly, I get dressed in high-waist jeans. I tuck in a graphic T-shirt and go to grab my boots before remembering that they're ruined. So, instead, I opt for a pair of white sneakers from the back of my wardrobe—they're tight, but they'll have to do. As much as I don't want to leave my apartment ever again, my fridge is empty, the gin I bought last night is shattered in some alleyway and now I need to get another pair of boots, some clothes, I guess, and some new bed sheets.

Maybe I might stop by the library to see if Mallrie's story is true, but first, I need a drink!

I look at the clock. It has only just chimed nine o'clock, but I guess it's five o'clock somewhere where there aren't flesh-eating monsters. Either way, I now appear to have a long list of jobs I want to do before sunset. I grab a trash bag from a cupboard in my kitchenette. It's small but perfectly sized for someone who lives alone. I forcefully shove my sheets, clothes and boots into the bag and bind it in a double knot.

"Eliana, are you alright?" I jump suddenly at the sound of my name, dropping my keys and the trash bag. Placing a hand over my pounding heart and turning, I press my back against my door. The old lady who lives two doors down from me is peering around her door. "I heard screaming from your apartment earlier," she says, her glasses making her eyes look twice their size.

I don't think Mrs Kaminski has ever left her apartment. I have seen people come and visit occasionally. And yet, I have never witnessed her poke more than her head out from behind her front door. When I first moved into this building, I assumed her neck would be as long as a giraffe's by how she craned around that door. For someone who never leaves her apartment, she knows an awful lot about the people who live around her. Probably because she does nothing all day but spy on her neighbours. I take a deep breath and force a smile on my face.

"Oh, yes. I'm okay. Sorry, I just slipped in the shower."

"Oh, dear, you ought to be careful. Especially a young

woman living all alone like yourself," Mrs Kaminski says, her tone anything but concerned. She's probably just fishing for information to see if I have *taken myself off the market yet*, as she so elegantly put it once. "If you hurt yourself, who knows when someone will find you? No one ever comes to visit you, dear. It's so sad."

Sweet old lady, my ass! I think, internally rolling my eyes. If I ever brought a man home, I'd make him climb through the window just to avoid her interrogation.

"What have you got there, dear?" Mrs Kaminski stretches her neck around the door to get a better look. "Bit early for garbage day, isn't it?"

Nosy old bitch, mind your own business!

"Just some old sheets and clothes I no longer need." The sweetness in my tone will surely give me a cavity, and I shift the bag further away from her inquisitive stare. I lock my door and swiftly move down the stairwell before she can question me further. "Have a good day, Mrs Kaminski!" I call as I rush away.

After disposing of the trash bag into the communal bin on the ground floor, a slight sense of relief washes over me. I push open the heavy timber doors and squint into the bright sunlight. The alleyways are busy with the hustle and bustle of people making their way in and out of the centre of town, briskly trying to do everything they need to before nightfall. They look as though they don't have a care in the world that last night was just as uneventful as any other— or as uneventful as a night can be when there are nocturnal flesh-eating monsters prowling your streets.

I turn down another alleyway, not focusing on where I am going, just knowing I want to get into the centre of town where the Bottle-O is so I can get the biggest bottle of gin I can get my hands on. Then sit down at Christina's—

my favourite little café, and a much better alternative to Rowan's Haus of Pancakes—and eat my weight in waffles.

A sudden chill runs through me as the realisation sets in. *This is where the Flesh-Hunters attacked last night.* People walk around and bump into my body, frozen in place, as they squeeze past. They're all completely oblivious. *Can they not see what is lying in the street?* Seeing a dead Flesh-Hunter should cause a scene, mass panic and hysteria. Never has a dead Flesh-Hunter been found in the street before. Sure, the bodies of their discarded victims, but never a Flesh-Hunter itself.

I force myself to walk forward. My eyes focused on the oak tree—*the Enkanti Tree, Mallrie called it*—in the town centre. It feels like my whole life has been twisted and flipped upside down. The Flesh-Hunter's body should be here. I frown as I get closer to the opening.

I stop in a wave of bewilderment.

Someone knocks into my back and curses at me as they walk around me. But I am too fixated on the pavement to acknowledge them. There should be a pool of black blood between the scurrying legs, but there is nothing. Looking around, I'm sure this is the right alleyway. But so much happened last night in such a short period that maybe I'm not as confident as usual.

I continue walking into the town square to the large oak tree. I longingly stretch my arm out, eager to bring back the innocence of my youth, of running under the large canopy as my grandmother stopped to speak to friends. Running my fingertips along the trunk, the rough bark caresses my skin.

Zap!

Ouch! A quick shock of electricity runs through my fingers and up my arm. I yank away my hand and inspect it;

my fingertips are black, the colour of ash. I rub my hand against my pants, trying to wipe off whatever has stained them, but it doesn't budge.

Trees don't have electricity running through them, do they? The thought runs through my mind, and I look around to see if a cable has come loose and fallen amongst the branches. Still, everything seems so ordinary. People move about their day, reading their newspapers, checking to see if any recent deaths or disappearances have been reported, and children play in the open space. I look at my fingers again and give them another rough rub on my jeans. A few zaps of static electricity run up my leg, but the black stain doesn't shift. I work up a big wad of spit, drop it onto my fingers and give them another rough scrub—nothing.

"*Touch it. Touch it again,*" a voice calls in the wind. I look around to see where it's coming from.

"Excuse me?" I say to a woman in her mid-thirties, her hands full of shopping bags. "Did you hear that voice?" She looks me up and down, her eyes landing on my fingers.

"What voice?" she asks warily.

"Someone saying, '*touch it*'." As soon as the words leave my mouth, I feel stupid. The woman clutches her bags closer to her chest and shakes her head.

"No. I don't know what you're talking about," she says quickly as she hurries off, glancing back over her shoulder.

Can no one else hear it?

Did I imagine it? Like the voices from last night?

No, that was just the adrenaline talking, my subconscious. But what could it be now? I shake my head and walk off. I need a drink.

"*Touch it. Touch the tree!*" I clasp my hands over my ears, trying to block out the clamour of voices calling out to me like claws trying to dig into my skin.

It's all in your head. It's just your imagination. Mallrie's story is just playing tricks on you.

Sitting in Christina's, light pours through the window, bathing the popular café in a warm, buttery glow. I slip a little gin into my coffee while I wait for my waffles. Wrapping my hands around the mug and warming my fingers, I gaze distractedly out at the oak tree in the centre of town.

Christina's is the only café with prime street frontage. Most other cafés or restaurants are on the higher levels or in the outer rings of the business district.

Yet, I can still hear that strange voice calling out to me. Thankfully, it's fainter within the café, but the eerie feeling coating my skin sends a shiver down my spine.

"Your usual waffles with fruit," Christina announces, causing me to jump out of my skin, my coffee sloshing over the side of the mug as she places the plate of food in front of me. "You alright, doll?" she asks, quirking her bright, blood-orange lips. Despite my rule about not making friends, Christina was kind of inevitable when I dine at her café almost every day. Not that I am ever the one to start a conversation with the woman. She drags out any conversation all by herself. Christina is a tall woman. She towers over me, but that could be because I am on the shorter side. Nevertheless, Christina stands before me, a hand propped on her hip, dressed in her take of a 1950s-style candy stripe waitress dress.

Not only does Christina make a mean waffle, but she is also very handy with a sewing machine and designs and makes her own clothes.

"I loved the vibe of those vintage uniforms, y'know? But like they were so... conservative. I wanted something a little sexy," she told me once when she tried to pry some information out of me. The skirt sits just above her knees and flairs with the most impractical apron sewn into the waist, where she places her notepad and pen.

"Yeah. Fine," I say quietly, dragging my left hand down by my side so she can't see what's happened to my fingers. Instead, she eyes me as I take another long sip of my gin and coffee, savouring the burn as it cascades down my throat, scalding my tongue.

"Okay, well, you know you can talk to me any time, doll."

I give her a dismissive nod, and she walks off, stopping by another table to chat.

That's why people love coming to Christina's so much. She knows everyone and loves to talk. Her customers are her family, and she'd do anything for them.

I love it for the waffles.

After devouring my meal and another cup of spiked coffee, I head on a successful shopping trip, then off towards the town's library. Mallrie's story keeps playing over and over in my mind, and I figure I can at least get some answers to silence his voice in my mind. Unfortunately, the voice in the wind calls to me again as I walk past the tree.

"Touch the tree. Touch it again," calls the wind. Instead, I lift my chin higher and ignore the voice.

The library is one of the largest buildings in town. Not that it is any taller than the others. All the structures in

Datura are the same height—five stories high—and all are equally beautiful. But the library alone occupies the entire building. Most structures in the business district share the occupancy between different department stores, offices, cafés and restaurants. They even split some buildings in the outer rings between residential and commercial. Even the government building is split between meeting rooms, the general disciplinary office and the mayor's office and penthouse.

I always found it strange that the library has its own dedicated building, especially when it feels like no one ever goes in there. I push open the heavy wooden doors, which creak ominously shut behind me.

Inside the spacious library, one can see all the way to the fifth floor and out the glass roof. It is also the only building in Datura that has a glass roof.

I remember coming here as a child with my grandmother and begging her to let me stay overnight so I could watch the stars.

"Oh, precious one. I wish we could, but you know the rules."

"Home before sunset," I reply sadly, reciting the universal rule of our town.

"That's right." She'd kiss my forehead, and we would walk back out of the library, arms filled with books, my eyes still cast towards the sky.

Each level of the library is exposed, with gold iron railings. Floor-to-ceiling bookcases line the walls, books overflowing and spilling onto the floor in stacks. How one tiny town can accumulate so many books, I cannot fathom.

On the ground floor, in the middle of the room, sits a large, round mahogany desk where the librarians sit. Five librarians—experts on all the books housed on one of the five levels—quietly chat amongst themselves as they work.

Being an expert on over 10,000 books must be arduous because they all are greying and old. Honestly, it feels a little cliché. I chuckle to myself whenever I enter the library —which isn't as often as I'd like. I try to get here at least once a month to borrow as many books as possible. Sometimes, when those nightmares plague me, I just need to escape into another world, and I can find some tiny fraction of solitude between the pages of a good book.

Walking to the front desk, I clear my throat. "Um, excuse me? Can someone point me to where I might find books about the town's history?"

All the librarians are busily marking books and putting them onto different trolleys and shelves with such speed and precision it defies how old they look. Only one bothers to look up—this must be his expertise.

"Town history?" he repeats, his voice soft and leathery like the book in his hands.

I smile at the thought and nod. "Yes, please."

"Haven't had someone interested in the town's history for a long time," he ponders, his eyes glazing over as if trying to remember the last time someone checked out the history books. The other librarians all murmur their agreement.

"Well, I'm interested. Now," I say, a little more demanding than I'd like.

All five librarians turn to look at me, and I feel I've done something wrong. "Please," I tack on sweetly. "Our town is filled with so much history. I think we all need to know about the brave first settlers and how we came here." I spin some bullshit, internally rolling my eyes, hoping it will get them back to helping me faster. I've found that—unfortunately, for me—being standoffish and abrupt around people rarely gets me anywhere. Other people still enjoy human interaction and relationships, even if they will only lead to eventual heartbreak. I don't want to be stuck here longer than I should be. I just want to borrow some books, get some groceries, maybe check out that new clothing store that opened a few weeks ago and get home. Shuffling my feet, the bags in my arms grow heavy and uncomfortable.

"Yes, yes, very good. However, no history books are to be taken from the library. You must read them here," says the old man, his brows coming together.

"That's fine," I say, though it is totally *not* fine. This throws a spanner into my entire plan. I take a deep breath. *I'll quickly flick through them to ease my mind.*

Ten to twenty minutes tops. Then, I am out of here.

The librarian walks out from behind the large desk, walking cane in hand.

"Well, follow me then. I hope you've got your walking shoes on," he jokes, glancing down at my white sneakers, the other librarians chuckling behind him. "We're off to the fifth floor."

I sigh a little too loudly. Of course the history books are on the fifth floor.

It will be nightfall before we even get to the top, a pessimistic voice in my mind grumbles.

We walk in silence up to the fifth floor, and I cannot help but look out at the windows covering the ceiling. The sky feels so close I could touch it.

"It's beautiful at night," says the timeworn librarian, breaking up the sound of his cane tapping rhythmically on the staircase. "Great for stargazing."

A small smile pulls at the corners of my lips. *That would be amazing.* I don't think I've ever actually seen the stars. Apart from last night, there have been only two times when

I was out after dark to potentially see the stars. However, when you're hyper-focused on trying to stay alive and not be eaten by flesh-eating monsters, stopping to look up at the stars isn't really at the forefront of your mind.

I sigh, internally kicking myself that I should have looked up last night on the walk home with Mallrie. Though the stars would be hard to see from the tight, winding alleyways and the light pollution, it would have been nice to look up and see what the sky beholds after the sun sets.

The librarian shows me a whole bookshelf. Rows upon rows of books containing the town's history from the first settlers to the recent mayor. Over a hundred years of history.

"Every mayor since Albert Charleston of the First Settlement has a journal about their service as mayor. Our current mayor, Edgar MacQuoid, comes in once a month to record in his journal. They're strictly off-limits to civilians until five years after his resignation." The librarian runs a wrinkly, bony hand over one of the many leather-bound books wrapped in black chains before levelling me with a stern glare. "Easy to know that they're off limits," he states. My eyes flick back to the chains and locks. *Subtle,* I think. He smiles at me and hobbles off back towards the stairs. I stare at the black journal encased in chains for a while, feeling a crease form between my brows. It is the most prominent journal, which isn't surprising since Edgar MacQuoid is the longest-running mayor Datura has ever had. A shiver runs down my spine as I stare at the iron-dressed book.

"Liar," the voice hisses around me, causing me to shudder, a sudden coldness washing over me.

I spin around and fall into the bookcase, looking for the person responsible. But I am all alone. I can hear the faint, rhythmic tapping of the librarian's walking stick on the stairs as he returns to the ground floor.

Dropping my shopping bags on the floor, I rub the back of my neck to ease the feeling of being watched. *I should have grabbed another coffee.* Instead, I contemplate having a swig of gin straight from the bottle as I climb the rollaway ladder and pull the first journal out. History always was my worst subject in school; I never had the knack of remembering dates and events.

I commandeer one of the small reading tables and chairs spaced out around each level and pull it over to the history section, the first journal tucked under my arm. It's thick—almost as big as Mayor MacQuoid's journals are. It's going to take me forever to read through all these books. *And I only wanted to be here for ten minutes, twenty minutes max!*

If I ever want to get a good night's sleep again and live in blissful peace, or maybe just blissful ignorance, I need to debunk Mallrie's story that keeps playing through my mind. *Why am I like this?*

Settling into the worn leather chair, I flick open the cover. The handwriting is small and cursive, depicting a writing style long since abandoned and replaced with something faster and simpler. I have to squint to make out some words. I was never good at reading cursive writing— I even had trouble reading my grandmother's handwriting, and I saw that daily. The pages of the journal have yellowed with age, making the writing harder to read. Still, the ancient pages have a nice, crisp feel, and the sound they make when I turn them is aesthetically pleasing.

This journal belongs to Sir Albert Charleston.

If this is not you, kindly return to where you found it.

A quiet chuckle bubbles out of me, feeling like I have just picked up a teenage girl's diary. I flick through the first few pages. The first book is a bust. Apparently, Charleston thought quite highly of himself and kept regular journals. When he decided to head out on his expedition, he deemed them all worthy of bringing along. I roll my eyes as I return the fifth book of pre-settlement ramblings. However, I would be a liar if I didn't say I lingered a little on those diaries. Reading about Charleston's mundane life in a town not riddled with flesh-eating monsters had my heart yearning to somehow be rid of this town. To find that quiet, ordinary life somewhere... safe.

I perch myself up on the ladder with my ass awkwardly resting on one of the rungs and my arm looped through the side as I flick through journal after journal. Climbing up and down to find they are just more dead-ends was getting exasperating.

Charleston really thought that his shit didn't stink. I'm partially in awe of his determination to go before his king and demand that he finance an expedition that he would lead to explore new lands. It took Charleston a good fifteen months before the king agreed. Snapping the diary closed, I twist on the old wooden ladder, cringing at how it groans. As I free the next journal, I try to block out Beckett's poisonous words about my weight.

The first third of the book is about Charleston's petition to the Crown for him to lead the expedition party. *How Charleston could walk anywhere when his head was so freaking big, I have no idea—over-inflated ego much?* I grouse internally. There are internal monologues on how, as loyal to the Crown as he is, their king is not actively seeking new territories to claim and how he would make for a respectable ruler. Charleston clearly thought that the king would allow him to rule over whatever land he found and acquired. My teeth grind against each other until my jaw aches. Charleston sounds like the biggest wanker, and his belief that he should have been *allowed* to rule over whatever land he *stole* has my blood boiling. Sticking my finger between the pages, I grab the following few books and return to the table and chair I commandeered.

Rolling my eyes, I flick through the pages of the journal. My newly stained hand drags along the page as I skim the words. Charleston has just left his motherland and set out in the name of the Crown to gain more land.

I find myself daydreaming again about some of the cities and towns Charleston wrote about on his journey, wondering what it would be like to live in a place not overrun by flesh-eating monsters. Shaking my head as a clock somewhere in the library chimes to midday, I take a sneaky swig of gin to clear the daydream and continue to flick through the book. *So much for ten minutes, tops!*

We've found a wonderful place to set up our newest township. The land is rich with great splendours. I have chosen a beautiful oak tree as our town's centre point. We know oaks are a symbol of strength and endurance. These are impeccable properties for a new town of the Crown. People will come far and wide to celebrate with us underneath its striking canopy.

Nightfall, however, proves to be complicated. Whereas on the other side of the Melsheim Forest, in which we came, the only things we feared of the night were wild dogs and the occasional wolf, which seemed to convey some sort of higher comprehension that we would kill them quickly if provoked. We obtained many splendid pelts which have made fine coats from their foolish attacks. However, here, I fear we are not at the top of the food chain anymore. The journey through the Melsheim Forest was arduous. Many creatures that seem to be straight from the deepest, darkest depths of Hell lurk within. By the time we made it out, our party of 1,000 of our strongest fighters and their families had dwindled to 300 persons. Combined.

Regrettably, a creature of the night stalks us and feasts upon our people. Taller than our tallest man, slender unlike any man, woman or child we've ever witnessed—even those riddled with sickness. A creature of bone and flesh seeking to devour more flesh.

A Flesh-Hunter, I've named it.

They have but not a face, only a serpent-like nose, and if you're calamitous enough to witness, a line in place of its mouth. A mouth that looks like someone has placed a blade and carved a smile onto that soulless face, a mouth that peels open to *reveal a row of incredibly sharp, pointed teeth—far sharper than we have ever been able to produce for a sword or spearhead. Its arms are the length of its body, and where its hands should be, this crea-ture slenders off into incredibly sharp points, creating arms like blades, which it uses to skin its prey while still breathing and devouring it. Slowly. So slowly, we have listened to our friends, family and comrades cry in pain, begging for mercy. Then, when we so generously deliver a deathly blow, the Flesh-Hunters leave the body. They seemingly only want fresh, live meat.*

Well, there you go. I sigh, and the leather chair groans under my weight as I lay back into its softness. *Nothing in there about witches.* Slamming the book shut, my brows knit together into a slight frown. I don't know why I am frustrated that this has proven Mallrie's story to be just that... A story.

An instinct in the back of my mind hints that something is not quite right. I'm too cynical to believe everything someone says. I have given my trust before, and those I have handed it to returned nothing but betrayal. My goodwill was used against me; people walked all over me and then blamed me for *their* actions.

Now, I like to just stick with the facts.

And the fact is right here in this book. No witches. No magic. *So why does it feel like something is missing?*

Resting my neck against the top curve of the armchair, I press my palms into my eyes, trying to recall the events of last night, as much as I don't want to.

Let's look at the facts.

The memories come back in a gin and adrenaline-induced haze.

Okay, so Mallrie was strong and fast enough to kill the Flesh-Hunters. It was impressive, really it was. My foot bounces nervously as I try to gather my thoughts, my hand itching towards the bag of gin.

But witches and fairies?

Did he think I was naïve enough to believe him?

I stopped believing in magic when I was a kid. When you have real-life monsters at your backdoor, you quickly stop thinking a knight in shining armour will come to save you.

No one will save you in the real world.

But Mallrie saved you. Twice!

I can still hear his voice calling me a good girl. Those two paltry words of praise rocked me, and something inside me that I had repressed for a long time awoke. I shake my head, dislodging the memory of his hands on me and the slight sound of hurt in his voice when I told him I wanted to forget everything that happened that night.

But of course, I can't forget. Something doesn't feel right. There is an annoying feeling in the pit of my stomach that won't let me just put this to rest.

"Why?" I groan, running my fingers through my hair and interlocking them at the nape of my neck to stop myself from reaching for the bottle of gin. *Why is this nagging at the back of my mind? Do I want it to be true so I can give reason to all the terrible memories of my past instead of just living with the fact that this is life in Datura? So I can shift the blame of all the people senselessly murdered by Flesh-Hunters onto Charleston? So I can believe that if he had just left the High Witchess alone, maybe all the horrible things that have happened to me that draw me to the drink wouldn't have happened?*

When Mallrie told the story, it felt like *his* story, not just a story or a legend he had heard. A shuddering breath leaves my body. He spoke about it with such emotion. As if he was actually there witnessing it. Even though that's impossible.

With a sigh, I pick up the last diary of Sir Albert Charleston. Flicking through the pages of the journal to the last entry, I scan over it quickly. The handwriting has changed. Charleston's eldest son is writing on behalf of his father. The calligraphy was bloody and messy as if it had been written hastily. Scanning the page, I realise Charleston is passing the town's leadership to his son. A Flesh-Hunter has brutally injured him. Sucking in a shuddering breath as my fingers trace over the yellowing pages spotted with dark ink and aged blood—

As I lie on my deathbed, the heroics of my eldest son, Jeremiah, will not be forgotten, for his swift call to action has given me these last few moments. A Flesh-Hunter had me restrained. The beast devoured my flesh from my chest. Oh, the agony. The pain. I would not be here if not for Jeremiah and his quick thinking. He tied a noose around my ankle and suspended me in the—

An inkblot is smeared over the following few words, making it impossible to read. A knowing weight presses against my chest as I run my finger over it. I don't know how to explain it, but *something* inside me just knows something is wrong.

Curious.

Tracing my finger over the smeared ink, I see it looks different from the ink in which the words have been written. It's darker...

Could it—no.

I shake my head to avoid thinking that *someone* has gone back over the years and censored Charleston's diary in such a deliberately subtle way.

Where I clung to its boughs until the first light of the new day, alas, this last entry of mine is not to dwell on my suffering but to atone for my sins. If only by writing about my shortcomings.

Gentle reader, as I lie here, our best physicians unable to stop the extensive bleeding, I can only feel responsible for my fate. If not for my selfish actions, my people might have been able to live here in safety and peace.

Hastily turning the page, my shoulders slump in defeat. So that's where it ends. Not *quite* a confession. But it seems enough that Mallrie's story could have a sliver of truth. Maybe not about witches and magic, but Charleston wasn't the founder. I don't know. Perhaps I am just grasping at loose ends.

That inkblot has my mind spiralling. I turn the page to see if I can make out any indentation of the word on the other side of the page, but my eyes get caught up on my blackened fingertips. An effervescence of aggravation swells in my chest as I aggressively rub them against my jeans, but nothing budges.

What the fuck is this shit?

My frustration simmers away into curiosity as something catches my eye in the back of the journal.

I shouldn't be curious. I should let this go and continue living my life as it is. But there is an ache in my chest that has me almost desperate for answers. Tracking my non-blackened fingers down the crack of the open book... Pages are missing. So meticulously torn out with such precision that no one would notice or question that they were missing.

Sucking in a breath, my heart does a silly little flip. There may be something in those missing pages.

I quickly flick back through the book with a closer eye.

Pages are missing throughout the entire book!

CHAPTER SIX
ELIANA

The sound of leather colliding with wood fills all five levels of Datura's library as I slam the diary of Albert Charleston, the leader of the first settlers, onto the mahogany front desk. I flinch as the sound echoes back to me, and all five librarians' attention snaps to where I stand, my blackened fingers still curled around the journal. Their expressions are a mix between shock and irritation.

"Sorry," I exhale sheepishly. After running down all the stairs from the top floor, I am out of breath. I really am out of shape. Limping the short distance from the other side of the desk, his cane tapping rhythmically, the fifth-floor librarian stops short when he notices my blackened fingers resting on top of the book.

"Curious," he mutters as he carefully reaches out to grab my hand. Quickly, I pull away from his outstretched grasp and tuck it behind my back. I don't like being touched. Not if I can help it. Of course, I have desired it from time to time. *It's better to be alone,* I remind myself, even as the memory of Mallrie's big, strong hands around me floods my mind like a monsoon in a desert, sending a wave of liquid heat directly to my core.

"I have a question about—"

Before I can finish my train of thought, another librarian grabs my arm behind me. Their firm grip is almost painful as they hold my hand for the others to examine.

I cast the librarian assaulting me with an irate glance, yet he doesn't take any notice of me. Which just irritates me all the more. I would snap and tell him off, but I still need their help.

Today isn't going at all how I had hoped it would. Somewhat conscious of the time, I try to pull my hand away. But, unfortunately, all five of them are too busy scrutinising my hand and muttering in hushed tones between themselves.

"Do you see this?" asks the librarian, tightening his hold on my wrist, his tiny oval spectacles slipping down his nose.

"Oh, I see it, Caspian."

"Do you think it has started?"

"Certainly not. We would have known."

"But didn't the—"

"Don't say her name!" snaps another librarian with something akin to superstitious fear in his voice.

They look up, turning their heads from side to side like meerkats watching for a predator.

"What happened to you, dear?" questions one of the librarians. She's short and thin with long hair that falls like a sheet of silver down to her waist. I can't imagine how annoying it would be to have all that hair flying around all the time.

"Oh, um—"

Why can't I speak? The desire to remove my arm from

their intrusive scrutiny is almost unbearable. It has clearly affected my bloody brain's ability to speak. I try to pull away, but the grip on my wrist is firm. My skin feels hot and agitated. The librarian's moustache scrunches to one side as he waits for my response. Narrowing my eyes in his direction, I give my arm another subtle yank.

"I had a bit of an accident on my way here," I half-admit.

"What *type* of accident? Should we call the town practitioner?" urges the woman, her absurdly long hair falling over her shoulder as she tilts her head.

I shake my head. "Oh, no, no need for that. I just touched—" I stop myself mid-sentence, a thought sparking to life, blaring with alarm bells. *If Mallrie's story is true, and magic is hidden within the oak tree, could it be that whatever has stained my fingers is* magic?

The thought is ludicrous, but it could explain why it doesn't come off. Besides, if every mayor since Charleston knows about the existence of magic and witches but has swept it under the rug, so to speak, who knows what they'll do to me if I tell them I've discovered the truth. Send me straight to the mayor and the general disciplinary office, I assume. But then what?

The thought of having to go before the GDO—or worse, Mayor MacQuoid—has every nerve in my body lighting up on high alert. Every public address he has given has left me feeling uneasy. My back seizes up as if someone is hiding behind me. There has always been something about him I didn't like that left me feeling... slimy.

Maybe it's because Edgar was relatively young when he took over as mayor after his father. Edgar MacQuoid Sr. died in a tragic accident that never sat well with my grandmother or me. Something about his death always felt... wrong.

This year will mark Edgar's tenth year as mayor. An abnormally long period—mayors typically only stay for a three to five-year term. It's not like other people haven't tried to run against Edgar because they have, but no one has ever won. He has so much charisma that he could convince a terminally ill man he was in perfect health if he wanted to. It's a quality that just feels sycophantic.

The last person to run against Edgar as mayor, Robert Simpson, had an "unfortunate accident with a Flesh-Hunter".

"Mr Simpson was heading home late after a busy day of campaigning for mayor when he met his untimely death." It was blasted all over the news. Robert was the people's favourite to win. For years, he served in the temple of Achel and Vid as one of the high priests before deciding to run for mayor. Robert was a man of faith and was loyal to serving his community.

"It sorrows me deeply," Edgar announced over the public address system after the news broke. *"Mr Simpson was a wonderful man who devoted much of his life to his gods and community. A worthy opponent who I feel would have made a wonderful mayor for this town."*

I remember sitting in an armchair by the window, feeling utterly numb inside after another restless night battling my demons, a hot cup of coffee in my hand as I stared out at the bleak day. Storm clouds were forming high above the buildings as Edgar's voice reverberated throughout the alleyways from the public address systems. Again, I looked down at the coffee in my hand, my body seizing as Edgar's words filled me like poison.

"Are you okay, dear?" The librarian's voice snaps my

attention back to her. Our eyes meet; her bright blue eyes, against her aging skin and silver-grey hair, search mine.

"I touched the oak tree," I blurt without thinking. As the words leave my mouth, I instantly want to reach through the air and grab them before anyone can hear them. I know how preposterous that sounds. No doubt they'll send for a practitioner now. Or worse, the GDO.

The librarians react to my statement with gasps and murmuring amongst themselves. At this moment, I just want to run and hide. But that curious side of me wants to see where this will go. One of their earlier comments burns in my mind. *Do you think it has started?*

What did he mean by that? I look over to the librarian who spoke those words; his right eyebrow arched, a scar slicing through the grey hairs. He runs a hand over the side of his head where the hair is shaved short, the length on top gathered in an elastic. Despite his age, he is rather handsome. He looks like he might have been a warrior in a past life.

The old man gripping my arm—Caspian—suddenly releases it. My arm falls with a heavy thump to my side, snapping my attention back to him with a scowl. Caspian's salt and pepper hair is tied up in a neat bun on the top of his head, and tiny oval spectacles perch on the end of his nose. His grey moustache nervously twitches as he clicks his tongue in disapproval.

"This is not good," he mutters. "Do you know what will happen if—"

"Oh, shush, you old grump!" spits the librarian with the long hair.

"This is a good thing," responds the librarian with the scar.

"You all need to stop talking right *now*," urges the fifth-floor librarian.

"Look, I don't know what is going on, but I just need to know *where* the missing pages of this journal are." My tone is harsh and unsympathetic, and I honestly don't care.

I have already been here longer than I expected, and the librarians are wasting my time. I don't care *who* they're talking about anymore or *what* might have started. I just want my answers and to go home.

Maybe I don't even care about the answers anymore.

No, that's not true. I won't be able to let this go. I know that.

They look between themselves as if they are unsure about something. The feeling is mutual, and I now regret coming here.

"Why don't you come with me, dear?" asks the female with the sheet of silver hair. Her voice is kind, and when she looks at me, her eyes fill me with warmth, with a sense that I can trust her. The feeling is old and foreign and sends my stomach tumbling. The other four librarians are all staring at me intensely, and I feel like I'm being backed into a corner. Like I have no other option than to go with her.

"Um, am I in some sort of trouble?" There is a slight tremor in my voice, breaking the strong façade I've been trying to show.

"Oh, no, darling." She looks around to make sure no one is listening and then extends her arm, silver bracelets falling around her wrist. "We're trying to keep you out of trouble. Come with me."

CHAPTER SEVEN

ELIANA

The librarian, who introduced herself as Selma, leads me through the tall bookcases towards the back of the library. Her long silver hair glistens in the warm light of the scalloped wall sconces scattered between the bookcases.

My stomach twists into a knot as we near a heavily stained wooden door with gold writing reading "RESTRICTED ACCESS". My heartbeat picks up as Selma pulls a small gold key from her pocket. Throwing a coy smile over her shoulder, she carefully slides the key into the lock and twists it with a foreboding *click*. She holds the door open for me, her silver bangles bunching up at the end of her wrist. I take an exploratory step forward, peering into the doorway and down the staircase that descends into darkness, the beating of my heart drowning out the world around me.

I look back at Selma apprehensively, and she urgently waves me into the doorway. I peek over my shoulder at all the other librarians, who appear to be busily working again but keep stealing glances over their shoulders in our direction as if making sure I go with Selma. I wonder what would happen if I just said no. *Will they let me go? Surely, I can outrun them.* Flexing my wrist that Caspian had gripped unnaturally tight for someone his age, that thought evaporates quickly. There is just something about how he held onto me. The air surrounding the librarians just feels... unnatural. I shake my head.

You're being foolish! You've gotten yourself all worked up about Mallrie's stupid story. There is nothing supernatural about the librarians. They're just doing their job.

Biting my lip, I descend into the darkness. I take one last glimpse over my shoulder as the door swings shut, plunging us into complete darkness.

The lock clicks behind me.

My heart drops to the floor.

My breathing quickens.

The well-known feeling of anxiety's cold, bony fingers wrapping around my spine has my back straightening, trying to get out of its grip. I reach out for the handrail to steady myself.

I can't breathe, despite how quickly I am gasping for air like a fish out of water.

Squeezing my eyes shut until white spots scattered across my closed lid, I will my body to relax. I wish I had my gin with me to help settle these nerves. But I focus on my breathing.

What was that godsdamned breathing exercise again?

I feel Selma push past me, her cool arm brushing against mine as she swiftly descends the stairs as if the darkness doesn't affect her. For once, that brief brush of human contact has my body buzzing for more.

Come back, the scared little voice calls from deep within me.

The hum of electricity echoes around the basement. As the lights flicker around us, it is less reassuring than I had hoped, but at least I can see now. Selma looks back up the stairs to where I am still holding onto the rail as if it is the only thing keeping my body upright. It probably is.

That little voice gets forced back into the dark parts of myself. I unclench my jaw, and my breathing slowly resumes to an average pace.

"Well, come on then. You of all people should know we don't have all day." Her voice sounds more youthful down here as if the withered old lady's voice was all an act. *Of course, it's probably just the acoustics,* I try to reassure myself before my mind runs off on a tangent of what-ifs.

I cautiously hurry down the stairs. "Sorry, what do you mean, *'you of all people should know we don't have all day'*?" I ask, tilting my chin up, trying to re-establish some sense that I am not about to fall apart.

She gives a low chuckle. "Oh, dear, we know all about your little incident last night," she says in a mock-caring way. "Scary stuff, that was."

My eyes widen, and I wonder if following her down here alone was a mistake. Mrs Kaminski's words from this morning ring in my ears. *Who knows when someone will find you?*

She's not wrong, and acknowledging that has my stomach twisting into an uncomfortable knot. If something happened to me, who knows how long it would be before anyone noticed I was missing or dead. I don't have any family left, I have sworn off relationships after my ex-boyfriend turned out to be a psychopath and I try to keep my distance from people as much as possible.

Those you care about will either end up disappointing you or dead. My heart quietly aches for those I've lost. I take a deep breath to stop the tears from threatening to pool in my eyes and push the feelings away, as I've done over the years. I have gotten pretty good at disassociating from the trauma. Even if that is with a bottle of gin.

It all started when I was sixteen. That's when I first started drinking to help numb the pain. It wasn't a lot. Just one drink of sherry before bed. It was my grandmother's— the nutty and saline flavour would burn as I shot back the tiny glass. But when I turned twenty-four and...

A shudder runs through me as the memories threaten to break out of the little boxes I have carefully locked them away in for all these years. *Well, then, I need something more substantial.*

I look around the basement. It's what one would imagine a typical library storage room to be. One wall is lined with some extra bookshelves. Books that look as if they haven't been touched for decades line the shelves, covered in a thick layer of dust. Some old, broken ladders lean against the ends of the bookshelves, and spare trolleys are pushed into the corner of the room.

A sign browning with age catches my eye from the side of the shelves, reading "BANNED BOOKS". My curiosity is piqued, but I decide to continue my examination of the room. A small kitchenette is in the other corner, and a round rug and table sit in the middle of the room. There is one door off the side marked "Toilets" and another unmarked door. The entire room smells musty, like old books and herbal tea. Yet, despite my metaphorical hackles being up, the smell is rather soothing.

"Come, sit down." Selma tugs a chair from the table and walks over to the kitchenette to open a cupboard. I warily walk over and take a seat, glancing back over my shoulder at the bookshelf with the banned books. *Maybe that's where the pages from the journal are? If I could just get down here alone, perhaps I could—*

"Tea, dear? We don't make coffee, sorry. Too much caffeine can cloud your... *judgement*." She takes a moment, chewing her words, choosing them carefully.

"Um, no, thanks," I reply, my focus still trying to scan the bookshelf.

"You won't find what you're looking for over there, dear." I glance up, but the librarian still focuses on brewing the tea.

"I'm sorry. I don't know what you mean," I play dumb. I already feel disadvantaged down here, so I think keeping my cards close to my chest is best—the little to none I have, anyway. She turns to face me with a perfect smile, white teeth flashing as she walks over to me with a floral teacup. The smell of herbal tea fills the space as she sits beside me, tiny rose buds dancing around in the cup from where she's stirred it. The scent is familiar, but I can't quite pinpoint where that familiarity is coming from. An anxious feeling, like a rock sinking to the bottom of a lake, settles in my gut as the librarian stretches out her hand, her palm facing up.

"You're safe here, dear. May I?" She nods towards my hand with blackened fingertips. Cautiously, I place my hand in hers. The tension in the air is thick, making it feel as if I have little choice—*plus, they locked you in a basement.* She turns my hand over in hers, inspecting it.

"You said you touched the Enkanti Tree." Selma chuckles sweetly. "Pardon, I mean the oak tree," she corrects herself, but how she laughs makes me wonder if she meant the slip of the tongue.

"What did you call it?" I can't help but ask, tilting my head up and looking down at her. A small part of me curses myself for being so stubborn about figuring this out. *Why can't I just let it go?*

She gives me another attempt at a friendly smile, reminding me how a snake curves its lips up when it prepares to open its mouth and strike its prey.

"Ah, so he told you." Her eyebrows raise as an all-too-knowing smile seeps across her face before clicking her tongue and adding, "That man can't keep his mouth shut. But I guess he would only have told you if he sensed something in you." Selma gives me a long look up and down before waving a hand in the air, dismissing the thought. "Who am I to question his methods? He'll achieve what we need to be done."

I just stare at her in disbelief. Before last night, my life was perfectly normal. Now, I feel like I've fallen down a rabbit hole and into an alternate universe with magic, witches and faeries. My head feels like it is trying to float away from my body, and the world is spinning the wrong way. I swear, the waffles I ate earlier have sphacelated in my stomach. It's all too overwhelming.

My fingers start to tingle. Heat runs from my fingertips into my veins and pumps through my body. The sound of porcelain scraping across the wooden table is like nails dragging down a chalkboard. It resonates down the back of my neck as Selma pushes the tea towards me, and I press a hand to my forehead to steady myself and stop the spinning. All of this new information is a lot to process, and then there is my anxiety sloshing around in my stomach, wanting to just get out of here. Maybe coming here in the first place was a mistake.

"Drink. It'll help with the nerves and whatever sensation your hand is feeling." She places my scorched fingers around the cup. Her voice sounds distant from the roaring in my head, and I don't have the energy to make a snarky remark about her comment about my hand. Instead, the warm porcelain and my hand's heat collide, creating a tingling sensation like pins and needles. I pull the cup to my lips, the floral aroma filling my nose. A memory of my grandmother comes flooding back to me.

CHAPTER EIGHT
ELIANA

19 YEARS AGO

I have always loved visiting my grandmother. Something about being around her made me feel safe and loved. Her apartment was on the fourth floor of her building and always smelt like freshly baked biscuits and flowers.

Every Sunday, we would go into town, and she would let me pick a fresh bouquet of flowers. I'd then place them in little vases around her apartment. At the same time, she wrapped the old flowers in bunches and hung them upside down to dry on whatever available window or doorframe there was.

My father always thought it was a waste of money.

"Why spend hard-earned money on something that just dies?" he would tell her every Sunday as she let me pick the flowers.

"Simon, you never said anything when Nina would buy flowers," my grandmother would retort, which always seemed to shut him up. I'm sure my grandmother meant no ill intent in bringing her up.

Nina was my mother and her daughter. Who died giving birth to me.

A bit of guilt always clung to me when my mother was mentioned, even at a young age. I wondered if my father blamed me for taking away the love of his life when there was already so little to love in Datura. Everyone who knew my mother would tell me how much I looked like her, from my wavy blonde hair and brown eyes to how even our noses were similar. *"A mini-Nina,"* they would say.

It was just the three of us left. My father was an only child, and his parents died before I was born, so we visited my grandmother often. I spent most weekends with her; they were some of the happiest times I can remember.

When I was six, my father and I headed to my grandmother's house just before nightfall.

Everything about that day was strange.

My father was a logical man and a stickler for the rules. He ensured we were home well before sunset and double-locked all the doors and windows. So, when he came to me an hour before sunset that night and said we were going to my grandmother's place, and to pack my stuff, something felt off. But it wasn't my place to question his actions. He always knew what was best. Even as he looked at me like he had just seen a ghost.

I remember clinging to his jacket, terrified. My legs were stiff as I tried to keep up with his long strides. I'd never been out so late before.

"Hurry, Eliana," he pleaded, pulling at my arm.

"My legs are sore," I whined. We were almost at my grandmother's when my father abruptly stopped, which caused me to run into him. He looked around as if he heard something, but I was too busy complaining to hear anything over my panting and internal whining.

Father dropped into a crouch and held my shoulders, forcing me to look into his eyes.

"Oh, my dear Eliana. I am so sorry I have let you down." He looked around, and my body tensed up in response. I knew what he was looking for; every child in Datura was told horrible bedtime stories about the monsters that lurked in our streets. School children told rumours and tales of them, how if you were naughty, the Flesh-Hunters would crawl out from under your bed and drag you away. A shudder rocked through my petite body. "Whatever you do, whatever you hear, do *not* stop until you get to your grand-mother's house. Do you understand me?" Tears pooled in my eyes, and my voice had been stolen from me. My father gave me a gentle shake. "Eliana, do you understand me?" he demanded.

I nodded, the tears now falling down my face.

"And, my sweet little Eliana, remember, I have *always* loved you." He pulled me against him, hugging me tightly. And I knew it would be our last goodbye.

I didn't want to let go as he tried to push me away. Inhaling deeply, I tried to memorise how he smelt. The way this embrace made me feel safe and whole.

"Papa, no!" I sobbed, clutching tighter to his shoulders. He pressed one last kiss to my forehead and pushed me forward. I didn't want to move. I didn't want to leave him. But he gave me another push. That's when I heard what my father must have heard before.

I started to run.

Shame filled me and burnt my cheeks as tears streamed down my face.

I could see my grandmother's apartment at the end of the alleyway. Still, the sound of the Flesh-Hunter's sluggish footsteps echoed behind me. It felt like someone had reached through my back and taken hold of my spine, slowly squeezing it. Little did I know that feeling would haunt me for the rest of my life.

I almost reached the building before a blood-curdling scream sent an icy shiver through my whole body, seizing up all my joints until I couldn't take another step. I looked over my shoulder, tripping and falling into the cold, wet snow, soaking my clothes. Shivering, I pushed myself up and saw the tall, emaciated figure of a Flesh-Hunter standing in front of my father. I wanted to scream at him, but all that came out was a sob. The Flesh-Hunter raised one of its deadly arms, and my father fell backwards onto the snow-covered cobblestone, the monster gracefully dropping on top of him. I squeezed my eyes shut, my father screaming in pain, ringing in my ears and down into my soul.

I prayed that it was all a horrible dream.

I prayed to Achel and Vid, the gods of life and death, to save my father.

"Run, Eliana. RUN!" his voice shrieked and echoed through the street, his head tilted back onto himself like he was possessed. He looked at me with terror as the Flesh-Hunter tore bloody ribbons off his chest. Red blood fell into the snow, reminding me of my favourite fairy tale he read me every night before I went to sleep. My father was more afraid of the Flesh-Hunter getting to me than of his imminent death.

Why aren't the gods helping him? The thought burnt in my throat as I sat there, unable to scream for help and too afraid to go to him.

I couldn't pull my eyes from the scene unfolding before me.

Blood was splattered across the ground like a million

tiny rubies glittering in the streetlight, and bloody hand marks clawed through the snow towards me as my father screamed for me to run. My lip quivered.

I didn't know it then, but that scene of my father, who always seemed so much larger than life, was reduced to something so insignificant it would haunt me for the rest of my life.

A firm hand gripped my waist, lifting and pulling me backwards onto my feet.

"Papa! NO!" I swung out my arms and legs. "STOP! PAPA!" I screamed, thrashing and fighting against those warm hands, trying to break free.

I have to save him. He needs me to help him! I couldn't just leave my father there to die, not like that. The gods were of no help. They had turned their backs on us.

"Hush, child!" my grandmother's voice, soft like velvet, pleaded in my ear. I felt the warmth of the building wrap around my body. The thick wooden door shut behind us, and the audible click of the lock sliding into place felt so... *final*. That was the last time I ever saw my father. The last memory of him was seared into my brain: my father lying in the snow, bloody and screaming at me to run. To leave him. To save myself. The building had muffled his shouts and screams, but they would forever play through my mind like a scratchy record stuck on repeat, haunting me for eternity. With each piercing cry, my heart tore a little more.

My grandmother struggled against my writhing as she hauled me up the stairs. I screamed and wailed the whole way. Doors cracked open, and eyes peered around them to see what the commotion was about.

My body was thrust unceremoniously into a chair at the small dining table by the window. I tried to protest, to beg that she help my father, but my voice was hoarse, and only a ragged sob came out.

My grandmother rushed back over to the door and locked it. There was a flurry of commotion in the kitchen as she prepared a cup of rose and chamomile tea. The sweet, floral scent filled the small apartment, but the muffled screams of my father being eaten alive from the street could still be heard from inside. I squeezed my eyes shut so tightly it hurt and pressed my hands over my ears.

"No, no. Please stop. Please help Papa," I muttered to myself over and over and over. A prayer to a new God who would be merciful and kind.

The china clinked on the table, and the tea's floral aroma had me looking up at my grandmother, watching as she jerked the curtains together, blocking the view of the alleyway. Finally, she heaved a mournful sigh and pressed the teacup into my hands.

"Drink, my love," she whispered gently. I watched as she hurried around the small kitchen, collecting an array of white candles from the back of a cupboard and setting them on the island bench.

The candles were reverently placed in a circle. My grandmother's attention was fixated as she muttered something incomprehensible under her breath.

Each candle was lit with a graceful flick of her wrist, so elegant I didn't see the strike of the match through my swollen eyes.

The flames flickered as she rummaged through her cupboards. A circle of black salt was spilt around the outside candles first. Then, a ring of red salt that caused me to flinch at the memory of the blood on the snow was added inside the circle of candles.

Once the circles of salt were complete, my grandmother

returned her attention to collecting different herbs from the dried bundles hanging around her home.

She crushed the herbs in a pestle and mortar, then sprinkled them over the candles and rings of salt, all the while muttering to herself. The tea warmed my hands and body as I sipped, but there was still a deep cold inside me that warmth could ease.

Suddenly, as if a phantom gust of wind blew in out of nowhere, all the candles blew out one at a time.

Then, there was silence.

An animalistic cry came from outside. The Flesh-Hunter sounded angry, like a child when their favourite toy had been taken from them. I clung to my cup harder as I squeezed my eyes shut, tears falling down my face.

My grandmother's warm hand rubbed over my shoulders. "It's over, dear. He's with your mother now."

Dark circles hung under my grandmother's eyes that weren't there the last time I saw her. She appeared exhausted; the hard lines around her mouth looked like they were weighted, pulling her full lips downward. She slumped her body into the seat across from mine, and we silently drank our tea. Finally, she looked up at me and smiled.

"We will be alright."

CHAPTER NINE
ELIANA

Inhaling the floral scent of the tea Selma handed me has dragged up memories I've tried to repress for a long time. I cautiously glance at her over the rim of my cup.

"Your hand, dear," the librarian prompts, her eyes penetrating as she looks from me to my hand. "You said you touched the Enkanti Tree?" she asks again, her tone cracking a little with impatience.

All I can do in reply is give a slight nod, my heart weighing heavy in my chest with the past swirling in the forefront of my mind.

"Can you tell me what happened when you touched it?" she asks, tilting her head to the side.

I clear my throat and press my eyes together briefly, trying to compose myself before I speak. "I don't know why I touched it," I say more to myself before glancing up through my lashes. "Why do a bunch of librarians care anyway?"

Selma's body stiffens as she prudently tilts her head to the side. "We are scholars, dear."

I harrumph, not convinced by that response. "How do

you know Mallrie?" I question, raising my brows in the librarian's direction and placing the cup back on its saucer. "I'm assuming that is who you meant by '*he*' since you seem to know what I did last night."

"Let's just say Mallrie is an *old friend*. Your hand, dear."

"It felt like a shock of electricity. Then, a voice told me to touch the tree again," I say, straightening my back and looking down my nose at her.

"A voice?" Selma asks, raising her eyebrows. "Who are you, my dear?" She leans forward.

"Eliana Nightingale," I say softly before remembering the feeling I got last night that I shouldn't have told Mallrie my name so quickly. I instantly regret falling for the same mistake twice, but a soft smile brightens her face, making her look youthful and trustworthy.

"Ah, Matilda Halliwell's granddaughter. Beautiful woman. *Powerful.*"

I nod vacuously in acknowledgement. My grandmother was beautiful, and not just in appearance. She was kind and gentle, always happy to help a neighbour in need, though I am a little puzzled why the librarian would describe her as powerful. Yes, she was very opinionated and did things her way, and if you didn't like it, *"Well, then, that sounds like a you problem, not mine, doesn't it?"* as she used to say.

Selma loses a quiet sigh before looking around the basement. But we're the only ones down here. I follow her gaze around the room, not quite sure what she is looking for. "Look, it's unsafe to talk about all this here. There are powers greater than us that will silence anyone who dares to talk about this." She glances down at my hand. "Your *differences* will be exploited."

"What are you talking about?"

"I'm sorry you've been dragged into all of this. I am. You

seem like a lovely girl, albeit a bit standoffish. But you would have gotten caught up in all of it in one way or another." She continues ignoring my question, and I want to reach across the table and shake her. Demand that she answer my questions.

"I wanted nothing to do with this," I spit out, and she nods sympathetically, which only irritates me more.

"None of us did. How much did Mallrie tell you last night?"

I frown. "How *do* you know about last night?" I question. I can feel my anger rising like a spark in my chest. This all aggravates me—the secrets, the skirting around *my* questions but demanding I answer theirs.

She smiles sweetly at me. "We seem to have a mutual friend, dear."

"I hardly know him," I spit out, looking away, my gaze flicking back over the banned bookshelf. "I wouldn't call him a friend."

"Maybe so, but I wouldn't pass up the opportunity to make a friend there if I were you, dear."

"Why do you care if I make friends with him? As you can see, I don't really do the whole *friend* thing." Even the word sounds foreign, and the thought of letting someone else back into my life sends a shudder down my spine.

"You may have to put that mentality aside, dear," Selma says, once again avoiding my questions. The look she pins me with has me shifting in my seat as if she can read the thoughts rushing through my mind. "You may very well be needing one." She pauses, the silence heavy between us. "And Mallrie is a good friend to have," she says, smiling off into the distance.

"You still didn't answer my question. How do you know

about last night?" *Or care if Mallrie is my friend or not?* But I don't add that final thought.

"Our *friend*," Selma begins, and I can't help but cringe at the term. "He is good at what he does, but messy and young," she says bluntly, her tone filled with disapproval as she straightens up in her seat. "And we are here *trying* to keep him and his antics out of sight of those who would want to get their claws into him." I narrow my eyes at her, waiting for her to continue. "We're the ones cleaning up after his mess." Selma clicks her tongue in disapproval again. "Would be better if he wasn't so impulsive, but what can we do?" She shrugs, calming her expression.

"So what? He's out there every night, *killing* the Flesh-Hunters?" The thought of Mallrie out every night risking his life like some sort of vigilante... A strange feeling of concern rolls across the pit of my stomach. It's something I haven't felt in a long time, and I take a breath, pushing the feeling away and locking it back into its box. "And why would someone want to stop him from doing that anyway?" I look up at the librarian. She's shaking her head.

"They're called Kailadons, dear." Her tone turns chilly and condescending, reminding me of how exasperated Mallrie got when I kept calling the monsters plaguing our town Flesh-Hunters. "And yes, that's exactly what he does. He's trying to protect the townsfolk. Until he can fulfil a promise he made long ago."

"You still didn't answer my question," I grumble, folding my arms across my chest. "Why would someone want to stop him from killing the *Kailadons*?" I enunciate every godsdamned syllable for her benefit.

Selma reaches into her pocket and pulls out a gold pen and a piece of paper. Clicking the top, she scribbles something down. "Look, dear, it's getting late," she deflects, looking up at the ceiling as if she can see through it and out the glass roof. "You need to get home before dark. When you do, lock the doors." Selma looks up at me briefly and gives me a dry smile. "Don't trust anyone. Not that that'll be very hard for you," she adds in a sweet yet bitchy tone. She folds the piece of paper towards herself three times and slides it across the table. I pick it up and turn it over in my hands. Before I can unravel it, Selma is standing, her hands intertwined in mine. "No, not here," she says with a breath of urgency. "Wait until you get home. Burn it after you read it."

I blink up at her. *More secrets.*

She pulls me to my feet and ushers me towards the staircase. I take one last look at the bookshelf. I can't help but think there might be something there that has some answers.

"Forget about it," calls that eerily familiar voice.

The librarian retrieves the golden key from her pocket and slides it into the lock. She turns to look at me. "Put that in your pocket until you're home." She nods at the note still in my hand. I begrudgingly do as I am told, and then we walk back out onto the first floor of the library.

Selma freezes almost instantly. I follow her gaze across the room to where the other four librarians are standing behind the large mahogany desk. Two tall, bull-necked men dressed in black stand before them. With their shirts tight against their muscles, they look intimidating, like they have just stepped out of a mafia movie. They stand flanking a tall man dressed in an expensive-looking all-black suit. His dark blonde hair sits at his shoulders and has three neatly braided rows along his scalp, exposing a defined jaw. My heart skips a beat as a wave of something like fear mixed with—

"You need to leave, *now*," hisses Selma at my side. "Get home and lock the door. Do not open it for anyone."

I don't question her demand as I nod and creep along the library wall, trying my best to be inconspicuous. I have at least that much common sense to know that these three men are trouble.

Especially the man in the suit.

There is a presence emanating from him that screams danger. A subconscious *knowing*, like my intuition is on *Speed* and its twelfth cup of coffee.

I watch the librarian walk gracefully over to the desk to rejoin her colleagues, arms outstretched as if meeting an old friend. The brawny men reach for something at their side, and my eyes fall on the shiny metal of a gun.

Muscles tightening, a primal instinct freezes me where I stand as my body recognises that I cannot outrun a bullet.

The man in the suit turns to her. "Where have you been?" he growls, his voice deep and filled with a darkness that promises violence yet is surprisingly smooth. He glares at Selma as if he's been waiting for her return. "You are meant to be manning the desk," he reminds her softly, but his voice has a vicious edge like a double-edged blade. The force of his fist connecting with the desk echoes throughout the library, sending papers scattering to the ground.

Wait—that wasn't his fist, but a dagger. My lip quivers. Despite living in a town filled with flesh-eating monsters, the citizens of Datura don't carry weapons.

The librarians don't flinch at his outburst. Instead, Selma simply tilts her head to the side and says, "Oh, Cyan, are we not allowed breaks anymore? Or would your dear mayor rather us chained to the desk at all times?" Her words are icy, and her face is expressionless. She's got balls,

I'll give her that. The man in the suit straightens to his full height, towering over the small, frail librarian.

"You all know what you've done to deserve this fate."

A shrewd smile spreads across her face. "A funny choice of words you chose there, Cyan. *Fate*," she spits it back into his face. His body tenses, and he steps forward, looming over her.

"Watch it, Selma. Don't for a second think that you're not expendable. I'll have you tied to the Enkanti Tree at nightfall... *or worse*."

A gasp escapes from my lips—I cannot help it. *No one* has referred to the oak in the centre of Datura as the Enkanti Tree in the twenty-five years I've been alive. And yet the librarians and this man—Cyan—are all dropping this name as if it's common knowledge.

I quickly clasp my hand over my mouth, remembering I should be long gone already. Three sets of eyes turn to where the sound came from, and my eyes lock with that of the man in the suit.

A chill runs down my spine as his dark eyes burn into me. I turn on my heels and sprint for the door as his voice booms behind me.

"Get her!"

CHAPTER TEN
MALLRIE

I rarely head into Datura until after nightfall. That way, any prying eyes looking out onto the forest surrounding the township won't glimpse a strange man stalking out of the forestry with a sword strapped to his back. But there is a nagging feeling in the pit of my stomach, telling me Eliana is going to get herself into unnecessary trouble. I don't believe time elementals possess any sense of extraordinary intuition, so I can't really explain the feeling that has me making my way through the silent forest earlier than usual. Most creatures in the woods give me a wide berth as I make my way to the clearing between the Melsheim Forest and Datura.

If Eliana somehow got into trouble, I can't blame her. I essentially turned her world upside down last night when I told her everything she thinks she knows about her life in Datura is an unmitigated lie.

I didn't sleep well last night, wondering if I did the right thing by telling the truth about her town's origins. I decided not to take my sleeping draft in case I needed to return to town sooner than usual. After tossing and turning in bed, I went downstairs to conjure up the essence of the *Timeline.*

This magic is something I don't like to do often.

Time elementals are rare; our magic can be unpredictable. No one apart from the Fates should be able to see the future's possibilities. Therefore, our magic can have significant consequences.

Regardless, I pulled at the strings of time. I needed to make sure I hadn't altered it too much. Everything still seemed on track—exactly how I had planned it.

The trees of the Melsheim Forest thin out, allowing the sun to break through the dense canopy, warming my skin. As I step into the clearing, I see the tall buildings of the town across the vast field. I run my thumb under the strap that secures the sword to my back.

She deserved to know the truth, I remind myself. *At least the truth about her town.* Eliana is going to be a handful, and I decide some details are better left on a need-to-know basis.

Making quick work getting from the Melsheim Forest to the town, I keep a steady eye on the rooftops and exposed alleyways, confident *he* has a team stationed somewhere to keep an eye out for my arrival. If roles were reversed, I would.

Everything is clear.

The ease of the trek into town has me apprehensive. I effortlessly scale one of the buildings on the outskirts of town. After all, I have been doing this for more years than I care to admit. Once on top of the building, I turn my back on this godsforsaken town and look to the forest. I have about a half hour before the sun completely disappears beyond the trees. Closing my eyes and inhaling deeply, I soak up the last of that fresh air and pine scent before the smell of too many people living in too small a space suffocates me.

I wasn't born for the confines of a town. Not one as small and overly populated as Datura anyway.

A sense of gratitude washes over me as it always does before I head into town. The hand the Fates dealt me means I don't have to live in the cramped spaces of Datura. I turn my back to the forest.

Letting that *intuitive* sense be my guide, I make my way to the town centre, ensuring the structure I ended up perching on is not the government building. If I could, I would burn that building down in a heartbeat, but that is not why I am here. I have a job to do. A promise to fulfil. Even if that means I may become just as much of a monster as—

What the fuck?

Pushing myself out of my crouched position, I arch my head to the side to get a better view of that blonde tangle of hair I would recognise anywhere. Eliana jumps and falls— rather ungracefully—down the steps of the library. Apparently, that sense of *knowing* paid off and led me right to her. Moving around the rooftop to get a better view from around the Enkanti Tree, I see her clambering to her feet, rubbing her palms against her jeans. I notice the faint staining on her fingers. A wave of relief washes through me that the *Timeline* is on track, and I will not have to intervene.

Eliana is curious by nature, even though she has spent years trying to squash that curiosity.

The town is all but empty. Being this close to sunset, the

townsfolk have enough common sense to get inside. But *her*?

I run my hand through my short hair, fisting it in the back.

What the fuck is she doing?

I try not to look too closely at the events. However, Avark's warning still rings through me every time I conjure up the *Timeline*.

"Don't look too closely at the specifics. Doing so gives one too much knowledge, which then can cause significant change."

Being so young and knowing so much—that responsibility weighs heavily on one's shoulders. It had me questioning why one shouldn't look too closely. *Surely it wouldn't do too much harm?*

"Would you still accept it if you knew you would die tomorrow, and what caused your death? Would you accept the death of a loved one? Or would you do what is in your power to take that obstacle out of their way to ensure they survived?" Avark's raspy voice droned on, making me feel like I was about to nod off to sleep.

"Of course I'd save them," I replied, looking up at him with disbelief as he clicked his tongue in disapproval and waved his cane through the air in front of my face.

"You'd save them from one death, but it would only result in another. When the Fates decide our time is up, there is no way we can alter that. So looking into the Timeline and what the Fates have planned is impertinent and inexpedient. The Fates may see that as a sign of great disrespect, and the person you love whom you just saved?" His voice thickened with a warning that sent a wave of fear through me, *"They will most likely die a death even worse than one that was preordained for them.*

Or worse." His cane fell as he drove it into the earth, signifying the end of the discussion.

What was worse than a painful death? I knew the answer instantly: being stuck in *Vraska*. The space between life and death.

The heavy wooden doors of the library, adorned with false runes, slam against the brick of the building. Eliana has already scrambled to her feet and is off and running. Considering her history, you'd think the girl would have enough common sense to be home well before nightfall.

Sighing, I watch as she sprints across the courtyard as a tall, bull-headed man appears in the doorway moments after, calling out to her, "HEY, YOU! STOP!" I recognise him immediately, and a wave of apprehension goes down my spine. *What has she gotten herself caught up in already?*

I watch the two men, who look like they spend way too much time in the gym building up their muscles to compensate for the size of their brains, take off after her.

Curiosity piqued. I'd know those two pea-brains anywhere and whom they work for. Muscles tense and tighten with the urge to run after Eliana. *If Butch or Louis get to her...* I can feel the magic within me swell, demanding to be unleashed. Yet I linger on that rooftop to see *him* leave the library.

I know he's in there.

I take a deep, mollifying breath. Now is not the time to lose control. My magic is unpredictable if I let it surge and overflow. Who knows what type of disruption I could create to the *Timeline* I have so vigilantly tried to keep for all these years.

Rolling my shoulders, trying to work out the tension

settling there, I straighten up. *Where is he? What could he possibly want with the librarians?* After all these years, he has never shown an interest in them.

In what *I* did to them.

They have always been more like an unnecessary complication in his eyes.

Feeling restless, I open and close my fists at my side as I pace across the rooftop. *This is pointless. He mightn't—*

Whatever thought is forming in my mind disappears like smoke as I see him step out of the library, straightening the lapels of his jacket. I detect the faint tinge of red against his knuckles.

What have you done?

My jaw tightens with emotion. His hair is longer—still styled in the same way, even after all these years, with three tight braids along the side of his scalp. He looks like he has been working out more from how his impeccably cut suit hugs the muscles in his arms. He bounces down the few steps of the library without a care in the world before noticing the blood on his knuckles. Flicking out a handkerchief with a flourish, he wipes his hand clean before casually crossing the courtyard to the government building.

Cyan—

I squash the desire to jump from the rooftop to talk to him. It won't do any good. Cyan is no longer the man I once knew.

I stare toward the alleyway Eliana sprinted down, my mind drifting—*Fuck!*

I push off from the edge of the building and start off in the direction she went. Summoning a tendril of my magic, a small ember bursts to life before me as it shoots off after her.

I don't mind simple incantations like this on a whim.

Even with all my years of training, the more complex spells make me nervous. The *Timeline* is a very fragile substance. Summoning one's past steps won't affect it, but something more significant like slowing time or pausing one's aging process can cause serious ripples that alter the *Timeline*. I have tampered with the *Timeline* more than I would like, and sometimes, some events are just set, and no amount of intervention can prevent them from running their course. *Just like Avark told you.*

The time I have spent to ensure this *Timeline* stays uninterrupted has been strenuous. But what needs to be done will be.

A pang of guilt pulses through me. The tendril of magic picks up on Eliana's signature, showing me where she went. It stops—there is a warming in my chest where my magic hums. I look down into the alleyway.

Strange.

With a flourish of my hand, I summon a wisp of magic to reconstruct why she stopped here. The ember burns brighter as it grows and morphs into a six-inch-tall form. The curvy female leans against the wall before yanking off her shoes and socks and tossing them into the nearby trash can.

I have to stifle a laugh at how ridiculous this woman is. Two prominent men are *chasing* her, and she stops to remove her shoes!

The figure morphs back into an ember and shoots off again.

Eliana is definitely going to be a handful. I pray to the Fates that her antics will not disrupt my carefully curated *Timeline* too much.

I make chase after that little ember when I hear Louis shout further down the alleyway, "Hey! STOP!"

The sound of his voice calling out to her sends a trill of rage through my veins and my magic into a frenzy.

"We just want to talk to you!" cries Butch.

What kind of idiosyncratic name is that anyway?

Butch and Louis are not their real names, but why pick Butch? He must be trying to compensate for something.

I jump from building to building effortlessly before crouching down and watching Eliana round another corner. She's faster than expected. She's short, too, which we can use to our advantage when we start training.

Training wasn't a part of the plan, a small voice says in the back of my mind. I decide to ignore it and the conflicting emotions bubbling to the surface about what the future holds.

I push to my feet, but as I move to watch Eliana round another corner, her pace falters. I look around the alleyway to see if she has seen something I have not, but...

Nothing.

There is nothing there. The alleyway is entirely empty.

Why is she slowing down?

My magic thrums in my chest with the rapacity to reach out and summon her memories to figure out why this alleyway has caused her steps to falter. Shutting down that urge is difficult, but it is a line I try not to cross.

Even though I can use my magic to sift through a person's memories, it crosses a moral boundary. Besides, if done incorrectly, it can send the person spiralling into their own subconscious, which can be challenging to pull them from. That's not to say I haven't crossed that line before— invading someone's privacy for my own selfish benefit.

Butch and Louis are still hot on her trail. Eliana shakes her head slightly, clearing whatever fog had washed over her, and her pace quickens again.

My brows press together as my chest swells with relief. But then, there is a shift in the breeze. The scent of peppermint and the tang of magic burns my senses and my body tenses.

The *Timeline* has just shifted.

CHAPTER ELEVEN
MALLRIE

Keeping a close eye on Eliana, I continue to stalk her from the rooftops. She reaches out to help propel herself around the corner, and her bare feet splash in the water, starting to pool in the alleyway. The water catches her off guard. *Does she know the streets flood this evening because the Kailadons are making their way to the surface?*

Fighting the urge to yell at her to keep running, the muscles in my legs tense as they prepare to jump from the rooftop and grab her. I bite my lip, and the metallic taste of blood pools in my mouth, willing those urges away. I felt a shift in the *Timeline* already. Intervening would only make things worse.

Frustration builds in my muscles as I thumb the strap securing my sword to my back.

Why can't she just focus on the task at hand?

Doesn't she know that if Cyan's cronies catch her, she will wish I never saved her from the Kailadon? Something catches her eye in the water. She looks up. Our eyes meet, and my reckless heart stutters in my chest.

Fuck, am I starting to care about her well-being?

Those big brown doe eyes blink up at me in disbelief. The ghost of a smile tugs at the corner of her mouth. I press a finger to my lips, silently urging her to keep quiet about my presence—and to stop myself from smiling back. She nods, the slightest dip of her chin, as she refocuses her attention on the building before her.

She's got this.

I stop at the edge of the building I am perched on, diligently watching as Eliana leaps up the steps across the small and rare clearing from me.

She shoves her hand into her pocket, pulling out a set of keys. I lower myself on one knee, watching. *She's got this*, I tell myself again and again as if the more I repeat it, the more I won't have to fight the urge to jump down and take the keys from her trembling hands.

A rough chuckle echoes to where I am, like the malicious screech of a Nechkrappe.

Butch and Louis have caught up to her.

I focus on my breathing as I remind myself not to intervene. Something has already affected the *Timeline*. I don't need to add any more ripples. *You know what influenced the Timeline,* a voice whispers in my soul.

The adrenaline racing through Eliana's body has her hands shaking. She drops her keys at the sound of Louis' chuckle, her body tensing up, spinning on her heels to face her assailants instead of picking up the fucking keys. A growl rumbles deep within my chest, catching me off guard.

The girl mightn't be the brightest in these situations, but she's got spunk.

"Well, well, well, what do we have here?" taunts Louis.

"Gave us a good little chase there," chuckles Butch a little breathlessly. *Figures*. All that muscle is just for show, an intimidation tactic. My few altercations with Butch and Louis have established that their muscles are purely cosmetic, and they don't know how to use them. And here I thought Cyan was smarter than to have pea-brained gorillas doing his dirty work. Or at least put in the effort to make sure they are appropriately trained.

"Oh, look, she's shaking like a little bunny," taunts Louis. "Come here, bunny. We're not going to hurt you," he says, stepping forward, stretching out an enormous arm and wiggling his sausage fingers at her.

I'm going to kill him. I will cut off those sausage fingers and feed them to him. I'm going to kill them both.

The look on Eliana's face... I've seen it before, and it will forever be tainted on my soul. My heart aches. As she looks between the two nonsensically large men stalking towards her, her face twisted with fear. She's no doubt wondering why I am not intervening. Fates, I want to. I want nothing more than to end Butch and Louis' miserable lives. But I can't. I can't risk the *Timeline*.

"We're not going to hurt you..." says Butch as a revolting smile of rotten teeth spreads across his face. "... much," he tacks on with a wink.

"Fuck it," I mutter, ready to drop myself from the rooftop and rip their hearts from their chests, but Eliana moves—once again, faster than I expected her to. She drops to her knees, snatching the keys and turning towards the door. Eliana will definitely be a pain in my side, but I can't help the pool of excitement and anticipation at training her.

Muscles tensing and magic thrumming through my blood, it takes every inch of my self-control to watch this play out. There is this pull towards her. I've always felt it, but now... it feels different.

"Get her!" snarls Louis as Butch lunges forward. He grabs Eliana's shoulders and jerks her away from the door as a shriek erupts from deep within her—a sound I hoped I would never have to hear from her again. But she holds onto the door handle with all of her strength and determination. A rush of heat courses through me as she tries to fight off her attackers.

Fight. Fight, Eliana.

Butch wraps his arms around her waist and, with one wrench, pulls her away from the door. Eliana lets out another scream, not just with frustration at the situation she's found herself in but laced with pain.

He's got her. Red seeps into my vision. She's kicking, trying to free herself, but she does not know what she's doing. My vision blurs briefly in my anger. Her panic is overpowering any sense of direction.

"Fucking hell," I curse as I draw my sword and drop into the alleyway. The lilac glow of the blade hums in my peripheral vision as tendrils of my magic seep into the steel, summoning magic from the past.

I step out of the darkening alleyway, flexing my muscles.

Eliana's eyes widen slightly, flicking between the sword and me as I start stalking forward.

"Let. Her. Go," a growl rumbles through my chest that sounds more animalistic than human. At this moment, when something akin to fear flashes across Eliana's face, I allow myself to acknowledge that my actions caused the ripple in the *Timeline*.

A shiver runs down her spine, yet her plush lips curve at the corners at the sight of me. My stupid heart leaps at how she looks at me like she knows I am about to rip these men limb from limb for what they planned on doing to her. I will kill them slowly. They don't deserve the swift but everlasting death that would come from my sword.

A word comes to mind, and I have to squash it out of existence before it can affect the *Timeline* any—

Mine.

My jaw tenses as the word burns with the heat of a thousand suns in my mind. I can virtually feel another ripple forming in the *Timeline*. The plans I have carefully orchestrated for years slowly unravel with that single word.

Butch lets out a booming laugh, tightening his grip around Eliana, her arms pinned to her sides, her legs thrashing about aimlessly.

"This feisty bunny is coming with us." His voice chuckles with amusement.

The corners of my lips tug up, knowing I finally get to put these two bastards six feet under, or better... My grip tightens on my sword, knowing what will await them if I end their miserable lives with it. "Get him!" Butch shouts.

I feel a whoosh of air as Louis swings a punch, but all that useless muscle makes him slow. I easily dodge it, spinning on the ball of my foot. The metallic click of a gun loading vibrates through my body as my magic demands to be used. I summon a tendril of my power to flow through and out of me before Louis can pull the trigger. The lilac glow of my sword flashes as it falls, slicing through flesh and bone. His finger jerks, pulling the trigger. Louis screams as hot blood splashes across my body and face, coating my skin with the metallic scent of death.

Louis' hand and gun fall with a thump onto the cobblestone. Eyes wide, he looks down at the bloody stump of an arm. He clutches it to his chest for a moment before composing himself after Butch shrieks a string of expletive demands.

Sending the pommel of my sword into his stomach, the cocky smile I have fails as he hardly flinches.

What the fuck?

"A few things have changed since we last tussled, *witch*," Louis grumbles through gritted teeth.

His words catch me off-guard, allowing him to land a surprisingly sturdy punch to my shoulder. A ripple of pain shudders down my arm. The gun. I sheath my sword. It would all be too easy to keep cutting him down, but then I wouldn't get the satisfaction of delivering every bruise and broken bone, taking out years of frustration against Cyan on his lackeys.

Louis swings a leg towards my abdomen. I catch it, driving my elbow into his kneecap. A satisfying scream breaks from his lungs.

We move around each other, throwing and blocking punches and kicks like a choreographed dance.

Louis advances forward, swinging one punch after another, even using the *fucking nub* of his wrist. I fling my arms above my face, blocking his attacks, embracing the sharp sting of each blow.

The bloody nub hurts like a motherfucker when the exposed bone collides with my forearms, slowly tearing apart my flesh. The more punches he throws, the faster he will tire himself out—or the excessive blood loss will weaken him.

A smile pulls at Louis' lips as he cocks his arm back for what he thinks will be a final blow to break my defences. I break formation, catching his wrist in my hand and pulling him closer before connecting my fist with his face. There is a rewarding crunch, and I feel his nose crumble against my aching knuckles. Louis lets out an agonising grunt and curses. He stumbles backwards, clutching his face as blood drips between his fingers. I can feel the warm slick of his life force between my fingers as I stalk towards him. I swing my leg, a kick contacting his ribs.

Crack!

I will never tire of hearing Cyan's mens' bones breaking. Finally, Louis falls to his knees, groaning loudly in pain.

"Weak," I mutter as I stalk towards him.

As a child, my father trained my brother and me to fight. He'd always say never to let your enemy see you're hurt. As kids, it seemed brutal to be thrown into combat against one another, and no matter how many bones were broken, we just had to keep our mouths shut and grit through it.

Now, I understand the meaning behind the madness. I can clearly see Louis' weak points, where I need to strike next that will have him out cold or dead.

Louis tries to get up—

"I'll deal with you later," I growl as I drive my elbow down into his shoulder, hitting a nerve and knocking him out cold. Louis' body falls in an unconscious heap by my feet.

My eyes drag from the bloody mess to Butch—the idiot didn't run while he had a chance. Not that I expected him to. That would involve thinking. Plus, Butch was always one to sit back and enjoy watching the fight.

I step over Louis' body, stalking over to where Butch stands, holding onto Eliana. Her eyes track across my face, taking in every inch of me covered in blood—both Louis' and my own.

"Put. Her. Down," I hiss as something ugly rolls over in the pit of my stomach. When I see him holding onto her like that, I know without a doubt that I single-handedly have fucked up my carefully curated *Timeline* because I have gotten too close to *her*. She has unconsciously drawn me to her, and now I can't... I've never been one to believe in love at first sight, and maybe this isn't even that. Perhaps this is some other *pull* the Fates have designed to chart a new course of the *Timeline*.

All I know is I won't let *anyone* hurt her, even if that means my original plans have all gone up in flames.

Mine. Eliana is mine to protect.

She still hasn't given up the fight as she thrashes her small body around in his arms, and my chest warms with her drive, her desire to fight. *She'll need that if we're to finish what I started.*

"I won't ask again," I say through clenched teeth. I try to push the thoughts out of my mind.

"Sorry. Boss' orders," growls back the goon as he tosses Eliana against the building. Her head hits the wooden door with a sickening crunch that knocks her unconscious.

My vision blurs with rage—something that has only happened a handful of times before. A scream rips from my lungs as I run towards Butch. I am going to enjoy every inch of his death.

My fist collides with his jaw, and a sharp, stinging pain shoots up through my fist as two of his teeth fly through the air in a spray of blood. "I'm going to make you regret every choice you've made in your miserable life," I say, grabbing him by the shirt and flinging him into the building.

I don't have much time. An awareness shifts over my skin as my magic warns me of what's coming.

I pin Butch to the wall and knee him right in the kidneys, not once, not twice, but three times. I notice the sun has already set, and my magic hums over my skin with an ominous warning. The amount of blood coating the streets from Louis, Butch and myself will undoubtedly draw an unfavourable crowd.

All it takes is that split second of distraction, and fucking Butch breaks out of my embrace. I curse under my breath at the sharp pain in my arm. *Did that fucker actually just...*

I look from him to my arm; sure enough, there is a round bite mark on my forearm under where I have rolled up the sleeves of my black shirt. My eyes widen at the pebbles of red blood pooling around the bite.

"Did you just fucking bite me?" I ask as I punch Butch in the collar bone, hearing a satisfying snap. He spits a mouthful of blood onto my chest.

"Fuck you, *witch*," he groans as he knees me in the balls. I stumble back, cursing to be dammed by what my father used to say about not showing your opponent you're in pain. That was a low fucking move. I stumble backwards, cupping my balls, a wave of nausea washing over me.

Bitch is a sore fucking loser. I look up through the pain-induced haze as he circles me, forcing me back against the wall as he pulls something from his pocket. The metal swooshing, Bitch flicks open the blade of a small butterfly knife.

Sore fucking loser, I think.

Bitch punches me in the face before I can pull my hands away from my groin. To my surprise, he breaks my nose. Thankfully, the painful blow to my face has drawn my attention away from the ache between my legs, snapping me out of the stupor the pain had dragged me into. Blood pours down my face as I smile back at him, the metallic taste seeping into my mouth and coating my teeth.

Bitch raises the knife to my throat when we both freeze.

The sickly sweet scent of decaying flesh washes over the clearing between buildings. We both turn in unison as a Kailadon moves slowly over Louis' unconscious body.

"Don't. You. Fucking. Move," I whisper to Butch. My voice is low but nonetheless threatening. His hand at my throat trembles. I doubt Cyan's men have had too much experience dealing with the pest population of Datura.

The Kailadon moves its terribly thin and large body to position itself over Louis before inhaling deeply. The sound is like dried bones rattling in the wind. A small whimper escapes *Bitch's* lips.

The Kailadon flicks Louis' body onto his stomach and rips his shirt open with its long-bladed arms before it devours his flesh. At the first slice, Louis' eyes snap open as a guttural scream escapes his body.

The Kailadon drops onto its knees. The sound of Louis' bones crunching under the weight increases his shrieks.

Somehow, that seems to have drawn Butch out of his stupor. Quickly, I knock the knife out of his arm and kick it away.

"Eliana!" I shout against the arm pressed against my throat. "*Godsdamn it!* Eliana, run!" I am so fucking tired. I am becoming weak. I curse myself for pushing my body to its limit and then some. For staying up all night watching Eliana's apartment. For looking over every resource I have for an alternate solution to fulfilling my promise.

"Eliana!" I shout again as she pushes herself up, rubbing her eyes, trying to clear the fog no doubt settled in her head. A small trail of blood runs down from her temple. "Get. In. The. Building!"

Her eyes fall to where I'm shouting. They widen with distress as she takes in the scene unfolding before her. Louis has stopped shrieking, presumably from exhaustion.

Her gaze shifts from mine to his. Her hand flies up to her mouth. Butch looks back over to his acquaintance. With Louis' back bare, grisly insides and cream-coloured glimpses of his spine now exposed, the blood drips slowly down his back and into the street. The muscles in his back still flex under the pain of the Kailadon, slowly slicing sections of his flesh away. It raises a shaving of meat carefully to its mouth, those sharp, needle teeth shredding the flesh into smaller sections, blood dripping from its arms and face.

No matter how often I intervene in a Kailadon attack or how many lives I end with my sword or hand, the sight of one's insides never ceases to send my stomach rolling.

Over the years, I have learnt that death should always be *felt* and never be taken lightly. The day the sight of someone's torn, mangled body doesn't send my stomach twisting is the day my humanity has slipped too far, and I become as much of a monster as those I try to protect the people of Datura from.

"Eliana!" I shout again as I slip under a distracted Butch, twisting the arm, pinning me to the wall and pressing his enormous frame in my place. Then, bringing my knee up, I return the favour as I crush it between his legs and keep it there. "Inside!" I shout as I jerk my arm to force Bitch's mouth shut to muffle his screams.

How many times am I going to need to shout at her? Surely, she isn't too stupid to understand what sort of situation she is in?

My magic is a constant thrum just under my skin that I've learnt to tune out, so when Eliana screams, "Mallrie! Behind you!" I can hear the panic in her voice. I let my magic float to the surface, slowing time for a fraction. A crack of thunder echoes high above us, muffling her scream. I release Butch from my grip and roll out of the way as a second Kailadon swings its arm. Time resumes its average pace, and the sounds of flesh slicing open and the cleaving of bone fill the air.

Butch's head drops from his body and rolls to the side. The Kailadon straightens up, cocking its head to the side, blindly watching the head roll to a stop. My hair is damp from the rain, and it feels like a cleansing caress from all the blood and death. The Kailadon whirls on me, flinging its bloody arm at my chest. The rain falls harder, making the blood-soaked ground slick. I grab the beast's arm, stopping it from slicing my chest open. I take one step forward, then another as the Kailadon's feet slip across the cobblestone.

I reach up, drawing my sword. The lilac glow of the blade illuminates the puddles. I kick the Kailadon in the kneecap, knocking the creature slightly off-balance. I swing my leg out, sending it to its knees. Then, I swing my sword and allow my magic to infuse with the blade before drawing it high above my head. I let it fall, dividing the Kailadon down the centre to its stomach. Black blood sprays in every direction, coating my face and body. The monster's innards fall with a wet squelch onto the ground. I straighten up as I watch the two halves of the Kailadon hang on the torso, its body swaying with uncertainty before dropping with a thud. Blood seeps into the cracks of the cobblestone street.

I step over the body, looking up at Eliana. Fuck, if I wasn't so mad at her lack of common sense, I would enjoy the sight of her a little more as she sits against the steps of the apartment, her shirt soaked and clinging to her curves, the peaks of her breasts showing through the material and her blonde hair clinging to her face as she looks at me like I am both the monster and the hero. And maybe I am.

I grab her under the arm, my knuckles brushing the side

of her breast. "Get up!" I growl, more forceful than I mean it, but Eliana pushes herself to her feet, her eyes glued to me like I am some fictional character come to life that she cannot believe stands before her.

I carefully turn her towards the door before turning my back and raising my sword. The Kailadon devouring Louis has hardly moved, too preoccupied in its meal. I hear the lock click over, the heavy door opening and Eliana rushing inside. I let a small part of me relax, knowing she's safe. With that bit of tension eased, my body is starting to recognise all the aches and pains, especially one particularly painful ache in my shoulder. I push the pain aside. I haven't heard her shut the door, let alone fucking lock it.

What is she waiting for? A fucking invitation?

I stay where I am, ready for the Kailadon to realise fresher meat is available.

"Get in!" Eliana's voice snaps as if she is fighting with herself about whether to let me in or not. I glance over my shoulder as she stands inside the building, holding the door open for me. Those brown eyes watch me like she's holding it open for a wolf and questioning her sanity.

I grunt my approval and step over the threshold. Eliana moves instinctively, getting out of my way. I lock the door swiftly behind us, handing the keys back before jerking my chin to motion her to lead the way to the apartment.

Even though I know where to go.

She looks up the staircase, then back to me as if deciding whether it's better to have me leading the way or following her as if I am a fucking threat. The thought sends a rumble of a laugh vibrating through my chest. I clear my throat to cover the sound, but all that does is cause the pain in my shoulder to intensify.

Damn these fucking stairs! I curse every step as my

breathing becomes laboured. Using my sword to steady myself and my grip on the banister, I haul myself up one step after another. I can feel the hot, sticky blood pouring out from a wound at my side. I can't remember if Butch or the Kailadon—most likely the latter—caused it.

Eliana flinches with every rasp of my breath and the scrape of my sword on the timber stairs that echo through the stairwell. She looks over her shoulder at where I am dragging myself up. I arch an eyebrow at her as she moves down a step, saying, "Stop. Let me help you." My brows press together as I eye her up and down. I'm about to tell her I am fine and don't need her help when she rolls her eyes. "Don't be a jerk," she says sternly. "You're drawing too much attention." She pulls my arm tight around her shoulders. I look down at my boots, trying to hide my smile at her boldness.

We struggle up the rest of the stairs. I am taller and heavier than her, but she keeps a firm grip on my arm around her shoulders and clutches my sword in her other hand. I try to tell her I am fine, but her determination is admirable, leaving me in awe of her. Eliana is stubborn, and I can see the caution plastered over her face about helping me, yet she does. She's been burnt in the past by those she loved, yet here she is, helping a perfect stranger.

We reach the fourth floor, and Eliana unceremoniously dumps my body against the wall. Closing my eyes, I draw in a shaky breath, slowly regaining my strength as I chew on the medicinal herb I had stashed in my pocket. The thump of a foot kicking in the door has my eyes snapping open. "I'm good," I grunt, walking past her into the small, two-bedroom apartment. It looks even smaller inside.

"Doesn't sound it," Eliana mutters, the sound of a series of locks clicking into place behind her.

Like that would stop anyone. I glance over at Eliana as she slides the chain into place, her blonde hair wet and a little dishevelled, before I move into the kitchen and start raiding the cupboards. I need to tend to this wound at my side, and fast. Kailadons carry many diseases. The thought of the effects of an untreated Kailadon wound scrape at the back of my skull like an Ashga's bony fingers. It starts with a headache, which most dismiss, but can quickly turn into a fever. When the nausea and vomiting start, it's too late. Inky black veins spread like lightning across the skin, white, pus-filled boils dotting around the wound that, if popped, excrete a discharge so acidic it burns the skin.

I toss herbs, spices and dried flowers onto the bench, trying—and failing—not to think about the potential infection. *No one has lived in this apartment for years*, I think to distract myself as I move an out-of-date box of cereal—

"Sit down. Let me help you," Eliana's voice cuts through the fog invading my brain, suppressing the smile wanting to tug at my lips at the sound of frustration. She isn't even remotely trying to hide in her voice. I step out of her way, knowing when to pick my fights, and lean against the bench, exhaling. I'm drained. I cannot remember the last time I was this exhausted.

That's a lie.

"Boil some water."

Eliana arches an eyebrow in my direction. I nod towards the kettle, and she pops a hand on her generous hip. It takes everything in me not to smile at her. "Please," I add, softening my tone and noting how her full lips twitch in the corners as she represses a smile. Spinning on her heel, I can see the tops of her ears turning pink as she fills the kettle and returns it to the stove.

"I think there is a first aid kit in the bathroom. I'll be

back." Her voice quivers slightly as she walks off. I tilt my head back against the overhead cupboards, not bothering to tell her I won't need it. Instead, I savour this moment of silence. The medicinal herb has removed some pain, but I still feel the dull ache. My pulse feels too close to the surface, and I know how badly I'm injured by how the blood has my shirt unpleasantly sticking to my side.

Eliana returns, holding a small first aid kit as I tug off my shirt and toss it into the sink. Her footsteps stop, and I look up to find her frozen where she stands. Cocking an eyebrow, I ask, "Are you okay with blood?" I have a pretty good idea that it is not the sight of the blood covering my body that had her stopping in her tracks with her mouth slightly agape and her cheeks flushing a sweet, rosy pink. Instead, her eyes wander down my body, taking in every inch of exposed skin, and I cannot stop the smile that spreads across my face. There is something so primarily satisfying about watching Eliana, so strong and stubborn, become so speechless over the sight of me. Even if, at the moment, I am covered in blood. *Maybe she likes that? Does the picture of me covered in blood, fresh from a fight have her little body writhing with desire?*

She clears her throat in an adorable but awkward way. "Um, yeah, I think so."

"Where are the bowls?" I ask.

Eliana places the first aid kit on the bench and moves around me, pulling out a glass mixing bowl. I nod my thanks and start ripping some herbs and tossing them into the bowl with the boiling water. I always hate this part. The strong, minty smell of the herbs burns my senses as I reach around Eliana. I can almost see her holding her breath as I pull a tea towel hanging over the oven handle.

"You don't have to help," I say matter-of-factly. I'd

prefer if she didn't, but I like that she *wants* to. My tone, however, comes out cold and distant, and I internally cringe at how her brows crease together. "You can get yourself cleaned up," I add, looking her up and down.

"I'm fine," Eliana replies, watching me intently.

"Do you like this?" I hold up the hideously floral tea towel, trying to dismiss the awkwardness.

"This isn't my house," she blurts out innocently.

"Breaking and entering, are we?" I can't help but smile at how her voice sounds a million miles away.

"Oh, no. It's my grandmother's house. She passed away, and I just... I couldn't get rid of it."

I know, I want to reply, but I hold my tongue. Instead, I nod, only half listening as Eliana rambles. I add the remaining herbs I collected to the water and mumble the healing incantation to turn back time and draw out any infections.

"Are you a witch?" Eliana blurts out. I arch an eyebrow in her direction. It took her less time than I thought it would to start questioning me. "Sorry, you just seem... I don't know, you—"

She's rambling again. *Put the girl out of her misery.* "Yes," I say coldly. I frown as I plunge my hands into the hot water, wringing out the towel, cursing myself for my harsh tone again. I guess I am a little out of practise communicating with pretty females. Especially one whom I had no intention of developing feelings for. I'm still at war between keeping to my original plan and throwing it out of the window to accommodate this woman standing before me.

She stands there in stunned silence. *Maybe I should have—*

The sting of the damp towel against my shoulder ceased all thoughts. I carefully drop the towel back into the bowl and wring it out as I carefully clean the wounds, the magic turning back time and ridding my body of any potential infections.

"Is there anything I can do to help?" Eliana asks sheepishly, and a pang of guilt drags its claws through my gut at her tone.

You have no idea...

"Do you know how to sew?" I don't tell her this brew I just made will heal the wounds better than any first aid she knows. That pang of guilt has me wanting to let her feel helpful. The blood from her face looks like it's all but drained away.

"Is-is that bone?" Eliana sways a little.

"You alright?" I wrap one arm around her waist and the other around her shoulders, steadying her. "I asked if you were okay with blood," I remind her as I lean down to get a better view of her face. She pushes me out of the way with more force than I expected as she rushes to the sink and vomits.

The damp strands of her hair feel nice between my fingers as I scoop it away from her face. My other hand rubs small circles on her back.

"You're okay," I whisper into her ear, the heat of our bodies mixing together. Despite Eliana throwing up her guts, I can't help but marvel at how her pink cheeks show off her freckles. Then, she runs the back of her hand over her mouth. I scoop her into my arms, savouring the feel of her curves as I gently place her on the island bench.

"By the pantry," Eliana mutters weakly as I open and slam the cupboards, cursing that there isn't a universal place for cups.

I yank the cupboard she said to open, and sure as eggs, there are the cups. "Why aren't they near the sink?" I ask as

I hand her the glass of water, and she takes it without hesitation. *That'll be a first.*

Her hand trembles as she lifts the glass to her lips and delicately lifts one shoulder. I swipe my thumb across the corner of her mouth, clearing away some of the sick. Her big brown eyes meet mine as I brace my arms on either side of her hips, my thumbs gently brushing against her thighs as a slight shiver runs through her.

Her mouth hardens and then pulls into a sarcastic smile. "I'm fine. But you need to back up unless you want me to throw up all over you." Then, as if her cheeks can't get any redder, she blushes again under my gaze. My eyes drop to her plump lips as they part on an inhale, and she subconsciously leans in.

"Yeah, you'll be fine." I chuckle as she glares at me through slitted eyes, tilting her head to the side.

"Funny. He's funny." Eliana tries to put some bite in her tone, but it doesn't quite come off the way I think she expected. She slides off the counter between my arms, and I wish I could keep her there. Her breath catches as if she thought I would have stepped away. I hold her there for a heartbeat before I move, shifting my attention to the first aid box.

"Sorry," she mutters. The half-hearted apology has a smirk pulling at my lips and conflicting emotions raging war against each other.

"Why are you apologising?" I ask as Eliana continues to clean my wound.

She raises her shoulder in a half-shrug that pulls at my heart. Suppressing a sigh, I lay out the stitches kit.

Eliana's hands tremble as she wrings out the towel. Her eyes linger on the black droplets of blood floating like oil in water. "Kailadon blood," I explain, "isn't as dense as ours. The fuckers stain everything."

Her head snaps to meet my gaze, and I internally curse myself for how incensed my voice came out. I'm not used to this—to *her*. "You don't have to do this," I say as I wrap my hand over hers, reaching for the needle and thread. "You should rest. It's been a difficult night for you." *And my mood isn't helping, I'm sure.*

Thank the Fates, my voice comes out softly, but her hand still trembles beneath mine. I give it a gentle squeeze and a small smile.

"That's probably a good idea," she mumbles, pulling her hand away from my embrace. Before I know what I am doing, I lift her back onto the counter.

Don't leave. Not yet, I think sadly.

She gives me a stern look, but I don't regret manhandling her. On the contrary, I like how her soft body feels in my hands.

"You don't need to pick me up. I'm fine." She juts out her chin defiantly. I can hear the aggravation in her voice, but I ignore it, instead moving my attention back to these infernal stitches. I should have just kept my mouth shut. *She already figured out I'm a witch. Do I have to waste time with these stitches? I'll just rip them out when I get home.* But I don't want to upset her any more than I worry I already have.

"Don't look if you're going to be sick," I say. I can see her watching me intently out of the corner of my eye. The glow of the streetlights coming through the windows illuminates the side of her face, making her look otherworldly.

Tossing the bloody needle in the sink, I turn to Eliana. "Your grandmother was a witch," I announce, softly cursing at my half-assed job, stitching up my wounds and the insensitive announcement. But I am tired, so tired. I can see a trickle of blood oozing from the half-assed stitches out of the corner of my eye.

"What?" Eliana's gaze flicks to mine. "No. No, she wasn't." So much fire in her tone. I like it. Probably a little too much.

"Hm." I nod in fake contemplation before a playful smile pulls across my face. "Could have fooled me."

CHAPTER TWELVE
ELIANA

My grandmother was NOT a witch, I think as Mallrie roams about her apartment shirtless. His body is a homage to his hard work and dedication, golden muscles peppered with small white scars that make my stomach pinch uncomfortably, wondering how he got them. He doesn't seem to care that he's covered in blood and gore. Mallrie tentatively opens trinket boxes with a single finger, careful not to get any blood on them, and looks at the photos scattered around the room. *If she were, I would have known. I lived with her for twenty-three years before she passed. She was my flesh and blood. I would have known.*

Mallrie stops in front of the bathroom and turns to look at me, pointing his thumb over his shoulder towards the bathroom. "May I?" he asks humbly as if he hasn't just dropped a bombshell on me.

"Oh, yeah, of course. Towels are under the sink."

He nods and shuts the door behind him. I slump into the lounge, flinging an arm over my face. *Why is this happening to me?* I wonder, letting out a deep sigh. *I don't want to be running for my life every night. Who would want that? Mallrie, obviously.*

My chest feels heavy, and I'm exhausted. I'm getting soft. I promised myself when I was six that it would just be my grandmother and me. That's all the room my heart could take. I couldn't watch anyone I cared about to be eaten alive by the Flesh-Hunters.

But watching as Mallrie risked his life for me?

My heart does a happy little flip in my chest, and I let out a silent groan.

Not that this is the first time my heart has broken that promise. When I was thirteen, I made a friend at school.

Chelsea Huang. Neither of us intentionally wanted to become friends, but unfortunate circumstances brought us together. Chelsea's mother was killed the year before by a mob of Flesh-Hunters. Her father was badly hurt trying to protect them both. He got Chelsea out safely but then killed himself a week later.

By the time we turned sixteen, Chelsea had enough. She had heard stories of towns beyond the Melsheim Forest that were safe from Flesh-Hunters and begged me to run away with her. But our whole lives, we'd been taught two things: never go out after dark unless you want to die a slow and painful death from a Flesh-Hunter and *never*, under any circumstances, go into the Melsheim Forest. Besides, I couldn't leave my grandmother. She was the only family I had left, and she wasn't well.

Chelsea packed her bags and left town. I never saw or heard from her again. I grieved for weeks with the pain and agony of not knowing if she was okay. If she had died. Unable to give her the funeral she deserved.

Then, my heart betrayed me again at twenty-two. That time, it almost killed me.

I fell in love.

CHAPTER THIRTEEN
ELIANA

I was eighteen when I met Beckett Peiris. He was everything I could have hoped for in a boyfriend. Beckett understood my past trauma and was still kind and patient. He would hold me in the middle of the night when the nightmares felt too real, and I woke in a tangle of sweat-covered sheets. I even imagined that I could spend the rest of my life with him. That he could be "*the one*". The one I would love, and no matter how awful things got in this godsforsaken town, he would love me unconditionally in return.

The first few years were incredible. Sometimes, though, I would just lash out and push him away. Not because I wanted to, but because I was scared. I feared if I let him in, I'd end up hurt. Because those you love always end up being the ones who hurt you the most when they leave.

Beckett knew about the nightmares that chased me in my sleep and about my drinking problem. At first, I tried to hide how I'd try to chase away the bad memories and nightmares with a bottle of gin, but these things always have a way of revealing themselves eventually.

Beckett *helped* me.

He helped me reduce my consumption, and he encouraged me to see a therapist—not that I went until *after* Beckett's *accident.*

I wasn't ready to talk about it all yet. *"But when will you ever be ready, babe? Think of the first session like a Band-Aid and just rip it off."* I hated when he'd talk to me like that. It always felt so condescending. Beckett was *good* for me though. He made me feel like life wasn't as bad as it was. It wasn't until the last year or so before the *accident* that things between us got... *messy.*

We started to fight. But every couple has its issues, right? No relationship is perfect. At least, that's what I tried to convince myself of. We would fight over the silliest things, slowly making Beckett more insecure and... dangerous.

Three years ago, I got an internship as a marketing assistant for one of the high-end department stores. It was my dream job, and a hard one to get into. Living in a small town, there isn't much need for marketing jobs. They usually do their marketing in-house, but they wanted a *"fresh perspective"*, and I had it. They loved me, and I loved the job. I worked hard, but Beckett didn't understand. He would get annoyed about the long hours I'd put in. I'd leave as soon as the sun was up and come home a half-hour before sunset. My drinking almost became non-existent because I enjoyed the job so much. The nightmares couldn't touch me because I was so engrossed in my work. I was feeling good. I felt how I imagined most people would feel. But Beckett didn't understand.

3 YEARS AGO

"Babe, if I want to actually get the job at the end of the internship, I have to put in the hard work!" I throw my hands in the air, frustrated that we keep having the same fight over and over.

"Yeah, fine, but being gone from sunrise to sunset. Come on, Eli, you can't have me seriously believing that you're '*working*' that whole time? Do I look stupid to you?" Beckett's voice rises with every word, making me nervous the neighbours will overhear our argument. Of course, they have already heard it a million times over by this point, but it's still embarrassing.

"No, I'm not. It's just that you're not—"

"It sounds like you're calling me stupid, Eli!" Beckett looks as if he might actually turn red soon.

"Beckett, please, just *listen* to me. I need to—" I take a deep breath, trying to speak softly, hoping it might calm him down, too, so we can discuss this civilly.

"So who the fuck is it then, Eli? Huh?" He shouts. "I'm not stupid! I know you're fucking someone!" Beckett slams his hand down on the dinner table, the cutlery jumping from the impact. I flinch, squeezing my eyes shut. In the last year or so, Beckett has started to get a little... physical. He always feels so bad and apologises afterwards, promising it will never happen again, spoiling me with flowers and fancy dinners enough to make the abuse seem like an accident. Accidents Beckett deeply regrets.

He loves me. He never means to hurt me.

But something is different this time. There is a... viciousness in Beckett's eyes like he *knows* he will hurt me, and it scares the living shit out of me.

I try to take a steadying breath. He seems to get a kick out of intimidating me, of reminding me I am nothing without him. That I'm a nobody with no family or friends. I try to stay calm, but there's a small lump in my throat, and I can't seem to breathe properly.

"Beckett, there's no one else. I love you, you know that."

"Bullshit!" He is yelling now, and that lump in my throat grows, threatening to suffocate me. He runs his fingers through his short, curly hair and sighs as if trying to calm himself, but it feels *forced*.

"It's Dylan, isn't it? You're always saying how funny he is and—"

"It's not Dylan!" I shout, trying to be heard over Beckett and his paranoia. He's been slowly baiting me for weeks now that I am cheating on him with a colleague. I've tried telling him I am not sleeping with anyone, that Dylan has a boyfriend, but he won't listen.

"Why are you getting so defensive, Eli?" Finally, his voice evens out, sending a shiver down my spine.

"Beckett, you've met Dylan *and* his boyfriend. You—"

"You're fucking him! Just admit it!" He picks up the steak knife and stabs it into the table. I jump back in my seat at the outburst. My heart is in my throat, tears pricking at my eyes as I stare at the blade embedded in the surface. *Beckett, he... He's never...*

A shudder runs through me. I want to run. At this moment, I want to be as far away from here as possible. I want to be back in my apartment. But it's late, so I try calming myself and Beckett.

"B-Beckett, I am not cheating on you. I promise," I

speak slowly as I carefully push myself to my feet. There's nowhere for me to go. His apartment is identical to mine. The wooden chair groans as he pushes it back, forcing himself to his feet and rounding the table before I can move.

"Where do you think you're going?" He presses his hand hard on my throat, cutting off my air supply. Beckett's done this before. I try to stay calm, to ride it out like I always do, but he's not letting go. He forces me back against the wall. My head cracks against the plaster.

"You are *mine*! You are nothing without me!" Beckett whispers in my ear, sending all the tiny hairs over my body to stand. My vision starts to blur. I grab his arm, trying to pull him off, but he squeezes tighter.

My head spins with the lack of oxygen, my chest constricts... I'm about to pass out when he releases me, and I fall in a heap on the floor.

"I gave you a home, unconditional love, a family and this is how you repay me? By fucking some guy in your office?"

I clutch my throat, trying to force air back into my lungs, but it's all coming out in short, painful gasps. I look up at Beckett, my eyes watering from the pain as he paces before me, my vision still blurry. He runs his fingers through his hair, and I can see his mouth moving, but I can't make out the words over the loud ringing in my ears. I feel like I might pass out.

I need water. I crawl over to the table and reach for my glass of water. Beckett's hand wraps around the long pony-tail hanging over my shoulder and yank backwards, hard. A slightly strangled sound breaks through the ache in my throat. Tears prick at my eyes as I gasp for air.

"You want a drink, Eli?" Beckett picks up the jug of

water and pours it over my head, the water forcing its way down my open mouth, gagging me. "Are you even listening to me?" he shouts.

I gasp for air under the water. Beckett tosses the jug against the wall behind me, shattering it into a million pieces. There is no doubt the neighbours have heard the commotion now. But I know there will be no intervention. It's too late in the evening for the general disciplinary office to send someone out. He releases my hair roughly, and I almost hit my head on the table. A little sob bursts out of me. I look up. He's walking away, still yelling and cursing at me. My gut tells me to run, to get out of here as fast as possible. *To hell with the Flesh-Hunters.* If I leave, there is a tiny chance I can survive this night.

My grandmother's house is close, I think, looking up at Beckett as he breaks plates into the sink. *If I stay here... he's going to kill me.* I know that for sure.

It's now or never, I think, psyching myself up. Beckett turns on the water as he throws more dishes into the sink. I take that as my chance and turn and run for the door. Something whooshes past my head as I grab hold of the handle. The wood groans, and I scream as a kitchen knife pierces the door. I turn around, pressing my back against the exit, watching in disbelief as Beckett stalks towards me.

He threw—He threw a knife at me!

"Where the fuck do you think you're going?" Beckett reaches beside my head and dislodges the knife. He presses the cool blade against my arm and drags it across my chest. I try to take a deep breath.

"You—" My eyes blink rapidly. "You threw a *knife* at me," I stutter in disbelief.

"I wouldn't have hurt you, Eli," he coos softly as if

trying to calm a small child. "Where could you possibly be going at this hour?"

"I-I—" Beckett isn't even looking at me. He's too transfixed on the blade in his hand as he applies pressure on the knife over my left breast, slowly carving an *x* on my chest. Whatever I was going to say dies on my tongue as I suck in a sharp intake of breath.

I will not scream.

I will not give him that satisfaction. Blood slowly drips down the blade. Beckett lifts the knife to his lips and slides the blade down, catching my blood on his bottom lip.

My mouth drops open in bewilderment. *Never* would I have thought Beckett would be like this. *Never.*

"A kiss," he whispers.

"What?" I breathe, feeling lightheaded.

"To remind you that you are *nothing* without me, Eliana." He smoothes his thumb over the cut, pressing in just enough that my breath catches. "No one would even care if you didn't show up for work tomorrow. Which is a good thing..." Beckett tilts his head to the side as his voice trails off. He grabs me at the back of my knees and throws me over his shoulder, screaming.

I am thrown onto our bed with such force that my neck strains from the impact. Beckett is there before I can sit up, running the knife up my leg and splitting open my stocking. Tiny droplets of blood follow the knife's path.

"Look at the slutty clothes you wear, trying to impress *him*." Beckett's words are cold and dark. Something has snapped inside of him.

There is absolutely *nothing* slutty about my clothes. I am dressed within the company's guidelines: stockings, a knee-length pencil skirt and a white business shirt. Beckett runs his hand up my inner thigh and yanks my skirt over my hips. I am shaking violently. He stabs the knife into the mattress next to my head.

"Eli, darling, you *need* to relax. It's just me. You *love* me, remember?" His voice is dark and violent, a horrifying juxtaposition to the words spilling from his lips.

He's going to kill me. That thought plays over and over like a song on repeat. Then, finally, I take a deep breath.

"I-I do love you," I stutter out, but it's barely louder than a whisper. He presses his thumb into the x-marked wound above my breast.

"I *own* you. Nobody else wants you."

I have got to get out of here. I don't want to die like this. No matter how hard I thrash, Beckett has me pinned to the bed too well. There is no way I will be able to break free of him. He wraps his hand around my throat, squeezing tightly as his other hand rips my stockings and underwear off. I can't breathe. I try to suck in air, but he's suffocating me.

Stay calm. You can do this! I try to tell myself. My eyes water as he squeezes my throat. A rough hand teasing me, I clench my thighs together tightly. I don't want this. I need to get away. Slowly, I reach up and grip the knife. *I will only get one chance.*

I try not to think about what I am about to do. The handle of the knife is warm in my palm. I will my hand to stop shaking, but it won't listen. *Don't think. Just do.* My lip quivers as I carefully stretch out my arm and plunge the knife into Beckett's back. His screams fill the bedroom. The apartment. The building. My *entire* soul.

Stabbing someone is more challenging than I thought it would be. My eyes snap shut at the resistance of the knife plunging through flesh and muscle. It hardly went in deep enough. *Do I need to do it again?* I quickly pull it back out.

Beckett screams, his hand tightening around my throat.

My eyes water, and a horrible sound comes from my lips as I am being choked. His blood drips off the knife onto the side of his face and my chest.

I have to do it again. Gods, I don't want to do this.

I plunge the knife into his back again—harder and deeper—shuddering at the way it *feels*. I try to lock down the thoughts and feelings raging through me like a storm.

Beckett releases my throat, rolling off the bed, screaming and cursing in pain.

"I'm sorry," I sob as I scramble off the bed. "I am *so* sorry."

As I make my way out of the bedroom, a firm grip seizes my leg, causing me to fall face-first into the ground. Twisting my body, I see a bloody hand clutching onto my ankle, the knife still sticking out of his back.

"You fucking bitch!" Beckett screams as he pulls me back towards him. With my free leg, I kick him hard in the face. The feeling of his nose crumpling under my bare foot sends a shiver down my spine and bile rising in my throat. He loosens his grip on me enough that I scramble to my feet and scurry for the door, snatching my keys off the hook as I go. I sprint down three flights of stairs, two at a time, fearing even more for my life.

I don't doubt that if he catches me, he will kill me.

The door banging against the wall three flights up has a scream erupting from my chest, echoing in the stairwell. Terror sizzles inside me. I look up the stairs to find Beckett chasing me down, bloody knife in hand. My hand shakes profusely as I unlock and push open the front doors to the building and escape out into the darkness.

It's death either way. I might as well take my chances against the Flesh-Hunters.

Laughing like a maniac, Beckett is hot on my heels as he

chases me down the dark alleyways, swinging the bloody knife as he runs. My grandmother's building is not far away. I round the corner of the alleyway, my bare feet stinging against the pavement, the cold air caressing my legs. *The building should be here.* My vision blurred from the adrenaline and horror, I run straight into something. Something tall and unnaturally gaunt. We both fall back onto the cold, wet ground. The throaty, clicking sound paralyses me where I lay sprawled out on the cobblestone.

Flesh-Hunter.

My eyes feel like they're practically bulging out of my head, unable to blink at the monster scrambling to its feet. My whole body trembles as I try to clear some of the blankness from my mind. I shuffle to my feet, backing away from the flesh-eating creature still struggling to regain its footing, its long, knife-like arms making it difficult for it to get a grip. Tears stream freely down my face as memories come flooding back of the night Papa was killed. The Flesh-Hunter makes an irritable clicking sound. I press my hand over my chest, *trying* to block the scent of my life force, but it won't do anything. I know the monster has already tasted my blood in the air.

A large crack of thunder, like two boulders being thrown together, snaps my attention. The Flesh-Hunter lunges towards me from its knees. I quickly step out of the way as icy rain falls around us.

I've got to run. Now.

I lunge for my dropped keys—

"Eliana!" Beckett's sing-song voice calls wrathfully from behind. Not wanting to take my eyes off the Flesh-Hunter before me, I quickly glance over my shoulder at Beckett. The heavy downpour has saturated him. His shirt clings to his chest, spreading the blood, reminding me of when I was a child and would colour in napkins, then pour water over them and watch the ink bleed. The bloodstained knife glistens in the rain and moonlight like liquid rubies. The Flesh-Hunter jerks its head up, and the guttural clicking sound intensifies as it smells Beckett's blood. Finally, it scrambles to its feet in a state of hysteria.

It wants him, not you, I tell myself as I press my body hard against the wall, out of the monster's way—just in time—as it lunges forward, knocking Beckett onto his back with a sickening thud as his head hits the concrete, cracking open and spilling blood. The knife skitters just out of his reach.

"Eli! Eliana! Help me!" Beckett cries, his words slurring from the impact. The Flesh-Hunter gradually raises its long arm and slices open his shirt as it makes a clicking sound of contentment. It's found exactly what it was looking for. It pulls itself closer to Beckett's chest, and its long line of a mouth slowly unzips, revealing its sharp teeth. Pulling itself closer to his face, the Flesh-Hunter's long tongue darts out and, for the first time in what feels like forever, Beckett looks small, scared. That is exactly how he has made me feel for the last few years.

A part of me wants to help him because, despite the abuse, I still love him—or the part of him that was kind and caring. The old Beckett I fell in love with. But I know he wouldn't hesitate to sacrifice me to save himself.

I won't let him hurt me or anyone else ever again.

"Eliana, you bitch! Help me!" he screams as the Flesh-Hunter takes a deep, slow breath. It pulls away and slices pieces of Beckett's tanned skin off his chest.

"I'm sorry, Beckett. I loved you. I really, really did." My voice is lost as his screams fill the alleyway. I turn and run for the building.

I lock myself inside my grandmother's apartment, my back firmly pressed against the door. Safe.

I am safe. I am alive! I think as my body goes into shock. I start shaking and crying hysterically at what I have done. As Beckett's screams filter into the apartment, I slide down the door, pulling my knees up to my chest. I press my hands over my ears, squeezing my eyes shut, praying for it to stop. A half-hour passes so slowly, and suddenly, there's an animalistic shriek. Then silence.

I'm a monster, the voice inside me says over and over as I sit on the floor of the shower. *I just left Beckett there to die.* The water falls over me, drowning me in guilt.

"He would have killed you," says a voice around me, and I know that to be true.

CHAPTER FOURTEEN
ELIANA

The water in the shower shuts off. I open my eyes to find Mallrie leaning against the wall, watching me, his arms folded across his bare chest, a towel wrapped low around his waist. Indecently low. His muscles glisten with droplets of water, his hair damp, causing the strands to curl around his face. I drag my gaze back up his body to his face. He's frowning at me. My cheeks redden under his stare, even as I wonder what *his* problem is.

"What were you dreaming about?" he whispers, but his voice's gentleness doesn't match his expression. His eyes bore into me as if he's holding onto whatever restraint he has not to pry open my mind and see what is troubling me.

He can't do that.

I try not to squirm, but I do not know what *magic* he possesses. I repress a shudder at that thought and force it away to analyse later when I have a potent drink in my hand.

I hadn't realised I had fallen asleep. I sit up a bit more on the lounge. My head aches like invisible hands pressing on either side of my skull, trying to crush it. My whole body is stiff—probably from falling asleep on the couch. I press my hand to my forehead. "Um, nothing," I lie, squinting and rubbing my eyes. *When did it get so bright in here?*

"Looked like you had a bad dream." Mallrie crosses the room and pulls my hand away from my face as he gently cups my chin, tilting it so I look up at him. He cautiously turns my head to the left and then to the right. I should push him away. I don't know him, and I don't *want* to know him. But his gentle touch, how he looks at me as if he... *cares. Don't be stupid,* I tell myself. *He—*

"You've got a mild concussion." Mallrie sighs as he releases my face, cutting off the thoughts rushing through my mind.

I can still feel the warmth of his hand against my skin as he walks into the kitchen. I move to follow him, but before I can push to my feet, Mallrie's voice calls from the kitchen, "Don't even think about it. Sit down." There is enough bite of authority in his tone that I obey.

Pouting like the mature adult I am, I open my mouth to protest that I am fine, but my head is spinning. I slump back down, leaning over the back of the chair with my head resting on my arms. I watch silently as Mallrie walks around the kitchen in just a towel. My body burns with desire. *It's just the concussion making you swoon,* I tell myself, trying to remind myself that I do *not* trust him.

Even though he has saved your life... twice? that annoying little voice in the back of my mind remarks. *Does he know what he's doing to me?* I repress the groan that wants to rip itself from my lips and rest my head on the back of the couch. It really is pounding, and I want to go back to sleep.

Mallrie makes a cup of tea and brings it over to the lounge. Placing it on the coffee table, I turn around and raise an eyebrow.

"Tea?" I question, tilting my head to the side. "A cup of tea is going to fix my concussion?"

"Not yet," he says as he walks off into the bathroom. I pull my legs up under me as I reposition myself on the old couch, the movement causing the scent of dust to perfume the air. Mallrie walks back into the lounge room, tossing his black pants onto the nearby armchair and retrieving a small glass vial with a cork lid.

The jar is filled with a thick green substance with gold speckles. I scrunch up my nose at the sight of it. Mallrie removes the lid with a *pop* and carefully pours two thick droplets into the teacup. The smell of the green and gold substance mixing with the hot water makes me want to be sick.

"I'm not drinking that," I announce, folding my arms across my chest and narrowing my eyes at the man before me. Mallrie doesn't respond to my refusal. Instead, he picks up the teaspoon resting on the lemon-print saucer and stirs it twice to the left and once to the right. He taps the spoon on the cup's side three times, places it back on the saucer and hands me the matching teacup.

"I'm not drinking that," I repeat, scooting myself further into the couch. Mallrie sits across from me on the coffee table. The towel wrapped around his waist pulls up a little, showing off his thick, muscular thighs. *Not that I am looking.*

"Yes, you will," he says, that sharp bite of authority returning to his tone. "Otherwise, you'll have to go to the practitioner. Would you rather do that?"

I glance from the cup in his outstretched hands to his solemn face. "Maybe I would."

Mallrie moves with swift gracefulness—which is truly remarkable for someone his size. He puts the cup back on the saucer, and my head spins. "As you wish." He gets up and is at the armchair where his discarded pants are in an instant. With his back turned to me, I watch as the muscles in his back and arms shift as he—

"What are you doing?" I snap, and his hands freeze on the towel, along with my breath.

"What does it look like?" he asks, looking over his shoulder. "I'm going to take you to the practitioner."

"Now? It's still dark," I say, panic rising in my voice. I jerk my head towards the window, and the sudden movement intensifies the spinning feeling and that aching pressure.

"Doesn't bother me," Mallrie says indifferently, with a slight shrug of one of his muscular shoulders. I'm tired and hungry, and I definitely do *not* want to go back out into the darkness again.

Sighing heavily and a little dramatically, I ask, "What is it?" as I jerk my chin to the cup—which I instantly regret. Mallrie drops his pants back onto the chair and readjusts the towel as he walks back over and sits on the coffee table.

"A potion. It'll help." I carefully sniff the teacup as he hands it to me; it smells sweet now, like honey and lavender. "It's fine, trust me," he says, watching me with that intensity that makes me want to squirm.

"*It'll help. It's fine. Trust me,*" I mock, rolling my eyes. "That's real convincing, you know? And a lot to ask of someone you just met."

Mallrie rolls his eyes—there is something amusing about seeing this man roll his eyes. I suck my bottom lip in and bite down on it to stop myself from smiling. He mutters something under his breath about me being stubborn and how much trouble I will be as he reaches across, takes the teacup from my hands and takes a sip. "See? Safe." He pushes the cup back into my hands and lifts it towards my mouth. I can see where his lips had pressed against porcelain, almost smelling his scent over the honey and lavender. A shiver runs through my body as he drags his thumb over the back of my hand and sighs, *"Please."*

I take a tentative sip. The warmth of the tea slips over my tongue and runs through my body. All the aches and pains slowly melt away, just like magic. I chuckle into the cup. *It's just like magic,* I think to myself again, another giggle bubbling out of me. Mallrie raises an eyebrow in silent question. I just close my eyes and carefully shake my head. A quiet, *"never mind,"* and take another long sip.

Mallrie sighs with relief. "Thank you."

I try not to smile down at the cup, at how marvellous whatever he put in there is, but it is all but impossible. I feel great—well, not great, but significantly better. The pounding in my head is gone, and I no longer feel like someone is trying to blow my brains out like I am a human pimple.

Mallrie slumps onto the couch next to me, kicking his feet up on the coffee table, and closes his eyes. "So are you going to make a habit of me needing to save you?"

I choke on the tea, coughing and spluttering back into the porcelain cup. I think a little even came out of my nose. With that thought, I return the cup to its saucer, feeling slightly disturbed about having to drink the rest.

I turn to face Mallrie, eyebrows raised, eyes widened and mouth slack with a lack of words at the audacity of this man. "You going to keep stalking me?" I recover and glare at him, but he just smiles, eyes still shut. *Amused, and is he... blushing?* I bite my lip at the idea of making this man blush.

My traitorous eyes take this moment to explore his body. I know little about First Aid, but the stitching on his shoulder and the side of his abdomen looks rushed. But the other wounds that pepper his skin… I blink hard. They're practically healed or gone. Faded into soft pink scars. *How is that even possible?*

My eyes keep exploring down, down—

"I think the words you're looking for are *thank you*," Mallrie's voice interrupts me just before—

I shake my head, dragging my focus back to his face, eyes still closed. Thankfully. "I didn't ask for any of this," I snap back.

Mallrie shrugs. "Maybe not, but it was bound to happen."

"Excuse me?" I jerk upright, cursing as a sharp zing of pain slices behind my eyes. Mallrie opens an eye lazily and studies my face. "I *never* wanted this. I *don't* want this," I say, putting more force into my tone.

Mallrie sits up a bit more, kicking his feet off the table. He grabs my blackened hand and lifts it in front of my face. "Too late," he says coldly, and he drops my hand tersely. He gets up and heads back towards the bathroom, picking up his pants as he passes.

"Hey!" I shout as I push off the couch, stumbling over my feet from getting up too fast, and stalk after him. "Don't you walk away from me! You can't—"

As I round the corner, my voice gets clogged in my throat. Mallrie stands there, pulling his pants back on, his bare ass squeezing into his black jeans. He turns to face me as he zips up his pants and fastens the button. I'm shamelessly staring.

I can't pull my eyes away from the dusting of dark hair trailing down, *down* his body.

He's probably the most handsome man I've ever seen.

I can't help but blush, even if I don't trust him and he

irritates me. Mallrie smiles as he walks past me and puts one finger under my chin, tenderly pushing my mouth shut. "It's rude to stare," he whispers in my ear as he steps around me. "Besides, you might have been able to avoid all of this, though I highly doubt it," he calls over his shoulder. It takes me a moment to remind my body how to breathe. "But the moment you touched the Enkanti Tree, well, you're in the thick of it now, baby," he says, walking back into the kitchen.

My eyes blink rapidly as I try to process what he has just done and said. He didn't seem phased at all that I just walked in on him getting dressed. He didn't care that I just stood there gawking over him. If anything, his expression looked as if he found it all a little amusing.

I finally free my feet, the disbelief being replaced by anger.

"Okay, first of all—" I spit as I meet him in the kitchen. I slam my hands on the island bench. "*Never* call me baby again! I am *not* your baby. Second, how about you actually *explain* to me what the fuck is going on? Who are you really, and what the fuck are you doing?" He gives me a small, crooked smile.

"You're so easily fired up." Amusement laces his every word.

"No. You're just frustrating," I deadpan as I watch Mallrie walk past me and snatch one of the many candles my grandmother decorated her home with. Flipping the tall pillar candle as he returns to the kitchen, he places it on the bench between us.

I shake my head irritably. "Well, are you going to answer my questions? Or would you rather redecorate?" I want to reach across the bench and wring his neck as he lazily bends down until his eyes are the same height as the candlewick. Instead, he looks up at me, wide-eyed and waiting.

"If you be a good girl, calm down and ask me nicely," he torments with a smirk.

"*Stop!*" I shout, digging my nails into the wooden benchtop. "I think I deserve some answers!" He just sits there staring at me with one dark eyebrow arched.

"Say please." His voice is dripping like honey, thick with amusement as if he finds pleasure in pushing my buttons and getting a reaction out of me.

My body feels hot with rage. Finally, I slam my hands on the bench and walk away. *There's no winning with this man. He's taking the piss!*

Well, fuck him! I am not *involved in anything. I am going to go to sleep, and when I wake up, I am going to pretend as if I never met him.*

Mallrie lets out a small, delighted gasp. Something in his voice changes. It's kinder when he calls my name. "Eliana, come back." I turn on my heel, about to start yelling and cursing at him, but nothing comes out. My arms hang limply at my sides, my mouth falling open at what sits on the bench between us.

CHAPTER FIFTEEN
ELIANA

There is only an island bench standing between a witch and me. My body's inert as the candle between us is now alive, the flame dancing in the dim light.

My eyes widen as I look between Mallrie and the candle. "I didn't do that!" I raise my hands defensively. His eyes soften as he rounds the bench, closing the distance between us. I try to back away, but I run into the couch.

His voice is low and calming. "Yes, you did, Eliana. It's okay."

I shake my head, side-stepping around him, and march over to the candle and blow it out. "No," I repeat, "I didn't."

Mallrie cocks his head to the side. "Are you saying I did?"

"Well, you're the one who admitted to being a witch," I spit. I can feel my eyes widen, and imagine how they'd look with too much white showing around the iris as panic bubbles inside me.

"Hmm, well, your grandmother seemed to like candles," he muses as he looks around the room.

"So what? Lots of people like candles. They're relaxing," I say over-sensitively.

"Did you ever see her light them? Where are her matches?"

"I—um—well—" I stop short, racking my brain for a memory of her lighting a candle. But I can't remember. It is such a mundane action. Who actually remembers lighting their birthday candles? No one. You remember blowing them *out* and the taste of the cake. Mallrie nods as if confirming what he's trying to say.

"Your grandmother was a fire elemental," he continues.

"No. Impossible. She—" I begin, but Mallrie gently leads me back to the couch. He's not even touching me, but the way his hand hovers at the small of my back... It's thoughtful. Not that he knows about my past, but I appreciate him not overly manhandling me—like in the kitchen. *"But that was different, wasn't it? You enjoyed the way he took care of you. The way he made sure you were okay over himself."* I look around, trying to find where that voice is coming from. Gods, what I wouldn't do for a bottle of gin right now.

"Sit," he commands. I fall down with him onto the couch, crossing my arms over my chest.

"Did you just use some mind control magic on me?" I demand before I can even stop myself.

Mallrie's dark eyebrows crawl up his face. "Excuse me?"

I look over my shoulder at where we were standing in the kitchen, then back at him. One eyebrow has dropped, leaving only one arched in speculation. I stumble for my words, incoherent mumbling tumbling out.

Mallrie stifles what I guess is a laugh with a cough. "No, I didn't use any mind control magic. We can't do that."

"Oh," I breathe, feeling a little silly.

"Your grandmother *was* a witch though," he continues,

angling his head to better look at my face. "A fire elemental, to be precise," he repeats softly, as though if I keep hearing it, that will make it true. That I will accept it.

He softly tilts my head so I am looking at him, his other arm wrapped affectionately around the back of the couch. Mallrie is not touching me—except for the featherlight touch on my chin—but he's close enough that I can feel his warmth, and I hate how good it feels to be close to him. I've spent too long distancing myself from people, and being this close to another person— to *him*—feels almost sinful.

"You want answers?" Mallrie asks, his voice low and calm, breaking the silence between us.

"Yes." I give a soft nod. "Please." I'll reprimand myself later for my inability to let this go. The feeling of unease settles in my chest. I don't want to have any part of this. Mallrie, sitting shirtless in my grandmother's apartment, has me itching to push him away. To say or do something to make him leave because this is starting to feel too... *intimate*. But if he can answer the questions I don't want forming on the tip of my tongue...

Mallrie returns my nod, releases my chin and sits back in the chair, his hand rubbing over his stubbled jaw like he's wondering where to begin so as to not overwhelm me with information. My fingers nervously fiddle, picking at my nails and the skin surrounding them.

After a long silence, Mallrie sits forward, his elbows resting on his knees. His muscles are tense as he searches for the right words. His dark brows draw together, a faint line forming between them. "Do you remember the story I told you the other night when I walked you home?" he asks quietly, his elbows pressed into his knees, looking down as if praying. I give a slight nod, even though he isn't watching me.

"About the Enkanti Tree and the first settlers," I reply.

He nods slowly. He looks sad. "I know that story is true because... I was there." He finally looks up at me, his eyes filled with darkness and regret.

I shake my head. "No. That's impossible. If that were true, you'd be, what—" I try to do the math in my head. It makes little sense. *There is no plausible way...*

"198 years old," he finishes for me.

I push myself back on the couch, trying to distance myself as much as possible.

What the fuck did he just say? What was in that tea?

I glance at the lemon-print teacup sitting on the coffee table. I drank most of it. The aching pressure in my head is gone, but now I must be hallucinating. Or maybe it killed me. Because there's no way...

Mallrie gets up, walks across the room and leans against the wall, giving me much-needed space. I have seen this man in battle; he's quick and strong. I *just* saw him practically naked. But, no... I can't even comprehend that age. He's almost *200 years old*, and he looks *that* good.

It's inconceivable!

"But you don't look..." I say breathlessly. Panic is building in my chest.

Mallrie takes a deep breath and continues. "I'm a time elemental," he says casually, shrugging as if that answers all my questions—which it certainly does *not*. He deliberately lowers his head, studying my expression. "170 years ago, when Charleston burnt my coven at the Enkanti Tree, I performed a spell to freeze my *Timeline*. I will not age until I fulfil a promise I made. I will right the wrongs that were done to my people." His voice sounds strange... Almost distant. "And I have not aged since. Forever in my thirty-fifth cycle around the sun." The way he speaks now... His voice sounds like he is talking from another time. Lost long ago.

Silence grows between us as he waits for me to say something. I lick my lips and open my mouth, then shut it again, unable to form a complete thought.

This is too much.

I'm at war with myself. The logical part of my brain is screaming that this is *wrong* on so many levels. I need to tell Mallrie to leave, to put as much distance between us as possible. But the other side of me—the stupid side—wants to know what he has to say. Even though I don't trust him, I feel... I feel safe with him.

It's just because he keeps saving your life, I remind myself.

"*Please* say something," he finally says, his arms folded across his bare chest as he tilts his head.

"Keep going," is all I can manage to get out. Those two words are barely audible.

He nods and continues, "You might remember I said they burnt all the witches at the tree. Only a few relinquished their magic and lived a mundane life under Charleston's rule."

I nod, letting him know I am keeping up, even though it feels like my brain is being scrambled.

"Well, I was one of those who didn't burn. Obviously." A small smile plays at the corner of his lips as he gestures to his semi-naked body. "But I didn't give up my magic either."

Obviously, I add silently.

"I used my magic and cursed the five other witches who refused to stand with my mother." He frowns at the memory, looking at the ground.

"Wait," I interrupt, rubbing my temples. "Your mother? Your mother was the High Witchess?" He looks at me and nods, a small smile at the corner of his mouth, impressed that I made the connection. But there's sadness in his eyes.

"The five witches didn't know I put a curse on them, but I was young and angry. I wanted to keep my promise and make things right, but I needed their help. I needed all five elemental witches. Fortunately for me, the five traitors happened to be one of each elemental." Mallrie mumbles something under his breath that I don't catch. Something about fate or Fates? "I left the township Charleston was building and moved into the Melsheim Forest, where no one would come looking for me. Of course, I conjured a protection spell so no one could enter unless I deemed it," he says, waving his hand as if that's just common sense, that only a fool wouldn't put a protection spell around their home. Mallrie looks up at me, making sure I am still following. I give him a slight nod, and he continues. "I waited. A time elemental who has stopped their *Timeline* can be pretty patient." He gives a soft chuckle at what I'm guessing was his way of trying to ease the tension in the room.

It doesn't help. My back is aching from how stiffly I am sitting.

"I let them all remarry, have kids, grandkids—great-grandkids, even. That was a good year." Mallrie smiles at the memory and is momentarily quiet as if his mind has returned to that point. Then, finally, he clears his throat and continues, "When they thought their time was up, they waited for death to take their souls to the Afterlife." Mallrie's eyes darken with a viciousness. "That's when my curse kicked in. Freezing them in time—ageless, like me—wiping them from the memories of their loved ones."

A small gasp slips out of me, and I slap a hand over my mouth as I stare up at him with wide eyes. Mallrie dips his chin in acknowledgement of my horror. Somehow, it silently conveys something like, *"You have every right to be afraid of me, but I won't hurt you."* How a single subtle dip of a chin can convey so much, I cannot explain. Or maybe I'm just reading too much into it. Trying to convince myself that he's not here to hurt me.

"I needed their bloodline, not *them*," Mallrie continues. "Their magic filtered down into a new generation. Although it would be weak from years of breeding with mortals, it would be enough for a start. I would train this new generation of elementals and bring back the balance. Eventually, they searched for me, pleading that I lift the curse. I told them of the High Witchess' plan to restore peace and order. That's when they all took up the positions as the librarians."

I can't believe what I am hearing. "The librarians are witches?" I drawl. Mallrie nods. "The librarians are witches," I repeat, shocked. "It kind of makes sense," I whisper, remembering how tightly one of them gripped my wrist.

"My curse stripped them of their magic so they'd never be able to recall it again. Their magic is stored in the Enkanti Tree for their descendants to inherit. Also, so the time elemental won't try to undo my curse," he adds quietly, as if he was so clever to tie up any loose strings.

"Wait a minute," I say, sitting up straighter in the chair. I look at my blackened fingertips and then back to Mallrie.

He nods, not needing me to finish my thought. *He's probably seen how this conversation plays out already.* "Yes, you're a descendant of a fire elemental. But, honestly, I am surprised your grandmother possessed any magic at all. Most of the descendants have traces of magic still, but it is so dormant they don't even notice it is there. But you... You're special."

The way he says that has my blood thrumming, my heart beating a wild and untamed song.

Beckett's words replay in my mind, reminding me I am nothing.

But how Mallrie said it, like I am the missing piece in a larger puzzle that he's been searching for... I want to believe him.

I clear my throat. "Time out," I call, pinching the bridge of my nose. "No pun intended." My eyes flick up to his. "Please don't stop time."

Mallrie chuckles. "Don't worry. I rarely, if ever, do that."

I let out a relieved sigh. "Have we had this conversation before?" I ask. "Or, like, have you seen how this conversation plays out?" I know it's not essential, but it will bug me if I don't know the truth.

Mallrie's brows press together. "No, we haven't had this conversation before. And no, I haven't looked into our *Timeline* to see how this plays out. So whatever you think or feel, I won't know until you tell me."

Well, fuck. Now I have even more *questions.* But one pushes all the others aside. "What do you mean by *our Timeline*? What is this *Timeline*?"

Mallrie explains his powers. How they say time elementals were gifted their magic from the Fates. That the *Timeline* is like one giant spiderweb that interlinks different people's lives and how one small action can send the *Timeline* off in a completely different direction.

Honestly, the whole spiel has my head spinning.

"Can I finish our original conversation?" Mallrie asks. "Or are you wanting to throw the *Timeline* of this conversation off on another tangent?"

It must be horrible, being able to feel the different shifts in the *Timeline*, so I decide to keep my hands and feet inside the ride for the remainder of this conversation. I nod sheepishly.

"Thank you. Witches have specific powers that fall into one of the five elements," Mallrie continues. "Time"—he gestures to himself—"Fire"—he nods towards me—"Water, earth and air. The High Witchess possessed all five. You'll need to touch the Enkanti Tree to gain the remainder of your magic. The first touch is kind of like a test. If you are worthy, the tree will check your bloodline and determine which element you belong to. The second touch gives you the rest of the magic." He points at my blackened fingertips, a small crease forming between his dark brows. "Curious side effect I didn't account for," he says quietly, slightly tilting his head as he looks from my fingers to my eyes.

"*Magic?*" I ask with a sigh. "So, what? You want me to believe I am what? A witch?" The word sounds funny to say out loud. Mallrie smiles, but I continue to look at him in disbelief.

"After everything we've discussed this evening, you still don't believe it?" he asks, a little stunned that I am not jumping up and down in my seat. Like I get to live out some childhood fantasy or something.

"Well, that's just it, isn't it? We've just talked." I wince at how dirty that sounded, and I hope he doesn't take it the wrong way.

Mallrie chuckles dryly. "Is seeing really believing for you?"

I shrug a shoulder nonchalantly while internally screaming, *WHY DO I CARE?* I don't want this. I don't want to be a witch—well, maybe, when I was a kid, I did. Who didn't want to get a letter saying they had magical abilities and got to be shipped off to some magical boarding school to fight dragons and save princesses? But this is real life, and as horrible as it sounds, I have come to terms with my reality of living amongst flesh-eating monsters with no white knights.

Mallrie moves, carefully sitting in front of me on the coffee table. "Eliana." My name is like a song that has me inching towards him. "You were born a witch. The Enkantian elemental magic runs through your veins. Whether you believe it is up to you." He sighs, running a hand through his dark mass of hair. "However, if you need proof…" Mallrie holds out his hand, palm facing up, and closes his eyes. The air shifts around us, sending a chill running down my spine. Suddenly—dare I say it, like magic—a purple, glittery orb of air rises out of his hand. I gasp loudly, and Mallrie's eyes snap open.

His cerulean eyes swirl with a mix of purple and gold flecks. He's looking at me, but I am unsure if he's looking at me or into my soul. It's a little unnerving.

The orb in his hand grows until it's the size of a soccer ball. Then, the thick, glittery air shifts, and inside the ball is…

Oh, gods! It's me!

I am standing in a clearing surrounded by trees, and flames surround me. Ribbons of fire float around my legs and arms like I am controlling them.

My mouth drops open at the vision. "Wh-what is this?" I whisper, too afraid to speak more.

"A vision from a section of your *Timeline*," Mallrie replies calmly. "I'm training you to use your magic." A little Mallrie steps into the frame, his mouth moving as he points to wooden targets, and my flames lash out and find their marks.

"Stop! Please, just stop!" I shout, pushing to my feet. The orb bursts like a bubble, and I realise I now stand between Mallrie's legs. A wave of heat rushes through my body, curling low in my stomach. I place a hand on his shoulder to steady myself. His skin is hot under my palm as I step over his leg and storm into the kitchen. I rifle through the cupboard for any sort of alcohol.

Right at the back of the cabinet is a bottle of tequila. I take a large swig of the rich, golden liquid and gag, remembering why I hate tequila so much. I cough and splutter as I clutch onto the kitchen bench like it will stop the world from falling out from under my feet.

This can't be real! I must have spoken the words out loud because Mallrie is here, leaning a hip casually against the bench next to me, saying calmly, "It is real, Eliana."

CHAPTER SIXTEEN
ELIANA

"It's getting late. You should get cleaned up and get some rest," Mallrie says after I've thrown up again in the sink. I really fucking hate tequila.

Turning off the tap, I turn to lean against the bench. "But wait, what about—"

He raises his hand to silence me. "Another time. You need rest. It's been a big night. Lots of information for you to process." A sly smile spreads across his handsome face. "Besides, I can't start training until we're in the woods, and you need to be well-rested and ready. Fire can be... unpredictable."

I open my mouth to protest. *The woods. Surely he doesn't expect me to go into the Melsheim Forest! And who says I even want to train?* Mallrie carefully leads me into the bathroom. "There'll be plenty of time for all your questions later, I promise."

The butterflies in my chest flutter at his promise. *Ugh! What the fuck? Why am I getting excited about knowing I will see him again?*

"Shower. Rest. We'll talk again soon." Mallrie reaches around me, pulling the door shut. I grab it, stopping him.

"Why do I feel like this is goodbye?" My heart is beating so loudly in my chest it's a miracle he cannot hear it. I am also fully aware that my heart and brain have ceased communication with me. They've teamed up to work against me. *Traitors.*

Mallrie gives me one of those half-crooked smiles. "Are you asking me to spend the night with you?" His voice is a deep, sensual caress with a hint of innuendo.

I scowl at him. "No." The word flies out of my mouth so quickly. *I just don't want to be alone.* The thought of being by myself scares me after the flashback of Beckett and being chased by the man in the suit's thugs and then the many Flesh-Hunter/Kailadon attacks. I don't trust Mallrie, but he makes me feel safe. And that has become a rarity in my life.

"I can stay if that's what you want," Mallrie's voice pulls me out of my head. I drop my eyes to the tiled floor. I can feel my cheeks flushing red. I give a slight nod.

"Shower," he says as he shuts the door.

I lean against the closed bathroom door and take a deep breath. *What have I gotten myself caught up in?* I can lie to myself all I like, but the truth of the matter is that I find Mallrie attractive.

He's indisputably gorgeous, but there's something more than just physical attraction. The way he keeps checking in on me, the way he keeps breaking down my walls, making me vulnerable. My mind wanders, and I can almost feel the warmth of his body against mine as I undress and step into the shower, pulling the curtain behind me. I try to shake away the fantasy blooming in my mind.

"You don't know him," I tell myself. "You *knew* Beckett, and look how that turned out." The water runs down my chest, and I roll my head back as I run my fingers through my hair. "Plus, he's a witch! A witch that is nearly 200 years old! Who carries a sword!" For some reason, that just makes him even more appealing, and I try not to think about the whole age gap thing. It's one thing for it to be sexy in fantasy novels, but in real life? I'm not quite sure how I feel about it.

My mind drifts again as the water caresses me. *Mallrie's fingers chase the warm droplets of water down my body. His lips leave a trail of kisses as they follow his fingers down, down... slowly... sliding down my legs. His arms wrap around my waist, his head between my thighs.* The thought is so fucking hot, I feel like my whole body is on fire.

Wait.

Something burns my senses as I open my eyes.

The heat is real.

The *fire* is real.

I let out a shriek and fall back against the wall. The shower curtain is on fire, sizzling against the water from the showerhead. Smoke is quickly filling the room. Mallrie bangs against the door.

"Eliana? Is everything okay in there?" he calls from the other side of the door. I grab the curtain and yank it off the rod into the water with a loud, clanging sound.

Everything that happens next happens so fast.

I'm jumping over the flaming shower curtain as it hisses and smokes.

Calling out to Mallrie that I'm fine.

The room is rapidly filling with smoke.

I am coughing as it invades my lungs.

The loud crash from ripping down the shower curtain has Mallrie bursting through the door.

I shriek at the unexpected eruption. His eyes fall over

the scene of the water pouring over the burnt shower curtain and then to me as I scramble to pull a towel over my naked body.

Mallrie quickly looks away, and I swear his cheeks redden.

"Sorry, I—um—" He clears his throat nervously, and I can't help the smile that blossoms on my face. "I saw smoke. And there was a bang," he rambles. The man is nervously rambling. He looks away from me, but his feet seem glued to the floor.

I press my knuckles over my mouth to hide my smile at how embarrassed and uncomfortable he looks at this moment. Forget being over a hundred years old; he looks so young and boyish. Whatever red flags were popping up have dissolved away.

Running my fingers through my wet hair, pushing it out of my face, I try not to laugh as I say, "It's fine. I'm fine."

"Good, good. I'll—um—I'll leave you to it," he says as he walks back out and tries to shut the door that's now hanging on half of its hinges.

Thankfully, I have finished cleaning myself, so I don't have to jump back in the shower. I quickly pull on my old dressing gown that has fallen off the back of the door.

When my grandmother passed away, everything was just too much. So I left all of my belongings here and started afresh. New apartment, new clothes, new furniture, everything.

I carefully push open the door as it hangs precariously on its hinges and walk back into the lounge room. Mallrie is sitting on the couch, his head resting on the back cushion, eyes closed. I try to tiptoe towards my old bedroom beside the kitchen, hugging my old pink and white flower dressing gown closer to my body.

"What happened in there?" Mallrie cautiously opens an eye. He's regained his calm demeanour.

My entire face turns red thinking about the truth—not that I will tell him I was having a dirty fantasy about him between my thighs.

"Oh, um. I don't know." I shrug, trying to sound casual and perplexed. "The curtain just caught fire." I meet his stare. He's not buying what I am selling.

"What were you doing?" he insists. I run my fingers through my hair, trying not to think about how they felt between my legs. I keep my eyes on my old bedroom door and walk. *Gods, I wish I had a strong drink right now.* Well, that's kind of a lie. The two mouthfuls of tequila I had are still weighing heavy in my stomach. I don't think I could stomach it anymore.

"I was just showering," I say unconvincingly as I walk past where he is sprawled on the couch. He gets up and follows me to my room, and my pulse quickens.

"What were you *thinking* about?" he continues to question.

I turn to face him and raise my eyebrows. "That's a bit personal, don't you think? What do *you* do in the shower?" I ask, instantly regretting the words because they sound absolutely filthy. I walk into the dark room, shutting the door between us. Leaning against the wood, I exhale heavily.

Mallrie presses his head against the door with a quiet thud. He keeps pushing for information. I'd rather tie myself to the oak tree at nightfall than tell him the truth.

Eventually, he stops, and his footsteps recede.

I turn the light on, and it's as if it has transported me back in time. I walk over to the antique wardrobe. The wood creaks as I pull open the doors.

I cringe at what I behold in the wardrobe and thank the useless gods that my sense of fashion has changed since I moved out. Sweet, innocent sixteen-year-old Eliana was flirtatious and feminine.

Nowadays, I wear jeans almost all the time, no matter the season. I prefer to keep my scars covered. It helps to block out those painful memories and avoid the pitiful or curious looks people throw my way. I sigh as I rummage around the wardrobe. I settle on a short black skater skirt and a black-and-white gingham print top with puffed sleeves. Then, I find some lingerie and dress quickly.

I walk over to the mirror to check out my outfit choice. Wrapping my arms around myself, struggling to maintain eye contact with the girl staring back at me, a hopeless feeling of being overly vulnerable washes over me in an almost painful wave.

When my relationship with Beckett started to dissolve into something more... toxic, we'd fight over the smallest things, and he became more controlling. It started off with small, throwaway comments. Little things that, at the time, I quickly dismissed, not even realising what was happening.

Beckett would make a backhanded compliment or question my choice of clothing. Then he started to recommend books for me to read, commenting that reading fantasy or smut was not actually reading or as stimulating as reading non-fiction books. I quickly learnt that it was easier to just wear what he approved, to keep my preferred books at work and read his intellectually stimulating books at home. I have a small scar behind my left ear where he threw a book at me. My fingers trace over the raised tissue; I can still feel the thick, hardcover book slamming into the back of my head.

However, my eyes fall onto the scars on my legs—Beckett's preferred place for "discipline" when I did something he disagreed with. It was the easiest place to cover so no one would see the cracks in our relationship.

I know I should have left him at the first sign of abuse, but he always seemed so sorry, and I was young, naïve and utterly alone. Also, I believed he loved me.

I reach down and trace my finger down a long, red burn. It has long since healed, but the memory is inescapable.

CHAPTER SEVENTEEN
ELIANA

3 YEARS AGO

The small kitchen smells of bacon and toast as we make breakfast in silence. I can tell Beckett is still mad about last night. I've apologised about a hundred times. These fights are getting ridiculous. I wish my grandmother was here. Maybe then I wouldn't feel so alone.

I let out a sad sigh as I wait for the toast to cook, my fingertips tapping mindlessly on the benchtop.

"What's *your* problem?" snaps Beckett, looking over at me from the stove.

Oh, just that your silent treatments are getting on my nerves. I did nothing wrong! Well, not nothing, but far less than you. These stupid little fights we keep getting into are grating on my sanity.

If you don't want to be with me anymore, just break up with me. Just stop nitpicking over every little thing that I say or do! It's making me feel—

"Nothing," I reply, knowing that if I really spoke my mind, it would just blow up into another argument. Plus, I hardly slept last night between staring mindlessly at the ceiling just waiting for Beckett to talk to me, to talk through these issues like grown adults, and finally falling asleep to the nightmares that clawed their way through my subconsciousness. I don't even have the energy to fight this morning.

"Doesn't sound like nothing." His voice is tense, and against my better judgement, my mouth just starts talking.

"I just don't want you to be upset with me anymore. I told you I needed to work when I got home. That proposal is due on Monday, and we didn't have any plans, so I thought it would be okay."

"You thought it would be okay," Beckett scoffs, throwing my words back in my face.

"I'm not fighting about this again! You know how important my job is to me," I snap. I'm over all the fighting and then acting like the happy couple in public. I turn to walk off to the bathroom. Beckett's hand wraps around my wrist before I can get far, pulling me back into him. He smells like bacon and the faintest hint of scotch. *Has he been drinking already this morning?* He got up before me, but I didn't think I slept in that much.

"Where the fuck do you think you're going?" he growls.

I try to pull my arm free. "I'm going to have a shower. I am not fighting with you about this anymore." Beckett pulls me tighter and forces me onto the kitchen bench next to the stove, his fingers digging into my thighs.

"Do *not* walk away when I am talking to you!" he shouts.

"You're not listening to me, so what's the point?" I yell back, trying to unclench his hands from my thighs.

"Because *you're wrong!*" he barks. I roll my eyes and click my tongue, looking out the window.

He's so stubborn, but I guess I can be too.

Suddenly, there's a sizzling sound, and something hot and slippery runs down my leg. I let out an excruciating cry as I watch Beckett pour the hot fat and oil from the bacon down my leg. I reach for the pan, trying to push it away, but he just holds it there until all the oil has run out and down my thigh to my ankle.

I scream in pain, begging him to stop. Instead, Beckett tosses the pan back onto the stove top with a loud clang. My screams reverberate through the apartment and through my head. He walks away from me as if nothing happened, as if we just resolved this argument pleasantly, grabbing a piece of toast and the bottle of scotch and slamming the bedroom door behind him.

I am left sitting there in shock and agonising pain as my leg starts to blister. I carefully slide off the bench but crash to the floor on my throbbing leg under the weight of my body.

CHAPTER EIGHTEEN
ELIANA

"Eliana?" Mallrie cautiously knocks at the door. It sounds like this isn't the first time he's called my name from the hint of concern leaking through his tone. I push to my feet from my sitting position on the floor at the end of my bed. Straightening my skirt, I walk over to the door and cautiously open it. Mallrie stands there frozen, my hourglass figure accentuated by the shape of the skirt. If I wasn't feeling so self-conscious, I'd blush at the way he's looking at me.

I wrap my arms around myself. "What do you want, Mallrie?" I ask quietly, wondering if this is the first time I've said his name out loud. My heart beats wildly.

"Sorry, you look—" He clears his throat nervously.

"What do you want, Mallrie?" I repeat, getting impatient. I don't need his flattery.

"You look good," he says firmly.

I roll my eyes and look behind him, not wanting to meet his gaze. "I don't need your compliments. My body isn't here for your pleasure. Now, what do you—"

A fantastic smell is coming from the lounge room.

"What is that?" I point to the coffee table in disbelief, a small line forming between my brows.

There are two plates of lasagna on the table. Mallrie looks over his shoulder to where I am pointing and looks back at me, offering an apologetic smile. "Dinner," he says simply as he walks back to the couch. I watch him walk away in disbelief.

Where did he get the food?

He's still just sauntering around my grandmother's apartment in *just* his jeans.

"Yeah, okay," I drawl. My mouth feels dry, and my voice sounds strange as I follow Mallrie back to the lounge. I would slam my door back in his face if I wasn't starving. "Where did you get this?" I ask as he hands me a plate. "There's no food here."

"Your grandmother's neighbours have food," he says with a boyish smile. I look between the plate in my hand and him, shocked.

"You..." I suck in a deep breath, trying to reboot my brain. "You broke into someone's house and stole their dinner?"

Mallrie chuckles. The sound is so light it makes me want to smile, but there's a heaviness in my chest, urging me to push him away. To hurt him, if only to protect myself. "You needed to eat. What did you want me to do?" I look at him, stunned. "Besides, I believe these are technically their leftovers, so—"

"*Nothing.*" The word comes out flat, and hangs in the air between us as I hold the plate of warm lasagna. Mallrie looks up at me from where he's sitting on the couch, casually eating. "You didn't need to do anything," I clarify.

He cocks a dark eyebrow at me. "So you're not hungry?" he intones as his tongue drags across his lower lip. I'm starving, but I just can't wrap my head around this man. He is like a puzzle I don't know where to begin solving.

Or if I *want* to solve it.

"I am not your responsibility. You do not *need* to look after me." My voice is cold and defensive. Mallrie looks me up and down with an expression I can't quite make out.

"You've made it *remarkably* clear you don't need anyone's help. But asking for help is not a sign of weakness. This is where you want to stay for the night, and you need food to recover. So, I got you food."

"How?" I keep my voice down as if not wanting anyone else to hear. Mallrie smiles mischievously and leans forward like he is about to tell me a secret, and godsdamn it, I can't help but lean into him to hear what he's going to say. It is like he has some spell cast over me, where I want to hang on to every word he says. As much as that feels ludicrous, even though he's literally proven he is a witch, I know it is not some magical spell. No, this spell he has over me is one of my own making. I didn't think pushing everyone away would make me so stupid over the first person showing me a lick of kindness.

"I climbed through their window." He points to the roof, breaking me out of my thoughts. I look up and then back at him and point to the ceiling.

"You broke into the apartment *above* me? And stole their lasagna?"

Mallrie lets out a small laugh, amused at my shocked horror. "Yes. That is exactly what I did, and you should eat it 'cause it's fantastic." He takes another mouthful. I can't help but feel apprehensive around him. I don't want to trust him; I can feel my walls going up to protect myself. But there is just something so genuine about him.

"Are you opposed to clothes?" I snap. "Put your gods-damn shirt on!"

Mallrie raises an eyebrow. He's looking at me as if trying to figure me out. "You want me to put a shirt back on that's drenched in blood, sweat and *your* vomit?"

I open my mouth to speak, but I've got nothing. Of course I don't want that.

"Does it bother you?" Mallrie asks, amusement lighting up his voice and face as the corners of his mouth twist into a smile.

I bite my lip. It doesn't bother me; it does the exact opposite. I obviously can't trust my body not to spin wild fantasies about him.

"It's late. Shouldn't you be going home?" My voice is cold and hard, my defences back up, locking him out. *Couldn't he have stolen a bottle of wine too?*

"Thought you wanted me to stay?" he replies.

"I changed my mind."

"Because I got you some lasagna?" All the amusement has vanished from his voice. His head tilts slightly as if he can pry open my mind and sift through its contents.

"No, you—" I stomp my foot in frustration like the mature adult I am.

"Because I don't have a shirt on?" Mallrie suggests. I don't know if he's just being annoying or actually trying to understand why I've suddenly changed my mind.

"I just don't think it's a good idea. You should leave," I snap.

Mallrie nods somberly and puts his plate back on the table. "As you wish."

Those three little words hang between us as I quietly suck in a breath.

Silently, I watch as he walks over to the kitchen and

wrings out his shirt, tucking it into the back of his pants. Then, he grabs the sheath, his sword already safely away, and secures it onto his back.

"Please eat," he says, gesturing to the plate still in my hands as he pushes open the window.

"We have a door, you know," I say, motioning to the front door.

When Mallrie speaks, his voice is bitter and calculated as if it's taking all his self-control not to say what he wants to, to protect my feelings. "Our friend hasn't finished his dinner yet, and I am not in the mood for any more fighting."

My shoulders slump.

I am not in the mood for any more fighting.

The air runs out of my lungs, causing me to suck in short, sharp breaths. *How many times had I said or thought that about Beckett? Have I become as twisted as him?*

"Good night, Eliana." Mallrie's voice is like a beacon drawing me out of the darkness of my thoughts.

My lips parted slightly, but I didn't know where to begin or what to say.

My ears strain to listen for the sound of the Kailadon downstairs, still eating one of the thugs. Mallrie doesn't give me another look as he climbs out the window and up towards the roof. I wait a moment before running over and sticking my head out to watch him run off over the rooftops towards the edge of town.

As soon as I said it, I instantly regretted it.

I slam the window shut and slump back onto the couch. The apartment suddenly feels even smaller, so cold and empty.

CHAPTER NINETEEN
ELIANA

I take my time washing the plates as I let my mind wander, trying to figure out what I am meant to do today. After bombshell after bombshell yesterday, I feel so lost and alone, despite being surrounded by reminders of my grandmother.

I have woken surprisingly well-rested, considering I fell asleep on the couch last night.

Mallrie was right—though I hate to admit it, the lasagna he stole from the neighbours upstairs was terrific. So much so that I ate his serve too.

I stare at the soapy suds covering my hands as I mindlessly scrub the same spot on the plate I've been working on for the last five minutes.

I shouldn't have kicked him out, I think. Mallrie was injured, and I selfishly just kicked him out into the night—well, early morning. I know why I did what I did; to protect myself from letting him break down my walls and avoid getting hurt over some guy. Even if Mallrie seems nothing like Beckett, I won't let myself get hurt again. No matter how attracted I am to him. I should *not* be attracted to him.

I have tried so hard to be strong after my grandmother died. The black cloud of depression that hung over me for months after her death felt like it would never leave. Until I met Beckett. And, well, we know what a shitshow that turned out to be. I don't want to be the type of girl who lets a man fix all her problems. I don't want a man to fix my problems.

I don't want a man. I don't want anyone!

But Mallrie isn't just *a man, is he? NO! He's a godsdamned WITCH!*

A witch! Oh, gods, there was a witch in my grandmother's apartment. My grandmother, who was a witch!

I'm spiralling. I can feel a panic attack coming on. I clutch onto the side of the sink, my head dropped between my shoulders, focusing on reining in my breathing.

This is too much. Gods, I wish I had someone to talk to. I wish my grandmother was here, or Chelsea.

Gods, I miss Chelsea.

I have had two friends in my life, but Chelsea's friend-ship was always different. We bonded over mutual trauma and grief and shared similar outlooks on life and dreams of getting away from all of this one day.

Hot tears prick at my eyes and trickle down my face. I turn away from the sink and fall into a mess on the floor. Covering my eyes with my wrists to not get the soap bubbles in my eyes, I sob loudly into the surrounding abyss. "I can't do this. I don't know what to do." Pulling my knees up to my chest, I hug them tightly.

The memories I've carefully locked away all these years of my father's death, Beckett's abuse and death... Every-thing has been flashing back. I just—I just can't take it anymore.

I can feel my attentively constructed walls crumble

around Mallrie. Part of me wants to let them go, be vulnerable around him and work through all this baggage. But I don't know him. How can I trust someone when I know nothing about them?

I promised myself I wouldn't be that scared twenty-two-year-old running for her life from her abusive boyfriend ever again. No matter how different I feel Mallrie is.

I wipe the soapsuds off my hands so I can dry my face. I haven't cried like this in a long time.

It feels so good. Cathartic.

The sun shines cheerfully into the small apartment, warming my skin. Such a contrast to the cold emptiness inside.

"What do I do?" I cry, letting my head fall back against the cupboards.

"*Read the note,*" calls the eerily familiar voice in the wind, and this time, I don't flinch when I hear it call out to me. *Maybe it's a witch thing.* Honestly, I should be concerned with how normal hearing voices is becoming, but right now, I'll take any advice I can get.

I give myself a stern nod as I push myself to my feet, listening to the voice.

The faint smell of smoke clings to the air as I walk into the bathroom. The burnt shower curtain still lies in the shower, pools of water sitting in the folds. I shove my hand deep into the pocket of my jeans and retrieve the note. Clutching the letter between my teeth, I scoop up my clothes in one hand and the burnt shower curtain in my other arm as I walk out of the room. I find an old overnight bag and stuff my clothes in there to take home, then toss the bag by the door and fold the shower curtain over the top to take to the trash as I leave.

Leaning against the back of the couch, I pull on my knee-high boots. The note is still sitting between my teeth with the weight of my potential future. I run my fingers through my hair, detangling it as I try to calm myself enough to open the note.

Once you open this, there's no going back.

I give myself one last chance to back out. Whether or not I have magic, I am still in control of my life.

Only I can control what I do.

"You are strong enough," whispers the voice. *"Open the note."*

Sucking in a lungful of air through my nose, I carefully unravel the piece of paper with trembling fingers.

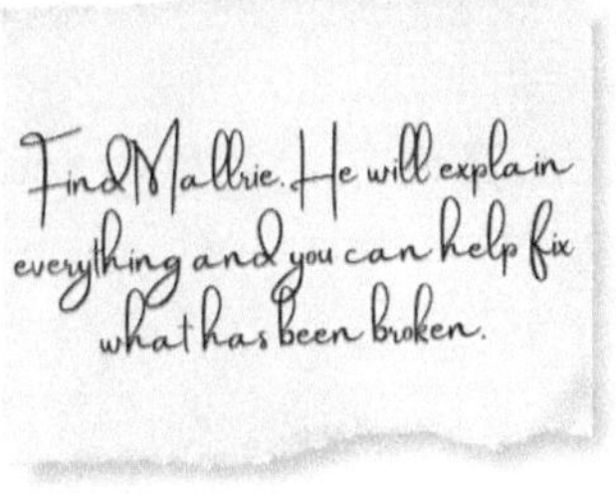

A rough laugh bubbles out of me as I look over the note and the map with directions for finding Mallrie. "Yeah, nah, I'll pass," I say aloud to the deafening silence. "He's already told me everything... right?" Doubt fills my voice. Acid burns my throat as I look over the map, which looks like it was drawn some time ago, as if the librarians had been trying to find Mallrie's home. I wait for a reply, but the apartment is silent. The only sound is the distant footsteps of people in the apartment above. *Most likely wondering where all their leftovers have mysteriously disappeared to.*

I run my hands over my face. I don't know what to do. The

librarians—who are witches—clearly want me to talk to Mallrie. *But what more is there to say? How do I just show up at his house after kicking him out last night? He said I needed to touch the Enkanti Tree again to gain the last of my magic. Honestly, I wonder if I can just avoid the tree for the rest of my life and forget about all of this. I'm sick of running away from imminent danger.*

But my stomach has a nagging feeling that if I don't claim the rest of my magic, my life will spiral into chaos. *As if it could get any more chaotic.*

I scrub my face with my hands, trying to clear my head. The paper scratches against my cheek like a child pulling on their mother's skirt for attention.

"Home via the tree," I say, folding the note and stuffing it down my bra for safekeeping. One day I might actually need to know how to get to Mallrie's house.

I doubt it though.

I grab the overnight bag and shower curtain, locking my grandmother's apartment door behind me.

My hand freezes, holding the handle to the building's front door. Through the narrow windows on either side of the entrance, I glimpse two bulky men dressed in black. My body flushes cold as I remember how the man from last night grabbed me and threw me against the building. The scuffle. Mallrie fighting off my assailants and the Kailadon. The blood and gore.

The balustrade bites into my back. I didn't realise I had backed away from the door.

I could be wrong.

They could be anyone, waiting for anyone. Who's to say they work for that man in the suit... What was his name?

Shifting my weight to the left, I peer through the window from a distance. There is an air of ominosity about them. Or I could be getting paranoid.

Either way, I'm not feeling like being chased through the streets like some low-budget animated slasher flick where the dialogue doesn't match the mouth movements, and the female gets killed off in the first ten minutes. Especially when I am dressed like one of those women. I turn on my heels and head for the back door. I tentatively push it open and glance around. The alleyway is empty.

Slipping quietly out the door, I keep a steady pace to not arouse suspicion. I take the long way towards the centre of town, feeling a little silly as I walk in a big circle, but no one seems to pay attention to me.

The thing about living in a town plagued with flesh-eating monsters is that everyone keeps to themselves and those they've got attachments to. Which, luckily for me, makes me practically invisible.

Or does it make me stick out like a sore thumb?

I really could do with a drink right now. Pressing my thumbnail into my mouth, I chew on it anxiously. I can feel the corner of my nail break away under the pressure. The sharp sting of the break scrapes along my tongue. I pull my hand out to tuck it into my pocket. I haven't chewed my nails since... Well, since I started drinking. My hand slips along the soft material of my skirt. I press my lips into a fine line, holding in my anger. *But of course I don't have pockets, not in this ridiculous skirt.*

I pass my apartment building. I could just go upstairs, curl up on my couch under a million blankets, watch a movie with the largest bottle of gin and forget the whole damn thing.

"*Go to the Enkanti Tree,*" that oddly familiar voice in the wind calls out to me.

I frown. "Really?" I mutter, more speaking to myself than expecting the wind to talk back.

"*Go to the Enkanti Tree,*" repeats the voice.

I pout to myself. "What if I don't?" I whisper.

Silence.

Smiling to myself, I start towards my apartment building.

Ha. Mark one for Eliana, Nil for the wind, I think, continuing towards my building when my stomach sinks. The two men in black round either side of my building as they survey the area. They must have seen me leave somehow. They are looking for someone, and I indisputably know that someone is me. I turn and head towards the centre of town. *Wind one, Eliana nil,* I amend.

It takes me less than five minutes from my apartment to the town centre. I'm not far. Over the hustle and bustle of people, I can see the top branches of the Enkanti Tree. I quickly glance over my shoulder to see if I am still being followed. When I lose sight of the men trailing me, I let myself relax a bit. But I am in no sense of delusion that I am not still being followed. What I will do after I get my magic from the tree, I do not know.

Not that I suffer from claustrophobia, but I always get a sense of released pressure from my chest when I step out of the narrow alleyways into the open clearing at the town centre. I inhale the sweet smell of waffles, bacon and coffee hanging in the air from Christina's.

Time for a game plan. I will pretend to head towards a department store across from where I am. That way, I can just brush my hand along the Enkanti Tree as I pass. Hopefully, I won't rouse any unwanted attention and then slip into the department store and out the other side.

It's a good plan, I think as I step into the clearing. The sun heats my skin, the light breeze lifting the strands of my short hair off my face and rustling the leaves.

Even over the commotion of everyone as they move about their day, my eyes narrow on my target, laser-focused on what I need to do.

I walk purposefully up to the Enkanti Tree, cautious of who could be watching. There's a couple on the other side of the tree making out.

"Ugh!" I roll my eyes with disgust. Public displays of affection have never been my thing. There is probably some trauma linked to it that I am not ready to acknowledge.

With the path I am on, I will practically brush past them. However, if I change the direction I am heading now, that might look suspicious.

Am I overthinking this?

The couple doesn't seem to notice the world moving around them. Their entire world is in their arms, in that embrace.

That would be nice. To have someone so caught up in you that the world just stops when you're around them. To be loved so unconditionally and wholly despite your flaws.

Ugh! What am I thinking?

I scrunch my nose in disgust as I move on. I go through the list in my head of all the people I have loved and lost. The reasons I don't want to get involved with anyone again.

The large oak tree in the centre of Datura stands before me, its thick trunk stretched high, the curvy branches breaking off in different directions. Even if you don't believe in magic, the way this tree has grown looks like it belongs in an actual fairy tale, not the middle of some cursed town.

Or maybe this is a fairy tale... One with a dark and twisted ending.

I stretch out my hand, running it along the rough bark, trying to be as subtle as possible. I can feel the magic vibrate under my touch. The power of my ancestors races through my fingers into my body. I don't flinch as the warm sensation runs through my fingertips and into me, warming my entire body. I watch my fingertips slowly turn black like ink dripping into water. It feels different this time. I close my eyes, relishing this moment. The Enkanti Tree recognises me and gives me my remaining powers freely and generously.

The strangest feeling washes over me. A sense of completeness. *Is that even a word?* It's hard to describe. It feels like a part of me that has always been missing has been found. Like the missing piece of a puzzle finally being slotted into place.

I give the tree one last caress, my fingertips all stained black. It looks like I've stuck my fingers into a fire and pulled them out, all covered in ash. Glancing around, everyone is going about his or her business as usual. I smile to myself, satisfied with how clever I am. Wrapping my arms around my chest to hide my hands just in case, I head towards the department store.

Suddenly, a powerful set of hands clenches tightly around my arms, forcing them behind my back so fast and hard that my muscles ache in protest. Before I can scream, they shove something soft into my mouth. It tastes sweet and smells like a strange combination of citrus and nail polish remover that makes me gag. My vision goes blurry, and my legs feel weak as I stumble into a soft, feminine body. She catches me under my arm.

"She's almost out. Let's go," her voice fades in and out. The rough hands readjust, supporting my weight as my legs give out entirely along with my consciousness.

My feet flop lifelessly under me. I am being dragged down a flight of stairs. I can't entirely open my eyes, and my jaw aches from the gag stuffed into my mouth. A little involuntary groan escapes my lips, which feel too dry. Someone tenses beside me. They struggle a little under my weight, long nails digging into my skin.

"Hurry up," demands a vaguely familiar voice. They throw my body into a hard chair, my arms and legs restrained against it. My wrists throb under the pressure of the ropes. "Search her," says that painfully familiar voice again. *Where do I know it from?*

Two sets of hands search every part of my body. I struggle against their invasive touch. Finally, a slender pair of fingers slips under my bra and across the scar on my breast, retrieving the folded note with the map and instructions to Mallrie's house.

I hear the metal clang as they drop my keys onto a table and the soft thud of my bag.

"Wake her up."

A sharp blow stings my face, the metallic, copper taste of blood as their ring splits open my lip. My vision is blurry as I open my eyes, trying to take in my surroundings.

A tall figure dressed in black is leaning against the table.

My belongings lie next to him. His arms folded across his chest. I blink harder, trying to get my uncooperative eyes to focus on him. My heart skips a beat.

Dark blonde, shoulder-length hair, the sides neatly braided. It's the man from the library. His name sits on the tip of my tongue, but I just can't quite bring it into existence.

I look around the room. On either side of me is the couple who was making out by the Enkanti Tree. They must be the ones who abducted me. I look back at the man in the suit as I struggle against the restraints.

"How are you, Eliana?" he asks, his voice intimidating and cold. My eyes fall over the shiny metal dagger he twists around in his hands. The way he's turning it so the light catches and reflects into my face must be to focus my attention. "Why the fuck is she still gagged, you idiots? How is she meant to talk with that foul rag stuffed in her mouth?" shouts the man in the suit as he pushes himself forward intimidatingly, making me jump at his sudden outburst.

The couple stumbles over each other as they pull the gag from my mouth. I cough at the sudden release, my lungs trying to suck in as much air as possible. The rag has left a bitter taste in my mouth. The man presses his thumb and finger to the bridge of his nose and closes his eyes.

"I am surrounded by idiots," he breathes. "Utterly incompetent." He sighs to himself as if trying to rein in his irritation. "Sorry about that, *love*," he drawls. The way he says "love" sends a tremor down my spine. The word does not hold any of the qualities it should possess, but is twisted with malice. "Eliana, yes? Please spare these morons their lives by telling me they managed to bring me the right girl." His voice regains its calm, ominous tone.

The man to my left makes a remark under his breath—too quiet for me to hear, but the man notices enough that he's standing before him in the blink of an eye. The man screams as a sickening, slicing sound fills my ears. Turning, I see the man holding his throat, blood spilling over his grip. Not enough to kill him, but it definitely sent a message.

"Did I ask your opinion?" he asks, eyebrows raised. "No, I did not. You are a fucking moron and unequivocally replaceable. Now, stand there with your pathetic mouth shut before I finish the job on that cut." The man in the suit roughly cleans the glistening blood off the blade on the shoulder of the man next to me, clicking his tongue. "Use your words, love. I asked you a question," he snaps as he walks away.

I lick my dry lips. "Why should I tell you anything?" I ask huskily. He smiles wickedly as he leans back against the table, twirling the knife in his fingers again.

"Oh, she's got spunk. I like that. I don't think we formally got introduced back at the library. My name is Cyan, and I work for our *beloved* Mayor Edgar." The word "beloved" sounds like poison on his tongue.

"I don't think the *beloved* mayor would like the towns-people knowing he condones kidnapping and torturing," I interject, regaining my voice a little and throwing the word back in Cyan's face with as much spunk and venom as he did.

He lets out a dark laugh that echoes throughout the room. He walks over and slams his hands over my restrained arms, his full weight bearing down on me. I let out an involuntary groan. The cool sensation of the knife presses against my overly hot wrist.

"Oh, we haven't even got to the fun part yet." He pushes himself away, waving the knife at me, gesturing to the restraints. "This is hardly torture. Do tell me if you want to play though. I can be very accommodating." His voice is like poison. Every word reverberates through my body and into my soul. Every nerve goes on high alert under his stare, and I can't help but wonder if he meant some hidden innuendo by the way his eyes are glinting. Cyan retreats, leaning against the table and crossing his arms over his chest again.

Cool, calm and collected.

"Tell me, Eliana, what happened to your fingers?" He points the knife lazily at my hands.

"I'm not telling you shit!" I spit. He smiles and lets out that dark chuckle again that seeps into my core.

"So you want to play? Oh, how I am going to enjoy this." Cyan slowly closes the distance between us, twisting the knife's point on his fingertip. He roughly presses a hand onto my shoulder and tilts the chair backwards so I meet his dark eyes. The blade lightly dances on my skin. The touch is so gentle it almost tickles, slowly making its way down towards my chest. Cyan's blue eyes widen slightly as he notices the mark left by Beckett. They flick back up to mine, filled with a murderous rage, but the knife keeps making its descent.

Down, down, down. Cyan's eyes never move from mine. It's like we've engaged in some sort of sick staring contest. I take a deep breath and keep his gaze. His fingers replace the coolness of the blade as he traces the scars on my leg from Beckett. The touch has all the air in my body pushed out on one heavy exhale. Tears prick at my eyes, but I won't let them fall. "You're a fighter, Eliana. You won't give anything up unless it's exactly what you want to do," Cyan says with conviction as if he knows exactly what I have been through from the scars adorning my body. As if he could possibly relate. "I respect that." His thumb traces small circles on my shoulder as he speaks. "I'm not asking for much, love. And if you're good, I might even spare your life." He releases the chair, thumping back onto all fours. "Hell, I might even offer you a position at my side." He gestures, showing where I'd stand beside him.

"I don't know if you heard me the first time or if your head is shoved too far up your own ass, but *I'm not telling you shit!*" I repeat, louder this time.

The amusement on Cyan's face melts away. He stands before me, cold and expressionless. I don't know why I don't just spill my guts and tell him everything. After all, he literally just slit a man's throat—albeit not killing him, but still—all because he mumbled under his breath.

"You didn't even hear what my questions were though."

I spit the blood pooling in my mouth towards him. "You think you're intimidating? You don't scare me," I lie through my teeth. "You're just some pretty boy with a knife." I'm talking too much shit, and I know it. But I know this is my way of coping with the situation. A fake-it-till-you-make-it approach.

If Cyan wants to play the big, scary, intimidating game, well, so can I... I hope.

A small, amused smile stretches across his face. "You think I'm pretty?" Cyan's eyes rake over my body. "Well, you're not too bad yourself, love."

Shit. This isn't going the way I thought it would. Why did I say that? He's not even pretty. He's handsome, in an I-might-kill-you-but-you'll-enjoy-it sort of way. Kind of like how people have a thing for serial killers. *WHY AM I EVEN THINKING THIS RIGHT NOW?*

"You talk a good game, except for one thing..." Cyan

snaps me out of my delusional thoughts, crossing the room so quickly it makes my head spin. "Your heart betrays you," he says as his knife slides over my chest, resting on the mark Beckett made.

Another sharp push. The chair is leaning dangerously back onto its hind legs. My heart is beating so fast, trying to leap from my chest.

"I can *see* the fear. You try to hide it behind your brave words. And behind those big brown eyes. But I *see* you, Eliana. I *know* what you've become." He runs a long finger gently down my face, the shiny blade flickering in my peripheral vision. "I can help you become the best witch possible." My body tenses under Cyan's stare, and my eyes widen like saucers.

"Yes, yes." He waves a hand in the air nonchalantly. "I know you have gained your magic back."

I let out a small, hysterical laugh. Cyan stares at me, bemused. I give him my brattiest smile. "Oh, Cyan, if you're so smart and already knew what happened to my fingers... why ask?"

His face twists with frustration, and his lips purse together tightly. His hand snaps to my throat, and his fingers press on either side, slowly increasing in pressure. A small choking sound slips from my lips, and Cyan's lips twist into a smile as tears prick at my eyes. "What powers did you get, brat?" he spits, suddenly releasing my throat, causing the chair to fall back on all fours. He pulls a matte black gun from inside his jacket. The sound of the safety being clicked off is as loud as a siren.

I need to figure out what Cyan's motives are—what Mayor McQuoid's motives are. *Maybe Edgar wants the witches gone?* But Cyan seems fine with me possessing magic. He even offered me a place *beside* him.

The gun is cocked.

Oh, gods!

Maybe Cyan is a witch too? What if they want all the elementals? Mallrie said there are five of us—

Mallrie!

What if they're looking for him? After all, he's killing Kailadons. My eyes flick over to the piece of paper on the table, an intense urge to protect Mallrie washing over me.

"Come now, love. I don't have all day," Cyan says, pointing the gun at my head. I go a little cross-eyed, staring down the barrel. I drag my attention up from the weapon to Cyan's face. He's watching me intently, reading every detail of emotion that flickers across my face and adjusting his reactions accordingly. *Fuck. He's so much better at this than me, and not just because he's the one holding the gun.*

"You want to know what type of witch I am?" I ask through gritted teeth.

How the fuck do I go about accessing this magic?

I need to embrace the fire within me. That sounds stupid. I don't know how to do that, but that just *feels* like what I need to do.

I *need* to burn that note to protect Mallrie. Cyan tilts his head, waiting for my answer. *Fire, fire, fire,* I chant. *How did I do it last night? Oh, gods. Now is totally* not *the time to have a dirty fantasy.*

Anger!

Mallrie pissed me off, and the candle lit.

"Use your fucking words, love," Cyan intones, looking utterly bored with this situation and ready to blow my brains out. "I'm not in the habit of repeating myself."

The tears I've held back well up and spill over my eyes. I think of every awful thing that has ever happened to me. Every dreadful thing Beckett ever said or did. How angry

Mallrie made me last night with his teasing. How angry I was at myself for kicking him out, for letting myself *feel* something for him.

I can feel the heat rising in my body. My anger is like a spark igniting the flame in my blood. It burns behind my skin. I can feel the power—the magic—running through my veins. It's there, right under my skin, ready to break free. I open my eyes and force a smile.

"I can probably show you better than I can tell you." His eyes narrow at my innocent tone despite the tears rolling down my face. Abruptly, the walls burst into flames, rapidly closing in around us. I look over at the piece of paper on the table as it burns and shrivels.

Mallrie is safe, I think to myself happily. That happiness feels... strange. *I am not a horrible person,* I try to remind myself, even though sometimes it feels almost impossible to believe. But suppose Cyan or the mayor really want Mallrie. I bite my lip. Cyan is clearly a really horrible person, and Edgar has always given me the ick. So I allow myself to relish in this little slice of happiness, knowing I saved him from them. Even if I don't trust Mallrie.

The flames rage around us. I stare wide-eyed. My gaze flicks around the room at the fire engulfing the small space. My muscles tremble against the bindings as I realise my mistake. That sense of happiness and pride in unleashing my magic disappears as if someone tossed a cold bucket of water in my face. The couple standing beside me are screaming in pain as the wrath of my flames consumes the room. I look back at Cyan, who's just calmly staring straight into my eyes. Thankfully, he has lowered the gun. The corner of his lip twitches with amusement. The couple screams at each other as they try to make their way across the room to escape the inferno. I watch in terror as the flames rage more vigorously, closing in on the space. My heart beats wildly in my chest, which only encourages the fire. The realisation washes over me like a cold sweat. *I have absolutely no control over what's happening.*

I have no experience with magic.

Would I even be able to recall the fire?

I didn't think this through. Cyan's booming laugh snaps my attention back to him. I've got his undivided attention. As if we're not about to be swallowed by the flames at any moment.

"What a cute little fire elemental you are." His voice rises so I can hear him over the crackling inferno and the screams. "But you've got no control over your magic. You're *weak*." He chuckles as the words cut deep, deeper than any blade.

The screams of the couple contrast with Cyan's booming laugh.

They're burning alive.

I'm killing them.

The woman is pressed against the wall, trying to pat out the flames on her clothes. The sizzling sound of her hair burning fills the room with the most rancid smell. The man tries to crawl towards the door. His clothes are ablaze. He screams as he reaches and pushes himself forward, leaving a trail of blood behind him like a snail.

Cyan's hand jerks my face back to his, demanding my attention. He's captivated by the terror in my eyes. His head slowly tilts to the side, taking in every inch of my face. Then, he jerks my head back towards the man who's now lying lifeless on the ground, and to the woman whose skin is burning and melting away under the heat, revealing muscle and bone.

Bile threatens to creep up my throat, but I force it away.

I'll be sick over this later when I have the *biggest* bottle of gin the Bottle-O sells.

"Look at what you've done, Eliana. You're *weak*. If Mallrie was a good mentor, he would have taught you how to control your magic." Cyan's words sting like salt water on a wound. A wound that is deep inside of me.

I can feel the flames closing in behind me, hot at my back. Yet Cyan looks perfectly at ease. He's hardly breaking a sweat. I look around us, terrified, but then I notice the flames keep their distance. It's as if there's an invisible barrier around us the fire cannot penetrate.

Cyan tugs at my face so I am looking at him again. "Ah, Mallrie hasn't taught you anything, has he?" There's amusement in his voice. He opens his mouth to speak again, but a booming crash interrupts him. The door falls from its hinges to the ground. A tall, dark silhouette stands in the doorway.

"Let her go, Cyan!" Mallrie shouts from the doorway, lifting his arm to shield his face from the flames, a bandana covering his nose and mouth.

"Or what?" tests Cyan from the safety of the other side of the room.

"This will not end the way you think it will." Mallrie's voice is filled with the promise of bloody violence as he growls through gritted teeth, "Let. Her. Go!" Smoke fills the room from the increased amounts of oxygen Mallrie has let in through the open door, and it is getting harder to breathe. Cyan lets out a booming laugh.

"If you want her so badly, come get her!" He kicks the chair I'm strapped into, and it falls with a *thwack*, my head hitting the concrete floor.

I writhe in the restraints, the flames closing in on me. I push myself one way, then the other, trying to fall onto my side. It takes two good attempts before I knock myself over. Mallrie uses his arm to shield his face from the flames as he races towards me. I scan the room, trying to find Cyan. He walks away effortlessly. The heat and smoke must distort my view because the flames bend and move at his will as he leaves the room.

Cyan turns and takes one long look back into the room. His mouth moves. "I'll see you around, love." His words send an ominous shiver down my spine despite the heat surrounding me.

Mallrie slides a small blade between my wrist and the rope, cutting me free. I push myself to my feet, but his arm has already wrapped around my legs, hoisting me over his shoulders. I punch at his incredibly hard back for him to stop manhandling me. I am overly aware of my short skirt and that my ass is probably exposed. But he doesn't seem to notice my attempts.

Mallrie pushes his way back through the flames. He drops me onto the stairs outside the room, now fully engulfed in flames, and pats out the embers on his clothes and pulls the bandana around his neck. Soot covers his face. Coughing into the crook of his elbow, I try to reassure him that I am fine. Mallrie's hands run over my body, checking for injuries despite my protests. I swat his hands away before he can reach my legs, even though I secretly enjoy his concerned touch.

"I'm okay. I'm fine, seriously," I snap as I push to my feet. But Mallrie scoops me back into his arms before I can get up. It infuriates me how shamelessly he manhandles me, but a small part deep inside me does a happy little dance that he wants to hold me. I try not to think of how the magic in me hums through my veins at his touch.

Mallrie climbs the stairs with me in his arms effortlessly. My arms wrap around his neck, my head resting against his shoulder, watching the flames pushing their way out the door.

"Mallrie, seriously, I'm fine. Let me go," I protest, but he keeps climbing the stairs.

CHAPTER TWENTY
ELIANA

Mallrie kicks open the door to the rooftop. A cool breeze fills my lungs, and the sun is so bright I have to squint. He carefully sets me on my feet, securing the door behind us. My legs feel weak. I can't believe I just set a room on *fire*.

Oh, gods! I killed *two people!*

Mallrie's in front of me in a heartbeat, down on one knee, looking up at my face. "Eliana, you need to breathe," he says, but he sounds like he could be on the other side of the Melsheim Forest instead of standing right before me. "Can you breathe for me?" His knuckles gently stroke my arm. The feel somehow has a grounding effect as I suck in a shaky breath. "Good. That's so good."

The haze of the panic attack eases away. I look around at the flat roofs that surround us. I've never been on any of the rooftops before. There's a decent view of the layout of the town, the farmlands to the east and the Melsheim Forest that wraps around the town like an ouroboros.

Leaning against the brickwork, I look down at the Enkanti Tree below, its foliage reaching almost to the top of the building. The leaves gently blow in the wind as people disappear under its large canopy before reappearing on the other side, utterly oblivious to the damage and lives I had just ended. Silent tears slip down my face.

Mallrie places a heavy hand on my shoulder. "We've got to go." His voice is rough and low as I look up at him, his face stoic.

"Where are we going?" I ask. His sun-kissed muscles peeked through his burnt shirt.

"Home."

"My keys—"

"Oh, not your home. My home," Mallrie clarifies, and a bubble of panic rises in my gut. *Focus on your breathing,* I remind myself, and my eyes focus on his stupid lips as I carefully regain control of myself. The stubble on his face. The curve of his lips, the slash of a scar through them.

"I'm sorry. We've got to go," he repeats, walking to the edge of the building towards the west of town. Mallrie gracefully jumps up onto the ledge and reaches his hand out for me to join him.

I hesitate, taking a step back. "What are you doing?"

"Do you trust me?" he asks.

"I'm still deciding," I say truthfully. Mallrie scowls.

"Still deciding," he scoffs. "I've saved your life about three times now, and you still don't trust me?"

"I said I'm still undecided," I snap back. *What is his problem?* "Trust isn't something that can be given automatically. It's not like giving a thank you card. How did you know where I was anyway? Are you following me?" My stomach twists into knots as the words leave my lips, afraid of his response.

"Yes," Mallrie replies matter-of-factly. I take another step back, the knots melting into a panic. I knew I was right not to trust him. Mallrie runs his hand down his face. "I also don't expect you to just give me your trust willingly…"

"I want to go home," I blurt out like a child. Mallrie gives me a long, sombre look. *Oh, shit.* My heart squeezes in my chest.

"I'm sorry," he says flatly, and my heart shatters into a million tiny pieces. Sharp, stabbing pains explode outward from it, a lump forming in my throat, and my eyes burn, desperate to release the tears forming behind them.

"What?"

"Cyan will have his people waiting for you."

"Well, I'll go—"

"He'll have people at your grandmother's place too. The only place I can keep you safe is with me. But, please, we've got to go." Mallrie steps off the ledge, holding his hand out for me again. "You don't have to trust me. Just know I have your best interests at heart." He sighs, scrubbing a hand over his face. "Cyan doesn't. No matter what he tells you."

I shake my head. "How am I to believe *you* have my best interests at heart when you just admitted you've been stalking me?" I snap angrily.

There's a rattling at the door behind us. A muffled voice is calling to someone for help. Mallrie dishearteningly advances towards me. My mind screams at my body to run, but I am frozen.

"I wasn't asking."

My eyes widen at the sudden harshness in his voice. I try to take another step back, but Mallrie's arms are already wrapped around my thighs and waist as he tosses me over his shoulder. I press my hands into his back, trying to push myself up to stop the blood rushing to my head.

"Let me go!" I scream, trying to free myself. My cheeks burn as cool air blows against my ass.

"No." Mallrie's upper arm firmly presses against the curve of my ass. I try to kick him, but instead, he grips my legs with his free hand. "Damn it, Eliana!" he curses as he strides quickly over to the ledge, disregarding my weight on his shoulder as if he is carrying a disobedient child instead of a twenty-five-year-old woman who likes waffles a little too much.

"Mallrie!" I protest, trying to cover my face as he gracefully pushes us up and over the ledge of the building in one fluid motion. My body feels weightless as we float across the sky, and my stomach feels like it is trying to make its way up and out of my throat. Panic grips me tighter than Mallrie's embrace. We land gracefully onto the next building, and the realisation that he just... *jumped* from one rooftop to another with me thrown over his shoulder sinks in. My stomach sits uncomfortably against his shoulder as I try to reposition myself.

There's a loud bang on the roof of the government building where we just were. I look up to see two burly men smash through the door.

Mallrie doesn't look back. He just keeps running and jumping effortlessly from building to building. My grip tightened against the fabric of his shirt and the leather strap holding his sword to his back. The men curse and rush back inside, the government building becoming smaller and smaller the further we go.

We're at the edge of town when I break the long silence, unable to take it anymore. I am uncomfortable, and the mix between weightlessness and the blood rushing to my head is getting too much. "Put me the fuck down! They're obviously not following us!" I snap impatiently. Mallrie's grip tightens around my ass, sending a rush of heat through me, and then he jumps from the building. I curse as I try to bury my face in his back. My stomach floats up into my throat as we fall.

I look up, expecting to still be falling, but Mallrie painlessly walks away from the town. I punch him in the back as hard as possible, but it feels like I am just beating a brick wall. *How much muscle does this man have?*

"Let. Me. Go!" I grunt with each blow.

Mallrie flings me off his shoulder. I fall hard onto my ass in the cool grass.

"What the fu—"

"Will you shut up for five minutes and listen?" he growls, towering over me, slowly stepping forward to stand on either side of my legs. I stare up at him apprehensively. We're quiet for a long moment before he speaks. "I won't force you to come with me, but I can guarantee Cyan has his people all over town waiting for you. You can choose. Either come with me now, or you can leave. I won't stop you. But I won't save you from Cyan again. Or the Kailadons." His words are bitter. I'm stuck between a rock and a hard place.

Mallrie will take me into the Melsheim Forest, where who knows what terrible creatures lurk.

If I return to town, I have no idea what Cyan will do to me.

I don't trust either of them.

I guess Mallrie is the lesser of two evils. He has saved my life and has only seemed to care about my well-being. But that scares me just as much as whatever torment Cyan will dish out. At least I know how to deal with that pain.

"Last chance," Mallrie says as he takes a step back. I give him a slight nod, and he stretches out his hand, helping me up off the ground. "You don't have to trust me.

Of course, I'd prefer it if you did. But we can work on that. But I *need* you to listen to me."

"I hate you," I snap, the words escaping before I can think about what I'm saying.

"No, you don't," Mallrie replies calmly, pulling me to my feet, a small smile playing at the corner of his full lips.

No, I don't—not really—I'm just so angry with him. At putting me in this position. Giving me the option of going with him into the Melsheim Forest, which they taught us at a young age to never go into, or staying where I will most likely get abducted again by some knife-swinging, gun-wielding psychopath.

We walk in silence across the vast, grassy field between the township and the thick forestry of the Melsheim Forest. I look over my shoulder as the town shrinks into the background, wondering if I have made the right decision.

Mallrie sighs. "You really have a problem with letting people in, don't you?" His voice is sombre. I look up at him. He's observing me.

Nervously, I clear my throat. "I just—people haven't really been the most reliable in my life, that's all."

"So you just shut out everyone?"

"Sometimes, it's better to be alone. That way, no one can hurt you," I reply bitterly. I look away from him to shield the sadness and hurt in my eyes.

"Well, that's a very despondent way to look at it."

I glance out of the corner of my eye. Mallrie looks as if he wants to reach across and comfort me. I make a move to step a little further away from him.

"You have obviously never had the ones you love hurt you." I cannot help the sadness in my tone, and I wish I could just stop talking altogether. I don't do the whole talking about feelings thing.

Mallrie rubs a hand along the base of his neck. "You don't live as long as I have without having your own heartbreaks." He gives me a sympathetic look, and we walk on in silence again.

"Would it help you feel more at ease if you knew more about me?" Mallrie asks, trying to bring some common ground between us. I look up at him. I can't help but feel sorry for Mallrie. He doesn't know my past. He doesn't understand why I *need* to keep everyone away.

"I don't do the whole 'friends' thing, sorry," I say coldly.

Mallrie shrugs. "Doesn't mean you can't know a bit about me. What would you like to know?"

"I'm not playing *Twenty Questions* with you." Trying to put some distance between us, I pick up my pace. But I'm aware I don't know where I am going. So I subtly slow back down, feeling downright foolish.

"Well, you know I don't age," Mallrie begins, ignoring my attempt at silence. "But that *doesn't* mean I'm immortal." I let out a small humph by his side, not looking up at him. "What?" Without looking, I can hear the smile in his voice. "You sound like you want to fight me."

A small smile dances around my mouth at the comedic thought of my small, voluptuous body trying to fight against Mallrie's tall, muscular build. "Who wouldn't want to fight you?" I snap, rolling my eyes.

Mallrie lets out a boom of a laugh. "Don't worry, you will get your chance." He looks at me, and it is so hard not to return his smile. "It won't be as funny as I'm sure you're imagining. You're small. We can use that to your advantage."

"I am hardly small," I whisper to myself, looking down at my curves. I curse myself for saying that out loud. Despite everything I hate about the world and myself, my body isn't one of them. I'm curvy. I'm bigger than most girls, but so what? Life is shit, and people are cruel. I don't need to be hating on myself when there is a lineup outside my door of people ready to do it for me. Clearing my throat, I ask, "What, you're going to teach me to fight Kailadons?" I emphasise.

Mallrie smiles at me like he's proud of me for not calling them Flesh-Hunters anymore. That smile. *Fuck.* It has my traitorous heart racing.

"That's exactly what I am going to do. And your body is beautiful." My heart sinks, partly because the thought of fighting a Flesh-Hunt—a Kailadon—is terrifying. But also because of the compliment. I roll my eyes. *Maybe I'm just overthinking this.* I open my mouth to bite back. To blast the wall between us, to protect myself, but Mallrie continues speaking. Like he knew what I was about to do.

"Cyan and his men too. And anyone else who tries to hurt you. I will teach you that you don't need your walls up all the time to keep yourself protected." I freeze, paralysed by his words. *Okay, maybe I wasn't overthinking anything.* My body trembles at the thought of never feeling defenceless again. Mallrie walks over to me, and this time, puts a comforting hand on my shoulder. "I promise I will not hurt you like the people from your past."

I push his hand from my shoulder. "Don't make promises you can't keep."

"You don't know that. So why worry about something that's out of your control?"

Mallrie is the first to break the silence again. "Anyway, what else?" He clicks his tongue playfully as he thinks of things to say. "Obviously, I live on my own." He gestures towards the Melsheim Forest, still far ahead. "Oh, I have a cat," he adds.

The thought of this lone wolf-type of man sitting at home by the fire with a cat curled up on his lap is strangely sexy and a little humorous. "I guess you could say I kill Kailadons for a living." He shrugs with a slight chuckle, attempting to lighten the mood. As if it's just any other regular profession. The memory of him fighting the Kailadons flares to life in my mind.

"Why does your sword glow?" I finally speak. Mallrie gives me a mischievous smile as if to say, *I knew I'd get you talking eventually.*

"If you want a question answered, you've got to tell me something first."

I roll my eyes. "What?"

"How did you get those scars on your leg?" he asks quietly, like he's worried his question will shatter me into a million tiny pieces.

"Wow, way to go straight in with the hard questions," I mutter, rolling my eyes. "What happened to 'what's your favourite colour?'"

The thought of talking to him about my past scares me. *If I tell him about my dark past, will he look at me differently? Treat me like I am some fragile person? One wrong move from collapsing into madness?*

"Well, what's your favourite colour then?" he asks straightforwardly.

There was a painting of a beachscape behind the counter in an antique shop my grandmother and I used to go to. I dreamt of one day finding that beach and swimming in the crystal clear waters.

That is my favourite colour. The cerulean blue of a tropical ocean.

I look up at Mallrie, and my cheeks redden. Of course, inadvertently, that is the same colour as his eyes. I clear my throat, trying to make my voice as steady as possible. "Cerulean," I say, swiping a hand across the back of my neck. "Like the colour of the ocean," I add quickly, as if to justify myself.

"Orange," Mallrie replies calmly. "Orange like the sunrise. Sometimes, I like to sit on the edge of town and watch the sunrise. Watch as everything becomes peaceful again." I smile at him.

"That would be nice to see." I don't think I have ever seen the sunrise. Between the compact buildings stacked one on top of the other, it's hard to get a good view other than the brick façade of the next building. Or worse, someone's bathroom.

"Maybe I can show you someday. When you're ready."

It's a promise that one day, when I trust him enough, he'll share that little piece of his heaven with me.

We look at each other for a long moment, and a part of me wants to talk to him. Tell him everything. He seems genuine... but so did Beckett in the beginning.

"Okay, I answered your question. So, your sword? Why does it glow?" I ask again.

"Uh-uh!" Mallrie skips in front of me, walking backwards. I am having trouble picturing the man in front of me as 198 years old. "You never actually answered *my* question," he says with a boyish charm and a crooked smile.

"Um, yeah, I did. Favourite colours, remember?" I remind his clearly senile memory.

"Yes, yes. The same colour as my eyes," he says, waving his hand in the air as if it's no big deal. But, unfortunately, his tone is anything but. *Motherfucker.* My face flushes. I truly hoped he wouldn't actually make that connection.

"*No!*" I snap defensively. "There was this painting. I haven't even noticed what colour your eyes are." My voice is high—an unconvincing lie. A half smile spreads across Mallrie's face like he enjoys trying to get a reaction out of me. I can feel the fire burning inside me. "Are you always this bigheaded?"

"I actually asked how you—" Mallrie says matter-of-factly, ignoring my insult.

"Yeah, yeah. I remember the question," I spit, interrupting him. I don't need to hear him repeat it. I had hoped he would have the decency to not bring them up, but I feel Mallrie isn't one to shy away from asking the tough questions.

"You like interrupting people, don't you?" he asks.

I laugh sarcastically. "Oh, yeah, like you're one to talk."

We walk silently, clearly getting on each other's nerves.

Mallrie breaks the silence with a sigh. "Look," he says, "I get you've got your reservations about me. I'm sure this is a lot to process. I'm just trying to help—"

"I don't need your help." Without thinking, the words come pouring out. I have worked hard to be strong enough to support myself. Help means weakness, and that's something I never want to feel again.

Mallrie grabs my wrist hard enough that I jerk to a stop, but he doesn't hurt me. "Everyone needs help sometimes, Eliana." The rasp of his voice sends goosebumps cascading over my skin. My name on his lips sounds like a sin, something I know I shouldn't want, and yet...

I free my arm from his grip, but I know he's letting me go. If he wanted to keep me restrained, he easily could.

"What's your problem? Have you got a hero complex or something? Quit trying to save me!" I can't help but bite back. I've spent too long putting up walls to protect myself. Even though, deep down, a small, repressed voice tells me Mallrie *is* different and that I can trust him. I am not brave enough to put myself out there to be hurt again. Even if, sometimes, late at night, when the nightmares have chased me to the bottom of a bottle, I imagine sharing myself with someone. Someone to confide in, to share a drink or two with a friend.

Mallrie's expression is dark and dangerous. My body tenses, ready for the attack. "Just because you're strong enough to handle the pain, Eliana"—his gaze flicks down to my thighs, where the scars of my past continue to haunt me—"doesn't mean you deserve it."

Something in my chest flutters in response. Tears prick at my eyes. I swallow hard, trying not to let them fall.

"I've had my fair share of heartache. I've had my loved ones killed in front of me, and I've had my family betray me. Hell! They've even tried to kill me. You think the best thing is to shut yourself off from the world? You're wrong. *That's* what makes you weak." My breath is caught in my throat. I am not entirely sure I am even breathing anymore. I completely forgot about his past. How shallow do I seem to him? I want to shake some sense into myself. "Not asking for help. Closing yourself off from your emotions, from human interaction. You'll never be able to control your magic. I won't support you down that path."

I turn away from him. I have to so he doesn't see how much his words affect me. The tears break free in silent sobs as my heartaches. No one has tried to comfort me like this since my grandmother died. His words are brutally honest, but… I think I need them to be.

Mallrie's arms wrap around me, pulling me close. I bury my face in his chest. He feels safe and warm. I pull him closer as if hugging this man will chase away the emptiness inside me, the years of hurt and abuse. He smells how I imagine the forest would: sandalwood and a hint of citrus. Hot tears fall from my face, soaking his shirt.

Mallrie runs his fingers gently through my hair, his words still ringing in my ears.

"Okay, we've both got trauma from our past," I finally say, breathlessly through sobs.

Mallrie laughs sadly. "Yeah, I guess we do." He pulls me away just enough so he can look at me. His thumb caresses my cheek, wiping away my tears. I feel helpless in his embrace. It feels good to let down my walls—even if it's just for this fleeting moment.

"You don't have to tell me what happened. But do I need to go back into town and sort someone out?" Mallrie's voice is filled with the promise of violence. I can't think. I can't do anything but stare up at him, at his dark, windswept hair and those piercing eyes that scramble my brain. He holds me close with this offer of vengeance. I open my mouth to speak, my throat so dry that nothing comes out. "Just give me a name, Eliana, and his head will be yours. Literal or otherwise."

My knees go weak under the weight of his words. Mallrie catches me under my arms, pulling me close again. Fuck, *why does this feel so right?*

"Eliana?" he whispers my name like a fine wine on his lips. I can't look at him. I don't want to see his face when he realises I'm just as much a monster as Beckett was. It takes me two attempts before I can find my voice. Even then, all I get out is, "He's dead."

Mallrie sighs, the tension in his body melting away. One single word leaves his lips, sending goosebumps trailing over my skin. "Good."

CHAPTER TWENTY-ONE
MALLRIE

"He's dead."

Those two words are like a prayer I never knew I asked to be answered. Of course, I knew of Eliana's piece of shit ex-boyfriend, Beckett. I knew they had broken up or *something* had happened between them, but no specifics. He seemingly disappeared into thin air, and good riddance too. Yet, hearing her say those two words feels like a weight has lifted from my chest, even if there was pain in her voice over it. I don't know the specifics of his disappearance, but whatever happened, it seems to trouble Eliana. Her hand trembles in mine as we walk silently through the Melsheim Forest. I should have given her the space she so clearly craves, but I now realise I am too much of a selfish bastard to give it to her. She needs me just as much as I need her.

She feels good by my side, and I intend to keep it that way. Eliana doesn't shy away from me either. If she gave any indication that she needed space, I'd—albeit reluctantly—give it to her.

The further we go, the more the temperature drops as the trees grow closer together, blocking the sun. Eliana subconsciously moves closer to me. Whether for my warmth or protection, I don't know, nor do I care.

I stop at a tree I carefully hollowed out many years ago. With my free hand, I pull out a large staff with a red fire crystal. Fire crystals are rare to come by. Charleston destroyed all those my coven had. I was lucky to have come by this one from a Lorkreig—a type of Elf living within the Melsheim Forest—being mauled by an Ashga. The seven-foot-tall creature had the Lorkreig gutted, but still alive. What their conflict was, I don't know. I put the Lorkreig out of his misery and shamelessly took the fire crystal.

I give the red crystal a hard thud against the tree to awaken its mysterious magic within. Even after all these years, I am still unsure how Lorkreigs' magic works. The crystal sparks to life, a balmy glow emanating around us with a subtle warmth. A bubble of laughter works its way out of Eliana, causing my head to whip in her direction. That sweet sound is far too rare. It makes me want to fall to my knees before her and beg her to do it again. Instead, I arch an eyebrow in her direction. "Something amusing?" I ask as she stifles her laughter. I wish she wouldn't.

"You just look like you should have long grey hair and a cloak or something with that thing." She nods at the staff in my hand.

"Ha. Ha. Very funny." I can't help but return her smile; it's contagious. I wave the staff towards her playfully. *Fates! How long has it been since I have been able to joke around?* She lets out a little shriek and tries to bat it away.

We proceed deeper into the woods. The upturned roots make walking hard as they twist across the trail, but I know exactly where to step. I am surprised a path hasn't been worn from the years of me trekking the same route. I pull Eliana along after me. The trail has narrowed down, so we have to walk single file, but that doesn't stop me from holding her hand.

"I'm going to need your help," I say quietly, mindful that even though we're deep within the Melsheim Forest, that doesn't mean that Cyan hasn't got eyes and ears out here.

"Whatever you need," Eliana says as if without thinking, and I can't help but give her hand a slight squeeze. *Could she be willing to let her walls down around me?*

"We need to find the other elemental witches."

"Water, earth and air?" Eliana asks.

"Water and Air," I correct as a pang of grief stabs me in the back.

"Who's the earth elemental then?"

I can't help how my face twists with irritation at the sting of betrayal, and I am grateful Eliana cannot see it. "Cyan," I say, practically spitting the name out.

"Oh." Eliana is quiet for a while, no doubt processing this information. I feel somewhat of a hypocrite, asking for her trust when I only give her bits and pieces of information. *She doesn't need to know the whole truth,* I try to remind myself since the truth has changed drastically over these last two days. I glance up at the canopy stretching high above us. The sky has turned a deep shade of orange. Night is approaching.

"I need to find the last two elementals before he does," I say, breaking the silence. The trees have thinned out enough that we can walk side by side, and I can feel Eliana's gaze heavy against the side of my head. Meeting those brown eyes is a mistake; they're filled with questions. Questions I know I can't answer. Not yet, at least. "Now, he knows that you've regained your magic. So it'll be a fight between us to find the remaining elementals first."

"At least it's almost nightfall. Surely he won't be looking for them today... right?" she questions, and I can't help but smile down at her.

"Right," I agree. "Besides, he'll have to report to Edgar about why the basement of the government building caught fire." Eliana's cheeks burn bright red. "You did..." She looks at me with those big brown doe-eyes. "Alright." She chokes on a little laugh, which could be the cutest thing I have ever seen. "I just mean I am surprised you could summon *that* much magic without training."

"What's Mayor Edgar got to do with any of this? Is he a witch too?" asks Eliana, clearly wanting to change the subject.

Clearing my throat, I reply, "He's just a power-hungry bastard. Edgar wants all the elementals under his control. He knows of my bio-indefinite mortality. He wants the same so he can remain in power. Have the elementals do his dirty work for him." Sighing, I reluctantly release Eliana's hand to run my hand through my hair. "The one thing we both can agree on is that we want the Kailadons gone. But the only way to do that is for all the elementals to resurrect the magic in the Enkanti Tree and perform the protection spell again." I can't help the notes of sadness in my voice. I've spent *hours* poring over manuscripts Charleston hasn't destroyed, trying to find *anything* on the ritual to restore the magic to the Enkanti Tree. *But, of course, there is little, if any, information I don't already know. Finding an alternative—*

"But if Cyan is a witch, isn't he more powerful than Edgar?" Eliana asks, cutting off my train of thought. The way she tries to hide the quiver in her voice makes me want to wrap her in my arms. *This* is why she doesn't need to know the truth. "What power does Edgar possess to make Cyan do what he wants?"

Fuck. I internally curse at her inquisitive nature. Massaging the kink in the back of my neck, I need to fight back the smile. I love that she's got questions and wants to help solve this—even if she swears black and blue that she doesn't. "I don't know," I lie a little too blatantly. "I've tried to talk some sense into him over the years, but he's stubborn. Cyan seems to have his own plan." I glance over at Eliana and fear what Cyan has planned for her. "Remember, everyone has their weaknesses, no matter how powerful they may seem."

CHAPTER TWENTY-TWO
ELIANA

Mallrie and I continue to walk through the Melsheim Forest in silence. The powerful aroma of damp earth and bark fills my nose as the needle-covered path crunches under our feet. I take in a lungful of its earthy scent, realising just how bad Datura smells.

"How much further?" I question for what feels like the millionth time. The trees have thinned out even more, and the last rays of sunlight illuminate the path. I haven't eaten all day. Hunger and fatigue are overcoming me and making me grouchy. As I drag myself across the uneven trail, my legs grow heavy, tripping over upturned roots.

"We're here," Mallrie says as he reaches his hand out to me. I look around, confused. There's nothing here. It looks just like the rest of the forest we just spent a good half-hour hiking through. I raise my eyebrows, waiting for clarification. Finally, he offers his hand to me again, and I take it hesitantly since he doesn't seem to say anything else. His warm and calloused hand, from *way* too many years of training with a sword, gently wraps around mine. The thought that Mallrie is closer to 200 years old than thirty-six is still a hard pill to swallow. It boggles my mind if I think about it too much, just like the fact that when he holds my hand or the subtle touches we've shared, a small thrill goes through me. I have lost everyone I have ever cared about. I don't *want* to feel a little thrill when my hand brushes against Mallrie's. I don't *want* to feel the heat rising to my cheeks when he compliments me or looks at me like... *that.*

"This may sting a little the first time," he says, dragging me from my thoughts, his eyes searching my face with a gentle kindness I don't deserve.

I don't have time to say anything before Mallrie pulls me further into the woods. A shockwave of pure energy jolts through my body, leaving me breathless. My vision is blurry with an array of colours. Every hue I could imagine, even some I can't name, flashes before my eyes.

As I blink them away, we have emerged into a clearing. It's as if Mallrie has transported me to another world. There is a small two-storey cottage made of carefully hand-carved stone. Whoever built the house used the same stone as a path leading up to the porch. The wood and glass front doors are open just a crack, a soft amber glow emanates from inside and the chimney is lazily puffing smoke.

It looks as if we've just stepped inside a fairy tale. Wild-flowers cover the iron rails of the balcony, jutting out from the second floor. Beside the cottage, there's a small fenced area with fresh fruit and vegetables growing. Another fence separates the chickens and their small coop.

The trees hug the area, creating a sense of safety and isolation. Which, for me, have never been two feelings that coexist. I sigh as I slowly turn, taking it all in. Envious of this little slice of heaven away from the Kailadons, away from the hustle and bustle and the reminders of my past. I can't help the tears that well up, but I quickly blink them away, not wanting Mallrie to see.

He is already heading up the path towards the front door, pulling his sheath off over his head. It is a picture-perfect moment. I wish I could freeze time—except for the part where I feel like I might be sick. Whatever we stepped through has my empty stomach turning on itself. Straightening up, I force myself to take deep breaths and appreciate my surroundings.

The serenity is shortly interrupted. The front door is nudged open further. A large, light brown and black-spotted cat that reminds me of a photo I once saw of an Asian Leopard Cat—but the size of a cougar—lunges off the front porch at Mallrie.

He stumbles backwards as he catches the beast. The giant animal keeps pushing its weight onto him as he stumbles backwards until he falls onto his back, dropping his sword with a loud *clang*.

I gasp in shock. "M-Mallrie?" I don't know whether to run over and try to pull the animal off him. Surely he's got it under control. He fights Kailadons for a living, after all. I take a cautious step forward when he lets out a booming laugh. I am frozen where I stand.

Rolling over, the giant cat pounces on his back, trying to keep him pinned to the ground, but Mallrie pushes himself to his feet, hoisting the animal across his shoulders like he's just slayed the beast. A contented purring rumbles in the creature's chest as it gnaws at his ear playfully.

Mallrie walks over to me, still laughing. He seems different here. He's relaxed and happy.

This is his safe place. His *home*.

"Eliana, meet Winifred." The considerable cat pushes its head back and growls as if it protests the name. "Sorry.

Winnie," Mallrie corrects. The cat rubs its head over his, ruffling his hair.

I stare at the two of them in horror. Words are beyond me. I have never seen a creature like this before.

"What?" Mallrie asks, his voice light despite holding the large animal on his shoulders. "I told you I had a cat." He runs a hand over the creature's head, and it chews on it affectionately, exposing its large teeth that could easily tear flesh from bone.

I finally find my voice. With a little nervous laugh, I ask, "Have you ever *actually* seen a cat?"

Mallrie laughs, and Winnie makes a throaty purr resembling a laugh. "Yes, I've seen a cat before. Winifred is a Misnac."

I blink in confusion. "I'm sorry?"

Mallrie chuckles as he lets the cat go. "It's a species of magical cats. A very long time ago, before I was born, every witch of nobility owned a Misnac. They were a symbol of status because they only obeyed noble bloodlines," I watch the large cat as she stalks around Mallrie with feline grace. "People got resentful, wanting their own because not only are Misnac exceptionally loyal, but they also possess magic witches do not. So they killed them all." Horror and realisation jolt through me. "Winifred was just a babe when we found her." The magical cat rubs up against Mallrie's leg, tenderly purring. I look up from Winifred, who looks thrilled to have Mallrie home.

"Nobility, huh? Should I be calling you Sir... or Your Highness?" I smile teasingly.

Mallrie returns my smile, cocking a devilish eyebrow. "Don't tempt me." His voice is a low, sensual rumble as his eyes subtly dip and roam down my body. His eyes darken, and his gaze is heavy like a caress, sending goosebumps prickling all over my body and a pool of heat rushing between my legs. "Come, let me show you around," he says, clearing his throat as he walks towards the house. Mallrie flicks his sword into the air with a careful kick, catching it as he goes.

What the fuck just happened?

I stare in awe and disbelief, fully aware that my jaw hangs loosely. *Mallrie said he was going to train me to fight. I wonder if he can teach me to do that. The sword flicky-kicky thing, not the eye-sex thing. That was... impressive.* And not at all helping with the wave of arousal that has crashed over me.

Winifred walks at his heel. She turns to watch me follow and gives me an approving mew. I return the gesture with a slight bow of my head. Being a creature that finds its loyalty to royals, it only feels fitting to bow to it. Even if I feel somewhat ridiculous.

"Over there are all the fruit and vegetables. Behind that is a handful of chickens. They give us eggs and meat," Mallrie says, pointing to the birds lazily pecking at the dirt. He looks over his shoulder as a slight gasp slips through my lips. I must look a bit shocked because he explains, "I've got to eat something, Eliana, and those old cronies in the library don't exactly let me into town." He gives a slight shrug. "It's all self-sustainable. Behind the house is a cow, Delia, though Winnie doesn't like her very much." Winnie gives a disapproving growl at the name, and Mallrie pats her head reassuringly. There's a beautiful bond between the two of them that shows a softer side of him. "And here is the house."

He jumps up the little step and pushes the door, holding it open for me. I walk inside and am surprised at how warm and cozy it feels. Despite living on his own,

Mallrie's home is spotless and tidy. Not at all like the state of Beckett's apartment when I first met him.

A small, round table sits in the centre of the room. Behind that is an old leather sofa and a small kitchen and bathroom to the left. A wooden staircase stretches up to the second floor. The balustrade has been carefully carved from a tree, the trunk and branches wrapping up the stairs.

"It's beautiful," I breathe as Mallrie points out the different areas around the small cottage but doesn't mention the door behind the staircase. "And upstairs is the bedroom." I open my mouth to ask what is behind the door under the stairs, but Mallrie is already heading upstairs, taking them two at a time, calling out behind him, "Make yourself at home."

I stand awkwardly between the staircase and the lounge room, staring at the mysterious door and chewing my lip. Quickly, I glance up the stairs to where Mallrie had disappeared. There is a small landing at the top, the door closed beyond that.

The floorboard creaks under my weight as I walk towards the mysterious door under the stairs. I bite down harder on my lip. I have no idea where Winnie has gone, and I wonder what the temperament of a Misnac is like as I slowly approach the door. Then, carefully, I wrap my hand around the doorknob and press my other hand against the wooden frame to steady myself as I quietly try to open the door.

The knob resists any attempts to open it. It's locked, but not like a lock has just been switched on the other side. Instead, it feels like a force around the door is trying to push me away.

"It's magic," Mallrie calls from behind me, and I almost jump out of my skin. I didn't even hear him come back downstairs. I turn and instinctively knot my hands together in front of me, my eyes falling to the floor.

How did that floorboard not creak for him?

"I'm sorry, I shouldn't have—"

Mallrie waves a hand dismissively. As he walks over to the fireplace, he's changed his clothes, and I am *very* appreciative of the pair of black lounge pants he has put on as he bends over and adds some more logs to the fireplace.

Get a grip on yourself, Eliana! I reprimand. *What the actual fuck?* I press my fingers to the bridge of my nose. Suddenly I've just thrown caution to the wind, and I am what? Daydreaming about him? *Gods, NO! Snap out of it!* I throw myself onto the leather couch.

"You're fine, Eliana," Mallrie says before I finish my shameful apology. "That room used to belong to someone, and before you ask, I do not wish to talk about it. Please do not try to go into that room again."

"Yeah, of course," I say quietly, chewing on the inside of my cheek as he prods and adds a few more chunks of wood to the fire.

I pull off my knee-high boots and sit them on the floor beside me. Winnie jumps onto the couch—practically out of thin air—startling me, and lies beside me, her large head in my lap, purring.

"She likes you," Mallrie says as he runs a hand through his hair. His voice is distant like he's lost in thought.

"Once you get over the fact that she's a small lion and *not* a cat, she's rather lovely." Winnie places one of her enormous paws on my leg and shuts her eyes as I idly pat her head. I stretch my body, feeling tender and sore, and yawn.

"When did you last eat?" Mallrie asks, walking into the kitchen.

"Honestly?" I call after him. "I have no idea. Probably the lasagna."

He washes his hands in the sink under the window that looks out onto the moonlit vegetable garden. Different dried herbs hang from the window. Mallrie pulls a knife from the block and starts chopping vegetables, preparing dinner for us. I try to push myself to get up, but Winnie presses another great paw onto my lap, her weight pinning me to the couch.

"Is there anything I can help with?" I call, straining my neck to watch him busily in the kitchen. The long black sleeves of his shirt rolled up to his elbows, he throws the knife into the chopping board with a *thump* as it stands in its place.

I flinch at the memory of Beckett throwing a knife at my head and it missing me by *inches*.

He glances up at me as he moves on to preparing the meat. "You okay?" he asks, concern crinkling his handsome features. I can't help but stare at the knife lodged in the wood. My pulse quickens, and my throat feels swollen as I try to swallow. "Eliana?"

Blinking rapidly, I force my gaze away from the knife to Mallrie. "Yeah, just... please don't do *that* again," I say, nodding towards the knife.

Mallrie quickly removes the blade and places it on the chopping board. "Sorry."

I scrub my face, trying to calm myself. "It's fine, just..." *Gods, why is it so hard to talk to him about this?* "Can I help with anything?"

"I don't think Winnie will let her new friend out of her sight."

I smile to myself. For once, the word doesn't sound foreign. The exact opposite, actually. This giant feline curled up on my lap, purring sleepily, likes me. It makes me feel all warm inside.

"Mallrie?" I call, straining to look at him again. "If Misnacs only like noble blood, why—"

"You're warm," Mallrie cuts me off before I can finish my thought. "We found Winnie during one of the coldest winters I think I have ever lived through. My brother and I found her hiding in a hollow tree and brought her home. She stayed close to our fire for months, hardly moving. So you feel like home, I guess. A safe space." Mallrie shrugs as he keeps cooking, tossing the frying pan over the wood-burning cooktop, but I can tell he's holding something back. He is not saying what he really thinks or the whole story.

"You never told me you had a brother," I say.

Mallrie's body tenses. Did he actually just *flinch*? "You didn't want to play—what was it called, *Twenty Questions?*" he replies, and that's the end of the conversation.

"Winnie! Let her up." Mallrie's voice is the first sound that cuts through the haze in my mind. The second is the sound of plates, knives and forks sitting against the table. I hadn't realised I had fallen asleep on the couch with the big, magical cat resting on my lap. The smell of roast chicken and vegetables fills the room. The Misnac grunts as she gracefully pushes to her feet, gently pawing into my leg. I stand up, and pins and needles cascade through my legs. I stagger precariously over to the dining table, trying to avoid the tingling sensation in my feet and legs. Mallrie holds a chair out for me, smiling wickedly. Like he has been in this position many times himself. I give him a small smile as I take my seat.

The food looks fantastic, and my stomach makes a very loud protest for me to fill up my plate. Everything tastes even better than it looks. The flavours burst in my mouth. The herb-encrusted chicken is juicy, and the vegetables are tender. I shovel the food in my mouth, finally realising how hungry I actually am.

After a while of stuffing my face and grabbing a second helping of chicken, Mallrie speaks softly. "As I said earlier, I will need your help." I look up. His elbows rest on the table, his chin resting in his hands, trying to figure out the best way to effectively accomplish our goal.

"Finding the air and water witches?" I ask.

He nods solemnly. "It won't be easy, and I don't want you going into any situation feeling unprepared, but—"

I place my knife and fork on the side of my plate. "But we have little time for training," I finish his sentence for him.

Again, Mallrie nods solemnly.

I shrug. "Teach me something simple. Not whatever was happening in that vision. That looked... complicated. Maybe a ball of fire or something. Is that hard?" Mallrie smiles, and I drop my gaze to my plate. "Or just show me how to use a sword or knife."

"It's called a dagger." Mallrie chuckles. "And a fireball is something we can achieve quickly. I'll also show you how to use a dagger." I look up through my lashes to find him resting against his chair. "You can't always use your magic," Mallrie clarifies. "The people of Datura need to stay in blissful ignorance about the existence of witches."

"Why?"

He rests an elbow on the arm of his chair and his chin

on his fist. "How did you cope with finding out the existence of witches, Eliana?"

I purse my lips. *Not well,* I think to myself, and I already know where this is going.

Mallrie nods as if reading my mind. *Which I haven't ruled out that he can actually do. Despite him saying he can't.* "It'd be chaos. We're already working against Edgar. We don't need the whole township on his side too."

I clear my throat. "Okay, so, tomorrow we start basic training. Then, we find the other elementals. How do we do that?" Mallrie says nothing. He just stares off behind me towards the fireplace, lost in thought. "How did you know I was a witch?" I prompt.

"I didn't." His attention slides back to me. "It was the strangest thing. I was on my usual patrol when a bird appeared out of nowhere."

"A bird?" I ask. It's very rare to find birds in Datura. The small alleyways and heavy foot traffic are not particularly appealing to the tiny creatures. Then there is the fact that no wild animal is game enough to linger in a town where flesh-eating predators lurk in the streets at night. I guess they have a better sense of survival than the hundreds of people living in Datura.

So a bird appearing, especially at night, is very peculiar. Mallrie leans in closer. "A nightingale." He levels a pointed look at me that makes me shift uncomfortably in my seat. "It kept flapping around my head until I followed it. It led me to you," he says, his voice filled with thought as he leans back and lounges in his chair.

"So I guess no other birds are going to help us?" I say sarcastically as I pierce a potato with my fork.

"I don't think you understand, Eliana." Mallrie's voice is

low. "The nightingale was your grandmother. She led me to you. She wanted me to find you."

I drop my fork with a clang onto the table. "No, that-that's impossible."

"The only things that are impossible are those which we allow ourselves to believe," Mallrie says, sounding wise beyond his looks. "I told you she was a witch. She died of natural causes?" I give a slight nod. My mind is spinning out of control, and my heart is beating wildly. I grab the glass of water and take a big sip, cursing that it's not gin. "Now, I can only speculate, but I think that if she was sick, she knew her time was ending, but wasn't ready to leave you. She knew you still needed her." Mallrie rubs his eyes. "You must understand, Eliana, that magic extends back eons. Some of it has been long forgotten. Some magic is dark and should never be used. Some magic is unpredictable, so it should be used with caution. Magic is not just in black and white, so to speak. Do you understand?"

"I-I think so," I whisper, afraid of where he's going to go with this.

"Don't worry, your grandmother didn't break any of the witches' code. However, I believe she found a spell. An ancient spell that allows one to take their life force and transfigure it into a familiar."

"Like a cat?" I ask dumbly. "You're telling me my grandmother is a cat?"

Mallrie chuckles. "No, a nightingale. Your family must have a long line of familiars to do the spell. Your last name is not just after some bird, but after your family's long dedication to their familiars." Mallrie's head rests against his fist as his arm perches on the table. I'm confused. Mallrie said my grandmother was a witch, but Nightingale is my father's family name. There is a thrum in my chest, a warming sensation. I place my hand over my heart. *Could it be that my father's family were also witches? Or at least descendants of witches?* I remember my father saying how his father used to paint birds. He'd venture to the edge of town and watch them with a set of binoculars as they flitted around the edges of the forest and in the fields.

Mallrie is again looking off into the distance, lost in his thoughts. Then, meeting my gaze, he says, "From what I've read about that specific incantation, you also have to take the life force from another being."

"My grandmother wasn't a murderer," I snap defensively.

"Did I say she was?" He raises a dark brow. "I'm not talking murder or sacrifice. It's got to be *given* with the purest of intentions. Few have been able to do it successfully before. People are selfish, and there can be... complications."

I remember the night my father died outside my grandmother's apartment. That cry the Kailadon made after my grandmother extinguished the flames of the candles.

I remember thinking that it reminded me of when a child's favourite toy was taken away—a pained, spoilt cry.

I look up at Mallrie. "I don't know what actually happened, but..." I take a deep breath, trying to swallow the lump in my throat that's suffocating me with the memory. I explain that night to him, spilling every painful detail. He sits there quietly, letting me get it all out.

Once I'm finished, Mallrie hands me a napkin to dry my eyes and asks if he can ask me a few questions about that night. I am terrified by what they might be, but also that burning desire I have within to learn the truth has me agreeing.

"Do you remember what herbs she used?" Mallrie asks

as he moves to a bookcase in the lounge room and pulls an old tome from the shelf.

"Um... cinnamon, fennel and marjoram, I think. I'm not too sure."

My grandmother ensured I had an extensive knowledge of different herbs and botanicals and their healing properties. We would mix little concoctions and put them by the windows to be enhanced by the energy from the full moon, then drink from them in the morning. She made me swear I would *never* tell anyone what we did. Or about the knowledge she passed on. A part of me wants to keep that promise to her, to keep it our little secret. But a more significant part of me knows Mallrie won't use this truth against me. That maybe he might help me decipher what we were actually doing.

He looks up from the tome in his arms, smiling at me, nodding slowly. "She saved your father. Your grandmother sent him to the Afterlife, and I'm guessing he gave her his life essence as a token of appreciation."

Hot tears fall down my face, knowing my father didn't suffer long. Mallrie pulls me into his chest, dropping the tome onto the table. I suck in jagged breaths as I cling to the fabric of his shirt.

For years, I've lived with the guilt that my father died a slow and painful death all because of me.

Mallrie strokes my hair. "Good girl, let it out." My arms are wrapped around his waist. I'm a blubbering mess. I hate how he makes me feel safe enough to let down my guard. I hate crying in front of him. I hate how he says, "good girl," and it sends my body into a mess of butterflies.

He reaches down, scooping me up into his arms. I tense at the closeness and the vulnerability. Mallrie walks over to the couch, carefully sits and pulls me close. His strong arms wrap gently around my body, forming a warming cocoon, his scent enveloping me.

And I don't hate it. Even though I know I should.

I exhale shakily and look up at him. "I'm sorry," I mutter, wiping the tears from my face.

Mallrie tilts my head up gently to look at him. "You have nothing to be sorry for." He presses a cautious kiss to my forehead, sending an electric shock through my body. I hate myself for enjoying how it makes me feel. The way he makes me feel.

I have deprived myself of human connection for so long that I feel like I am jumping into this headfirst and not even thinking about what I am jumping into. *Sharp rocks? Shark-infested waters?* I try to push the pessimistic thoughts from my mind.

Please, just let me enjoy this moment. A moment where I don't need to think. Where I can just be held. Where I can feel safe. Just for a moment.

CHAPTER TWENTY-THREE
ELIANA

"Come, let's get you cleaned up for bed," Mallrie says after the fire has reduced to embers, pressing me against his body and lifting me effortlessly.

"Put me down," I whine, my cheeks burning with shame. "I don't need to be carried." I try to push myself out of his embrace. "Please. I'm too heavy," I protest. I know Mallrie is strong, but this is embarrassing. I know I am not light. Beckett told me that plenty of times. I enjoy food too much, and in a town where I can enjoy so little, the single pleasure I allow myself is precisely that. Good food and good gin—not including anything from Rowan's Haus of Pancakes, I've officially learnt my lesson... until he brings out his next crazy concoction, and I will *have* to try it. I'll indulge in spending an obscene amount of money on soft cheese, smoked meat and dried fruit and call it dinner. I splurge for the top-shelf bottle of gin, and I will treat myself to waffles at Christina's every morning. I manage to get out of bed and get dressed at a reasonable hour. All things Beckett didn't understand.

It shames me sometimes to look back on our relationship, how different we were as people, yet I blindly stayed.

Mallrie's arms tighten around my soft curves. "I enjoy the way you feel in my arms." His voice is a lush growl in my ear, purely sinful. I look up at him, and his eyes are filled with a heavy heat. His gaze is like a caress, causing my skin to prickle with goosebumps. My lips part, and I am speechless.

Could he find me as attractive as I see him?

Gods, I just want to kiss him. Is that so wrong? I have spent so long alone, pushing everyone away from me. The only intimacy has been from my own touch. Thank the gods for whoever invented the vibrator. My heart is bursting in my chest, trying to break free, which only causes my face to redden even more because he can surely feel its untameable beating. If not, he can definitely see the blush on my cheeks.

Mallrie gently kicks the bathroom door, exposing a sizeable cast iron bath before a massive window overlooking a small field of wildflowers. He sets me on my feet, leans over and draws a bath. Steam starts to fill the room.

"You're a gardener as well?" I ask quietly, attempting to distract myself.

"It's an aeimweriah."

"I'm sorry, what?" I ask, not even attempting to repeat what he just said in what I can only assume to be Enkantian.

"An aim-wer-i-ah," Mallrie repeats slower. "It's an elemental shrine for those who have passed. Generally, aeimweriahs are gardens, but they can also be water vessels or an altar of candles. Depending on the elemental." Mallrie nods towards the garden, his voice dropping so low I must strain my ears to hear him. "My brother planted it."

He checks the temperature, then grabs a vial of salt and lavender from the shelf at the end of the tub and tips a handful in. I open my mouth to ask more about his brother, and a million questions form on the tip of my tongue. *Where is his brother? Did he lose him too? Did he teach Mallrie how to garden?*

But the memory of Mallrie dismissing my earlier query has me shutting my mouth. Forcing those questions back down.

He swirls his arm in the water, dissolving the salts.

My heart races as my mind fights my body. I know I shouldn't want him. I made a promise. A promise that is hanging on for dear life and growing more precarious with every moment I spend in Mallrie's presence. My body burns hot with lust and *desire* as my mind wanders scandalously. Trying very hard to recall how it felt to have a man inside me instead of my vibrator, which I called Anita Dick.

He said he enjoyed the way I felt in his arms. Butterflies flutter across my body as his words bounce around in my head like a ping-pong ball. I run my hand across my chest. My fingers slip beneath the collar of my shirt, tracing the rise and fall of my breasts, causing my nipples to harden.

My skin feels feverish against my touch. Mallrie takes a step away, and I think he's leaving the bathroom when he whispers in my ear, "Do you trust me?" It sounds like pure sex. My eyes roll back as my head lolls, colliding against something hard... and warm. *Mallrie's chest,* I realise, sending my breathing to rise into rapid, silent gasps.

"Yes," the word slips from my lips, but it doesn't even sound like my voice. It's too husky and sensual. I don't even know if I have ever heard it come out that way before. A sudden wave of comprehension splashes over me like a bucket of cold water, dousing my arousal at what I just said and what Mallrie asked me.

"*Do you trust me?*" *Gods, do I?*

My mind spirals out of control. Mallrie has saved me more than I would like to admit, but does that give me a reason to trust him? Do I even know *how* to trust someone anymore? After everything that has happened in my past, and not just the shitstorm of my relationship with Beckett, but my history with Chelsea too, I am just—*Oh, gods! What if I am reading this all wrong?* I am probably just reading into this all too much. It has been *years* since I have dated. *What if Mallrie is just being nice? Why would he want me anyway? I am just a human dumpster of fucked-uppery.*

A soft growl rumbles at the base of my ear as Mallrie's hands run idle circles along my back, pulling me out of my hurricane of thoughts. "Where did you go?" he breathes.

"W-what?" I stutter, his voice skittering along my skin and reawakening that fire deep within me. *Gods, I shouldn't be getting this turned on! I hardly know the man!* I try to reason that it's just a normal reaction, that I haven't had any human intimacy in so long that my body is... *Gods, I can't even come up with a reason as to why this is happening.* I am attracted to Mallrie. It's plain and simple. But I cannot stop my body from reacting to the littlest things he does, like speaking in that soft, gravelly way that reminds me of a man holding on to the last scraps of his self-control. *Okay, I think I've been reading too many dark romance novels.*

His hands massage my rock-like shoulders. "I asked if you trusted me. You said yes, and then you froze up." He works a knot away with his large and clearly *skilful* hands.

"I'm fine," I lie—sort of. *What has gotten into me?* I am a mess of conflicting emotions, but at the base of all of it, I am fine.

I feel safe with Mallrie, for some reason I can't quite place my finger on. I know that if I didn't want something to happen, it wouldn't. That I am entirely in control here. Mallrie murmurs at the base of my neck, "Where did you go? What are you thinking?"

"I just—I—um—I'm not quite sure—" I splutter incoherently as his hands move from my shoulders down my arms. How am I supposed to have any coherent thoughts when he touches me like *that!*

"I'mnotquitesurewhat'shappening," I spit out as quickly as I can.

Mallrie's nose traces along the column of my neck. "Breathe, beautiful girl. We're going to have a bath." His hands trail down my body, stopping at the waistband of my skirt. "Are you okay with that?" he asks.

"Are you?" I reply. The words come out so quickly that I know it's my way of putting another brick in the wall around my heart. Turning the question back on him, making him feel uncomfortable about the situation. I blink a few times, refocusing my gaze on the aeimweriah, on the splattering of coloured flowers gently blowing in the evening breeze.

It was a deflection—one that backfired when Mallrie's responding chuckle sent a shiver of awareness through my body, making me realise how slick I am between my legs.

"I am more than comfortable sharing a bath with you, Eliana."

Pressing my legs together, I think, *fuck it!* I've spent so long forcing myself to keep my distance from people. *What if Mallrie was right? That I am only hurting myself by pushing everyone else away? How can I give someone a chance not to hurt me if I never let myself take a chance?*

"So am I." I am not ashamed of my body, I love my

curves and soft stomach, but I am afraid of Mallrie seeing me so bare, so... vulnerable.

Mallrie growls his approval against my neck as he carefully slides my skirt down my legs. My fingers twitch, tempted to stop him as he pulls the shirt up and over my head slowly—almost torturously slow. "Breathe, beautiful girl, you're safe," he whispers in my ear as he tosses my shirt into the corner of the room.

My breath hitches in my throat. When was the last time someone called me beautiful? It sure as hell wasn't Beckett.

His fingers trace idle circles around the clasp of my bra, causing my nipples to harden underneath. "I want you to release your control tonight. You overthink everything. Just let go of all the thoughts smashing around in your mind and *relax*," Mallrie whispers into my ear, sending a wave of goosebumps prickling my exposed skin. "Stop thinking, Eliana," he adds as if he knew my mind was about to lose control and spiral into a mess of self-doubt.

But that... makes little sense. If Mallrie wants me to release my control, won't my mind spiral? If I relax, won't the thoughts and, worse, my fears plague me until I am sweating and clawing for the closest bottle of gin?

"Beautiful girl..." Mallrie coos. "You're overthinking everything, aren't you?"

Of course I am! Nothing makes sense anymore!

I open my mouth to explain that there is *no way* I can release control and not have my mind spiralling out of control when Mallrie's lips press against the side of my neck.

Suddenly, I forget what I was about to say. My eyes drift close as his teeth graze against the sensitive skin, and my nerves light up.

"Relax," he reminds me. The pressure across my back

and chest is released, and my bra straps slip away. The release of tension my bra was pressing into me is so euphoric I need to bite back my moan as cool air caresses my peaked nipples. One of Mallrie's hands wraps around my stomach, painstakingly close to the underside of my aching breasts.

My body slumps against his chest as he continues to place strategic kisses along my neck and behind my ear. "When a thought enters your mind," Mallrie murmurs between kisses, "acknowledge it and let it go. Focus on your breathing." His teeth grazed against every sensitive bit of flesh, his tongue stroking up my earlobe. "Good job," he growls, and I swear I can feel the press of his erection against the small of my back.

Mallrie's hand moves away from that space just under my chest. The cool air that replaces the warmth of his hand is too much as a pathetic little whimper breaks free from my lips.

If my brain could make some sort of coherent thought, I would remind myself to reprimand myself for how desperate I sound. But my brain can only focus on the direction that warmth has gone.

Down, down, down.

Mallrie's calloused fingers—from years, *literally years*, of wielding that magical sword—slip beneath the waistband of my thong. The kisses from my neck also migrate down my body as he carefully pulls my underwear down. "Step out, Eliana." His voice is a dominant command I can't help but obey. "Good girl."

Fuck. The heat and slickness pooling between my legs from those two little words alone could send me over the edge.

What the fuck is happening? I feel like I will spontaneously combust from the ecstasy of his touch. After so long with no human intimacy, my body vibrates with every touch, every word and every whisper of his breath on my skin.

I should not *want this,* I try to remind myself. *But* gods, *it feels so fucking good.*

CHAPTER TWENTY-FOUR
ELIANA

"We're going to play a little game." Mallrie's voice is a deep rumble of sensual desire as he guides me into the warmth of the bath. My muscles relaxed under every inch of water, the scent of lavender floating around, stroking my senses. I watch the flowers in Mallrie's aeimweriah dance under the moonlight in the gentle breeze. I run my hands along the water's surface, feeling the ripples beneath my palms. My mind is... calm.

"What sort of game?" I ask. Despite my body relaxing in the water, the back of my neck prickles with anxiety. I don't love games.

"I'm going to give you an instruction, and we'll see if you can follow it."

I scoff. "That sounds easy."

Mallrie's hum is unconvincing.

"What's the instruction?" I ask as I turn to look at him.

"Don't turn around," Mallrie says with a snap of authority. I have to bite back my giggle as I return my focus to the garden.

Don't turn around? Seriously? How hard can that be? I lean back, inhaling the sweet aroma of the bath salts and lavender deeply, and rest my head against the side of the tub.

The door clicks shut, snapping me out of the peaceful trance I was under. Turning at the sound, my mouth dries out as Mallrie's broad and muscular frame pushes off from the doorway. His black shirt is unbuttoned, showing off those beautiful golden muscles with a scattering of white scars, and his pants are untied and pulled down low enough that my body burns as my gaze falls on the dusting of dark hair.

He looks like someone has spent years lovingly carving him out of marble, taking particular care in etching out the definition of his muscles. I bite my bottom lip hard to stop my mouth from dropping to the floor as I lower myself further into the tub.

Mallrie clicks his tongue in disapproval. "I thought you said this would be easy?"

I blush under his gaze. "Sorry." I can't help but smile like an idiot.

"Turn around," he commands in that dominating tone that has my body aching to submit. As he tosses his shirt across the room onto the pile of my clothes, I surrender. The sound of his pants dropping to the floor makes breathing hard. My chest feels constricted, and I am so glad that my last brain cell could tell my body to turn around before I *saw* any more of him or else...

The water ripples around me as Mallrie carefully slides into the bath behind me, his legs bracing the sides of my body.

As he slides into the water, he whispers, "Are you alright?" His chest rests against my back. I nod stiffly. "I can leave if this is too much too soon?"

"No," I whisper back, afraid that if I speak any louder, my voice will be a breathy moan. I can feel the hardness of his erection against me, and gods, my mind is spiralling out of control. This can't be real. I am sure I will open my eyes at any moment, and this is all just going to be one crazy dream. My chest aches at the thought. *What if I don't want this to be a dream?* My brows press together. *This isn't something I want,* I remind myself. *I am better off on my own. No one can hurt me if I'm alone.*

Mallrie's hands are rubbing my shoulders and—*Oh, gods! It feels so, so good.* The thought of having someone doting after me, looking out for me. Someone who would put up missing person posters when I mysteriously disappear...

"What are you thinking about?" Mallrie whispers in my ear.

"I don't want this." The words spill out of my mouth like word vomit, my voice nearly breaking with each syllable. I didn't mean to say them aloud. I was trying to quiet those raging thoughts of a life *with* someone. Someone who will love all of me, even the darkness that rests in my soul.

Mallrie's hands freeze on my shoulders, and he readjusts himself in the bath, pushing himself further away from me. *Fuck. Why does he have to be so considerate?*

"I'll leave," he whispers.

Fuck. I've hurt his feelings.

Why does that make me feel so bad? I've never felt bad when I've pushed people away before.

"No. Please don't. That's—that's not what I meant." Ugh, I hate myself for how pleading my voice sounds. So desperate. Mallrie's hands return to my shoulders, massaging out all the knots, but he's still keeping his distance.

"What did you mean?" His voice is soft with caution. It is so gentle it coaxes me to lay down some of those walls I have built and speak freely.

"I keep telling myself I don't want any of this." Lifting my hand from the bath, I inspect my fingertips. "I don't want to be running for my life. I don't want to be caught up in some witch uprising. My grandmother... kept her magic a secret from me for *years*. She *lied* to me..." I'm rambling. My throat is getting tighter, strangling the breath out of me.

"Your grandmother was *protecting* you," Mallrie whispers as he gives my shoulders a reassuring squeeze. I turn to look at him. My mind is such a mess that I've forgotten where we are. That we are sitting in a bath together, *naked*.

And his stupid rule about turning around.

"How do you know?" I sob. "How is lying to those you love protecting them?"

Mallrie's quiet for a moment. His cerulean eyes turn dark and distant. "Sometimes, not telling the ones you love the whole truth is better than hurting them with it."

"It's still lying," I say breathlessly. "My grandmother could have told me. Prepared me for all of this. Did she know? About you, and Cyan, and Mayor MacQuoid?" My head is aching, and tears threaten to spill.

Mallrie's hand cups my face. "No. She knew nothing." He tilts my face so I am looking directly into his hypnotizing eyes. "No one apart from Cyan and Edgar knows. She did the right thing by not telling you."

"I've kept myself away from people for so long. I wanted *no one* for so long. And now..." my voice trails off, and I try to look away, but Mallrie catches my face, turning me to look at him again. Gently encouraging me to keep breaking down those walls.

"It's okay. You are allowed to change your mind. I'm

sorry if you feel like I am pushing you into anything you don't—"

"No. I want. Trust me. I..." I bite my lip again. Deep down, I *know* I want to love and to be loved. I am just *so scared* of history repeating itself. Maybe I'm not meant for a great love story. Maybe only tragedy is to follow me like a shadow.

Mallrie brushes his thumb over my lip. "You are allowed to change your mind," he repeats, turning me back to face the window.

We sit together in companionable silence in the warmth of the scented bath, looking out the window at the dancing, moonlit flowers. I focus on my breathing, acknowledging any thoughts that come across my mind and releasing them.

As the water cools, Mallrie starts to wash my body. His hands caress every curve, and my head rests against his strong shoulder—a shoulder that could carry the weight of my trauma if I dared to bare my most naked self to him.

My throat feels dry as I bite my lip hard to stop the thoughts from ruining this moment.

"You have no idea how you've infected my thoughts," Mallrie whispers against my neck. The raging storm of thoughts withdraws like the tide before a tsunami crashes.

What did he just say?

I open my mouth to ask him to repeat it, but his hand trails along the side of my breast. His lips gently press against the base of my neck as he murmurs. "Meeting you was a blessing and a curse."

My body goes tight and hot, and I try to press my thighs together, but that only makes the craving for his touch burn hotter.

"Eliana." The way he growls my name has the heat

rushing through my core between my legs. It sounds so sexy and forbidden. I trap a moan behind my lips through sheer force of will. I run my fingers down my leg towards my—

Mallrie's hand catches my wrist. "Eliana!" His voice is stern and a little... panicked?

My eyes snap open as he jumps from the bath. Water bubbles around me, but it doesn't feel hot. I look up at Mallrie with his back to me, his body pink from the heat as he wraps a towel around himself.

I know I shouldn't laugh, and I try so hard not to. Mallrie angles an eyebrow at me. "Something funny?"

I can't hold it in any longer. A fit of giggles ruptures from my lips as I slip back into the warm water.

Did I seriously just... boil the bath?

Another wave of hysterical laughter bubbles up and out of me. I cannot remember the last time I laughed like this. It feels so good that my chest hurts and my cheeks ache.

Mallrie leans against the wall, arms folded across his chest, waiting for me to calm myself. "Okay, that's enough, Eli." Mallrie extends a hand. "Time to get out."

"I'm sorry," I say around my laughter. Mallrie's body is returning to its natural tanned colour, but the image of him jumping out of the bath, his body all pink and flushed, will forever remain a core memory. A memory that may be a little exaggerated in his exit, with little cartoon bubbles around the corners. I can't wipe the stupid smile from my face as the memory plays over and over again.

Mallrie pulls a towel off the rail with a sharp flick, resulting in a snappish little crack. I bite my lip to stop from laughing. The action, which usually would have my back straightening and my nerves coming alive with apprehension, actually has the opposite effect. Mallrie smiles devilishly at me. I don't know if it's the fit of giggles threatening to take over me again, or if the smile lighting up Mallrie's face has me knowing he is enjoying this moment just as much as I am. That crack of sound he made with the towel? I know he did it playfully. He didn't do it to threaten me. My heart gives a happy little wiggle in my chest at the thought of being able to *laugh* and *play* with someone else.

But my past is a dark cloud reminding me why I must keep my distance. The scars Beckett left, both visible and under my skin and in my heart, have me biting back another smile.

Reaching out for the towel, Mallrie gives a stern shake of his head as he drops to one knee, looking up at me through those dark brows. "You lost the game."

My mouth pops open as he dries my body. All of my laughter ceases on a breath.

"Your emotions and your magic work in harmony together. If you want to control your magic, you must control your emotions." Working his way up my body, he looks up at me again with an arched eyebrow.

"But you told me you wanted me to release my control." I look down at him, and if the sight of this man on his knees for me doesn't end up being my undoing, I don't know what will be. "So what is it, Mallrie?" I purr. My voice is all sultry as I tuck a strand of short, blonde hair behind my ear. "Do you want me in control or to submit?"

Mallrie pinches my thigh, causing me to yelp. "*You* need to do both. You're too caught up in your own thoughts. They're fighting against each other and yourself. You need to be able to release them and still have control over your emotions." He wraps the towel around my body and tucks it into my cleavage. "You need to be the rock when the storm comes."

CHAPTER TWENTY-FIVE
ELIANA

Leaning against the doorway, I take in Mallrie's spacious bedroom. A large king-sized bed with crisp grey linen sheets sits against the wall, looking across the room and out the beautiful glass doors—doors that are open, letting in the cool night air from the small balcony. The scent of the wildflowers growing over the black iron railings fills the room. A handmade dresser sits next to a matching wardrobe. The dresser has beautiful, intricate designs carved into the drawers... The first three, anyway. Unfortunately, the last drawer is incomplete. On the opposite wall is a wooden desk—well, what you can see of one. The desktop is littered with papers, books sprawled across its surface. The side of the desk facing the bed has a knife sticking out of it and various knicks. I can imagine Mallrie lying in bed tossing the blade at the side of the desk in frustration over whatever all the books and papers littering the desktop are about.

Cautiously, I enter the room, a hand gripping the towel tucked into my chest. I am drawn to the desk like a stupid moth to the flame. My curiosity is definitely going to get me in trouble one day.The worn leather is soft under my touch as I trace my fingers over an insignia of some sort. It resembles a pentagram, but has replaced each point with a unique symbol. I run my fingers over each of them as I mouth my recognition. Fire, earth, water, wind and... the swirl at the top of the pentagram must be time. In the centre, there's a symbol I don't recognise.

I am a fucking cat, I think as I pick up the strange book. *My curiosity is going to get me killed.* Thumbing through the stiff, textured pages, staring blankly at the unknown language that looks almost alien, I pause, unable to pull away my gaze from the freakishly lifelike sketch—well, as realistic as a man with a lion's head can be. Above the Lion-Man is a circle with two axes crossing with symbols at the top, bottom and on either side of the ring.

"There are clothes in the dresser," Mallrie says, silently slipping into the room like a wraith. I jump out of my skin, screaming and dropping the book. It lands on the plush-carpeted floor with a muted thud. *Fuck.*

"I-I'm so sorry. I was just—"

Mallrie waves a hand, dismissing my apology as he picks up the book by my feet.

"Enkantian," he says as if answering the question I was about to ask. "The writing is in Enkantian." He places the book back on the desk, exactly where I picked it up.

"As in the tree?"

"The tree and my coven, yes," Mallrie says as he walks to the dresser.

That's right. I blink as my brain catches up. *They named the oak tree in the centre of Datura after his coven.*

"So that book was..." I say, dragging out my question, waiting for him to answer before I say something potentially stupid.

"My grimoire," Mallrie replies, finishing my questions with an answer. I bite back the smile pulling at my lips as I lean against the lip of the desk, careful not to rustle the papers, watching Mallrie sift through the drawers.

"Wow, you really are a witch." I laugh. "Am I going to find your broomstick under the bed?" I mock.

He tosses a grey T-shirt at my head. "No," he says, pulling on a pair of grey sweatpants, "it's behind the door."

My mind is at war with itself. One part of me wants to stay where I am and continue to drool over Mallrie's muscular body as he drapes his towel over the wardrobe door. Which, by the looks of things, is not just housing clothes. The other part of me—the one with the inability to let something go—wants to check behind his door to see if there actually is a broomstick.

Mallrie turns around, leaning against the dresser, holding a handleless ceramic cup, a crooked smile sprawled across his handsome face. "Eli..."

"Mm?" I murmur absent-mindedly as I do my best impersonation of Mrs Kaminski. I crane my neck to see if I can spot a glimpse of a broomstick poking out from behind his bedroom door.

"Eliana," Mallrie says again with a bite in his tone, and reluctantly, I drag my attention back. And, sure as eggs, he's still smiling at me like *that*, and...

I press my lips into a tight line as the heat rushes to my cheeks and the butterflies migrate between my legs.

"The only broomstick I have is in the kitchen," he says, "that I use to clean."

I run a hand through my damp hair before quickly pulling the shirt over my head and letting the towel drop to the floor. "Of course I knew you were joking," I say whilst my head is in the material because I won't dare let him see me when I blatantly lie to his face.

A rumble of laughter skitters off my skin. Mallrie bends and picks up the towel, hanging it over the other wardrobe door before climbing into bed. Awkwardly, I lean against the desk again. Mallrie's shirt hangs down to my thighs, and his scent of sandalwood and citrus clings to it. Pretending to look out the glass doors, I steal a glance at him. He's lounging with one arm behind his head, the other holding an *ancient*-looking tome with a wooden cover.

"Are you going to stand there all night?" Mallrie asks, resting the book against his bare chest and looking at me.

"Oh, um... Where do you want me to sleep?" I ask sheepishly. The thought of sleeping in the same bed as him is a little overwhelming. I haven't shared a bed with anyone since Beckett. I can feel my chest closing in. My hands start to sweat, and I can't breathe.

Mallrie flicks the covers down next to him, answering my question.

Get your shit together, Eliana. You literally just shared a bath with the man. He washed you!

"Problem?"

"Oh, I, um—I just—" *I think I'm going to faint.* I take a deep breath.

"There are plenty of pillows. Feel free to build a wall if it makes you feel better?"

That doesn't make me feel better.

My fingers mindlessly rub the hem of the shirt. Usually, I don't mind pushing people away, saying whatever I need to get the *"leave me the fuck alone"* point across. I never give a second thought to how that affects them. But Mallrie...

My toes squish in the plush carpet. I am starting to *care* about not wanting to hurt him. "I'm not going to bite, Eli,"

Mallrie says, drawing my attention back to him. "Unless you ask me nicely," he adds with a dark, playful chuckle that sounds strangely familiar, but I can't quite place. A flash of white teeth and a cunning smile has a little of the tension easing out of me.

"Do you have any gin?" I ask. *Gods, when was the last time I had a drink?* Mallrie scrubs a hand over his face, and he looks... sad.

"No. I don't," he breathes. "That's something I was hoping we could talk about, actually."

"Oh." My stomach twists and knots painfully. I know I have a drinking problem, but I can't stop. I need the alcohol to help prevent the memories from chasing me in my sleep. Everything starts to blur around my peripheral. My knees feel weak, and I lean a little more heavily against the desk, papers shifting under my grip.

"Eliana." Mallrie's voice feels so far away, even though he's standing only a few feet from me. "Eliana, are you okay?" Strong, warm arms wrap around me. My feet leave the ground.

Breathing in the grounding scent of sandalwood and citrus, Mallrie's scent, I realise he's carrying me over to the bed. It shifts under our weight, and he pulls me closer. His hand brushes over my feverish head, dragging damp strands of hair behind my ear. "Breathe, Eli. You're safe. Remember, you're the rock when the storm comes. This is just another storm. You can withstand it."

"I am the storm when the rock comes," I mutter, sucking in deep breaths, trying to calm myself.

Mallrie's chest rumbles against my cheek. "Try that again, beautiful girl."

I frown, trying to remember what I said. "I am the storm..."

"You are the rock when the storm comes," he corrects softly.

I repeat it over and over until my breathing settles, and I don't feel like I am going to puke all over Mallrie and his bed.

"You're safe. You're safe here and with me." Mallrie's voice is soft, yet that undertone of dominance laces it.

"No." The word slips from my lips, and I try to push myself out of his embrace, but he holds me close.

"Yes, *safe*. I will not hurt you, Eliana."

My mind races to my dark past, pulling me deeper into my panic. Deeper into the darkness.

Mallrie's hand traces small circles on my back. "Breathe, beautiful girl. Breathe." His voice is low in my ear as my body slowly melts into his.

I don't understand how I want to run as far away from this man but also never leave his side again. The push and pull of it all is giving me emotional whiplash. I try to focus on what Mallrie said about acknowledging the thoughts and then letting them go. Breathing in, I count. *One, two...* When a thought or a wave of panic disrupts me, I acknowledge it and imagine it floating away. Then, I start again. *One, two, three...*

I always thought that being alone meant never getting hurt—and, to some extent, I still believe that—but having Mallrie hold me while I ride the waves of this panic attack... *Fuck!* It just feels so good to have someone *here*. To hold me, help coach me through my breathing. Someone to just support me. He's honestly not doing anything extraordinary or anything I couldn't do on my own, but the fact that he's *here* and willing to *help*? I think it means more to me than I realise.

Finally, I exhale slowly, and Mallrie runs his fingers up and down my back in time with my breathing.

"Good," he murmurs. I relax deeper into his embrace.

"I-I'm sorry," I whisper between breaths.

Mallrie cups my face and turns me to look at him. "You have nothing to be sorry for. I'm sorry," he apologises.

I look up at him, shocked. "W-what?"

"I shouldn't have pressured you—"

"You didn't," I interject. "It's me. Um, my ex was..." *How do I even begin to explain?* My voice trails off as I try to form a plan of how to explain my past, my trauma.

Mallrie lifts my chin so I am looking at him again. "I am not him," he whispers, his cerulean eyes locked onto mine, "but that is still no excuse for my actions."

"I know you're not him. But, look, it's not that simple," I snap defensively. *Gods, why does he have to be so nice?*

Mallrie slides out from behind me, giving me the space I didn't know I needed. He appears to be intuitive about what I need, as if he's examining my every move.

"Then make it simple. *Talk to me.*"

I give a protesting sigh as Mallrie pulls the blankets up around the two of us and props his head up on his arm.

"Look, I know this is difficult for you to talk about. And if you're not ready, that's fine. I'll sleep on the couch."

"No, you don't have to do that." I sigh, my brows pinching at the uncomfortable feeling in my chest at kicking Mallrie out of his bed. *When did I become so soft? When did I start caring about how my words affected others?*

He tucks my hair behind my ear. "I want you to feel safe."

I grab Mallrie's hand and coax him to lie beside me. "I do. And that's what scares me."

The sound of songbirds wakes me from my sleep. A gentle breeze blows the gauzy curtains around the open glass doors. I roll over in the large, empty bed, breathing in Mallrie's scent. The earthy scent mixed with a zing of citrus is comforting. Last night, I gathered all my courage and told him about Beckett. How I promised myself I would let no one close enough to hurt me ever again. He lay there, head propped up on his fist, with a sympathetic ear and kind eyes. He held me when I cried, and in the end, he didn't look at me like the monster I have felt like I am every day since Beckett's death.

It was a relief to share the horrible things that have happened to me with someone.. It felt like a weight had been lifted from my chest.

When we finished talking, Mallrie got me a glass of wine, then went downstairs and slept on the couch. Even after I told him he could sleep in his own bed, he insisted, pressing a soft kiss to my head. *"It's fine, you sleep. You won't get a good night's rest if I am here with you, and I want you to feel safe."*

The memory sends butterflies through my stomach.

Mallrie really is nothing like Beckett.

Stretching my arms out wide across the king-size bed, something crunches under my weight. Rolling to my side, I find a note with a wax seal on the pillow beside me, the same elemental pentagram on the front of Mallrie's grimoire pressed into the green wax. In the centre is that emblem I do not recognise. It looks like a double-ended arrow with the symbol for infinity wrapping through it. I run my fingers over the rise and fall of the sigil before carefully running my finger under the seal, breaking it. The crest is embossed on the corner of the paper too. I idly trace my fingers over it as I read the note.

I climb out of bed and walk over to the dresser. Sitting on the top are two sets of jeans, three graphic T-shirts and a few lingerie sets. A pair of black lace-up boots sits on the floor beside the dresser. A stupid smile spreads across my face, making my cheeks ache. Mallrie, at some point, went back to my apartment and got me a selection of clothes. It also doesn't pass me that he clearly picked out his favourite lingerie sets. I bite my lip and pick up the purple lacy thong and matching bra. *This one*, in particular, was at the back of my drawer. A part of me wants to be disgusted that he sifted through my underwear drawer and picked and chose which ones he preferred. But there's another part of me— one I have suppressed for so long I thought I might have finally snuffed it out once and for all—that has my cheeks warming and my skin tingling with magic as my arousal gathers low in my belly.

Creeping over to the bedroom door, I flick the lock before falling back onto the bed and pulling up Mallrie's borrowed shirt. The soft fabric pools under my breasts, exposing my soft, rounded tummy and bare pussy. I don't think I could concentrate or even be around Mallrie for a moment if I didn't take care of myself right now. I wish I had Anita Dick—my vibrator—with me. It would make this so much faster and more enjoyable. Slowly, I press two fingers inside myself, my thumb circling my clit ,and I bite my lip to repress the moan clawing at my throat. Memories of Mallrie come flooding back from last night, of us in the bath, as I slowly plunge my fingers inside my wet folds over and over. My back arches as I imagine all the things we *could* have done in that bath. I imagine Mallrie's thick fingers working my needy pussy instead of my own. I press down on my clit harder as my fingers work faster. I imagine how delicious it'll feel to have his cock stretch me. My free hand claws at my skin, my nails dragging against the sensitive scars that run down my thigh. I must have a masochistic streak because even after the years of pain Beckett put me through, I don't want to be treated like some delicate flower in the bedroom. Arching my back into the pillows, my orgasm comes crashing down around me with a wave of release. I moan loudly from the intense relief, unable to stop myself.

I swiftly clean myself and get dressed before bouncing downstairs, feeling much lighter. I didn't realise how much tension my body was holding onto.

Winifred purrs loudly, greeting me at the bottom of the stairs. The large Misnac tries to curl herself between my legs, but she is so much larger and stronger than a regular cat, and she has me tripping over myself. Winnie doesn't seem to care. She just continues to purr, pressing her weight against me until I bend down, matching her height and giving her a pat.

"Good morning, Winnie. Where's Mallrie?" I ask, feeling a million shades of stupid, talking to an overgrown cat. I run my hand through her soft, spotted fur. A small part of me can't help but feel that she might actually understand what I am saying. Winnie saunters off through the kitchen towards the front door. My eyes fall on a brown paper bag with a familiar logo stamped on the front. The concern of where Mallrie has gone falls from my mind, replaced with a warm feeling swooping through my chest. Heart beating wildly, I slowly walk towards the table as if a serpent is curled up, waiting to strike. Magic zaps against my fingers as I reach out to the bag, causing me to suck in a sharp inhale of breath. As if that simple touch broke the spell around the bag, I can smell the delicious scent of Christina's waffles inside. My hands rip open the brown paper to find a takeaway container, the transparent lid filled with steam and condensation. Slumping into the chair, I d place it reverently on the table. Popping the top off, the sweet aromas of maple syrup and fruit fills my senses. Tears prick at my eyes at the familiar scent, and my heart squeezes almost painfully at the kindness. Slicing my knife through the soft, fluffy centre to the crispy edges, a moan slips from my lips as the buttery goodness slips across my tongue.

Sitting back in my chair, Winnie paws over, looking up at me with pleading eyes. "Can you even eat this?" I ask. I have no idea what a Misnac is allowed to eat. Winnie mewls happily, gently pawing at my leg, "Well, don't tell Mallrie," I whisper as I cut a slice of waffle and hold it between two fingers, terrified of Winnie's fangs. The Misnac peels back her lips, revealing those terrifying canines, but carefully takes the offering.

I take the rubbish to the bin and put my cutlery in the sink. Winnie gently paws at the glass doors, careful not to scratch the glass with her sharp claws. I wonder, as I spy some scratch marks on the glass and the wooden frame, how many times she's been told off for clawing at the door. I wouldn't be game enough to reprimand the Misnac before me. Not with her sharp claws and elongated canines that could easily tear through flesh. Winnie stalks out into the yard with feline grace. I watch as she takes in her surroundings like a queen surveying her land. I step off the porch onto the sun-warmed stone path. Covering my eyes, I glared up into the sky, enjoying the sun's warmth on my skin, wondering how long I slept. Winnie sits at the path's edge, looking into the woods past the invisible magical barrier hiding this little slice of heaven from the hellish world beyond.

She makes a sound deep within her chest that is somewhere between a purr and a growl. "Has he gone out?" I ask, unsure if that is a happy or angry sound. She makes it again, and I assume she is just missing him. I look around. *I guess it could be lonely here if you like other people's company.* Personally, I couldn't think of anything better. "Come on, Win," I say, running my fingers through her fur and walking a little way back towards the house. I sit down in the dirt and grass and pat my knee, calling her over again. I've always liked cats. Winnie falls beside me, and I run my fingers behind her ear, which she seems to like. The sun was warm on my skin, the fresh, floral scent of the flowers caught in the wind, and I wondered—selfishly—if Mallrie would mind if I asked to just stay here, hidden away, for a few more days before I have to join him in this maddening quest to find more witches and restore the magic to the Enkanti Tree.

A heavy weight settles in my chest, and even the deep sigh I push out doesn't relieve it. I know that isn't an option. Not when people are terrorised and dying from the

Kailadons. Even though I wanted nothing to do with this, it is now my *job* to save the fucking world—well, Datura.

I may not have a few more days of peace, but I have now. Resting back against my elbows, lifting my face towards the sky, I close my eyes and take in this moment. The rustling of wings has me peeking through my lashes as a large black crow perches itself on the fence, cawing softly. Winnie shifts her weight, and I look out the corner of my eye to watch her stalk towards the crow. She pounces, lunging for the large bird, which squawks angrily and tries to claw at the Misnac.

"HEY!" I shout, pushing to my feet to shoo away the bird. The closer I get, I realise this cannot be an ordinary crow. It is much, *much* larger, with milky white eyes. It appears to spot me and flies off. "You okay?" I ask Winnie, giving her a scratch behind her ear as she continues to hiss in the direction the crow went.

"Well..." I groan, stretching my arms above my head. "How about we try to figure some of this magic stuff out, yeah?" Winnie tilts her head to the side, narrowing those all-too-knowing eyes at me. "I'm open to suggestions on where to start."

"How about asking your mentor?" a deep voice says from behind, the sound like a caress down my spine, sending all the nerves in my body on high alert in the best possible way.

I turn to find Mallrie standing at the edge of the magical barrier as he swipes his arm across his brow.

"Where did you go?"

He drops his sword to the ground as he strides towards the well beside the house. "Looking for the other elementals," he says casually, and my stupid heart deflates slightly at his words.

I swallow hard around the lump trying to form in my throat, and internally curse myself. "I thought we were going to do that together?"

"We are. But you were sleeping, and I thought you needed to rest. Especially after everything..." Mallrie's voice trails off as he pulls a rope attached to the well. He doesn't need to finish his thought, and I appreciated the sleep-in. After everything that happened, I was sure I was in for another restless night's sleep. But remarkably, after our conversation, I slept relatively peacefully.

"Well?" I ask, placing a hand on my hip.

"Well, I found someone," he says around the wooden cup attached to the bucket. I watch his throat work as he downs a second cup of water, and I could suddenly do with a drink myself. Instead, I blink away the thought, trying to focus on something—anything—else.

Control your emotions. He said he found someone. "Really? Who?" I ask, my voice a little hoarse.

Mallrie cocks an eyebrow. "A water elemental, I'm guessing. I'm not really in a position to jump down and ask her for her name, am I, now?" he murmurs with a sideways glance at me before taking another mouthful of water.

"Why *can't* you go into Datura—well, you do, but why do you hide?"

He looks over at me, his eyes filled with years of darkness, and all the common sense in my body screams that I take a step away.

But I am not scared of him. I won't back down.

I square my shoulders and raise my chin, waiting for his reply. Instead, silence fills the space between us as Mallrie seems to carefully choose his words. "Apart from the fact that Cyan is ordered to bring me into Edgar if I ever step foot in the city..." his voice trails off as he looks at me as if he's studying every slight reaction I have. "I'm more afraid of what *I* would do."

"So you don't go into town to protect everyone from... you?" It sounds reasonable after seeing how he can dismember a Kailadon. No one would be safe against Mallrie's wrath if he unleashed it. "I don't think you'd hurt anyone," I say quietly. "You haven't hurt me."

He looks at me. His expression seems to say, "*yet*," and my stomach hollows out.

I swallow hard. "You won't hurt me," I say, ending whatever dark thoughts are raging in his mind. A veil of dark lashes lower over his hauntingly beautiful eyes. He clears his throat, and when he looks at me again, the pain in his eyes has receded a little. But it is still there, simmering behind those cerulean eyes. "She was being followed," Mallrie says, breaking the chest-tightening silence. He turns back to the well and grabs another cup of water, pouring it over his face, running his fingers through the dark strands of his hair.

"The water witch? You mean she already has some of her magic?"

"I think so. She kept her hands concealed but ran her fingers through her hair. They looked like yours"—Mallrie glances down at my hand—"except hers were blue."

"Well, what are we waiting for? Let's suit up!"

Mallrie cocks an eyebrow. "Excuse me? Suit up?"

I shrug. "Would you prefer 'wands at the ready!'?"

A choked laugh escapes his lips. "Fates, no!" he laughs.

I shimmy my shoulders as I head towards the barrier, feeling so light and more like myself than I have in... Well, forever.

Mallrie's hand clamps down on my shoulder. "Love your enthusiasm." *Oh, if you only knew how much I wished I could just stay here forever. To hell with Datura.* "But you forget we agreed on basic training first."

He leads me around the other side of his home, where three wooden busts stand near the barrier. The one in the middle wears what looks like a fireproof jacket. "Daggers or magic?" Mallrie asks as he leans his sword against the house. He jimmies a stone from the wall, revealing a metal compartment. About six daggers are inside the secret compartment. He pulls three out and turns to look at me. I blink at the sleek metal design, suddenly afraid of what I am about to do. Memories of killing those two in the basement of the government building by my fire flash before my eyes. Stabbing Beckett in the back has the waffles threatening to climb back up my throat.

"I can't," I breathe, shaking my head. "I can't kill any more."

CHAPTER TWENTY-SIX
MALLRIE

E liana looks at me with pleading eyes. I drop the daggers and pull her tight against my chest.

"I just can't," she whispers against me as her arms cling to my shirt like a lifeline.

"I know," I breathe into her hair.

Scoffing, she pushes away from me. "You kill Kailadons *every* night. I watched you kill Cyan's men."

"Doesn't make it any easier," I reply. "I carry every death with me. Even the lives of the Kailadons."

Eliana kicks a pebble with her boot, watching it scoot across the dirt as she whispers, "Then how do you do it?"

The question rocks me to my core. *How do I kill? How can I determine whose lives are worth saving and whose aren't?* I don't have the answer. I don't think anyone—excluding the Fates—has the answer. One life is not worth more than another. Even those of the Kailadons. Despite being monsters who mindlessly kill anything that crosses their path, they're still living creatures. They're still deserving of life.

We stand in silence while I think of how to best

respond. "I do it to protect those I love." Eliana's tear-rimmed eyes snap up to mine. Her big brown eyes are my undoing. Bending down, I pick up a dagger and hand it to her handle first, the blade biting into my fingers. "Love yourself enough to learn to defend yourself."

Eliana sniffles as she shakes her head. I realise she does this to dislodge whatever thoughts are troubling her. "Acknowledge the thoughts and let them go," I remind her. "You are the rock when the storm comes."

She steels herself, tentatively takes the dagger from my outstretched hand and inspects it before twisting on her heel. With a frustrated yelp, she pitches it towards the wooden busts. Breathing heavily, she turns to look at me with determination in her doe eyes.

"What?" she pants.

"N-nothing." I clear my throat.

A blush creeps across her cheeks. "Why are you looking at me like that?"

"Like what?"

"Like…" She looks down, embarrassment colouring the tops of her ears. "Like you want to kiss me."

"Would it be so bad if I did?" I ask, desperately wanting to touch her, hold her, kiss her. I want all of her. Never have I felt this strongly about someone.

Suddenly, I understand how my brother felt about Morana. The pain and grief that struck him when he lost her is easier to understand. I don't know what I'd do if anything happened to Eliana. *Nothing is going to happen to her,* I remind myself. *I'm finding a solution.*

"I guess it wouldn't be horrible," Eliana says, looking up at me through her dark lashes. "Unless you're a horrible kisser."

Wrapping my arm around her waist, I pull her tight

against me. Her hands splay out on my chest, and I give her curvaceous side a gentle squeeze, which causes her to squeal in delight. Taking that as my cue, I lean down and press my lips against hers. Eliana is stiff under my kiss but quickly melts into my arms. She feels better than I thought possible. Tastes better than I've ever dreamt. She parts her lips when my tongue caresses their softness. I let her lead the kiss now that it has deepened.

Eliana kisses me fervidly. Her tongue is warm with the fire within her blood. It consumes me like a drug. I never want this to end. I quickly consider any potential ramifications if I slowed time down for this moment. So we could savour it. But, unfortunately, even for a time elemental, time is against us.

As if Eliana is thinking the same thing, she pulls away. I keep my arms tightly wrapped around her. She looks up at me through glazed eyes, with swollen lips. "Well"—she clears her throat in that cute way she does when she's embarrassed about how aroused she is—"you're not a horrible kisser."

I chuckle. "I know."

She hits my chest playfully and picks up another dagger. "So what do I need to know? Apart from the pointy end going in the other person?"

CHAPTER TWENTY-SEVEN
ELIANA

Mallrie runs through the basics of handling and defending with a dagger. My arms feel like they're going to fall off. I am not ambidextrous, but he firmly believes in knowing how to handle a blade with both hands. His father told him and his brother that they needed to be ambidextrous in all aspects of life. I, however, am as capable of using my right hand as a four-year-old.

The last half hour has been a nightmare. Mallrie even went to the extent of binding my left arm behind my back. Needless to say, I missed every target and almost stabbed myself in the foot.

"Your left side is great," Mallrie chuckles, wiping sweat from his brow as the mid-morning sun beats heavily in the clearing beside his house. "We will work on your right side when we have more time."

"Do we have to?" I groan from the ground, dagger still in my right hand, flung over my eyes, blocking the sun. "I'm so tired!"

"Get up, Doe—" That little pet name kind of slipped out

in the last hour of training. Mallrie looked almost shocked that it did, but he covered it in his usual suave arrogance. "I got a present for you."

Well, that has me sitting upright and sheathing the dagger. "A present? For me?" I can't remember the last time someone got me something. Beckett tried but wasn't the best at gift-giving and eventually gave up.

Mallrie pulls a small, black leather-covered book from his back pocket. "Well, actually, your grandmother has a present for you. I'm just the delivery boy. Sorry, it's a bit squished," he says, handing me the small book. My initials —*E.N.*—are embossed in gold on the front cover.

I look up at Mallrie. "Where did you get this?" I ask breathlessly, my heart working double time.

"Last night. After I got you some clothes. I stopped by your grandmother's house. She hid it under the floorboards."

I cock my head to the side, trying to figure out how he gets everything done. "Do you ever sleep?"

Mallrie lets out a booming laugh. Birds resting in nearby trees scatter at the unexpected sound. "Of course I sleep."

"Well, you just seem to be everywhere all the time." I shrug.

Mallrie smiles, and it makes my heart skip a beat. I will never tire of seeing this man smile at me like that.

"I'm a time elemental. I can alter my time."

I raise my eyebrows, waiting for him to continue.

"I can get a full night's rest in about five minutes. Give or take."

My mouth drops. "That sounds... amazing. But if you can alter time, why don't you just use your magic to go back in time and stop Charleston?"

He sighs, giving a sad little shake of his head. "Time elementals are... Well, as my brother used to say, useless."

"Your brother sounds like a dick," I say.

A dry laugh leaves him, but it's laced with bitter sadness. "If I ever talk to my brother again, I'll tell him you say so."

Mallrie goes to retrieve the daggers from the wooden busts. "Our magic is the most limited. We can't create balls of water or fire or control the trees or wind. Our magic needs to be infused into something to be effective. To achieve *Hypreslep,* I need to infuse my magic into something I can consume. Like a cup of tea."

My face must resemble a small child experiencing snow for the first time because his lips twitch at the corners before continuing. "Still, as wonderful as it sounds, when one is in *Hypreslep,* they move into their most vulnerable state." Looking at him and having just experienced his demonstration of handling a dagger, it's hard to imagine him ever being weak.

"You asked me why my sword glows." He walks over to his sword, leaning against the house. Mallrie pulls the blade partially out of its sheath to expose the glowing, lilac blade. He returns the blade and settles his gaze onto mine. His cerulean eyes bore into me. "Do you want the reason it was crafted or why it glows?"

I'm confused by the question. My brows press together. "I don't understand."

Mallrie rubs at the stubble on his chin. "Someone created it long ago, with the magic of the Enkanti Tree, to help protect its people from creatures like the Kailadons."

I nod and shrug my shoulders simultaneously. "Makes sense. Magical sword to kill monsters."

"With the magic now gone in the Enkanti Tree, I've had

to channel my power into the sword to retrieve that magic from the past," Mallrie says.

"How does that work?" Just trying to wrap my head around that statement is hurting my head.

He smiles smugly. "It's too complicated to get into now. We're on a schedule."

Right. We still need to find these other elementals.

"The reason it glows is a little more... sinister." He pauses as if waiting for me to shrink away from him.

"I'm not afraid," I say, and I know, deep within my soul, I am not.

Mallrie sucks in a breath. He clearly weighs up whether to tell me the truth. "It holds the souls of all those I've slayed."

Oh, shit.

Well, I wasn't expecting that!

"When someone dies, the magic I've infused within the sword—which makes it glow—stops time briefly for the person I kill. The sword then *grabs* that person's soul and traps it in the sword instead of allowing it to move onto Vraska and then into the Afterlife."

"So, the pretty glow is... people's souls?"

Mallrie nods gravely. "I was young and angry when I cast the spell—"

"Then undo it!" I demand.

Mallrie's back stiffens at my outburst. "It cannot just be undone. Those souls have lost their chance of entering Vraska. They're to be trapped within the sword forever. If I were to reverse the spell, it would destroy the sword and the souls. Which would leave everyone defenceless against the Kailadons. Do you want that?"

"I suppose not," I mumble, still unable to drag that

mental image of *actual* people's souls trapped for eternity in his sword.

"We're getting distracted," Mallrie says, gesturing towards the black leather-bound journal in my hands.

He's right. Plus, who am I to judge his past? My hands aren't exactly clean. I guess I brought this upon myself. I asked why the sword glows. Maybe he's right about keeping some things a secret in order to protect others because now that I know, I don't think I'll ever be able to look at how he yields that sword the same way again. Which is a damn shame because Mallrie looks so freaking good when he's fighting, even if a part deep down inside me gets nervous that he'll get hurt.

I flip the small black book over in my hands, carefully flicking through the pages. "Is-is this a grimoire?" I look up at Mallrie.

He looks at the book in my hands. "The most intricate grimoire I've come across. Your grandmother has given you *very* detailed instructions on harnessing and controlling your magic." He reaches across me and flicks to a page towards the front of the book. My grandmother's elegant handwriting fills every inch of the page. Beautiful illustrations help explain how to do different charms and harness my magic.

"You practically don't even need my help," he says quietly. I look up at him. Something flashes across his face but is gone before I can place that emotion.

"I'm sure your help will be invaluable," I say softly. Mallrie smiles down at me as if he's glad to hear me say so.

"Using your emotions helps you to control your magic, but is not essential. Try to think of a happy memory, then channel that energy into something physical," he recites from my grandmother's grimoire. As if he's already read through the book a dozen times.

"Sadly, there aren't too many of those memories," I say woefully.

"*But some new ones have started, have they not?*" that voice whispers.

"Your grandmother has covered that." Mallrie points to a spot in the margin, disrupting my thoughts. I follow where his finger is pointing. The writing has changed direction, using every available space on the page.

Age ten: You decide we will have sunflowers this week. We got home, and Mr Fletchinson, who lives next door, was coming home too. He was wretched because his son had just passed, and you gave him all your sunflowers keeping just one for us. You showed such kindness and love. I am so proud of you for sharing your happiness with someone who needed it just as much as us.

My chest is burning, but not like I've felt before. Instead, it is soft and comforting, like my heart is smiling. I run my fingers over the writing, feeling the rise and fall of the pen imprints.

"Put your hand out," Mallrie whispers in my ear. I didn't even hear him move. I lift one of my hands, and his fingers slide under my hand, turning it palm up. "Clear your mind. Any thought that comes, acknowledge it and let it pass." We stand there silently for a moment, then, Mallrie's voice caresses my ear again. "Good. Now, use that energy." His free hand moves over to the burning sensation in my chest. "Focus." His whispers fade out as he takes a step away.

That mild burning fills my body. I focus on directing it

towards my hand, following Mallrie's hushed directions. I can feel it move through my body. And then, a spark.

An ember flies out of the palm of my hand and into the air.

Then another, and another.

Suddenly, a flame emanates from my palm. I smile, tears falling. This feels so different from when I set the basement on fire. This feels whole and stable. But more than that, it feels like *love*—something I haven't felt in a long time.

Winnie was not impressed when we left her behind. Mallrie promised to take her hunting when we returned, which sent a chill through me. I didn't even wonder what the size-able magical cat ate. Apparently, something large enough that it needs to be *hunted*.

"So what's next?" I ask as we walk through the dark undergrowth of the Melsheim Forest. Mallrie gifted me with my choice of a dagger, which now presses heavily against my side, making me feel stiff when I walk. "You going to teach me to conjure a flaming dragon to sic on my enemies?" I slip on a mossy rock. Mallrie catches me under the arm before I fall straight on my ass. We freeze like that for a moment. He looks at me like I just asked if I can raise the dead to start the zombie apocalypse.

"Umm... Like, I guess you could conjure something along those lines." His voice is distant, like he's unsure if I am joking.

I'm not joking. That would be amazing. Imagine a dragon or a phoenix made entirely of flames.

"But forming something as large as a dragon will take a *lot* of practise."

We continue through the forest in companionable silence. I switch from looking through the grimoire to looking around the forest. Despite all the stories we've been told about it being a dark, horrible place filled with death, it doesn't really seem that bad. Of course, it is dark, and there most definitely is an ominous presence that clings to your body like a second skin. I would hate to find myself in the position of wandering the Melsheim Forest at night. Mallrie has reassured me that the stories are warranted, but most have been exaggerated.

"Can I ask you a question?" Mallrie asks, holding out his hand for me to step over a fallen log. I nod. "Back at your grandmother's apartment, when you set the shower curtain on fire, what happened?"

Oh, gods!

My blood heats with the memory of my desire for Mallrie. I was hoping he had forgotten about that night.

Before I can think up a half-decent lie, I whisper, "You." I focus on my feet. I don't want to see what expression crosses his face.

"Me?" Mallrie repeats, slowing our pace even more. "Well, I hope you weren't angry," he drawls, giving me a playful nudge.

I shoot him a glare. "No, I wasn't angry." My cheeks burn hotter. There is a buzz under my skin, in my veins, as I feel my magic stirring with each thought.

"Mm, *lust*," the word falls like the darkest silk from his lips, and I suddenly want to bite his bottom lip. "Still an unstable emotion, but better than anger."

I roll my eyes and click my tongue.

Mallrie's eyes drop to my lips as if he wants to taste

them. I realise we've stopped walking. My breath hitches in my throat as he leans in closer, "You really need to stop rolling your eyes at me," he says, his voice filled with dark promise.

"And why's that?" I breathe. Heat floods my body, and I press my thighs together but prop a hand on my voluptuous hip in an attempt to hide what he is doing to my body.

Mallrie takes a step forward, causing me to take one back. The bark of a tree bites into my back as he braces his hands on either side of my head. A sense of feeling trapped should have washed over me, a panic attack following. I hold my breath, waiting for it... but it doesn't come. Instead, my body floods with heat at how Mallrie looks at me like I am his salvation. My stomach tingles with the flutter of a hundred tiny butterflies.

I don't understand what is happening. *"You're trusting him,"* whispers the mysterious voice on a phantom wind. If Mallrie hears it, he doesn't let on. His gaze is wholly on me, drinking in every inch of my face, my neck and the press of my breasts against the material of my T-shirt.

I know deep in my heart that if I asked him to stop, he would.

It is such a strange feeling, knowing someone for such a short period and yet feeling like you've known them for a lifetime.

Mallrie presses me further against the tree—not hard enough that it hurts, just enough that I know that he's the one in control and that I can submit. If I want to.

"Because, little doe, I need your respect." His hand presses to my dagger-less thigh, and he slowly drags it up my body. Fingertips trace my collarbone, then my mouth. His thumb presses down on my chin, parting my mouth slightly. His muscular body closes the distance between us, pressing his weight against me. I can feel the hardness of his erection through his pants. Mallrie tilts my head a bit and leans in so close that our lips almost brush against each other.

So close.

He is so close I could kiss him. But the way he has my arms pinned down by my sides against the tree has him in complete control of this situation.

"Shouldn't we be going?" I breathe. "Wouldn't want Cyan getting the elemental before us,." I tease, but my voice comes out all breathless and needy.

Mallrie chuckles. "Is that what you want, beautiful girl?" His voice is hot against my neck, and his lips brush up towards my jaw.

"No," I moan softly. I can't hide the smile that tugs at my lips. Suddenly, Mallrie's lips press against mine. His hands move under my hips, lifting me and wrapping my legs around his waist.

He kisses me vehemently as if he is drowning and I am his only chance of survival.

My skin feels hot, like I am going to burst into flames. I push away ever so slightly as my body turns molten deep between my legs.

"Mallrie, wait," I moan. Instantly, he places me back on my feet, his face searching mine.

"Are you okay?" he asks as he runs his hand down my face soothingly. I press my hand against his, holding it to my cheek.

I've deprived myself of that human connection for so many years. Now, I just want to be wrapped up in this man's arms all the time. I shake my head, still feeling the fire burning under my skin.

"No. Yes, I mean... I just felt like I was going to lose control," I say with my eyes closed, trying to take deep breaths.

"Good job," Mallrie says, kissing my lips softly before straightening back up. "You passed the test."

My eyes flash open to find him smiling proudly at me.

"Wait, what?" I look up at him, bewildered. Mallrie's trying—and failing—to suppress a smile.

"Just wanted to make sure you're able to control those emotions. Like I said, lust can be just as powerful as anger."

I slap him against his chest as I push past him. "Asshole," I mutter.

Catching my wrist, he spins me back into his arms. "Oh, don't tell me you didn't enjoy it, Doe?"

"I'd enjoy it more if it did not leave me with all this pent-up energy."

Mallrie's eyes darken as they rake down my body. "I think I can help there."

He presses me against a tree, and the bark scrapes against my arms. The sudden movement and pressure in my back knocks the breath out of me, my lips parted, and Mallrie is there, unapologetically taking what little air was left in my lungs. My hands fly to his hair, threading through the soft strands as I pull him tighter against me. I don't know who needs this more, him or me. His hands move to my jeans, quickly unbuttoning them. His fingers brush against my thong, and he groans into my mouth. Pulling away, Mallrie looks down at the purple scrap of fabric peeking out of my black jeans. "Do you like it?" I murmur.

He drops to his knees, tugging my jeans as far as they'll go before the dagger gets in the way. A throaty laugh escapes me. "I'd think so," I say, taking that as a yes. "After all, I stuffed them in the back of my drawer." I can't help but mention that he actively looked through my underwear drawer. Mallrie's eyes go dark as his thumb presses over the fabric, and I can feel how wet I already am. Suddenly, his hands grip my ass, and my world is spinning. I scream as he lays me down over a fallen tree. The soft, damp moss tickles my exposed skin.

"You can be such a brat, you know that, right?" Mallrie growls before tugging my jeans around my knees, forcing the dagger and holster down too. Then, he grabs my thighs and throws them over his head so they're resting on his broad shoulders. Mallrie tugs my thong to the side, and then his mouth is against my centre, his tongue gliding through my wet folds to find my clit and circle it slowly. My back arches against the tree, and I moan loudly, unable to keep quiet despite his warnings every time we enter the forest.

Monsters be damned. If this is how I die, with Mallrie between my thighs, it will be a good death. Beckett never ate me out like this. Mallrie feasts on me like I am his last meal.

He looks up at me through thick lashes, and I grip his hair with one hand, silently begging him not to stop. Mallrie pulls away enough to press two fingers to my lips. Obeying, I open my mouth and suck them deeply. "*Good girl,*" he growls, readjusting himself before plunging his wet fingers inside me. My back arches, and my pussy clenches at the sensation.

"Mallrie, *fuck,*" I moan. This is *nothing* like I imagined this morning when I finger-fucked myself.

"Yes, beautiful girl," he murmurs, his breath hot against my centre. "Are you going to be a good girl and come all over my face for me?"

I nod my head eagerly, desperate for the release

building low in my stomach. Mallrie doesn't waste any more time. His mouth is on me in an instant. His tongue is hot, circling my clit as I writhe under his ministrations.

"Oh, *fuck*, Mallrie... I... I'm *so* close..." my voice echoes around us. I glance between my thighs to find his cerulean eyes pinned on me. His lips curve at the corner as his teeth clamp down around my clit, and I scream his name as I come.

We walk in almost silence across the clearing, back into town. My cheeks are still a little flushed. What Mallrie did to relieve my pent-up energy felt absolutely scandalous .

Mallrie's hand tightens on the nape of my neck as he gently guides me around a small boulder. I drag my thoughts back from the orgasm he gave me, pressed over the tree in the middle of the forest, and back to the book my grandmother left me—which turns out to be a tremendous help because by the time we make it to the edge of town, I can successfully click my fingers together and produce a small flame—*perfect for lighting candles*, my grandmother noted—and make a small fireball in the palm of my hand. It did not impress Mallrie when I got so excited that I formed the flaming orb, but then freaked out that I couldn't extinguish it and threw it across the open field. We had to stomp out the flames as they danced along the grass for about a minute before we managed to extinguish them all. With every giggle escaping my lips, the fire took on a life of its own and jumped a little further away from Mallrie. "Maybe you need to learn to recall the fire before throwing it," he said as he stomped out the last flames.

"You are going to have to find her on your own," Mallrie says as we stand close to the buildings at the edge of town. The long, stretching shadows provide the perfect cover from any wandering eyes. "If Cyan or his men see me —well, let's just say it won't be pretty." He chuckles. I feel like I am missing out on the punch line of his joke. "She's petite. Long, dark hair, porcelain skin. She's about your height." Something ugly rolls around in the pit of my stomach as I watch Mallrie recall the woman. I can feel an angry, unpredictable heat rising in my neck and into my eyes.

"She sounds pretty," I say flatly, unwarranted jealousy seeping into my tone.

"Yeah, she is," Mallrie agrees. I let out a disapproving grunt. I know he's not mine, and I have no right to get jealous if he finds another woman attractive, but the way he just agrees with me has me seeing red.

"Got it," I spit the words out like venom and start off into the alleyway.

"Whoa. Hold on there, feisty pants." Mallrie grabs my arm and pulls me back behind the building. "What's wrong?" He grips my shoulders, holding me in place, his eyes searching mine for the sudden coldness in my actions.

"Nothing." I shrug nonchalantly. "Got to go. Can't let Cyan keep the pretty girl all for himself." I storm off again, pushing myself free from Mallrie, but he blocks my path.

"El. Seriously? Are-are you jealous?" Shock and amusement fill his voice.

Yes. Of course I am, I want to say honestly, but instead, I say coldly, "Don't flatter yourself! You may be able to give a half-decent orgasm, but I'm sure—"

"A *half-decent* orgasm?" Mallrie scoffs at my attempt to push him away, to put another brick in my wall to protect myself. "Little doe, you squirted all over my face." He licks his lips as if remembering my taste.

Mallrie pulls me close, holding me tightly against his brawny chest. "You have no reason to be jealous. She's pretty, yes. Do I find her attractive? No. Do I find *you* attractive? Fuck yes!"

I shove him away from me and roll my eyes, even though my heart is dancing happily at the fact that he finds me attractive.

"Gosh, you've got a big head. You can find her attractive if you want. It's not like we're together or anything."

Mallrie tilts his head slightly to the side like he can see straight through me. Through the walls I throw up to protect myself from being hurt.

"We could change that though."

My heart sinks at the thought of *being* with someone again.

"You know how I—" My chest tightens, panic slowly consuming me.

Mallrie's hand strokes my cheek. "*I am not him*, beautiful girl," he says firmly. "I will not hurt you. I won't let anyone hurt you again." There he goes again, making promises he has no right to. And I find myself wanting to believe the pretty words he says. I know what I want, but I'm unsure if I am strong enough to voice it.

The shadows from the building cast his face in partial darkness, making him look even more hauntingly beautiful and mysterious than the night we met. I'm grateful that we're alone since no one really travels the alleyways at the edge of town, in fear of being too far away from the safety the town provides. I reach for his face, pulling him closer into an embrace. Mallrie pushes me against the building, running his fingers through my hair.

Oh, gods!

My mind races, and my legs feel flaccid. Mallrie runs his hands down my body, caressing the sides of my breasts as he passes them. His hands linger on my hips momentarily before he pulls me up and wraps my legs around his waist. I let out a small moan of pure lust and ecstasy. Mallrie breaks our kiss and starts kissing my neck.

"You haven't given me an answer, beautiful girl." Another moan slides from my lips, and my desire for him grows. I can feel wave after wave of warmth rushing through my body.

Beautiful girl. Two little words send my body into a frenzy. I try to remind myself that I don't need a man's recognition of my appearance. That I present myself how *I* want to. But it is nice to hear it. Especially the way Mallrie says it, his voice on the edge of pure desire.

"Yes, yes." His lips press against mine hard, pushing me against the wall, his powerful body holding me still so I cannot move. His hands slip down to my ass, giving it a firm squeeze. "I *want* you." The words glide from my mouth, all but a whisper.

Mallrie's voice is full of lust against my lips. Through his pants, I can feel the press of his erection. "I want you too. I wish I could fuck you right here," he breathes his words, dark and sinful. I let out a whimper. *Gods, how I want this man to fuck me.* It's scary though. Taking that step feels like the final brick to come down in my defences. "But we've got a job to do," Mallrie says, breaking me out of my thoughts, and I can tell by his voice that he wishes the troubles of our world could just slip away, at least for a few hours.

I let out a disapproving groan and meet his eyes. "I know."

Mallrie carefully returns me to the ground and readjusts himself. "I'll be keeping an eye on you." He jerks his chin upwards towards the rooftops. "Find her. Be safe." He kisses my lips, then scales the building like he's a superhero ripped straight from the pages of a comic book until he is out of sight.

CHAPTER TWENTY-EIGHT
ELIANA

Keeping my steps light, I navigate my way to the centre of Datura as quickly as possible. Even though it's midday, the streets are still packed with a sense of urgency as people cram as much as they can into their day. Teenagers hang out on the corners of alleyways. Women walk arm in arm, catching up on the latest gossip, and children play in the rare open spaces where alleyways meet up. Jumping over a ball and kicking it back to a group of bright-eyed kids, I can't help but worry. *Did we waste too much time spending an hour training at Mallrie's house? Then the trek through the Melsheim Forest with a... minor distraction. Well, it wasn't really minor, was it?* My body still hums with the afterglow of the orgasm, and I can feel a blush creep up my neck.

Not that the time spent was unproductive. The weight of the dagger pressed to my thigh makes me anxious. I don't like standing out in a crowd. The blade feels like a giant neon sign over my head with an arrow pointing at me. The people of Datura just *don't* carry weapons like this so... visibly. But there was nowhere else to hide it unless I wanted to shove it down my pants, which was just not an option.

The smell of Datura plagues my nose with death and cramped living conditions. I never noticed how pungent it was before until I spent time away from it. I glance up to the rooftops to catch a glimpse of him, but he's nowhere to be seen. My heart skips a beat as I worry something has happened to him. *Was Cyan waiting for him? What if he's hurt?*

The realisation hits me like a tonne of bricks, causing my pace to falter. *Am I in a relationship?* A bubble of fear prickles in my chest as I realise I care about what happens to Mallrie.

Focus! I remind myself. "I've got to find this elemental before Cyan," I grumble under my breath as I continue into the heart of town.

The description Mallrie gave me could have been more specific. How many women live in Datura with long, dark hair? It'll be a miracle if we even spot her again.

I press my hand on the back pocket of my jeans to make sure the grimoire my grandmother left me is still there. All the confusion I felt last night about her lying to me about our heritage has slipped into the back of my mind.

I am still angry. She could have told me. But I am grateful she left me this grimoire. I feel more confident in producing my magic on command and using it practically and safely.

As I lean against a building in the centre of town, one foot propped on the wall at my back, I watch people pass by as I pretend to flick through the grimoire. The leaves of the Enkanti Tree rustle in the wind, picking up loose papers and blowing strands of hair in my face. A small whirlwind of leaves and old, discarded papers dances around people. A rouge page from a newspaper blows past, catching on my leg. I reach down, picking it up, the headline blaring me in the face.

I scrunch up the page, that sense of dread weighing on my chest, and toss it into a nearby trash can. Hopefully, we can find the other elementals and stop this.

I scan the area for the woman who is supposedly the water elemental. Surely, she's long gone by now. The chatter of people going about their day surrounds me like a fog. I walk around the Enkanti Tree, trying to inconspicuously look for a woman with long raven black hair and skin like porcelain.

I sigh heavily as I complete my circuit around the tree, unsuccessful. Well, technically, I saw about five women who fit that description. However, none had blue-stained fingers. I glance up at the rooftops. Mallrie is still nowhere to be seen. I tell myself not to worry, that he's *way* older than he looks. He knows how to take care of himself. *He's been doing this long enough.*

My stomach protests at this fruitless venture, and the sweet scent from Christina's is sending my stomach into a frenzy.

Well, Christina knows everyone. Maybe I could ask her if she's seen something? I convince myself as I push open the door to her café. The bells jingle overhead, announcing my arrival.

Slipping my hands into my pockets, I call out to Christina, who's carrying two empty plates and a hot cup of coffee. "Hey, Chris, can I sit anywhere?"

Christina's mass of curly, dark hair flicks around at the sound of my voice, a welcoming smile like sunshine lighting up her tanned face. "Eliana!" she exclaims. "Of course, girl. Anywhere you like. Your favourite spot's free."

I nod and give her a small smile as I head across the brightly lit, 50s-style diner to my favourite table by the window. Not bothering to pick up the menu since I already know what I will order, I fold my hands under the table and continue to scan the streets.

"Hey, doll. Haven't seen you in a while," Christina says brightly.

It hasn't been that *long,* I think to myself. "Yeah, I've been a little busy."

"Love that for you. What have you been up to? Have you met someone? Mm, I could just see you with a tall, dark, mysterious man. Rugged, you know? Slight bad boy vibes," Christina rambles. Usually, her ramblings and attempts to prod into my personal life don't bother me. I just let it slide off my back, but the fact that she's basically described Mallrie has me feeling a little on edge.

"You know me, Chris, got no time for people," I say, clearing my throat and running my fingers through my hair —which I realise I haven't brushed yet this morning. *Gods! I must look like a mess.*

Christina shrugs. "You still got time for your usual?"

"Of course," I reply. "You know you make the best waffles and coffee in all of Datura." Christina smiles smugly and ever-so humbly agrees as she walks off.

Shit! I didn't get to question her. I watch as she saunters off. Her skirt sways as she walks. She throws a last glance at me over her shoulder.

Waiting for my food to arrive, I focus on the people making their way through the hustle and bustle of the heart of Datura.

This was a good idea, I think proudly. There is nothing unusual about me sitting in this spot with waffles and coffee, people-watching.

"Here you go, doll," Christina says, placing my food on the table. I smile up at her, but sorrow twists her naturally pretty features. "I'm sorry," she whispers as she steps away, and the chair across from me scrapes across the black and white linoleum flooring.

I go to push myself out of my chair, but a firm hand grips my knee under the table. "Now, now. Let's not make a scene here, love." I glare at Cyan sitting across from me. His hand moves from my knee to the chair between my thighs, pulling me back in. The table bites into my stomach. He leans in casually, still holding onto my chair. His free arm rests on the table as if riveted by what I have to say.

I smile bitterly at him. "You're looking good, Cyan. Come here often to ruin people's appetite?" *He really does look good though,* I think, then instantly curse myself for thinking that. Cyan's eyes are a striking shade of blue— eerily similar to Mallrie's. His shoulder-length, dark blonde hair is tied up in a man bun. Usually, men with long hair don't do anything for me, but the left side of his head still has those three tight braids pulled up into a messy bun. Between the hair and his impeccable suit that hugs the muscles that must hide beneath—*Gods! Shut the fuck up!* I internally yell. *He had a gun pointed at your face the last time you saw him.* With that final thought, his presence really has put me off my food.

His laugh is like a rumble of thunder with the promise of a destructive storm. It skitters down my spine. "Oh, how I love your witty tongue. I've said it before, but you're not so bad yourself, love." Cyan picks up my fork, pierces a strawberry off my waffles and pops it in his mouth. "Don't let me keep you from your food," he says, handing the fork back to me.

I take it from him between my thumb and forefinger as if it has been contaminated before making a show of wiping it clean with the red and white gingham print napkin.

"Well, you are interrupting, so"—I carefully cut into the waffles, syrup oozing down the middle—"how about you" —I wave my hand as if to shoo him away from the table.

Cyan laughs again, his hand snaking up my leg and seizing my knee in a camel bite. I gasp at the sudden pressure and sting of pain. "We need to have a little chat."

"Then talk," I seethe between my teeth.

"Eat. Then we can go somewhere a little more... private."

"I think I'll pass. If I remember correctly, you don't play particularly nicely with others," I say around a mouthful of waffles. "So you better talk. I can eat rather quickly when I want to."

Cyan chuckles almost sweetly. "If I remember correctly, you also have a little *fire* within you," his tone drips with condescension before he flashes a serpentine smile. "I'll admit, however, that our last few encounters have been rather... unfavourable. *Please,* let me show you some real hospitality."

I narrow my eyes. "How did you know I was here? Stalker much?"

Cyan waves a hand in the air. A moment later, Christina returns on silent feet and places a cup of coffee before him. Her mouth is pressed into a hard line as if she's trying not to speak. She looks at me, her eyes rimmed with tears, silently begging for forgiveness. "That'll be all," Cyan says with another wave of his hand, dismissing her. "I don't need to resort to following you around like a lost puppy, unlike some."

My back stiffens. I can't help but worry that something horrible has happened to Mallrie. I glance back over to where Christina is serving some other customers. She's trying to act normal, but I can see the tightness of her shoulders, and her walk is missing its usual bounce.

"Does she work for you?" I ask, turning my attention back to Cyan. *Everyone you let in will eventually hurt you,* I remind myself.

He tilts his head to the side as if he can pry my mind open and spill out its secrets. "No," he scoffs as if I am a fool to think he'd employ her. "I just paid her a little visit the other night."

My heart thunders in my chest. "You went out at night?" I ask, raising my eyebrows in surprise. "That's bold of you," I add, trying to school my voice and face back into neutral boredom. "Unless you have a very particular set of skills that can help keep you safe?" I subtly taunt, letting him know his secret has been exposed.

Cyan chuckles, causing goosebumps to pebble over my arms. "Oh, I have a lot of skills, love." His eyes rake over my body, and I bare my teeth in a feral snarl. "I'll make you a deal," he drawls, waving off that conversation.

"I'm not making anything with you," I spit, cringing internally at how dumb that sounded.

Cyan ignores me and continues. "You eat, and I'll

answer all the questions burning on the tip of your tongue." He winks at me, and my body flushes with anger.

Fuck him, I think, picking up my fork and stabbing a strawberry. "I'm eating 'cause I'm hungry. *Not* because you say so," I seethe, popping the sweet fruit in my mouth. "But feel free to talk. I know how you love the sound of your own voice."

Cyan laughs again in that way that reminds me of the dark promise of a summer storm. "I do enjoy our little chats," he says, his elbow resting on the table, his chin cupped in his hand. A long finger slowly rubs his top lip. My eyes are transfixed. "You asked me a question, love," he says, breaking my trance. I roll my eyes and focus on the food in front of me. I need to figure out how to get out of here. "Since you're being good, eating your food, I'll answer you."

"I really couldn't care less, but, honestly," I say, looking up and meeting his piercing gaze again, "you'd be doing the whole town a favour by getting eaten by a Kailadon."

Cyan straightens up in his chair, pressing a hand to his chest. "Ow. You wound me," he says mockingly.

"I got to pee," I say, kicking my chair back and walking off to the bathroom at the back of the café before he can get up or say anything else.

The panic attack comes on as soon as I lock the door behind me. *I need to get out of here! I need to find Mallrie. I-I need...*

I need to breathe!

I am the rock when the storm comes, I recite to myself as I focus on my breathing. I acknowledge whatever thoughts enter my mind and move on, clearing my head and concentrating solely on breathing.

Calming myself down enough to clear the fog in my

mind, I look around the bathroom. There are three stalls to my left and three basins on my right. Ahead is a small window.

Here we go! I think with a bubble of laughter bordering on hysterical. I'm about to climb through a bathroom window to escape the bad guy like a cliché.

Praying that no one saw that fumbling mess of an escape, I scramble to my feet and double check the grimoire is still in my back pocket. I sigh in relief that it didn't fall out as my ass scraped against the window before I fell on my face in the side street. I rub my arms where I broke my fall and sneak around the back of a building to return to the centre of town. I need to find Mallrie and tell him we need to get out of here. Cursing under my breath that I can't see from this position, I move so I am as far away from Christina's as I can be and lean against the Enkanti Tree. Glancing around the large trunk, my heart falters in my chest. Cyan is gone. I won't have much time. Panic is seeping into my vision, making it blurry.

"Look up," the soft voice calls in the wind. I look up and see Mallrie on the roof of the government building, struggling with the dark-haired woman.

No freaking way!

She's putting up a good fight, but Mallrie is considerably bigger and stronger than her. I put my hand over my face to block out the sun's glare to get a better look at the scene unfolding on the rooftop of the government building. Mallrie is glistening in the sunlight. *She's definitely a water witch.* His hair is flat under the weight of the water that has drenched him.

The woman struggles as Mallrie tries to drag her over to the edge. A bubble of water forms above his head, getting bigger and bigger until it drops. My heart stops as I watch him hold his breath and try to keep his grip on the woman.

I snatch my grimoire from my back pocket, flicking through the pages. *There was a spell I was reading—*

I glance back up at Mallrie, who's loosening his grip on her as he struggles to breathe. *Fuck, there is no time to practise.* I continue flicking through the book.

Found it!

It will be dangerous and evident to anyone who sees, but I don't have time to think of a better plan.

I take a deep breath and draw my arms up high as if holding a bow. I pull back the imaginary bowstring with surprising resistance for something invisible. A warming sensation wraps between my fingers. Sparks ignite from the space created. A flaming arrow slowly appears. I let out a small chuckle, amazed that I managed to produce this on my first try.

But it's unstable. I could hit Mallrie. My fingers start to tremble, and the arrow flickers erratically.

"Trust your heart. Aim strong and true. Let your heart be your guide," calls the voice in the wind. *"FIRE!"*

I release the precarious arrow.

It flies through the air, popping the water bubble around Mallrie's head. He drops one of his arms that is restraining the water elemental.

I curse aloud as the realisation that I hit him washes over me. The woman flicks her head around, looking for the source of the flaming arrow. We both freeze as our eyes meet, giving Mallrie the upper hand as he wraps an arm around the woman's throat, putting her in a sleeper hold.

She struggles momentarily against the embrace before her body goes limp. Mallrie tosses her over his shoulder. His shoulder is bleeding, and my heart pangs with guilt. He walks over to the edge and looks down at me. Despite the wound, he smiles at me as he jerks his head as if to say, *"let's go,"* before running back towards the Melsheim Forest.

It takes me a moment to regain control of my body. My mind is racing. *It can't be.* But she stares at me with the same shock and recognition plastered across her face that is on mine. The only real friend I ever had growing up. Who *allegedly* fled town because she didn't want to live in fear of the Flesh-Hunters anymore. Anger and confusion wash over me.

Chelsea.

CHAPTER TWENTY-NINE
ELIANA

I watch in stunned silence, my grimoire at my feet, as Mallrie runs off with my—supposedly dead—best friend. *No way that was actually Chelsea Huang. Not my Chelsea Huang.* It feels like the world has slipped on its axis, like I'm being thrown upside down and falling down a rabbit hole all at once. For a long time, I worried about her. I cried for her, mourned her death.

The building that Mallrie and Chelsea were fighting on just moments ago is now empty. My fists clench by my side, my knuckles turning white.

A hand wraps around my waist, pinning my arms to my sides and pulling me back against a firm body. "Here you are. I've been looking for you, love," Cyan whispers in my ear. I try to struggle, but he's bigger and stronger than me. He bends, picks up my grimoire and slides it into the inside pocket of his jacket. "I'll look after this for you. Looks like your hands are a little tied up at the moment." Suddenly, something wraps around my wrists, pulling them tight behind my back. A strangled gasp leaves my body.

He spins me so my back is pressed against the tree,

and he steps closer, glaring down at me, his eyes darken-ing. "Looks like you've figured out how to use your little gift."

"Looks like you've been keeping secrets from me, Cyan," I ground out.

"I'm not the only one keeping secrets," he whispers, angling his head down. His breath dances along my jaw, sending a shiver through me. I try to heat my wrists to break the bindings, but something sharp digs into them. "I wouldn't do that if I were you, love," he tsks. "Come, let's go have that chat."

The heavy wooden doors open with a push of Cyan's free hand, and we walk into the marble lobby of the govern-ment building. Thankfully, I've never needed to enter before. I look around the marble foyer, taking it all in as he continues dragging me like a disobedient child. The lobby is open-plan, cold and businesslike. Though I personally have never had to step foot in this cold, lifeless building before, I have watched documentaries on it. Courtesy of Beckett, who thought Mayor MacQuoid was the best thing to ever happen to Datura.

The first floor is a modest foyer, a large marble desk in the middle of the room with two security guards flanking the receptionist sitting there. Behind them is a staircase winding to the other floors and into the basement. Above the foyer, there's the general disciplinary office—the town's law enforcement. Then there are a series of conference rooms on the third floor. The fourth floor is the mayor's office, and the people who work directly under him also have small offices there. The top level of the building is the penthouse belonging to the mayor.

It once used to have more offices, but when Edgar's father became mayor, he took the whole level for himself. Dedicated to his job but paranoid about getting stuck at the office late at night, he decided it was in all the mayor's best interest to live and work in the same building. It was a humble residence until his son took over. Edgar stripped the modest home and transformed it into a penthouse fit for a king. The documentary showcased the renovation of the area, complementing Edgar on his exquisite taste and eye for detail. I remember sitting there and thinking how selfish he was. No one needed that much *stuff*, *especially* at the expense of the town's people.

The receptionist lowers her eyes compliantly as we walk past as if not wanting to get involved in what's going on. The two burly security guards step aside as Cyan drags me—now kicking, screaming and making quite the scene—through the lobby towards the staircase into the basement.

The room at the bottom of the stairs is charred, caution tape draped across it, the broken door leaning against the wall. This is where our last confrontation happened—where Cyan had two people drug me. Where I set the room on fire. Their screams fill my mind, the lingering stench of sulphur and burnt wood still hanging in the air as we pass. *I am stronger now,* I tell myself, steeling my mind, pushing the memories away. I focus on the breathing techniques Mallrie's taught me, on stilling my mind, determined not to let it consume me.

Cyan wrenches me to the left, towards another door. He reaches into his pocket, pulls out a gold key, unlocks the door and pushes me into a tasteful office. A large bookcase fills one wall, and a black marble desk sits in the middle of the room with two sitting chairs. Cyan pushes me into one of them. Vines poke through the carpeted floor, creeping around my legs and waist, fastening me to the chair. I try to heat my body enough to burn the vines, but they slowly tighten in an agonising grip. Thorns gradually appear from the plants, piercing my skin. The pain is unbearable. I thought I had a relatively high pain threshold after living with an abusive ex for so long, but this...

"The more you struggle, the worse the pain will become." Cyan runs a finger over my chest, where the vines and thorns dig in. "You see, this is my personal variation of Gymnosporia Buxifolia. A particularly nasty plant with poisonous thorns."

"I really don't care about your stupid plants," I hiss, interrupting him.

But Cyan pays me no attention as he keeps talking. "I suggest you be good and *sit still*," he growls out the last two words. As soon as I stop struggling, the thorns stop digging in. Puffing out an aggravated breath, I lean back in my chair in an attempt to get comfortable. Whatever he calls this stupid vine, the poison must affect my magic—when I try to summon it into the palm of my hand, it feels so far away. As if I am looking for it down a deep well.

Cyan carefully slips off his black suit jacket and tosses it onto the desk with a muted thud from my grimoire. He leans against the black desk, rolling his sleeves up to his elbows, exposing a sleeve of tattoos. His black shirt hugs against his body, showing off his physique.

He studies me as he loosens his tie like he wants to peel away layer after layer of my skin like a Kailadon and poke around inside my head. It leaves me feeling irritated and itching to run away. It takes all of my self-control to keep his gaze. I wriggle my wrists, hoping to find some weakness in them. Finally, Cyan breaks the silence. "Come now, Eliana. I told you there's no need to struggle. You're only going to hurt yourself." His words send the thorns digging in deeper, penetrating my skin. A small whimper escapes my lips, betraying my attempt at a strong façade. Tears prick behind my eyes as the poison stings against my blood. The vines loosen as soon as the cry leaves my mouth, retracting the thorns.

"I am not the cruel man you think I am, love," Cyan says almost softly. I struggle again under the restraints, trying to free my hands, but the thorns don't dig in as aggressively this time. Instead, they press against the raw skin they penetrated before but don't push in any further.

"You could have fooled me," I grunt.

Cyan sighs as if he's trying to calm himself. He folds his arms across his chest. "Fine. Call me cruel. Make me a monster. But know this." His eyes turn dark. "Mallrie is *not* the protagonist you think he is." His voice is deep and rich with a lethal warning. "You think he's your guardian of the night, protecting the innocent from the monsters that lurk in the shadows, but he's just as much a monster as I am."

"You're wrong," I spit out.

"Oh, am I?" Cyan leans forward, anger flickering in those dark eyes. "Did he tell you how he fled like a coward after watching *our mother* burn to death? How he sat by and watched as they slaughtered our sisters like animals with the other children?" he shouts.

"M-mother?" I stutter. I knew the High Witchess was Mallrie's mother and that he had a brother... but... he never mentioned who that was.

Siblings. Mallrie and Cyan.

The shock rattles me, and I am speechless.

Cyan lets out a small, pained laugh. "No. Big, brave

Mallrie left out how he was too afraid to fight or bow to the new powers-to-be. So, instead, he talks up how he's *protecting* everyone. When really he's just trying to atone for his sins."

"I-I didn't know Mallrie had sisters. He n-never—" I stutter, trying to wrap my head around this new information.

"*We,*" corrects Cyan, "had three younger sisters. Alinta, Abeline and Adriana." He looks away, but I can see the pain in his eyes. The longing and sadness that will never truly heal. "After Charleston burnt the witches on that godsforsaken tree, he got drunk on the power. On the fear of those who bent their knee to him. But, of course, we'll always be superior," Cyan opens his arms dramatically, emphasising that we are one and the same. "Even if we claimed to make our magic dormant, we could always call it back. Charleston wanted to ensure we feared him enough to never challenge his leadership. He gathered all the children and slaughtered them like pigs, vowing that our future children would suffer the same fate if we ever recalled our magic." Cyan turns his back to me, his body tense as he grips the bench along the back wall, his knuckles going white. "It's better to be feared than loved," he whispers. "I pleaded for Mallrie to use his magic to go back and save our sisters—"

"Mallrie's magic can't travel back in time," I whisper, interrupting again.

Cyan swings on his heels. "*He's a liar!* Don't you understand?" he shouts in a fit of rage, sending the thorns deep into my skin. I scream in agony as the icy toxins mix with my blood. Then, suddenly, they're gone. The briefest emotion flashes across Cyan's face as if he lost control for that split second and didn't mean to hurt me.

"He's not lying. Mallrie carries the guilt of his sisters' death in his heart. Has carried it since the day they were murdered," the voice whispers into my mind.

Cyan takes a steadying breath, his mask of calm composure slipping back into place. I must have imagined that brief look of concern. The toxins must be messing with my brain. He doesn't care what happens to me.

"Mallrie *can* travel back in time, but he claims that no matter what he *tried*, our sisters always met the same fate." Cyan clicks his tongue and rolls his eyes in disbelief that his brother tried to save their sisters.

I know this to be true—well, not about him going to save his sisters, but Mallrie's explained how his magic works. Yet, I find myself shaking my head. "You're wrong! Mallrie would have done anything to save his family!" I refuse to believe he would have just run away. That's not who he is.

Cyan walks back over to the desk and leans against it again, crossing his arms over his chest. "'The will of the Fates cannot be changed,'" he says as if reciting what Mallrie has told him a million times. "Time magic." He scoffs as if it's the greatest insult one could be given. "An unnatural and useless power. What good can be done with it?"

"More good than you do with *your* magic," I seethe.

Cyan looks me up and down, examining me. A strange look washes over him. Realisation, disgust and... jealousy? "You have feelings for him," he says in a way that feels like he is telling a small child that what they did was wrong. My cheeks redden under his stare. He clicks his tongue. "Who am I to tell you what to do? You've already painted me as the villain of your story."

"And a liar," I add matter-of-factly.

Cyan's eyes turn dark. "And why do you think I'd lie to you, love? Because you've deemed me to be the villain?" His voice is slow and calculated, making every word he says hang in the air like molasses as he slowly stalks towards me.

He leans into me, pressing his hand firmly on my shoulder. "If I am the villain, then I have nothing to lose. What would I gain from lying to you?" Cyan tilts the chair I am secured to back a little so I'm facing him directly, unable to break eye contact. "See, that's the difference between *villains* and *heroes*. A hero will lie to protect those they care about. A villain will always do what they say." He drops the chair back onto all fours. "Besides, I *respect* you enough for you to know the truth."

I scoff. "Yeah. You respect me, sure. That's why I am tied up."

"Don't get respect and trust mixed up, love. I respect you. I know the trauma you've endured and what you're capable of. But trust?" He presses his finger to his chin in faux contemplation. "What were the words you used? 'I'm still deciding.'"

My heart freezes at the words I said to Mallrie on the rooftop.

"Besides..." Cyan bites his lower lip. "I kind of like seeing you all tied up."

Anger rises in me. *Fuck him.* He knows *nothing* about who I am and what I've been through. I spit in his face. "Fuck you," I growl.

He straightens up, smirking like a cat that caught the mouse, his eyes glistening. Clearly pleased he got a reaction out of me, he walks back to his desk, leaning against it. Silence thickens in the air.

"Why am I here, Cyan?" I finally speak, breaking the silence, his face turning cold.

"Your *boyfriend*"—we both flinch a little at the word—"has taken something that belongs to me."

Of course, I know exactly what he's talking about—or rather, *who* he's talking about. "News flash, Cyan, *people aren't property.*"

He chuckles deeply, and I can see a resemblance between him and Mallrie. "They are when they *beg* for your help." His tone is almost regal, like the prince of hell. He implies that Chelsea would have done anything for his help, that she would have sold her soul to him. I don't believe it. That's not the Chelsea I knew.

"Chelsea never would have come to you for help." My tone's spiteful. I want nothing more than to rip the man before me into bloody ribbons. Cyan is like an animal though; if he senses fear, he will exploit it until you break.

"Oh, but she did, love," he says in a dark, mocking tone. "When I found her frozen with fear at the edge of the Melsheim Forest, she all but jumped at the chance to come home with me." Cyan's eyes darken, making me feel as if his words have more meaning than what he's saying.

"She's no fool—" I start to speak.

"No. She's not," Cyan snaps. "She's smarter than you." The words sting a little.

Two friends, two brothers. But who chose the right one? Is there even a right option?

"She was afraid of what became of her when she stumbled into the Enkanti Tree. Apparently, she tripped and used the tree to steady herself." Cyan waves his hand as if it's just a minor detail he didn't need to add but did so for my benefit. He smoothes his hands over his head, pushing some loose strands away.

"She was babbling about how the tree did something to her. How she felt a cool rush run through her fingers, 'like water or something,'" he mimics. "She was so bloody incoherent it gave me a headache." Cyan presses two fingers to his temple, slowly massaging the spot as if remembering the day. "She whined about how she kept making things flood in her apartment and didn't know what to do. So she was planning on running away. A little pathetic if you ask me," he scoffs as he walks around the back of his desk and pours himself a glass of whisky. "Thinking you can run away from all your problems. Such a mortal way of thinking. Pathetic." He takes a long sip. "Oh, well, c'est la vie." Cyan pauses, pressing his fingers to his lips as if waiting for me to say something. "Anyway," he continues, waving his hand when I don't entertain him. I continue to stare him down. "I explained our little predicament and gave her the ugly truths about the world. You know? There's no Santa Claus. Her government is built on a foundation of lies." He finishes his whisky and drops the glass on the bench with a soft thud. "She begged for me to let her come home with me. For me to *protect* her. Teach her how to wield her magic properly. She's quite the quick learner."

I roll my eyes. "Cute story, Cyan, but Chelsea would have contacted me if she stayed in town. Unless, of course, she was being held captive?" I raise my eyebrows, attempting to throw some sass, but in the back of my mind, a part of me knows he is telling the truth. What he said about heroes and villains makes sense. But Mallrie didn't lie to me. He told me he had a brother. Sure, he didn't mention his three sisters, but I understand. I find it hard to talk about losing my father. I hardly, if ever, mention my mother. Not that there is a lot to talk about. She died giving birth to me, and I look like her. That's about all I can say. But I get it.

I'm trying my best to free my hands at least enough to break the restraints. Nothing seems to work though. The vines are alive, constantly in motion, twisting tighter and then releasing when the pressure gets too much.

Cyan chuckles. "Oh, Eliana, you're so delicious when you try to be tough. Chelsea didn't *want* to see you. She was free to walk whenever and wherever she pleased. Instead, she found comfort here. With *me*."

Anger bubbles inside me, and I purposefully look around the room. "What? Here? I thought you said she was smart. This is just a hole in the ground. You can polish a turd, but—"

"Home is where the heart is, love," Cyan cuts me off. "Surely, you still don't consider your shitty studio apartment a home when a quaint storybook cottage is hidden in the woods." I can't help but flush. What he's saying is true. I always felt more at home with my grandmother than I ever did with my father. When she died, her apartment stopped feeling like home. My apartment never felt like a proper home. Beckett's sure as shit never felt like home, as much as I wished it would.

But Mallrie's place? With the sunlight dancing over the flowers, the gentle breeze waking me in the morning... Winnie. That felt more like home in the one night I spent there than anywhere else has in the last seven years.

If Mallrie offered, I'd move in with him in a heartbeat, never wanting either of us to leave.

Safe. Far away from the rest of the world.

"Anyway, enough chit-chat. You're to stay here until I get my Chelsea back."

My Chelsea.

My stomach twists in a mess of knots and butterflies.

"Maybe some time alone will help you, love. Give you some time to mull over what I have said. You might just decide you'd rather stay with me." Cyan picks up his suit jacket, flings it casually over his shoulder and walks over to me. He lifts my chin in his hand so I am looking directly at him. Cyan leans down close enough that I can feel the warmth of his breath. "I might even let you stay after you get on your knees and *beg*." His eyes burn into me.

I stifle a laugh. "I will *never* get on my knees for you."

"Hmm, we'll see, love. We'll see." Cyan releases my face with a slight, forceful push. His hand snakes up my thigh to the dagger Mallrie gave me. He unsheathes it quickly and taps the tip of the blade on the end of my nose. "You won't be needing this, Miss Nightingale." Cyan walks out of the room, locking the door behind him.

CHAPTER THIRTY

ELIANA

Cyan's footsteps recede as he walks back to the lobby, leaving me alone in the small office and finally giving me a chance to breathe. Whenever he is around, I am always on edge. There's something about him that makes the hairs on the back of my neck stand. The further away Cyan gets, the less the vines binding me to the chair squirm. They seem almost lifeless now that he is gone—presumably from the government building. They are still tightly bound to the chair, yet when I try to squirm, they no longer move like they're sentient and tightening or loosening their grip.

I focus on my energy. Looking down at that dark well where my magic felt lost moments ago, I call out to it, demanding that it respond. I envision my body becoming white-hot, the vines snapping under the heat. As I concentrate, I can feel the warmth of my magic run through my veins, heating my blood and pushing the heat to the surface. Cautiously, I open one eye as I hear the sizzling and snapping of the vines. Whatever toxin Cyan's climber plants injected me with suppressing my magic must only work when he's near—like the vines and their sentient-ness. Or they didn't inject me with enough to render me useless.

It has to be the first option, I think. There is no way that if Cyan controlled how much toxin to inject into me, he wouldn't have dosed me up so I couldn't escape the moment he left me alone.

I push my arms free and rip the remainder of the restraints away. It still astounds me that I am left unharmed after turning myself into a human torch—or boiling a bath full of water. That memory should have brought a smile to my face and a lightness to my heart. Instead, I am left with a sense of dread.

I hope Mallrie is alright.

Thrusting myself onto my feet, I head to the door. My hand hovers over the handle for a moment. This feels like a trap. I take a cautious step backwards, then another. Some-thing about this just doesn't feel right. It all feels a little too easy, like in those slasher films where the young female runs through the school away from the crazed masked man with a knife. All the doors to the exit are unlocked; the killer is nowhere to be seen. The exit is within her reach, and it, too, is unlocked. Only to find the killer waiting for her outside.

Walking over to the desk, I don't know what I am looking for or what I expect to find.

I guess I will know when I find it. I pull the chair out from behind the large black marble desk. *Who has a desk like this? It's so ostentatious!* It doesn't feel like Cyan's style. As much of a prick as he is, he doesn't scream *"money is power"*, unlike Edgar.

Sitting in the chair, Cyan's scent blooms from the soft leather. I scrunch my face, trying to dispel the grounding, earthy aromas of pine and... finely aged whisky. The top of the desk is practically empty apart from two small plants—lavender and a fern—a notepad and a pen. I stare at the two plants.

I know Cyan is the earth elemental, so it makes sense that he's got plants surrounding him, but these are the only two in this room. He is clearly a minimalist, so maybe he just doesn't like them cluttering the space?

No. Cyan is clever and cunning.

There is a deeper meaning behind why he would have these two plants. They're not small desk plants, so having them sit on the desk draws your eye. Luckily, the space is stupidly big.

I look around the room. There are no windows and no natural light. Not that I expected Cyan's plants to actually grow the conventional way. They're an extension of him. But I know lavender needs full sunlight.

I lean back in the chair, pressing my palms into my eyes, trying to remember what my grandmother taught me about flowers.

"Every plant tells a story, Eli. You can hide messages in them. Always be cautious of those who give you lavender. It's a sign of distrust."

Distrust? I look at the lilac flowers swaying under the air-conditioning. Their sweet, relaxing aroma mixes with that of Cyan's, making a fresh, unfamiliar scent that has my muscles wanting to relax into the leather chair.

Why would he have a plant representing distrust on his desk? Does he not trust Edgar?

I look over at the fern. I stretch over the large desk and run my fingers over its soft leaves.

"Secrecy," the voice on the phantom wind prompts me.

Ferns are a symbol of magic and secrecy. I let out a little

humph. The lavender has me stumped. I pull one flower off and twist it between my fingers before slipping it into my pocket. Then, heating my hands, I place them on the pots, causing the plants to wither and die.

There's a message for you, Cyan.

Flopping back in the chair, I notice two drawers on the side of the desk. Pushing myself forward, I pull on the first one.

Locked.

So is the second drawer. Chewing my thumbnail, I lean back in the leather chair, surrounded by Cyan's scent. Something is in those drawers. I just know it. I push to my feet, slamming my hands on the cool marble desk. I grab the bottle of whisky and fill a finger's worth into the glass Cyan used. Scrunching up my nose, I down it in one mouthful. I have an idea. I do not know if it will work or not. Sliding back into the chair with another glass of whisky, I press my finger against the key-shaped lock. My finger slowly heats until the metal of the keyhole starts to turn white. Working slowly and carefully to not damage whatever is inside the drawer, I push my finger into the hole. The metal melts and welcomes the push of my digit. I gently tug the drawer with my other hand, and it releases. A small, satisfied sound slips from my lips as I open it. My heart falls away.

Empty.

My brows knit together as I slam the drawer shut and pull open the second one with a forceful tug breaking away the melted locks. One folder. My heart beats loudly in my ears, and the air feels thick with anticipation. The aching grip of my anxiety clutches at my spine as I pull the folder out. Brown twine wraps around the thick file, keeping its contents contained.

I set the folder on the desk. My heart feels heavy as my hands hover over the folder, hesitating. Cyan's words ring in my ears. *"If I am the villain, then I have nothing to lose. What would I gain from lying to you?"*

Well, if he isn't afraid to tell me the truth, then he should have no problem with me reading whatever is in here, I reason as I pull away the string, opening the file.

My jaw hangs slack as I gawk at the contents of the file. Page after page, I slide out of the folder. The names and faces of Datura's missing residents stare lifelessly up at me. Some have black, inky veins spreading across their face. Some have thick, black liquid excreting from their eyes, nose and mouth. Dried blood runs like tears from eyes. The blackened, rotten look of gangrene. And the red and raw undersides of the flesh as if someone poured acid over their faces. My stomach twists as that glass of whisky weighs heavily on my stomach.

Oh, gods!

I lunge for the trash can under the desk, falling hard onto my knees. Thick saliva fills my mouth before the acidic bile comes flying out and into the bin. My body convulses from the retching and the involuntary stomach reflexes.

I keep my head low between my legs and push myself back onto the chair. Holding the bin between my knees, I suck in some deep, slow breaths.

In through my nose—hold—one, two, three, out through my mouth.

I wipe my mouth with the back of my hand, my throat burning from the acid and heavy heaving. I carefully look back up at the files on the desk, trying not to look too closely at the faces of the dead looking unseeingly up at me. They list names and ages at the top of the files. Under the names is a series of letters and numbers. Some sort of algorithm. Then, below that are the results, all ending the same way: Deceased. Subject Failed. Unsustainable Formula.

I press my fingers to my trembling lips as I run my blackened fingers over the photograph of the file on top of the pile.

Susan's eyes have turned a milky white, and bloody tears stream down her contorted face. Her mouth is frozen in a petrified scream. The inside of her mouth looks like it's been filled with some sort of black liquid. Whether that was poured into her mouth or her body produced it, I don't know. I don't think I want to know, either way. Susan lies on a metal table. I can see the top of a medical gown poking out from the bottom of the photograph.

It looks like they have been experimenting with people. Horror fills me as I remember the newspaper headline that clung to my legs earlier today. *INCREASE IN FLESH-HUNTER ATTACKS.*

I scan the rest of Susan's file. There are a lot of sections blacked out.

I skim-read over half the document because it's all just medical jargon that is going over my head. Then, there in bold letters, are the results. I hold my breath, even though I know poor Susan's fate. The FSXK24-56-75 serum was unsuccessful. Whatever this FS component is, it seems to be too high, causing severe subconjunctival haemorrhage. From what I can understand, the K24 formula is also unstable.

There are notes with many redactions where whoever is doing this to people has commented on what changes they should make for the next subject.

I feel absolutely sick to my stomach.

Have Cyan and Edgar been abducting people and experimenting on them? Why has this been done in a veil of secrecy?

What are they doing to the people? What are they hoping to achieve?

I scan the rest of the folder, but there is nothing else. I sigh, pushing to my feet. A dead end and wasted daylight.

"*No. Not a dead end,*" whispers the voice. "*You must stop these experimentations.*"

"I know," I reply.

I head back to the office door and rattle the door handle. *Locked.* I crouch down and look through the keyhole. I have never picked a lock, and I doubt it's as easy as people make it look. But I did just melt the locks off the desk drawers.

I sneer at the lock as if its very presence is mocking me. Heating my hands, I once again press my finger into the keyhole. Slowly, the metal softens and then gives way, allowing me to push deeper and melt away the lock. I can't help but giggle at the dirty thought that crosses my mind. . I must be losing it because the euphoria that hits me as the thick, warm goo runs down my fingers has me smiling, barely holding back another fit of giggles. As it drips onto the floor, I shake the last of the molten lock from my hand and try the doorknob again. *Nothing.* If anything, I made it worse. The handle won't even budge.

Stepping back, I take in the door. *The lock isn't the only thing mocking me now.* Frustration bubbles inside me, my magic swelling like an endless molten pit. I kick the door as hard as I can. It shudders against its hinges. I kick it again, and again, and again. The sound of wood splintering and the sharp clink and thud of metal resound in the empty room and the hall beyond. Finally, the door gives way. I jump back and press my back against the wall, my magic pulsing and ready to fight. I brace myself for Cyan or one of his men to storm into the room and restrain me again.

Nothing.

This feels like a trap, but I don't have time to wait for Cyan's attack. Instead, I dart up the stairs and peer around the corner. The foyer is empty and pitch-black.

"Fuck," I curse aloud. It's dark already. "That fucker left me here!" The lobby is empty, and my voice is too loud as it echoes off the walls. The mayor lives on the fifth floor. *Surely he's got security patrolling these halls.*

I don't know what I expected, but the thought of Cyan safely at home relaxing by a fire and sipping on a glass of cabernet makes my skin burn. I try to shake the image from my mind. Why I imagined Cyan lounging by a fire and drinking a glass of red wine is a mystery to me, but it burnt to life so vividly in my mind.

I head to the front doors, my footsteps echoing along the marble floor, sending an unnerving shiver down my spine. *Why is everything so loud?*

My hand freezes just before the handle. *Mallrie isn't here.* A surge of fear and panic races through me. *Would I be strong enough to fight a Kailadon on my own? Would my magic be strong enough?* A strange feeling whirls around me, and I sense I am not alone. I look around at the empty lobby.

"You're strong enough, Eliana. You can do this," calls that frustratingly familiar but soothing voice in the wind. But it sounds different this time. It's quieter, kinder.

My heart stops, and I look around frantically as recognition courses through me. "Grandmother?" I call. "Grandmother, is that you?" Tears fill my eyes, and my heart aches. "Please, I need you." I sob, the heartache overcoming me as I fall to my knees hard. The pain shoots up my legs, but I hardly notice.

"I am so proud of you, my Eli. You're stronger than I could ever have imagined. You were born to burn bright," my grand-

mother's voice echoes around me. *"I will always be with you."* I look around, tears stinging my eyes, but the voice is in my head.

"I miss you." As I struggle to form the words, I sniffle, my lip quivering. My heart feels like it is being ripped open. I can't breathe. I look around, desperately trying to see my grandmother's face one last time.

"I'll always be with you."

"I-I don't know what to do anymore."

"Trust your heart. It's strong and won't lead you astray," her voice echoes all around and inside of me.

I wipe my nose. "But—Mallrie. Cyan. Chelsea—I-I just don't know—" I wipe the tears as they fall. "So many people have let me down... *My heart* has let me down." My voice cracks as the shame of letting myself be hurt and abused all these years crashes around me.

"Listen to your heart. Look deeper. Cyan is not what he seems," says my grandmother.

"Yeah, I know that," I grunt. I don't trust him and I never will. I don't care if Mallrie says we need him to help revive the Enkanti Tree. Surely, we can do it without his help. Mallrie said there were still elemental bloodlines lying dormant. Surely we could find another earth elemental. We do not need Cyan.

"It's time to go now, Eli. Be strong." Suddenly, a gush of wind blows open the doors. I give a shaky, brief nod as I weakly get to my feet and head out into the darkness.

The air is cool and crisp as I leave the government building. It whips around me, sending my hair flying in every direction. Heading back to my apartment is the best option. It's closer than navigating through town and the Melsheim Forest to Mallrie's house.

However, I've got so many questions that can't wait till

morning. I need him to discuss all the thoughts and theories plaguing my mind. I want to tell him what I found in Cyan's office.

I *want* to talk to him.

I haven't felt the need to talk to someone for a long time. The urge to run into his arms and tell him everything is overwhelming, but I don't trust myself enough to navigate the streets of Datura *and* the Melsheim Forest. Honestly, I think I am more afraid of getting lost in the forest than coming across a Kailadon.

The click of the public address system snaps me out of my head as it turns on, and a recorded voice calls through the stillness.

"Attention. Please stand by for a message from our mayor." Another click and Edgar's voice, made tinny through the speaker, breaks the silence.

"Good evening, people of Datura. As I am sure you're all aware by now, there has been an increase in attacks from the Flesh-Hunters. Therefore, I would like to remind each and every one of you to stay home. Please do not leave your homes after sunset.

"I have been working closely with the GDO, and we fear these missing persons and the increase in Flesh-Hunter attacks may be linked. We fear there may be one or more people who are *feeding* citizens to the Flesh-Hunters. We are working diligently to track down these individuals. If you know anything or see anyone out after dark, please report it to the General Disciplinary Office during daylight hours. Thank you."

The Public Address System clicks off, and silence once again fills the air. I need to get out of here, and fast. I jog down the alleyway, my feet echoing around me. The hairs on the back of my neck stand up as I get the feeling I am being followed. I keep my head down and move faster, trying to keep my footsteps as light as possible, but even my breathing sounds too loud in the night's stillness.

I slide around the corner, and my heart beats viciously. The smells of death and decay hit me before I see it. At the end of the alleyway, slowly stalking towards me, is the tall, slender body of a Kailadon, its languid footsteps echoing off the walls. I stumble backwards, my body flushing with fear. It continues towards me, slowly hunting its prey. My heart races in my chest as I look around hopelessly.

I can't do this.

Searching for Mallrie on the rooftops, I pray he'll drop into the alleyway between the Kailadon and myself like my personal guardian angel and save me. I feel like a worthless piece of shit. I feel like I've turned back into that weak, helpless girl Beckett manipulated and abused for years. My heart sinks as the awareness that I am utterly alone and have backed myself into a corner washes over me like a cold shower.

The cold brick wall presses at my back as the monster closes in on me. I try to produce a fireball. Cupping my hands together, I try to construct enough heat, but the fear is too much. I look up just in time to see the Kailadon raise its long-bladed arm, ready to strike me down. I raise my arms over my head, terrified of the slow death awaiting me.

But it doesn't come.

Instead, the aggravated clicking sound comes from the creature's throat as if it is struggling against something. I cautiously peek through my arms. The Kailadon *is* struggling against something.

A vine.

The long rope wraps around its arm, holding it above its head. I spin around, searching the rooftops. Cyan stands above me, the sleeves of his business shirt rolled up to his elbows, his defined chest peeking through the top. His biceps flex in the moonlight as he holds onto the vine, saving me from the deadly blow the Kailadon was about to deliver.

"You're no good to me dead." Cyan's voice drifts down through gritted teeth as he strains against the flesh-eating monster. He looks down at me forebodingly, and I just stare back in disbelief. My body goes rigid under his gaze. "I'm not him. I'm not here to save you." He doesn't need to say his name. I know he's talking about Mallrie. My focus returns to the Kailadon as it cuts itself free from Cyan's restraints, lunging towards me.

"Fight it!" growls Cyan from above. I drop to my knees as the monster's arm smashes against the brick. I scurry between its legs to get away, pushing to my feet to run. There is no way I can fight a Kailadon. I'm not ready yet. I have only just inherited my magic, and, as Cyan has so blatantly put it, I have no idea what I am doing. I am not strong enough.

I go to run, but a firm hand grips my wrist, pulling me back, my legs kicking wildly in the air. The aromas of aged whisky and pine hit me in the face. Cyan's scent. His free arm wraps around my chest, pressing me hard against his muscular body.

"I told you I am not him. This is *your* battle," his voice is low and venomous as he spins on his heel so we're facing the Kailadon, stalking towards us, its arm poised to strike. "You're no longer the weak, powerless girl who let Beckett treat you like shit." My body tenses. *How does he know about Beckett?*

I want to run—every inch of my body screams for me to run. Cyan whispers in my ear like a trainer to a wrestler before a match, "You're stronger now. You've evolved." His fingers caress my shoulder, his breath hot in my ear, sending a shiver through my body, but his touch does not frighten me. *"Quit playing the damsel in distress,"* Cyan growls as he pushes me towards the Kailadon. My legs feel heavy under my weight without the support of Cyan at my back. I feel as if I am going to fall.

But I don't. I stand my ground. The Kailadon is all but upon me, its arm raised, ready to deliver a crushing blow. Cyan's words buzz in my head. *"Quit playing the damsel in distress."*

He's right. I am no longer powerless and weak.

Even before I gained my magic, I had created a stronger version of myself, promising I would let no one else hurt me like Beckett had. Why should the Kailadons be any different? *Cyan is right.* I hate to admit that, and I never would out loud, but in the safety of my own head, he is right. I don't need Mallrie to save me. I can save myself. The fire is burning through my body. Just before the Kailadon's heavy body presses against me, I steady my hands into position. The monster knocks my feet out from underneath me, forcing me backwards. My head cracks against the cobblestone street beneath me with a sickening sound that reminds me of someone dropping a watermelon from a window. I look up, and my vision is hazy from the fall. The monster threateningly unzips its mouth, baring its razor-sharp teeth. The putrid stench of rotten flesh suffocates me as it brings its face closer to mine. It makes a satisfying clicking sound. The Kailadon's sharp limb traces down my arm, the vicious sting as it slices the thinnest layer of skin from my body. I let out an agonised scream.

"Stop waiting for *him* to save you!" Cyan's voice calls irately through the alleyway. I crane my neck as he leans casually against the brick wall, his arms folded across his chest. His knuckles are white from his balled-up fists. It looks like it's taking all of his self-control not to step in and help. I look back at the Kailadon as it brings a sliver of my flesh to its mouth.

I can feel the fire burning through me. No one will save me. Cyan will watch me die before he steps in, and Mallrie isn't here. I was foolish to think he'd always be here to save me. Tears sting my eyes. I push my hips forward, trying to free my hands as I press them firmly against the Kailadon's chest. I look into its cold, faceless profile, its lips dripping blood onto my chest, its arm going for another piece of me. I grit my teeth as I feel the fire burning through my body into my hands.

"Fuck you!" I growl as my fingers ache from the heat. The Kailadon flings its head back as it lets out a blood-curdling scream. Its body convulses against my hands, and it stumbles, freeing me. I scramble to my feet. My head is spinning from getting up suddenly. I can feel blood dripping down my arm from where the Kailadon cut a section of my skin away. I raise my arms and draw my flaming arrow. This time, it's a burning blaze filled with my strength and fortitude.

I can feel its power between my fingers. I let out a steady breath and release the arrow. It flies straight and true through the air and into the heart of the Kailadon. The monster falls to its knees. Thick, black blood oozes from its mouth. As my arrow extinguishes, the lifeless body falls to the ground. I stare at the motionless creature before me.

I did it, I think, astonishment pulsating through me like a drug.

"I did it," I mutter, my legs weak and my head spinning from the high. My knees buckle under my weight. Cyan's arms slide under me, catching me before I fall. I look up at him. He looks different in the moonlight. Or maybe it's just the high of protecting myself and the encouraging push from him. My heart skips a beat. I can see a strange resemblance between Mallrie and him. They have similar eyes, yet they're different; Cyan's a deeper shade than Mallrie's. Where Mallrie's are bright, like how I imagine the ocean shines under the sun, Cyan's are how I guess the sea at night or during a storm must look. I push myself away on shaky legs. "I'm fine."

His lips curl into a sly smile. "Of course you are, love."

"I knew this was a trap," I spit.

He raises an eyebrow and gives me the same look Mallrie does when I've amused him. "A trap, you say?"

"Yeah, you wanted me to lead you back to Mallrie's." My voice breaks as his dark eyes look down at me. Cyan laughs like I just told him a hilarious joke, making my blood boil and leaving me feeling as if I have misunderstood this whole evening.

Fuck, I hate this man, I think. His laugh reverberates off the cold brick walls and damp cobblestone around us. I shove him away and storm off, heading towards my apartment. I'll have to wait till morning to get back to Mallrie's. Even if Cyan wasn't following me back there, I don't trust him enough not to have some ulterior motive.

Cyan matches my pace, walking casually next to me. "Do you seriously think I don't know where my own brother lives?" I raise my chin, ignoring him. I have no idea what his motives are. My head is spinning from the pain cascading through my arm and my head after colliding with the unforgiving cobblestone.

"Oh, what? Misnac got your tongue?" Cyan teases. "Where are we going?" I dig my heels as he spins to face me.

"*We* are not going anywhere. *I* am going home. I honestly don't care what hole you decide to crawl back into."

He presses a hand to his chest, the tattoos peeking under his black shirt illuminated in the moonlight. It takes all my self-control not to want to study every one of them. I always found tattoos alluring, like getting a glimpse into a person's soul. Something about Cyan's tattoos has intrigued me. "You wound me, Eliana. So spiteful. What have I ever done to you?" He chuckles darkly. I push him out of my way.

"Let's see, how about the kidnappings? Oh, you pointed a fucking gun at my head. You literally *just* tortured me a few hours ago. You're a fucking psycho, Cyan!" I can feel the fire burning inside me; I can feel myself about to lose control.

"Ah, yes, *that*," he says mockingly. "But *I* also just taught you to fight for yourself. You can't tell me our favourite hero has done the same?"

A feral growl passes from my lips. "We're working on it." Cyan's hand wraps around my mouth, pulling me tight against his body. I struggle under his grip. He shushes me impatiently.

He fucking shushed me while his hand is around my mouth!

His breath is warm against my ear, his scent enveloping me in pine and whisky.

It's intoxicating. *Fuck him!*

I bite his hand hard. The metallic taste of blood licks at my lips. Cyan curses, dropping his hand, and I run for it. "Godsdamnit, Eliana!" he curses. I glance over my shoulder. As he slowly looks up from his hand, a small trickle of blood runs down his wrist. Our eyes meet over the distance, and a slow curve of his lips turns into a satisfied grin as he starts chasing after me. I run faster than I think I've ever done in my life. There's something sinister about the way he is stalking me—like he's enjoying the chase. Like this is all just some game to him.

I know I shouldn't, but I can't help but look over my shoulder again. Hoping that he hasn't closed the distance yet, my heart sinks, entrapment biting at my heels as he chases after me. Finally, I round a corner and run headfirst into a Kailadon, its weight pressing me against the hard ground. It clicks favourably that it found the source of the blood it could smell. The monster's mouth slowly unzips as it drags its face up my bleeding arm. My stomach churns, and I grit my teeth as it runs its sharp fangs along the exposed skin, opening the wound more. I struggle under its weight.

Focus, Eliana! You can do this! I tell myself, anger heating my body. The monster scrambles off me onto the floor, and I rise assertively. The Kailadon is climbing back to its feet. I wait for it to regain its footing. I want it to feel like it has a chance—that's if it can feel anything at all. It finally rises onto its feet, towering above me. I draw up my arms, my flaming arrow burning strong as I release it swiftly into the Kailadon's head. It stumbles backwards into the wall, writhing in pain. I fire another arrow into its chest, then another. Finally, I stand over the lifeless body.

No longer the helpless damsel in distress.

Cyan's footsteps grow louder as I draw up another arrow in anticipation of him. He raises his hands in defence. Blood trickles down the side of his face, and his clothes seem damp as if he ran into a Kailadon of his own. Which wouldn't be unusual, but seeing Cyan all bloody and dishevelled when I know he'd be able to take down a Kailadon...

I look at him in shock. He was right behind me. If a Kailadon got him that fast, we must be surrounded... We look at each other for a long moment, examining one another's wounds.

"We've got to get out of here, love." Cyan's arrogant smile is gone. Instead, he looks... almost terrified.

I pull back the arrow tighter, ready to release. "*We* are not going anywhere," I say sternly. The heat of the arrow tingles against my fingers.

"Eliana, you don't understand," Cyan talks slowly, still holding his hands up in defence as if approaching a wild animal. Something moves behind him, tall and dark but too fast to be a Kailadon. I take a diffident step backwards, my heart racing with a fresh wave of adrenaline, primal instincts screaming at every nerve in my body to run from the danger. Cyan looks over his shoulder. Suddenly, a Kailadon smashes into him, knocking him to the ground. If my eyes could widen anymore, my eyebrows would surely fly off the top of my head. This monster was faster and stronger than the one I just slayed.

Its hard line of a mouth *cracks* open.

The sound of breaking bones ricochets inside my head, its jaw dislocating and opening wide enough that it would fit Cyan's entire head into its mouth effortlessly.

He struggles under its weight. Vines break through the surrounding pavement, binding the Kailadon's mouth shut. But the monster breaks them as quickly as if they were made from paper. More vines wrap around its body, fighting on behalf of Cyan as he struggles to get out.

"Eliana!" he growls. "Get the fuck out of here!" This monster is going to kill him. I know it. The way it aggressively attacks. The quick slashes as it breaks through his vines. The way its mouth is inching closer and closer to him as if it might die if it doesn't consume him. Cyan's vines cannot keep up with the rapidity of the Kailadon. Its mouth drops closer to his face, running its sharp fangs down his cheek, splitting it open. He cries out in pain. Something deep inside me stirs at the sound. Blood trickles from the wound down to his jaw and drips onto the cobblestone. The Kailadon's long, forked tongue darts out and laps up the blood. Cyan cringes as he continues attempting to fight off this monster.

I should leave him. Gods know he probably deserves this death. But there's a pull deep in my chest. I know I cannot leave him—not to die like this.

I take a deep breath and release my flaming arrow. It whizzes through the air and through the open mouth of the Kailadon. It looks up at me, and I can see where my arrow has burnt through its throat and out the other side. I draw another arrow, my fingers trembling as it lunges towards me, and fire it quickly again. Finally, my arrow finds its target right between where a pair of eyes should be. Firing again, my flaming arrow flies straight and true into its chest. The Kailadon stumbles backwards enough for me to dive forward, grab Cyan under his arms and pull him away.

"Get the fuck up!" I grunt at him as he staggers to his feet.

"What the fuck are you doing?" he yells back at me. I pull his arm as we start to run away. I glance over my shoulder and see the Kailadon push to its feet. *How is it still alive?*

"Saving your pathetic life!" I shout as I toss a fireball over my shoulder without looking. The sound of vines breaking through the cobblestone has me looking over my shoulder as a wall of thorns magically emerges from the ground. Cyan grabs my arm and pulls me down an alleyway, pressing me against the wall, his body hard against mine as he raises a finger to his lips. The manic clicking of Kailadons surrounds us.

"Fireball, that way!" Cyan jerks his head to the left. But I am already tossing a flaming orb, hitting a monster directly in the head, causing it to stumble backwards. Two large thorns with something oozing from the tips fly out of the ground as Cyan catches them and throws them in the opposite direction, hitting another Kailadon in the head and chest.

He grabs me around my waist, and I struggle against his embrace.

"Don't even think about it," he growls in my ear as I heat my body. A vine cultivates through the opening in the cement where the thorns have broken through. Cyan grabs it and flicks it towards the rooftop like a whip. It latches onto something, and suddenly, my feet have left the ground. I press myself closer to Cyan's powerful body as his magic has the vine pulling us rapidly up the side of the building. The wind rushes around us as I cling to him, afraid he'll let me fall to my death if I don't hang on. We land on the rooftop, and he releases me cautiously, but his arm hovers by my side, ensuring I have my balance. The agitated clicking sound of the strange, mutant Kailadon echoes through the streets as it claws at the building, trying to scale it.

Cyan looks over the rooftop's edge at the monster I just sent three arrows through. I step up beside him, feeling the heat radiating from his body as I join him, peering over the side. We watch as the Kailadon jumps frantically, clawing at the side of the building, trying to get to us.

"Fucking bastard," Cyan curses to himself.

"What?" I ask, but he ignores me.

He catches my wrist in a punishing grip and pulls me away from the ledge. "Has Mallrie taught you how to jump over large distances yet?" he asks darkly as if he already knows the answer.

My mouth pops open as I shake my head. I've seen Mallrie jump from rooftop to rooftop before. Hell, he's even done it while carrying me. But the thought of doing it myself... Well, it's as absurd as living in a town free of flesh-eating monsters.

Cyan pulls his black tie from his back pocket, and every part of me tells me to run, but my legs are frozen. He tugs my arm closer to him and wraps the tie around my wound. I stare at him blankly. My mind is spinning. The events of tonight don't make any sense. Cyan curses darkly, muttering something about Mallrie only thinking with his dick.

He pulls me tight against his side, one arm wrapping around my waist, the other holding my hand closest to him. And for the first time, I don't fight his embrace. Cyan looks at me with gentle, pleading eyes. Kind eyes that seem to say he will not hurt me.

"Stay with me," he whispers. I nod up at him, my skin tingling at his embrace. My grandmother's words echo in my head. *"Trust your heart. It's strong and won't lead you astray... Cyan is not what he seems..."*

His pace quickens as we head towards the edge of the roof.

"Ready?" he asks iniquitously into my ear.

"No," I answer honestly.

"You've got this. Don't think," he says as we fasten our pace. "Jump!" We leap onto the ledge and then push off, flying weightlessly through the air and landing on the next one. My knees buckle on the landing.

"I've got you," Cyan's voice is like silk in my ear as he holds me up, the next ledge getting closer already. "You've got this," he repeats as we push off the ledge and fly through the air. "Ready? Relax your knees." We land on the next roof a bit more gracefully. "Okay, Eliana. Last roof. You're on your own." My heart skips a beat at the way he says my name. Gone is the usual teasing or mocking tone. We press our feet onto the ledge, propelling ourselves over the edge, and my brain finally registers what he said as he lets go of my waist.

"Cyan!" I cry. I feel like I will fall, but I fly gracefully through the air, his hand resting softly on mine. My feet land on the roof, my knees buckling under the weight. His hand presses into mine tightly as he spins me around and back into his embrace. I press my face into his hard chest, shielding the tears pricking at my eyes from him.

"Good work, love." I don't need to look up to hear the smile in his voice. If the devil exists, he'd sound like a gratified Cyan. For a brief moment in the weightless bliss, I could have tricked myself into thinking he wasn't, well, Cyan. I push myself away, but his grip around my waist keeps me close.

"Let go," I grunt. A leopard cannot change its spots. He will never change from being an egotistical, psychopathic dick. He ignores my attempts to free myself as he leads us to the door on the rooftop. And just like that, Cyan is back to being Cyan. He pulls it open smoothly, hauling me inside and slamming the door behind us.

CHAPTER THIRTY-ONE
ELIANA

Standing in the entryway, I can't help but marvel that this apartment is beautiful. Not in the same way that the town is gorgeous. It is probably the nicest place I've ever been to, and I feel totally out of place in its modern and sleek design with all-black finishes.

Black like Cyan's soul, I think as he shoves me into the open-plan living, dining and kitchen area, locking the door behind us. Cyan moves nimbly into the kitchen—it, too, is immaculate. Black finishes form the bench tops to the splashback, and ven the tiny details like the faucet and power outlets. He flicks a switch as he passes, and the backsplash lights up with a warm glow, the marble bench tops glistening in the light. He kicks out a stool on the other side of the island as he rounds it.

"Sit," Cyan demands, his voice rough and pained. I take a wary step forward, feeling out of place, like I am going to stain it with my mere presence. "I said sit, Eliana!" he growls angrily like a switch has been flipped, and the Cyan from the alleyway has revolved back into the arrogant miscreant from the office under the government building. He throws his shirt into the sink, cursing. Long white and red scars brand his back. My mouth falls open on an inhale as I watch the muscles in his back shift the scars. It looks like he's been... whipped. Some are aged into white lines, but others are still red and raw as if he was beaten only recently.

I sit gingerly on the edge of the stool, my fight or flight instincts biting at my heels. I can't help but wonder if this feeling will always be a part of me.

My eyes fall over Cyan—seeing him without a shirt for the first time leaves me a little breathless. He's smaller than Mallrie but just as muscular. A sleeve of intricate patch-work tattoos stretches from his shoulder to his wrist on his right arm and across his chest. My eyes stop at the large open wound across his ribs, blood trickling down his body.

"Are you okay?" I ask without thinking. He clearly isn't okay. The wound is deep, and he's losing a lot of blood.

Cyan doesn't look up at me as he searches through a small first aid kit. "Do I *look* okay?" he replies coldly through gritted teeth.

"No, I just—"

"*Help him,*" my grandmother's voice calls, and I internally roll my eyes.

"*That is the* last *thing I want to do!*" I reply.

"*Help him, Eliana. He is not your enemy,*" she responds, and I wonder how much she can see from the Afterlife because, surely, she is thinking of a different person.

"Do you need any help?" I ask nervously through clenched teeth, remembering how much *help* I was with Mallrie when he was injured.

Cyan looks me up and down, a cocky smile playing at

the edge of his mouth. "I don't think you'll be able to handle this, love." I scoff and round the island. I am well aware that blood apparently makes me woozy as fuck, but I'll be damned if I let him think I can't handle something. I'm still riding a small high from killing that Kailadon all by myself.

Cyan towers over me. I snatch a towel hanging over the oven and run it under the sink. The cool water washes over my own blood-covered hands as I wet the towel. My eyes catch the sight of the water turning red. My stomach lurches, remembering how badly I handled stitching up Mallrie—well, how well I handled *not* stitching up Mallrie. His wound wasn't nearly as bad as this. I spin on my heel, taking a deep breath. Cyan leans casually against the bench, watching me.

What's with these men looking utterly unaffected when they're injured? They are definitely brothers, I muse, internally rolling my eyes. I press the damp towel hard against his wound. Cyan's quiet *oomph* is music to my ears.

"Enjoying yourself there, love?" I look up to meet his intense gaze.

I smile sweetly back. "Wouldn't want you to get an infection."

Cyan chuckles darkly. "And here I thought you didn't care."

"I don't," I snap sharply.

"Whatever helps you sleep at night, love." He rubs the back of his neck with his other arm, flexing his muscles in my face, and I have to look away before my face flushes.

Pressing the towel harder against his wound, he curses my name, and I have to bite my lip to stop from smiling. "Stop that," he growls. I pull away the towel. The wound is deep, and my stomach churns at the sight of it. Cyan's hand gently touches mine, his voice turning sympathetic. "You don't have to do this, Eliana." I push his hand aside, trying to figure out the best way to stitch this up, wiping up as much blood as possible around the wound. Unfortunately, my gag reflex is working double time, and I struggle to keep myself together.

"Do you trust me?" I sigh, looking up at him. I've got an idea. It's a bad idea, but I don't voice that. Cyan tweaks a dark eyebrow, examining me, and my heart flutters uncertainly. He holds his hand out for me. My stomach twists, and not just with the nausea of all the blood. I cautiously placed my hand in his. Cyan wrings our hands so he is on top. His warm hand leaves mine as he turns his palm face up. A small cluster of leaves appears out of thin air. He rubs them between his hands, crushing them, their aroma perfuming the air between us. He tips the ground herbs into my waiting palm.

"Don't get too carried away," he says quietly. His voice has a sceptical note to it like he knows what I'm about to do.

"Mm, don't tempt me." I tease. Cyan returns my smile, which helps ease the nervous butterflies fluttering in my stomach. He tilts his head back, shutting his eyes. I can hear him trying to steady his breathing.

He doesn't trust me. I can tell because his muscles are coiled tight, ready to strike. Why should he trust me? If roles were reversed, I wouldn't trust him.

I study his face for a moment while his eyes are shut, and he can't see. Not that it matters—because it definitely does *not*—but he really is handsome. The sharp line of his jaw is taut as he grits his teeth. His bare chest rises and falls in a steadier rhythm, though he occasionally sucks in a sharp breath.

Why shouldn't *I trust him?* As far as I know, he's been telling me the truth about everything.

I take a deep breath in through my nose as I carefully work the crushed leaves into Cyan's open wound and smear them around. The warmth of his insides on my fingers... *Oh, gods, I'm going to be sick!* Cyan winces at the pain, and I quickly withdraw my hand. The nausea is instantly gone, my stomach still stirring, but with concern. I look up at him sympathetically. His eyes are still shut, a pained expression pinching his face.

"No. Don't stop." Cyan wraps his hand around mine. My mind screams to recoil from his embrace, but I don't. Instead, I let him carefully guide my fingers back inside the wound. I bite down hard on my lip until the metallic taste of blood tickles against my tongue. For some deranged reason, I don't want to hurt Cyan—at least, not like this.

Pushing the concoction deeper into his wound, our fingers intertwine effortlessly from the slickness of his blood. He guides my fingers around the wound until the crushed leaves have dissolved. Cyan slides his bloody fingers out.

A wave of nerves crashes into me as I look up at him. I've never done anything like this before. I am not even sure it's the right thing to do. Bile rises in my throat. I barely lasted two days at medical school before I dropped out, unable to stomach the lessons or the memories they stirred up.

My fingers start to tremble. Cyan meets my gaze, and I can see the internal battle in his eyes. *I can't do this.* I know I can't, and so does he. I try to pull my hand away, but his grip tightens around mine. "You can do this, Eliana. I trust you."

My knees go weak, and my mouth parts. I drag my gaze up his body from the wound to meet his eyes. "What did you just say?" I breathe, unsure if I heard him correctly.

Cyan's brows bunch together, his eyes like a pair of green tourmaline stones. "You heard me."

My lip quivers, and I can't stop the swell of emotion that clogs my throat, but I blink hard, forcing it back down. I look at Cyan—really look at him, past the arrogant asshole, past him holding a gun to my head. My heart beats faster. "I-I don't want to hurt you," I admit quietly.

"You can't hurt someone who's already hurting," he says, not meeting my eyes as he guides my hand over his wound. My heart sinks. I know he's not talking about the injury. "Do it," he says as he gives my wrist a small, reassuring squeeze.

I take a steadying breath as I heat my hand. Cyan works with me as we try to close the wound as best as possible.

"Ready?" I look up at him. My hand is so hot my blackened fingertips have paled. He closes his eyes, bracing himself. His jaw is set tightly as he gives me a stern nod. I steadily press my fingers along the laceration of his skin. The blood sizzling underneath emits a burnt, metallic, coppery aroma. Cyan grunts and curses, his body tensing.

"I'm sorry. I'm sorry," I ramble. I want to stop. Every part of my body screams to stop as His body tenses and spasms at my touch. "Almost done. You're doing great," I say as I slowly and carefully run my fingers along the wound, the heat from my fingers sealing it closed. I'm not sure who I am trying to convince more. "Done," I announce, pulling my hand away and giving it a quick shake to dispel the heat.

Cyan's knees buckle under him, and he falls forward into my arms, his body tense and shaking. "Fuck, are you okay?" I try to look into his eyes as his forehead rests against my shoulder. Panic bubbles up inside my chest.

I did something wrong. It was too much. I should have stopped. Cyan places a hand heavily on my shoulder, forcing himself to stand. Still, the cauterization's shock makes him tremble and unsteady on his feet. "I'm fine," he grunts unconvincingly.

"Oh, shut it," I say as I steady his weight back onto my shoulder. "Which way to the bathroom?"

Cyan curses my name and mumbles under his breath something about me being stubborn and a pain in his ass, but leads me into the large bathroom down the hall.

Again, it is all finished in modern black marble. A large claw-tooth bath sits against the wall beside a walk-in shower. I lean him against the wall as I draw the bath. Cyan braces himself against the wall, his biceps flexing as he holds himself steady. His chest glistens with sweat and blood as he steps up to my side. As I test the water's temperature, various leaves and flowers fall from his fingertips like rain into the bath. He straightens up, his hands slowly undoing his pants.

"I've got it from here. Unless you'd like to join me, love?"

Gods, I hate this man. But my body hasn't gotten the memo. I bite my lip as Cyan's fingers slowly unzip his pants. I watch in disbelief as the zipper drops lower and lower...

I turn on my heels and head for the door, blinking rapidly, trying to rid that image from my mind. "Pass," I say sternly, slamming the door behind me. I lean against the wall, trying to catch my breath. My heart is fluttering wildly, and I've got a sick feeling of guilt in the pit of my stomach. I would never cheat on anyone. I've been on the other side and know how horrible it feels. The sounds of Cyan kicking off his shoes and his pants dropping to the floor snap me out of my head. I walk away from the sound of the water splashing around his body.

The shock of this evening's events comes crashing down around me as I walk back into the open-plan kitchen. First, finding that folder with people clearly getting experimented on in Cyan's office. Then, he encouraged me to fight a Kailadon, *actually* killing the monster. Then, being chased through the streets by Cyan. The mutant Kailadon, learning to jump across the buildings—which I still cannot wrap my head around—is humanly possible. Physics was never my strong subject at school, but even I know this should defy gravity's laws.

My whole body starts to tremble with cold flushes. My throat is dry, my chest feels tight and the ringing in my ears warns me that I am going to faint. I frantically search through the cupboards, looking for a cup. My hands shake violently as I clutch the glass and fill it with water. I need to steady myself. *What was that breathing exercise again?* My head is aching too much to focus.

Gripping onto the marble countertops tightly, the objects on the bench meld together as my vision blurs. I raise the glass, but before the water touches my lips, it slips from my hand, shattering on the floor. I drop, and the smooth, cold timber floors bite at my knees. Pushing myself back onto my ass, I pull my knees up to my chest and place my head between them, trying to steady my breath. The ringing in my ears is silencing everything else around me.

Suddenly, a hand caresses my back. Someone's calling

my name, but it sounds so far away, even though I know they're standing directly behind me.

"Mallrie?" I whimper, trying to look up, but the splitting pain in my head makes it unbearable. He scoops me up into his arms. I rest my head against his warm, bare chest, closing my eyes as I am carried off. I take a deep breath. The aroma of sandalwood and citrus surrounds me. "Mallrie." I breathe in his scent and relax in his warm embrace, but it's wrong. *Something* about his smell feels artificial; it has a subtle undertone of magic. My cheek is damp where it rests against his pectoral. *Am I crying?* I don't think I am. Another droplet of water runs down his chest onto my cheek.

Looking up, I meet Cyan's stormy green eyes as he carries me effortlessly over to the couch. I open my mouth to say something—anything.

"Don't," he says. The humming in my ears is still so loud, but I could swear he sounds… disappointed.

He carefully sets me on the couch and wraps a blanket around my shoulders. I watch as Cyan walks over to the window with just a towel wrapped around his waist, his body still dripping wet. He must have heard the glass smash and come running. He jerks open the window and makes a raspy, caw sound.

What is he doing? I must have really hit my head hard on something because I swear Cyan just imitated a crow.

The street. I remember cracking my head against the cobblestone alleyway when the Kailadon attacked. I must have some sort of concussion.

Suddenly, a large black crow with milky white eyes lands on the windowsill, cawing happily at Cyan. It's easily twice the size of a regular crow.

I try to sit up further. Cyan twists at the waist, pointing

a long finger in my direction. "Sit back down," he growls, and I instantly slump back into his soft couch.

He returns his attention to the crow—which surely cannot be real—and affectionately runs a finger down its back. "Tell Mallrie to come get his woman." His voice is bitter and distant. The crow caws, acknowledging the request, and turns, taking flight into the darkness. Cyan walks off to the bedroom without saying another word.

CHAPTER THIRTY-TWO
ELIANA

My mind is spinning from the events of the past few days. Gingerly resting my head on the back of the white couch, I close my eyes against the pounding ache that's settled behind my eyes. Cyan is bottling my mind. His actions are so erratic. One minute, he's got men chasing me down, capturing me, holding me hostage, torturing and tormenting me. Then, the next, he lets me go. He's encouraging me to *fight*. To believe in myself. He's *teaching* me to jump unnaturally over buildings. Letting me help. *Why did I help him?* I should have just let him bleed out. Mallrie and I would have found another way to restore the magic in the Enkanti Tree without him.

And the *flirting...* Cyan was undeniably flirting with me back in the bathroom. My cheeks heat at the memory. The heat spreading across my face abruptly turns cold. *What was it that attacked us?* That was no regular Kailadon. The way it moved so quickly, the way its jaw dislocated, the popping and cracking sound of its bones sends a shudder down my spine at the memory.

Cyan walks back into the living room in a pair of black sweats with a T-shirt flung over his shoulders, his blonde hair pulled up into a messy bun on top of his head. He tosses the shirt over to me as he passes into the kitchen. "You're getting blood all over my couch," he grunts. I lean forward and realise how much of his blood is on me. I practically jump off the couch, a pang of guilt hitting me in the chest that I've ruined his perfectly white sofa. But then I remember *whose* couch it is and whose blood I am covered in. I unfold the shirt but notice Cyan leaning against the bench, a glass of whisky in one hand and a very expensive-looking bottle on the bench. An arrogant smirk lingers at the edge of his mouth. I storm off to the bathroom.

"Egotistical prick," I mutter, loud enough for him to hear as I slam the door behind me. I swear I can hear him chuckle from the other side.

The bath is still filled with water. Cyan clearly jumped out when he heard the glass shatter in the kitchen. *Probably just didn't want me breaking his fancy crystal glasses,* I think. *He wouldn't give two shits if I fainted.*

My arm aches. I carefully remove the tie and inspect the raw flesh where the Kailadon tore bloody strips. I splash some water on the wound. I catch my reflection in the mirror. A splatter art of red and black blood splashed across my face, and exhaustion creeps in and around my eyes. I run my fingers through my hair in an attempt to smooth it out a bit and splash my face with water, but it doesn't help. I strip out of my bloodied clothes and pull on the shirt Cyan lent me. It smells like him, of the earth. The fresh, musky scent of pine with the hint of whisky—a pleasant mix. *How does he always smell of whisky?* I lift it up to my nose for a brief moment, inhaling deeply.

As a child, I always longed for these grounding, earthy smells. Being a prisoner in a town filled with cement and brick, the closest I could get to this relaxing aroma was when I would sneak to the edge of town after school and lay on the grass, careful enough not to go too far away from the safety of the buildings. The shirt is long enough to fall to my thighs and hang loosely off my shoulder. I tug at the collar, but it keeps sliding down. Finally, giving up the fight with a sigh, I walk back into the living room. Cyan sits in a grey provincial armchair in the room's corner, a large flat-screen television hanging on the wall beside him. He focuses on the amber liquid he's swirling musingly in his hand. I sit back on the couch, noticing that the dirt and blood stains are gone, replaced with a damp patch and a strong scent of fabric cleaner. I fold my arms across my chest. "What the fuck attacked us, Cyan?" I ground out through clenched teeth.

"Move over," he says, not looking up from his glass. "Don't sit where it's trying to dry."

I glare at him. If he looked up from his stupid drink, he would have seen that I wasn't stupid enough to sit in a wet patch.

I'm angry. I feel like I am getting totally screwed over. I'm sick of living in the dark. I want answers, and I want them *now*. There's a long silence. I don't break eye contact with Cyan. He's sizing me up, seeing if I will crack. But even if we have to sit here all night, I will hold my ground. I will not be the first to break. "I'm not telling you shit," he says darkly, downing the amber liquid and pouring himself another.

"I just fucking saved your life from whatever that was!" I seethe.

"You mean a Kailadon?" Cyan raises a single eyebrow.

"Or are you still naively calling them *Flesh-Hunters*?" he asks jeeringly.

"That's bullshit. You and I both know that wasn't a Kailadon. What was it?"

He chuckles and sips his whisky. "You're a little presumptuous, aren't you, love?"

"Cyan," I prompt as he finishes his drink, pouring glass number three. "Would you have preferred I left you to die, huh?"

He chuckles darkly. The sound skitters along my bones as he raises the glass of amber liquid to his lips. "Would have made my life easier," he says as the whisky brushes against his lips.

"Don't say that," I say before I can think. My heart aches to imagine Cyan lying in the street, the mutant creature. I don't even know what it would have done. It didn't act like a normal Kailadon. It had a hunger in how it moved, like it would have only been satisfied once it *devoured* Cyan whole, wiping his existence from the earth. I shake my head, the idea making me feel sick.

"Don't act like you wouldn't have enjoyed watching the show," he says darkly. My stomach twists angrily, and my magic burns under my skin.

"No. I wouldn't. Even if you're an asshole, you don't deserve that."

Cyan chortles loudly. "Yeah, bet you didn't think the same about old Beckett."

My brows knot together hard. "What did you just say?" My tone is as cold as ice, my skin hot like the flames of hell.

Cyan leans forward, resting his elbows on his knees. "I said. I. Bet. You. Didn't. Think. The same. About. Beckett."

The way he deliberately speaks each word with meticulous care makes me want to watch his entire apartment burn to the ground, a primal anger rising in me. Cyan smiles, sitting back, satisfied with the reaction he provoked. "Don't get me wrong, the bastard got what he deserved." He lifts the glass, taking a careful sip, muttering around the glass, "And then some." He downs the rest of the alcohol, a smirk tugging at his lips as he pours another. I have to repress the urge to roll my eyes. The way he's downing whisky, I won't get any coherent answers from him. "I just wish I was able to get my hands on him first... Oh, wait."

"What the *fuck* is wrong with you?" I shout, sitting up straighter on the couch, tucking my feet under my ass.

Cyan glances at me over the rim of his glass, his features turning deadly serious. "A lot, love."

I shake my head. I know there's a lot wrong with him. "You don't get to say shit like that. You *hate* me!"

He presses a hand to his chest mockingly. "You think I hate you? Frankly, Eliana, I'm hurt." His voice is a deep rumble as he suppresses a laugh.

I roll my eyes. "I know it's hard for you, but can you *try* not to be an asshole?"

"I'm serious though. *If* I got my hands on him, I would have taken him somewhere cold and dark. Somewhere no one would hear him scream."

"STOP!" I'm on my feet before he can finish his sentence. Cyan looks up at me, stunned. His eyes scan over my body at how his shirt clings to the curve of my breasts and hips, to where it ends on my mid-thighs. "How do you even know about Beckett?"

Cyan nods towards the glass of whisky on the coffee table before me. "Drink with me, love."

"Tell. Me. How. Cyan," I say through gritted teeth.

He sighs. "I've been watching you." A chill runs through my body, paralysing me where I stand. His words bounce around in my head like a small ball bouncing off the walls. "So has Mallrie," he adds bitterly. The ice inside my body, freezing me in place, shatters into a million tiny pieces, and I fall back onto the couch. I open my mouth to speak, but nothing comes out. Cyan moves, picking up the spare glass and pressing it into my hands. "Drink, love. It'll help with the shock."

My hands are shaking, but I carefully lift the glass. The alcohol slips across my tongue, a warm, burning sensation following behind. It's not my preferred drink, but it's not unpleasant. I have always liked the smell of whisky, and I love it when it's in an iced coffee or a banshee.

"W-why?" I stutter. My heart beats loudly in my ears, and my head spins.

"Because you're *special*." The way he says it sends the butterflies in my stomach on a rampage, and my cheeks burn bright. "Remember how Charleston said any witch to reclaim their magic would pay the price with their child's life?" That sweet feeling in my stomach turns sour in an instant. The butterflies have twisted into knots. I take another sip of whisky, nodding silently. "Your grandmother."

I start shaking my head. "No. No," I blurt out. Mallrie has already told me my grandmother was a witch. I've got her grimoire as proof—well, had.

I know where Cyan is going, and I can't hear it. I push to my feet, pacing in front of the couch. "Edgar was more than happy to keep Charleston's promise."

"No. No. No. Cyan. No!" My voice shakes, but he just keeps talking, ignoring my protests.

"Where Charleston promised death, Edgar—well..."

"CYAN, STOP!" Tears stream down my face, and my body shakes with trepidation. "*Please*," I whisper.

Cyan sighs sadly. Before I know it, he's downed his glass of whisky and crossed the room, holding me close to him, shushing me quietly as I sob loudly against his warm chest. I should push him away. Slap him. Punch him. Run.

But I am so tired. This is too much. I can't do this. Cyan's arms hold me close. "I'm not going to lie to you, love, and I am also not going to fucking sugarcoat this." He pushes me away slightly, his fingers pinching my chin, forcing me to look at him. "This is *your* story. You deserve to hear it." Even with tear-rimmed eyes, I nod. "Your grandmother was smart, Eliana. She kept her magic a secret for a long time. It wasn't until your mother was pregnant with you that Edgar caught wind." My knees give way, but Cyan holds me up, and his hand gently caresses my back.

I take a deep breath. The smell of fresh rain on grass fills my senses as if it has just blown in on the wind, the aroma masking Cyan's of pine and whisky. It wraps around me like a blanket, calming me ever so slightly.

It has to be his magic, I think between sobs. "He... He killed my m-mother?" I look up at Cyan. His dark, mossy eyes are emotionless. I try to push away, but he holds me still against him.

"I'm sorry," he whispers into my hair, his lips brushing over my head. It feels as if someone has tossed me into a brick wall. My body gives out entirely, and I am a mess in his arms. He scoops me up into his strong arms. I don't protest. I can't. My entire world has just been pulled out from underneath me. I always thought I killed my mother. I blamed myself. I believed my father also blamed me for her death. But, if it weren't for Edgar, she would still be alive. I would know who my mother is—was. My heart cracks. I can literally feel it tearing itself apart with every heart-wrenching sob.

A blanket is wrapped around my shoulders, and I realise Cyan has carefully placed me back on the couch.

He sits on the coffee table before me and rubs the back of his neck. "Eliana," he says softly. "There's more."

I look up at him through swollen eyes, shaking my head. "No. No, I don't want to know." For once in my life, that sense of curiosity isn't burning in my chest, desperate for answers. "I don't want to know," I repeat.

Cyan looks at me, and I hate the pity I see shining in his eyes—eyes that remind me so much of Mallrie. "You need to hear this, love." I shake my head again. "You deserve to know, and if Mallrie won't tell you, I will."

I can hardly make him out of the fuzzy mess before me. "Edgar." Cyan takes a deep breath. "Edgar is sick of living in the shadows of witches. He fears there will be an uprising. He hates that he's powerless against the silent masses that walk amongst him. The paranoia that everyone he encounters has dormant magic just waiting to be unleashed on him. He thinks that if he can somehow grant everyone magic, he will be beloved by all. So no one would live in fear of being powerless, he plans to sell it to cities beyond the Melsheim Forest."

That... That's a lot to take in. My head aches around what Cyan is telling me. A part of me wants to just write off everything he is saying as one big lie. I look up into his stormy green eyes. There is no lie. Cyan is telling the truth. How I know he isn't lying to me, I have no idea. But I know in my heart he's not. He never has.

"What's that got to do with my family?" I don't want to hear the answer, but I know he will tell me, even if I don't ask.

"When your mother was pregnant with you, Edgar got the disquieting idea to do a series of faerie venom injections into your mother's womb. He bribed her physician, who convinced her there was something wrong with the baby. That these shots were going to save you. Instead, they slowly killed your mother. Faerie venom in small doses will temporarily weaken a witch, making their magic inoperable. In large doses…" Cyan doesn't meet my gaze. "It's a slow and painful death." I open my mouth, but he answers the question forming on my tongue before I can even get a syllable out. "Your stubborn ass adapted to the venom. It's truly remarkable how your tiny body extracted the magic. I've studied it for years. Eliana, you're the first ever faerie-witch hybrid."

I think I am going to be sick… My stomach churns, and there's a pain, urging me to double over. *So I killed my mother. Slowly and painfully.* If she wasn't pregnant with me, she would probably still have ended up dead, but maybe it wouldn't have been so torturesome. Cyan's hand is on my shoulder, forcing my head between my knees. "Breathe, love." I didn't even realise I slipped into a panic attack. "In and out. That's it," Cyan says in gentle encouragement. "Just like that." His hand strokes my back gently, forcing the sickening feeling to slowly subside. "You good?"

I nod self-consciously. This sensitive side of him makes me feel uneasy. I don't want to be comforted by him. He's literally had a gun pointed at my head. He's locked me in his office, tied to a chair. I should hate him. Yet, this sensitive, kind Cyan—the one who speaks of what he'd do to those who hurt me—well, he's alluded to what he did or would have done to Beckett. I don't hate it. I want to, I really do.

His hand is gone, and I hear the tap in the kitchen running. By the time I lift my head, Cyan is back, holding a glass of water. I give him a small, appreciative smile and sip it slowly. Damn him for being kind. *Who the fuck are you?* I want to scream in his face.

"Edgar wants you dead."

I choke on the water, spitting it all over Cyan, who tilts his head, giving me a displeased expression. "What?" I ask, wiping my mouth with the back of my hand. "You can't just announce someone wants me dead and not expect a reaction."

Cyan gives me a look as he wipes his hands down his abs. There is a desire, deep, *deep* within me, that's screaming to grab his arm so I can look at all the tiny tattoos that make up his sleeve. "Come on, love. You really hadn't put it together that he wants you dead?"

"No, why—"

"Why do you think I keep kidnapping you? For your sunny personality and riveting conversations?"

"I-I didn't think... Are you—*Oh, gods.*" I jump up, almost knocking him over. Then, running into the kitchen, I pull a large cooking knife from the knife block, hands shaking. I stare at the man who's going to kill me, knowing deep down I won't be able to kill him. Tears prick at my eyes as he advances towards me. "Cy-Cyan, please. I-I can't—I won't."

Cyan looks at me. His expression is soft. Which only makes things worse. "Eliana. Put down the knife," he says calmly. There's the sound of a lock clicking, the front door swinging open, and before I know what's happened, Cyan has disarmed me. The kitchen knife is in his grip as he spins me out of the kitchen, away from the knives.

Mallrie stalks over to us, and I run into his arms, sobbing. He gives me a once-over, obviously checking to ensure I am not hurt. His brows press together, and his eyes darken as he notices a single trail of blood tracking down my arm from under Cyan's tie. He quickly kisses the top of my head and steps around me.

Cyan drops the knife onto the island bench, backing up, his hands raised in defence. "Mal—"

Mallrie clutches Cyan around the throat and pushes him back against the wall.

CHAPTER THIRTY-THREE
MALLRIE

Cyan holds onto my forearm, my hand wrapped around his throat as I smash him against the wall of his apartment. The force cracks the drywall around his shoulders. I bare my teeth in a feral growl at him—

"Yo! Uncle C—"

I whip my head over my shoulder at the source of the interruption. He walks into the apartment with his arm raised in a peace sign, his fingers stained white from air elemental magic against his dark skin. His short black hair is spiked up, making it look like he stuck his finger in a power socket. *Which wouldn't surprise me.* He nervously wiggles the small, black piercing below his lip. His hand reaches down to the long stock whip wrapped up and attached to his belt buckle. "Read the room wrong," Tyler whispers as if that's an appropriate apology. He's young, not yet eighteen, and by Cyan's groan, he's as much of a pain in his side as he has been in mine for these last few hours.

Chelsea quickly wraps an arm around Tyler and steps in front of him, her small, lithe body ready to attack. A pain laces through my chest at Eliana's expression when she sees Chelsea. She thought her best friend was dead. She mourned for her, yet here she stands, healthy, whole and completely in control of her magic. Eliana's head whips from glaring at Chelsea to me. She looks at me with jealousy burning in her eyes. I turn back to Cyan because I cannot fathom what Eliana could be jealous of. I pull him away from the wall, only to smash him back into it again. "You better start talking, Cyan, or I swear to the Fates, if it was you who hurt her, I will be the last thing you see before you talk to them," I growl.

My magic thrums through my veins, urging me to drive my sword through his gut if he touched a single hair on Eliana's head. One of Cyan's vines wraps around my throat before I can even move. His Gymnosporia Buxifolia thorns press against my throat, injecting me with their toxins. I can feel my magic slip away. He was always forward-thinking about his herbology studies. His teachers always praised his ingenuitive thinking and research in his elemental field, even if it scared them.

A lick of heat presses at the back of my neck, and the vine withers and dies from around my neck. Cyan shoots Eliana a glare over my shoulder. I don't need to turn around to know she is probably returning his glare with one of her own that says, *"Mess around and find out."*

"Talk, Cyan," I say, gripping his throat tighter.

"Well, it's kind of fucking hard when you're cutting off my air supply," he chokes out.

That's fair, I think, dropping his sorry ass into a heap on the floor.

Cyan promptly jumps to his feet and pretends to dust off his lounge pants. *Arrogant bastard.*

"Speak, Cyan," I remind him, my voice dripping with

the promise of violence. I'm older and stronger than him, and he knows that.

"Oh, come on, Mal. Give the big hero act a break, will you?" He pushes past me, crossing the room and slumping back into a grey armchair. He lifts a bottle of single malt whisky and checks how much is left before pouring himself a glass. "You've got your girl. Now go before I call the GDO. I'm sure Edgar wouldn't mind sacrificing a few mortals to capture his time elemental and the hybrid."

I glare at him, lounging in the chair with his legs sprawled as he examines the amber liquid in his glass. I know he's only bluffing. Edgar wouldn't waste his resources dragging us in when he's got a tight leash around Cyan's neck.

"Cyan. Brother…" I soften my tone, looking at him with sympathetic eyes. *How did we get here?* He glares back at me, filled with both self-loathing and resentment towards me.

"Leave. Now. Before I change my mind." He rests his head back against the chair and shuts his eyes. I open my mouth to plead our case with him. Beg for forgiveness— again. Tell him to come home.

But I can't find the words. Instead, Eliana wraps her arm around mine, lacing our fingers together. "Let's go home, Mallrie," she whispers with a hint of urgency in her tone.

My feet are bound to the floor as I spot the angry red wound on Cyan's side. Eliana has done a very rough job of cauterizing the long laceration. There is a call deep inside of me to rush over to my little brother and ensure he is okay. But I know I lost that right long ago. "Cyan… what happened?" I breathe around the pain in my chest.

He skulls the whisky, pushes to his feet and pulls a dagger

from behind the armchair. "Last chance, Mal. I'm not playing around," he says. I can smell the alcohol on his breath, but I know he can handle his liquor better than most. "You know Edgar would love to get his dirty little hands on her. Don't give me a reason to deliver her head on a silver platter for him."

"Don't act like you'd win this fight, Cyan. We both know—" Before I finish my sentence, he has thrown the dagger through the air. My magic hums in my veins, instinctively throwing itself out to enhance my reflexes to protect me. I catch the blade by the handle, mere inches from my face. Anger rushes through me as I throw the dagger back with my elemental speed. It finds its mark in Cyan's shoulder, in the centre of a tattooed rose, the speed and force of my magic knocking his ass back into the chair. Blood seeps from the wound down his chest.

An orchestra of gasps fills the room behind me. I feel Eliana recoil away from me. She hasn't seen what damage my magic can cause. Chelsea steps forward in my peripheral as if she wants to rush to Cyan's side.

"Talk," I ground out through gritted teeth, crossing the room and driving the dagger further into Cyan's shoulder. He stares at me, seething, baring his teeth like a wild animal.

"Tell him what attacked us, Cyan," Eliana says. I glance over my shoulder at her. She stands there with her arms crossed over her chest, his shirt hugging every dip and curve of her body. Just seeing her in his shirt has me seeing red. I shift that anger back to Cyan as I loom over him and twist the blade.

"I told you, love, a *Kailadon*." His voice breaks under the pain, but his face steels into arrogant boredom. Our father was always secretly impressed that no matter what injuries

Cyan took, he always could school his features into a casual, bored expression.

"Bullshit," Eliana seethes. "What are those files in your office? What's FSXK24-56-75? What are you and Edgar doing to those people?"

"I already told you, love. Edgar thinks that if he can grant everyone magic, he will be beloved by all."

"So he's trying to grant mortals magic?" Eliana asks.

I stand as still and silent as a statue over Cyan, my hand still gripping the dagger. "Rise of the witches. Has a nice ring to it, doesn't it?" He smirks.

"It's not working?" I whisper. Cyan's eyes move from Eliana's back to me.

"Of course not. Now"—he grips my hand, holding the dagger—"get the fuck out of my apartment." In a blur, Cyan pulls the knife out of his shoulder and swings it, slashing me across the chest. He throws it towards Eliana, missing her head by mere millimetres before it slams into the wall next to Chelsea and Tyler. Eliana screams, and I know the flashbacks of Beckett are playing like a movie through her mind. I punch Cyan in the wound, sending him staggering back into the armchair. I stalk over to where Eliana has her arms wrapped around her head, protecting herself from the oncoming attack. Tucking her under my arm, I whisper in her ear, "Come with me, little doe. We're going home." Her body relaxes in my embrace as I lead her towards the door. I jerk my chin at Chelsea, signalling that she grabs Tyler and follows suit.

We leave the apartment in silence, Chelsea and Tyler following behind. The cool, crisp air greets us as I kick open the door to the rooftop. The streets below are unnervingly quiet. I knew Edgar was experimenting on people, but on the Kailadons, too? He does not know what he's fucking around with. Something Cyan told me years ago rings in my mind. *"It is better to be feared than loved."* I wonder if he came to that on his own or if he learnt it from Edgar.

I pull Eliana to a stop before me and cup her face in my hands. She's so small, still so fragile. "Are you okay?" I ask. "Did he hurt you?"

She is quiet for a moment as she fiddles with the hem of Cyan's shirt. I run my hands from her face down her arms, and she winces. I pull the sleeve of the shirt up to find the blood trail's source. Again, Eliana winces as the cool air rushes against the bloody, raw skin, which has my magic thrumming to the surface. The skin surrounding the wound is red and aggravated.

"It's fine. I'm fine," she says quickly and unconvincingly as she tries to move my hand away. A Kailadon got to her. It tasted her flesh. My vision blurs as rage pulses through me. *I should have been there to protect her.* Jealousy crashes through me, and my knuckles ache as I press my hands into fists. It should have been *me* there for Eliana, to clean her wounds and ensure she was okay. Not Cyan.

"It was a Kailadon, not Cyan," Eliana says quickly, as if it wasn't obvious. "I-I killed it." She smiles sweetly up at me, proud of herself. As she should be. Fuck, I am damn proud of her.

I return her smile and try to bite back the pain in my voice. "Impressive. And…" I gesture to Cyan's shirt. Her cheeks and the tops of her ears burn red, and suddenly, her body tenses as if she's expecting me to accuse her of fucking Cyan and to lash out in the same way Beckett would have.

I know she didn't fuck him. She hates his guts too much to even get close enough to kiss him. I open my mouth to calm her down, tell her I know it's not what she's probably thinking, but she beats me to it.

"Cyan got attacked by—well, I'm not exactly sure what it was. It was like a mutated Kailadon. It was ridiculously fast, and its jaw"—a shudder rolls through her—"snapped! And broke open. It took three of my fire arrows, and it was fine." She's rambling on in the way she calls word vomit.

"Little doe," I say, cupping her cheek in my hand. Her body relaxes at the gentle touch. "Are you okay?" I repeat.

She nods. "I was just covered in a lot of his blood."

My back stiffens, and I glance back over to the door. There's so much I want to do. I want to take Eliana home, get her cleaned up and safely tucked into my bed. But I also want to storm back into Cyan's apartment and demand answers. *A mutated Kailadon? What was he thinking, allowing Edgar to do such shit?* And yet, I want to check to make sure my brother is okay. I made myself a promise to protect him, and I've been letting him down.

I need to get Eliana home and clean this wound before it gets infected. Silently, I curse Cyan for not taking better care of her. Though he had Hesper relay a message to come and get her quickly. Wrapping my hands gently around the back of her neck, I pull Eliana closer and kiss the top of her head.

"Is there anything else?" I ask her quietly so the others don't hear.

Eliana's eyebrows pinch together, a small line forming between them. "He said... that you've both been watching me. That Edgar experimented on me when I was... That I'm a-a..." Eliana takes a step away from my touch. The pinch of her brows shifts from confusion to anger to... betrayal.

I rub my hand along my jawline. *Fucking Cyan. Why did*

you have to go tell her everything? Well, not everything, *I hope to the Fates.* I nod slowly. "A faerie-witch hybrid," I answer.

"So it's true?" Eliana takes another step away from me. I know all the trust we had slowly built has either entirely crashed away or is hanging on by a precarious thread.

"It's not what you think," I say, lifting my hands to show her I am not trying to hurt her.

"Oh, yeah?" she snaps. I can see the walls she's throwing up between us, breaking my heart. "How is it meant to look? You and your *brother* have been watching me for how long? Since I was born? No, before. You sat by and watched my family die! You sat by and watched as I mourned my only friend's '*death*'." Eliana throws a scathing look over my shoulder to where Chelsea and Tyler are standing awkwardly, pretending not to be listening in on our conversation.

I knew keeping these secrets would break her trust in me. I just hoped we would have more time to work through her past trauma, so when I told her the truth, she wouldn't... Well, act like this.

I was doing it to protect her.

"What about everything with Beckett? Did you..." Her voice breaks, and she looks like she won't be able to finish her sentence.

"Yes," I say solemnly. "We've been watching you since Edgar found out your mother was pregnant and started injecting her with the faerie venom." Eliana's bottom lip quivers as she holds back her tears. "Cyan came to me and told me what Edgar was doing. What the results from the practitioner were saying—that you were adapting to the venom." I straighten my back. There is no easy way to say this. "I'm sorry. We couldn't intervene. Time is a very delicate mechanism." My voice is cold and emotionless, and I can see the wounds my words are creating.

"*We* couldn't intervene, or *you* wouldn't intervene?" Eliana's voice trembles.

So she knows it was ultimately my decision to let the venom trials continue in her mother. Whether Cyan told her or she's reached that conclusion alone doesn't matter. "I wouldn't allow an intervention," I say.

Eliana opens her mouth to speak. "I did approach Beckett," I say quickly. "It was after he..." The memory of the smug bastard walking down the cobblestone street to the local pub and brothel after pouring hot oil down Eliana's leg flashes in my mind. I should have killed him there in the street. "After he gave you those scars." I nod towards her inner thigh. "He was going for a run." That's the story he gave her. She doesn't need to know the truth.

Eliana's brows press together, anger marring her beautiful face. "So when you asked me about the scars before... you knew?"

Guilt pulses through me, and I hang my head in shame. "I did." I look up at her through my lashes. "I just thought it was time for you to talk to someone about it. To start to work through that trauma." Running a hand through my hair, my heart squeezes tightly in my chest. "I wasn't there the night he died though," I say, lowering my voice so only Eliana can hear. She runs her hands through her hair, pulling it taut at the nape of her neck. She's quiet for a moment, processing what I'm telling her.

"I knew that whatever I was about to do would mess up the *Timeline*," I continue. She needs to know at least *some* of the truth. "But I couldn't just let him get away with that. I couldn't sit by for one more second while he abused you."

Eliana lifts a hand to her trembling lips. "Did you..." She

swallows hard, struggling to find the words. She sucks her lips into her mouth, wetting them. "Did you break his ankle?"

Fates, it's hard not to smile at the memory of him pleading for his life. "Would you hate me any more than you do right now if I said yes?"

Her eyes soften, and her shoulders slump as she blurts out. "I could never hate you." Those five little words weigh heavily on my heart. "You saved me, Mallrie," she whispers, looking at her feet. "You saved me when I didn't want to be saved. You saved me from myself." Those big, brown, doe-like eyes, my undoing, look up at me. I need to hold her in my arms. If I don't, I think I might die.

"Eliana, please," I say, holding my hand out. She puts her hand in mine, and I swear I feel a collective sigh from the Fates. I give her hand a gentle squeeze. "Yes, I broke his ankle," I tell her, and her doe eyes look at me with no fear. No anger. "I told him he needed to end things. That if he didn't, I'd report him for the abuse," I sigh. "I'm sorry."

"Wh-why are you sorry?"

"Because of my interference, your relationship escalated, ultimately leading to his death." I shrug. "Not that I'm saying his death is bad. I just wish you didn't have to get subjected to that trauma."

Eliana keeps looking at me like she wants to throw her arms around my neck. But there is an internal war going on. She's fighting with herself about whether to take this on and move on or throw her walls back up. Fates, I hope she picks the former.

"Thank you," she whispers, trying not to look directly at me. Her cheeks colour ever so slightly.

"You shouldn't thank me. I should have done something sooner. Taken you away from him. Killed him myself…" My voice trails off in thought. "Come on. Let's go home. I mean—" I look at her, afraid she mightn't consider my home safe anymore.

Eliana squeezes my hand before lifting it to her lips and kissing my knuckles. "Let's go home," she repeats.

CHAPTER THIRTY-FOUR
ELIANA

Blood coats my skin in a slick, oily embrace. It's suffocating me. I cough. The metallic taste fills my mouth and splutters onto the street before me. There is just so much blood. It's everywhere. I try to blink the vision away, but another body appears with every shutter of my eyes. My father. Chelsea. My grandmother. Beckett. Chelsea sits up, her head cocking to the side. "Look what you've done," she says, blood falling from her lips.

There's a guttural clicking sound coming from behind me. I turn, and the last thing I see is the lifeless face of a Kailadon as it lunges at me.

I jolt upright as I look around the familiar room, sweat coating my skin. My hands quickly brush against my arms, making sure it is just sweat and not blood. I fall back into the soft sheets caressing my body, the soft morning light filtering into the room. Mallrie's hand caresses my side. "Bad dream?" His voice is hoarse with sleep. I roll over, and he pulls me close.

"You're sleeping?" I ask, amused and avoiding his question.

Last night was horrible. I felt sick to my stomach all the way back to his place. Everything Cyan had said, then my conversation with Mallrie on the rooftop. I was throwing my guts up when we got to the Melsheim Forest. I was starving and tired, my arm was aching and I just wanted to cry. Mallrie offered to carry me the rest of the way. I didn't want to seem weak and pathetic in front of Chelsea, but I was just so tired that I agreed. Mallrie apologised practically the whole way home. He explained he didn't want to tell me until I had time to process everything else. I told him that was no excuse to lie to me. But a part of me softened, knowing he had thought about my well-being enough to want to wait to tell me the truth instead of just truth-bombing twenty-five years' worth of lies unto me. Unlike Cyan, Mallrie actually cares for my mental health enough to think about how telling me what happened to my mother and how she really died would affect me.

When we got home, Mallrie cleaned my wound and bound it properly. Then, he offered me the bed, saying I was welcome to lock the door, and he'd sleep downstairs with Chelsea and the kid called Tyler. I thought about it, but ultimately decided that if I wanted to give Mallrie and me a chance, I'd have to give him the benefit of the doubt. Even though I disagree with his choice to keep secrets from me, I still respect his reasoning for doing it. And I wasn't about to hold that over him.

"Mm... I was," Mallrie moans sleepily. "Are you sure you're okay?" He rubs his eyes, clearing away the sleep as I prop myself up on my elbow, the sheets falling around me. He smiles even though his eyes are shut, and I pull the sheets over my naked body. Of course, if he opened his eyes, my breasts would be right in his line of sight. Not that he hasn't seen them before.

"You didn't take your potion last night?"

Mallrie opens his eyes lazily, pulling me closer to him until I can feel his naked body against mine. *Did we? No. Surely not.*

"We didn't have sex," he says as if reading my mind. I sigh, relieved. I don't even remember getting into bed. I would have hated to miss out on all the fun. Mallrie presses a soft kiss to my lips. "And no, I didn't take my potion. I wanted to keep an eye on our guests downstairs." He pulls back to examine me. "And to make sure you were okay. Are you?" he asks for the third time.

I can't help but smile at him. Damn him for being so thoughtful. Damn, fool me for falling for him.

It! I meant it.

"Little doe?" I look up at Mallrie. He's so fucking handsome, lying here in the soft morning glow. I run my hand through his hair and down his face, pulling him into a kiss.

"I am now," I say between kisses. Damn, Stockholm syndrome has got nothing on this sickness. My hand traces the curves of Mallrie's muscles, my fingers following the curves down his chest. I tease a little, rubbing my hand around the inside of his thigh.

I want this so badly. I can feel my body heat with desire, the butterflies in my tummy slowly descending between my legs. But I haven't been with anyone for years, and—

Mallrie's lips move as he kisses my neck. *Fuck.* He wants this just as much as I do. I can feel him harden against me. I'm nervous. It's a strange feeling, wanting everything this man can give me. But will I be enough for him?

"What's wrong, beautiful girl?" Mallrie whispers between kisses against my neck. My body tenses as he kisses my throat under my chin, tilting my head back against the pillows. He pulls away and runs his fingers through my hair. "Eli. Breathe." I sigh heavily. I don't know how long I've been holding my breath, but breathing now feels unnatural, like I have forgotten how to do it. "You're safe, Eli. If you don't want—"

"I do," I say breathlessly. "I really, *really* do." This just feels so much more *intimate* than Mallrie going down on me in the middle of the forest, and, well... "It's just... I... haven't done *it* since..."

He nods. I don't need to say his name. I never have to. He knows who I am talking about.

Mallrie presses a kiss to my lips. "Have you ever used a safe word before?"

A safe word. A shiver runs down my spine. I've read about people using them in erotic books, but that's all been in really intense BDSM scenes.

"Breathe, Eli." Mallrie kisses my forehead, drawing me back out of my spiralling thoughts. "Pick a word. If you choose to use it at any point, everything stops. No hard feelings, okay?" I look up at him, shocked. I don't think I am ready for what he has planned. He pushes himself up onto his elbow. "What's wrong? Talk to me." His hand gently caresses my face.

"I-I don't... I haven't done any..." *Why is this so hard to say?* "I've never done any, like... kinky stuff before," I whisper sheepishly.

Mallrie chuckles. I look up to see him almost blushing with laughter. "Oh, little doe." He pulls me close. "I want you to feel safe. So, if you change your mind at any point or don't feel comfortable, I want you to voice that and know that everything stops. No hard feelings. Safe words don't have to just be for kinky stuff." Mallrie chuckles, the deep, rich sound tugging the corners of my lips up. "They can be there so everyone feels safe and comfortable, okay?"

I smile—really smile. My heart feels full of sunshine, and I could just float away. I never knew someone could feel like this before. Mallrie is so different from Beckett. I don't know how I got this lucky. I wrap my arm around his neck and pull him in for another kiss. His tongue caresses my bottom lip, and I open up for him.

"Now, beautiful girl," Mallrie says. I moan a little at him, breaking the kiss. "Have you got a safe word in mind?" His voice drops an octave, and a wave of heat rushes through me.

I say the first thing that comes to mind, "*Moonlight*." My mind reels back in time to that first night we met. Mallrie standing under the full moon's light, black Kailadon blood splattered across his face and chest with his lilac-glowing sword. *Gods, maybe I should be concerned about how hot that gets me, thinking of him covered in blood and with a weapon that contains the souls of those it's slayed.* But, even then, when I didn't know who he was or the horrors within that blade, my body flushed with desire for the tall, dark, mysterious man who had just saved my life.

There is a fluttering between my thighs, and I clench them tighter together, trying to get some friction to the spot that desperately needs to be touched.

Mallrie growls in my ear, "*Moonlight*, huh?" I can feel my body tense with anticipation. I just want to grab his hand and press it between my legs.

"Yes?" It comes out as a question. I didn't mean it to, but I'm practically vibrating, waiting for his touch.

Mallrie repositions himself so he's straddling my thighs. One hand is pressed into the pillow beside my head, and the other is making a torturously slow descent down my chest, down my stomach—

"What are you thinking about, little doe?"

Staring into his cerulean eyes, my heart flutters. "Just remembering the night we met."

"Mm?"

"How much you turned me on and how conflicted I was about that."

"Ah. And now?" Mallrie asks, his voice thick. His hand squeezes my thigh, and I spread them, desperately needing him to touch me.

"I want you." I gasp as his thumb presses over my entrance, slipping between my already damp folds.

Mallrie leans in, and I arch my back to meet his kiss, but he moves his lips to my ear, whispering. "What do you want, Eliana? Use your words." His tongue licks the sensitive spot behind my ear before nipping my earlobe, dragging two fingers up the centre of me before flicking my clit.

"I want all of you. I want you to *fuck* me." I moan loudly, not even caring if they can hear us downstairs.

"Not yet, little doe," Mallrie says as his fingers continue their leisurely exploration and teasing touches. A whimper leaves me as I arch into his touch, needing him to drive his fingers into me. *More. I need more.*

His fingers disappear. And another whimper leaves me at the loss. My head whips up to find him moving further down the bed. "Just getting a better view of your pretty little pussy." My mouth dries out at the sight of his thick, impressive cock. I lick my lips, wanting to taste it. Mallrie tugs on my legs, pulling me down the bed, a small scream rupturing from my lips. His fingers return, gently stroking up and down the length of me and teasing my clit before slowly pushing two inside. The stretch is so delicious that my back arches, and I moan loudly. He pumps his fingers slowly in and out of me. "Now I know how sweet you taste, let me see how good you feel coming around my cock," he purrs.

"Oh, gods!" My pussy clenches around his fingers. *Fuck, he's going to make me come if he keeps talking like that.*

"I'm not your gods who turned their backs on you. But you're welcome to get on your knees and praise my name." Mallrie leans in, kissing me fervently. His teeth nipped at my lip as his fingers sped up, hitting that spot within me that has my body arching and my legs trembling. He curls his finger while he kisses down my neck to my breasts. My body feels so hot I might burst into flames. Teeth grazing against my hardened nipples, I cry out as my pussy clenches again. Mallrie's name is like a prayer on my lips as my head falls back onto the pillows. I'm shamelessly riding his hand as I come all over it.

He pulls away, making a popping sound as he releases my breast from his mouth. I watch through my lashes as he lifts his fingers. Mallrie holds them up in the early morning glow, examining their slickness. "Fucking beautiful," he says, looking down at me as he puts them in his mouth, sucking them clean. "You need to promise to control your magic if you want to continue." He tilts his head to the side. His eyes are dark and hungry as he looks over my body. "You do want more, don't you?"

"*Fuck yes*," I mewl, desire and arousal gathering low in my stomach, causing my body to arch, desperate to be touched again and again until I am coming and screaming Mallrie's name.

"Promise to be a good girl and control your magic?" he asks teasingly.

"I promise." I laugh.

Mallrie gently spreads my legs wider, giving him better access as he runs his tongue up my centre. As his tongue explores, I let out a soft moan. I can feel the fire within me waking up again. I squeeze my eyes closed, trying to focus on keeping my magic at bay. Remembering all he has taught me, I try to focus on steadying my breathing.

Mallrie makes a guttural moan as he licks my pussy clean. Lifting his head, his face glistens in the soft light. "You know something, little doe?"

"What?" I whisper. My hand laces in his dark hair, wanting to push him back down.

"You taste even better than I remember, and I've been trying so hard to remember how sweet you taste every time I fist my cock." Mallrie lets me guide him back down, a sultry smile on my lips at the image he just painted. His tongue flicks at my clit, and my magic spikes in my veins, desperate to be unleashed.

"Shh, beautiful girl. You need to calm down," Mallrie says teasingly. "How are you feeling?"

"So fucking good."

"What do you want?"

My eyes snap open. "I want you to fuck me. *Please*," I shamelessly beg. *Gods! I need his cock inside me.*

Mallrie flips me over and lifts my ass into the air. "Spread your legs, little doe." I brace myself against the headboard, doing as he says.

"Do you remember your safe word?" Mallrie whispers against the sensitive part of my ear.

I nod, "*Moonlight.*"

"That's my good girl. Use it if this is too much or you want to stop."

"Just fuck me already, Mallrie." I roll my hips back into him, reaching a hand around to grab hold—

"So bossy." He catches my wrist and returns it to the headboard. He positions his cock at my entrance and slowly pushes himself in, inch by glorious inch. My pussy stretches around him. "Fates, you take me so well, little doe," Mallrie pants against my neck. "I don't know how long I will last. You feel so fucking good."

His hand rakes up my back as he starts to thrust. His cock stretches me with a delicious ache, and my body feels like a live wire. My magic buzzes and presses at my skin as Mallrie thrusts into me. His hand snakes around my stomach, his fingers sliding down my body to circle my clit.

Fuck! He doesn't know how long he was going to last? I think I am about to explode!

"Tell me you're mine," Mallrie growls in my ear with a primal sense of possession. My body tingles with the need in his voice. It should scare me; that dominating demand growled into my ear. But I want this. I want Mallrie. He's made mistakes, but so have I. No one is perfect.

"I'm yours," I pant. His pace picks up. He thrusts into me harder, deeper. It has me crying out his name again and again.

"That's fucking right, beautiful girl. That's fucking right," he growls. My pussy clenches around him, and I am shattering into a million tiny pieces. Mallrie runs his fingers through my hair and down my back, squeezing my ass tightly. That is my only warning before he pulls out, and thick, hot lashes gush across my ass and thighs.

No one has ever finished all over me like that. It feels so dirty but so fucking right that my pussy clenches around nothing.

"How do you feel, beautiful girl?" Mallrie whispers as his hand strokes my ass, rubbing his cum over me. He pulls me into his lap. His other hand cups my face and turns me to look at him. "Feeling in control?"

I smile and nod, a little loopy from the high of multiple orgasms. *Gods, Beckett* never *made me come like that before.*

"Are you sure about that?" Mallrie asks teasingly. I frown up at him. I swear I didn't just say that out loud. He smirks at me and nods towards the headboard. I follow his gaze, and my cheeks burn with embarrassment. Staring back at me are two blackened handprints gripping the headboard.

"Oh, gods! I-I'm so sorry. Mallrie, I—"

He laughs darkly. It rumbles through his chest and into my body. "Don't be," he says, gently turning my face back to him. "It looks better that way." He kisses me softly. "I can't wait until you blacken the whole thing with your handprints," he whispers between kisses. We fall back into the crumpled sheets, my legs tangling with his as I rest my head on his chest. Mallrie's heartbeat races in time with mine as we lie there in blissful silence, the morning sun creeping across the floor. At this moment, I've never felt so safe and loved. Despite the revelations of last night, I'm ready to move forward. There's no doubt in my mind that Mallrie kept those things from me to protect me. I look up at him, watching as his eyes flutter open and meet mine. In my heart, I know this man would never hurt me, not intentionally.

"Come, little doe," he murmurs, pulling me from my thoughts. "Let's get you cleaned up before you fall asleep."

"Says he who had his eyes closed," I tease.

Mallrie chuckles, slipping out of bed and walking over to the dresser. I greedily take in his strong form, from the muscles across his broad shoulders, down to his sculpted ass, and then his powerful thighs. It isn't fair that he looks this good. But then, I remember how old he truly is—how he's from a time when warriors trained every day with swords and shit. The thought almost entices a giggle out of me.

He returns—unfortunately pulling on a pair of sweats—and drops a pile of clothes onto the bed. A wicked smirk lights up his face. Before I can react, his hand snaps out, gripping my ankle and pulling me toward the edge of the bed.

My breath is knocked from me, and I laugh, panting as he lifts me effortlessly into his arms. "What are you doing?" I ask as he repositions me in his embrace, wrapping a blanket around me while grabbing the clothes. "You don't need to carry me," I protest though a wave of anxiety crashes over me at the thought of being carried like this. My cheeks heat with embarrassment.

Mallrie sets me on my feet, his hand never leaving the small of my back. I sway slightly, my knees weak. "It's fine," he says, picking me up again as if I weigh nothing. "I don't mind carrying you if I'm the reason you can't walk," he winks.

"Gooood Morning…" the teenager from last night says humorously. Tyler, I think Mallrie said his name is—is sitting on the island bench, legs crossed, holding a cup of steaming coffee. "Had a productive morning? Coffee, Eli?" He holds out a cup to me, smiling from ear to ear, all innocent and boastful. My whole body heats with embarrassment. He would have heard everything from down here.

"Shut it, Tyler, or I'll send you back to Cyan," Mallrie says sternly, kicking open the bathroom door.

"No, man, I'm—" Mallrie shuts the door, ending the conversation.

"Ignore him," he says, setting me carefully on the edge

of the bath while he turns to the walk-in shower tucked neatly in the corner, turning on the water that falls invitingly from the rainfall shower head attached to the ceiling. "Tyler is—well, young. Chelsea has kept him hidden from Edgar for the past two years. He's an orphan. Doesn't get out much," Mallrie says, as if that explains a lot. My heart aches a little at the thought of being orphaned and then being locked away from everyone else. Especially being as young as he is. "Tyler stumbled upon his powers breaking into a department store, then jumped into the Enkanti Tree, which then granted him his powers in one full hit." Mallrie rolls his eyes. Tyler seems like he gives both brothers a headache. "Anyway, luckily, Cyan and Chelsea found him before Edgar got wind of the situation." He chuckles to himself, shaking his head at the poor joke. My mind tries to wrap around what he just said. *Luckily, Cyan found him before Edgar...*

Mallrie checks the temperature of the water before walking back out the door. I strain my ears as I hear him talking to Tyler.

"Get down. You're acting like a wild animal."

"Sorry, man. I'm just saying, I'm on your side. Y'know 'Bros before—"

"Don't finish your sentence." Mallrie's voice is a low growl. I can imagine him standing there pressing his fingers to the bridge of his nose, eyes closed. I smile at the thought of him having to look after this teenager. Then he's back, shutting the door behind him. I open my mouth to ask what he meant by what he said before he left, but it looks like Tyler has put Mallrie in a bad mood.

"Drink." Mallrie hands me the large glass of water, removes his pants and steps into the shower. The water cascades down his back, and I drink the water, watching as he washes.

My questions wash down the drain, along with any other coherent thought that dares to invade my mind.

CHAPTER THIRTY-FIVE
ELIANA

It feels weird to have someone dote over me after sex, I think as I wring out as much water as possible from my hair before pulling on the shirt Mallrie brought downstairs. Beckett usually just rolled out of bed and stalked into the kitchen for a glass of rum.

My cheeks warm at the memory of Mallrie carrying me downstairs, gently setting me down on the edge of the bath, getting me a drink of water and then carefully helping me wash. The man even dried my body. Chewing on my thumbnail around the stupid grin plastered on my face, I am so elated, I just want to scream.

He cares. I am unable to fully wrap my head around the fact. It feels too good to be true. Sure, Mallrie has been watching me since I was a godsdamned embryo—a fact that I try not to think too long on because, yeah, it's creepy. But I can't help having feelings for him. It's so weird to feel this strongly about someone I have just met. If you had asked me a week ago if I believed in love, I'd have laughed in your face and told you what a fool you were. But now? Maybe, just maybe, I might believe.

The steam from the shower feels good on my skin, and the smell of lavender fills the air, relaxing my aching muscles. We leave the bathroom, Mallrie's arm draped over my shoulders.

His.

A swell of possessive pride fills my chest. I never thought I'd like the idea of being with someone again, yet here I am, smiling like a damn fool.

Tyler sits at the bottom of the stairs with Winnie curled beside him. I look around for Chelsea, but she's nowhere to be seen. Mallrie raises an eyebrow at Tyler.

"She's outside," he says a little sheepishly.

As soon as the words leave Tyler's lips, the door closes behind Chelsea. I can feel years of anger rising like molten lava to the surface as I feel her eyes burn into the back of my head. Mallrie traces small circles at the base of my neck with his thumb. "Calm down, little doe. Why don't you just talk to her?"

I shoot him a look. "*Talk to her?*" I repeat sourly. "Yeah, like you and Cyan?" I grunt, pushing out from under his embrace. All the happy, fuzzy feelings have sizzled and burnt away.

"Eli, please..." Chelsea calls as I storm outside, colliding my shoulder with hers as I pass. *The air was getting too stale in there.*

I can hear them inside. Voices overlap, but I can't make out what they're saying. *She lied to me. For how many years? She was my only friend, and she lied to me!* The bitter taste of betrayal has my stomach twisting, a sickening cocktail of anger and heartbreak.

"Eliana, stop! Please listen to me!" Chelsea calls, chasing after me. I stop—not because she asked me, but because there is nowhere I can really go. I linger near the invisible barrier, debating whether to risk whatever lurks within the Melsheim Forest or stay here and deal with my *dead* best friend. I pace in front of the barrier, the dirt pressing between my toes, hoping she will let this go and return inside.

"El, please," Chelsea says again, her voice soft and desperate for me to listen.

I whip my head around to where she stands on the last step of the balcony. She's aged beautifully, still as graceful as I remember. Her long, raven-black hair hangs like a sheet over her shoulder. Her smooth, tanned skin looks full of life in the morning sun, unlike the horrid images my imagination had plagued my mind with for the last few years. "There's nothing you can say, Chels! Nothing!" I spit back.

Silence falls around us. Not even the birds or crickets dare to make a noise as everyone holds their breath. Chelsea takes a calculated step off the balcony. I watch her bare foot as she carefully steps off the timber steps onto the dirt. My eyes flick up to meet hers as I send a wave of heat through the ground to where she stands—a warning.

Don't fucking *mess with me.*

Chelsea jerks away from the heat, meeting my gaze with an unyielding expression. A small smile plays around the edge of her lips as she steps back down on the dirt. The ground sizzles around her as she proceeds towards me. Mallrie leans against the wall with his arm outstretched over Tyler's chest, stopping him from coming any further.

"Just leave them to sort it out. They need to get this out of their systems," I hear him say quietly, which only makes my blood boil even more.

Get this out of our systems?

Get what? How she's a traitorous liar and a lousy best friend? I wish I had never met her. I wish I had never felt sympathy for her. I wish I had never mourned for her. I wish... I wish... I wish she were actually dead.

There is intensity in my hand, and I look down, realising I have a fireball ready. Chelsea's dark eyes glance down as she notices it, too, and her blue-tipped fingers twitch as if readying herself for a fight. *Well, if it's a fight she wants, then it's a fight she'll get.*

I fling the fireball through the air, aiming for her head. But she smothers it with a shield of water. "Eli, please. Just listen. I wanted to tell you. Really, I did," Chelsea tries reasoning.

Lies!

I throw another fireball. Another deflection. Chelsea walks calmly towards me. My back is pressed against the barrier. I can feel the pulsations of the magic behind me.

"Then why didn't you just tell me the truth? You were *supposed* to be my friend!" My voice doesn't sound like mine anymore. It's twisted with anger and... grief. I swallow hard. *No. She doesn't deserve these tears.* The lump in my throat is choking me, and I can feel the tears stinging behind my eyes.

She's close enough I could grab her. Her long, dark hair falls perfectly around her face as if she didn't just spend the night sleeping on a couch. Her dark, angular eyes are filled with sympathy as if she really believes she has done nothing wrong.

"I wanted to tell you. Believe me. But do you really think you would have believed me if I told you I had *magic*?" Her mouth forms the word as if she knows I wouldn't have believed her, that she hardly believed it herself. Of course, it would have been hard to believe. I am still struggling to wrap my head around the fact that *I* have magic. That this is all happening.

"Of course I would have believed you! You were my friend!"

Chelsea's mouth parts slightly, forming a small "o" shape as if my words offend her. "You *are* my friend, Eli," Chelsea insists. "It's just, Cyan…"

"Don't you dare bring him into this!" I spit, and a part of my stomach twists uncomfortably at the sound of his name. I can see Mallrie tense in my peripheral vision. *But Cyan hasn't lied to me.* He admitted he had no reason to. He said that Chelsea didn't want to see me. Full stop. End of story. Simple as that. "Don't use him as an excuse to hide behind," I snap. "Just own up to the fact that you were a shit friend!"

"I-I'm not using him as an excuse, just, *please…*" Chelsea raises her arms in front of her as if trying to calm down some rabid animal. I'm sick of her. *I'm so fucking sick of her.* I grab hold of her wrists hard and swing her out of the barrier, stalking after her.

The magic tingles through my body as I emerge on the other side. She mustn't have expected the attack because she's scrambling to her feet, wiping the dirt from her face.

"Eli. Don't! You won't…" Chelsea doesn't get to finish her sentence before I am upon her, throwing punches and swinging kicks. I've never fought anyone before, and she's clearly had more experience. Cyan has obviously been teaching her to fight because she blocks my assaults easily and kicks me hard in the stomach, sending me back into a tree. The wind gets knocked out of my system as the bark bites into my back. I gasp, trying to bring the air back into my lungs. I hear the mystic whooshing sound as Mallrie and Tyler follow us through the barrier into the forest. Tyler is pleading for Mallrie to step in, but he won't. He's going to let this play out, and I am glad.

Even though I am getting my ass handed to me, it feels too good to get years and years of resentment out. The physical pain somehow helps to soothe that emotional torment I put myself through, all because, what? Chelsea thought she was protecting me? I somehow get the upper hand and have her pinned under me, my hands wrapped firmly around her throat. Her arms are pinned to her sides between my legs. Tyler is shouting now, and I almost feel bad as I squeeze the life out of Chelsea while he watches. She looks up at me with pleading eyes.

"El... please... don't..."

"You were my *only* friend. The *only* good thing I had in this godsforsaken town!" I can't hold it in any longer. The tears fall hot and heavy, trickling down my face and onto her chest. "You have *no idea* what it's like to mourn your only friend. Then see them perfectly fine. Fighting your boyfriend!"

My heart tightens as I acknowledge Mallrie is my *boyfriend*. It feels weird to say it out loud, but it's true. I want him to be mine.

Suddenly, my mouth goes dry. My head starts to spin, and I feel faint. I glare down at Chelsea. She must be doing this. My head aches, and the temptation to sleep is agonising. She rolls us over, easily taking up position on top of me, my arms pinned firmly above my head.

"Eliana! Listen to me." Her voice is stern. The fatigue wears off a little, and the ache in my head is tolerable. She must be using her magic to control the fluid in my body. "I couldn't tell you, no matter how much I wanted to. Believe me, I tried. Cyan..." I make a face, and she presses her fingers deeper into my wrists, pressing on my veins and making them throb. "*Listen*," she growls. I can feel fluid rushing from her hold into my blood. My stomach churns briefly, making me gag, and then, suddenly, it's gone. "Cyan told me what you are! Do you really think if I told you everything—that I am a witch, that you're a hybrid destined to help save us all, that our mayor wants you dead—you would not think I'd gone insane?"

"It's a tale for sure," I grunt, my throat so dry my words are rough and quiet.

"Believe it or not, but Cyan and I were protecting you. Like he's been protecting me. Like I've been protecting Tyler." She glances over to Mallrie and Tyler, and I follow her gaze. Mallrie's expression is stiff as he holds back Tyler, who looks as if he will be sick. He cares for Chelsea. I can feel his anger. The heat is rising in his body with his desire to help her.

"Every time Edgar got close to you, Cyan stepped in. Created some sort of diversion, stalling him. And every time that happened, *he* got punished. Every time you got away from him, Cyan got punished. Injected with faerie venom, whipped, beaten and tortured. Edgar demanded Cyan and I find you and Tyler. We hid Tyler away so he wouldn't be able to use him, and guess who got punished? Not me. *Cyan.* Cyan has done nothing but protect us all." She scowls at Mallrie. "You think Mallrie *saved you.* Has been *protecting* you?" she scoffs. "Cyan has been protecting you all along. I don't even know what this jerk's been doing." She rolls her eyes. There is a sudden crack of thunder like two large boulders being hurdled together. It shakes the ground. Chelsea and I are propelled apart. Mallrie walks over and helps me up.

"What was that?" Chelsea growls at him.

"An intervention," he replies darkly.

"Yeah, because you don't enjoy getting called out," she says incredulously.

Mallrie presses his fingers to the bridge of his nose. "Don't be talking about things you don't understand, Chelsea. I'm sure Cyan would have taught you that if your parents failed to do so."

Chelsea scoffs, opening her mouth to bite back, and I am in half a mind to call him out for that low blow about her parents. That was uncalled for. But before either of us can utter a sound, Mallrie says, "Cyan and I have *both* been protecting Eliana. In our own way. There are things I am sure he hasn't told you," Mallrie leans against a tree and folds his arms, looking around the forest and ensuring the area is safe. "We had a plan. Return the magic to the Enkanti Tree and restore the protection spell against the Kailadons. We can all agree on that, yes?" He looks stoically between the three of us. We sheepishly nod in agreement. "I did a prophecy ritual. It revealed that the Enkanti Tree wouldn't release its powers back to the witches until the faerie-hybrid was born." Mallrie nods gravely towards me, causing my stomach to roll onto itself. "Until that happened, Cyan and I did what we could to keep the mortality rate down. When Edgar finally tracked us down, he demanded I grant him immortality. Not that it works like that, but..." Mallrie trails off, shrugging, clearly irritated at the notion. "It was Cyan's decision to stay in town to monitor the grimoire Edgar had stolen and hidden. He wanted me safe so Edgar wouldn't be able to use me or my magic. I came back every night. Cyan debriefed me about Edgar's movements and motives. Then, I'd take watch over the town, surveying the Kailadons, keeping any foolish mortals safe if they dared to venture out after dark. A few years ago, Cyan..." Mallrie sighs, and a desolate expression washes over him. "He met a woman. Morana. He fell madly in love. I told him to forget about Edgar. That being that close to him was dangerous. I'd watch over Edgar from a distance. But Cyan wouldn't listen. He knew, as well as I, how important it was to ensure Edgar got nowhere near you. It would have been all too easy to take you as a child. Make you disappear and make it look like an accident." Mallrie jerks his chin in my direction, and my stomach turns to liquid at his expression and the heaviness of his words. Mallrie rubs the back of his neck. He looks physically uncomfortable retelling this story.

"One winter's night, Edgar found Morana and Cyan... He assumed she was a witch. So he imprisoned them both and demanded I grant him 'immortality.'" Mallrie rolls his eyes, and air quotes the word as if he's sick of Edgar inaccurately referring to his magic as immortality. "It was an ambush. As soon as I stepped through that door, I was injected with a cocktail drug of Edgar's design—a mixture of faerie venom, barbiturate, paralytic and potassium. Which would be lethal to a mortal. It knocked me out for a good few hours, and when I came to, my magic was useless. I was weak. They beat Cyan an inch from his life and... Morana..." Mallrie runs his hand down his face. "She was dead."

My hand flies up over my mouth. My knees threaten to give out underneath me. No wonder Cyan loathes me so much. If it wasn't for me, Morana would still be alive. The weight of her death presses down on my chest, making it hard to breathe. I take a step back, then another until my back is pressed against a tree. The bark is rough against my skin through Mallrie's soft shirt. Out of the corner of my eye, I see Chelsea take notice of my reaction.

"It almost killed me to get Cyan out of there," Mallrie continues. I can barely hear him over the ringing in my ears. "I brought him back here and healed him. But things were never the same between us." Mallrie pauses, looking off into the trees towards Datura. "He blames me for her death, for not bringing her body back so she could get the burial she deserved. I don't blame him. I should have done more…" I open my mouth to say something, to comfort him, but surprisingly, Chelsea is the one who beats me to it.

"I… I didn't know," she breathes. "There was nothing you could have done. That injection…" Chelsea rubs a spot on her neck as if she can still feel where she, too, was pierced with it. "There was no way you would have been able to save her. Cyan would know that."

We all stand in the silent forest for a long time until the sound of crickets and birds slowly returns.

Mallrie clears his throat and looks up at all of us. "Well, the past is behind us, and unfortunately, I can do nothing about it. Otherwise, we all wouldn't be in this mess to begin with. So"—he claps his hands together loudly—"I need you three to train up. You all need to be masters of your craft. I expect you all to be able to fight and hold your own in battle because it may just come to that."

Chelsea and Tyler follow Mallrie and me back to the house in silence. The tension is thick in the air. I don't trust Chelsea. She doesn't trust Mallrie. Chelsea wants to make amends with me. And Tyler? Well, I think he's just happy to be out of Datura. He's quirky and bubbly, and as much as he looked like he was ready to kill me before, that seems to be all water under the bridge now.

I make my way straight up to the bedroom. I can't be in the same space as Chelsea again. The air feels thick and unbreathable when I am around her.

Slipping into the clothes Mallrie brought from my apartment, a cold flush rushes through my body. There's a flurry of commotion as I throw back sheets on the bed, rustle through papers on Mallrie's desk and look through the drawers of his dresser. Not seeing anything I touch, I'm single-mindedly looking for the grimoire my grandmother left me. A lump forms in my throat, and I feel like I am about to shatter. The only thing I had connecting this new life to my grandmother is gone. I try to think where I saw it last—

Cyan! That motherfucker took it!

I storm down the staircase, heading towards the front doors, ready to storm back into Datura, into Cyan's apartment and take it back by force if necessary. I ignore the sideways looks from the others as I push open the front door. To my surprise, that peculiar black crow with eerily milky white eyes that Cyan called to fetch Mallrie is waiting for me on the porch with my grimoire in its mouth.

I eye it for a moment before reluctantly taking a step forward and carefully taking the small black book from its beak. The crow tilts its head to the side, eyeing me momentarily through those seemingly sightless eyes before it hops up and down, cawing like a maniac. Mallrie appears in the doorway, his arms folded across his chest.

"Hello, Hesper," he says, unimpressed.

The crow hops back a step, cautious to keep me between Mallrie and itself. Its head looks between us and it continues to caw. "You need to slow down. You know I can't understand you when you screech."

I turn to look at Mallrie. "You can understand it?"

"Her," he corrects. "And yes."

Winnie pounces from the doorway, lunging towards the bird. Hesper flies out of the way, cawing angrily, losing a feather or two in the process. Mallrie chuckles. "Is there anything else, Hesper?"

The bird perches herself carefully on the vegetable patch fence and caws.

"Hm. Help yourself to the strawberries." Mallrie waves a hand dismissively towards the strawberry patch. "They're starting to turn," he adds quietly as he turns and walks back inside.

"What did"—I look over my shoulder as the large crow carefully pecks off a strawberry—"Hesper say?"

"Just that Cyan found your grimoire and wanted it returned to you."

"*Found it?* He took it!" I look at Mallrie suspiciously. *Surely, more than that was said, but he's got that tone that feels like that is all to be told and not to push the matter.* And as much as I know he isn't Beckett, I don't *want* to push the issue. I know what happens if you do. So, instead, I ask, "How can you understand it?"

Mallrie sighs, and a tiny ripple of guilt spreads through me for asking. "Hesper is a Nechkrappe. A particularly nasty creature. They don't make good familiars, pets or companions. They don't make a good anything, really. Best to avoid them where you can. If provoked, they can bring grave illness and death." Mallrie sighs again and rubs the back of his neck. "Of course, somehow Cyan befriended that one. Named it Hesper."

I nod to myself, but something in the back of my mind is still wondering what the bird actually said. I push the thought from my mind. If Hesper *did* say anything else, Mallrie would tell me.

CHAPTER THIRTY-SIX
ELIANA

The reality of this morning comes crashing down around me as I sit on the front porch, watching the Nechkrappe peck at the strawberries.

I need to get out of here.

The thought is so loud it cuts through the haze, slicing through the passion of having sex with Mallrie for the first time, of him carrying me downstairs and taking care of me, of my fight with Chelsea. Panic seizes me so forcefully I think I might pass out from being unable to breathe. My fingers wrap around the soft leather of my grimoire. Chelsea and Tyler have busied themselves mainly, I think, to keep their distance from me.

I lost control.

And that scares me. The way I attacked Chelsea; I didn't feel a lick of remorse. I still don't. I never wanted to hurt Beckett. I just wanted to be free from him. I can still feel the weight of the knife and the heat of his blood on my hands. I don't *want* to hurt people. But I was just *so* angry. Tears prick at my eyes as I continue to struggle for a lungful of air.

I am just like Beckett.

I let my anger get the better of me, falling into that darkness and allowing it to consume me. My hands twist around the leather grimoire as I chew on the inside of my cheek hard enough until I can feel the cool, metallic taste of blood filling my mouth.

Occasionally, Hesper raises her head and turns those unnerving, milky eyes towards me. Eyes that make the bird appear blind—but she gives me a feeling that she sees so much more. A shiver races through me as I look into those unsettling orbs. The panic attack has eased a little as my curiosity and frustration take over. *Mallrie never told me how he understood the Nechkrappe.*

I look over my shoulder. The front door is closed. He had gone inside to do something that I didn't hear over the roaring of my heartbeat in my ears. A weight is pressing down on my chest, and I feel like my heart might give out under the pressure. I look at the book in my hands. The gold embossing glimmers in the sunlight. "This... This is too much," I whisper to myself. *I need to get out of here.* I just need... I just need a moment to myself. To gather my thoughts.

Would Mallrie let me leave if I asked? I can't breathe, and I don't want to risk asking. I look over my shoulder at the house, guilt seeping into my bones, but the panic builds again. *If I stay, will I lose control again?*

Raising a finger to my lips as Hesper cocks her head in my direction. I silently get to my feet and make a run for the barrier.

By some miracle, I made it back to my apartment. Standing in the shadows across the alleyway, I stare at the building. That tension in my chest didn't abate the further I got from Mallrie's place. I don't know why I ran...

"That's a lie," my grandmother's voice whispers. She's right. I know exactly why I ran.

I'm scared shitless, The sex, the way Mallrie cared for me *afterwards*... It was too much. Then, throw Chelsea into the mix, and this kid, Tyler...

I can't breathe. The house suddenly feels so small.

Breathing in the stale air of Datura, I keep my head down as I walk into my building.

After years of trying to avoid Mrs Kaminski's ruthless scrutiny, I have learnt where to creep up the stairs to make as little noise as possible. Pressing my body as close as possible to the wall, I sneak up the last flight of stairs. My boots in my hands, I slide my socked feet along the wooden boards on the landing, trying to keep an even pressure.

I breathe in as I jump over two floorboards that, no matter what, *always* squeak. I am clutching onto my door handle like my life depends on it. I give it a little jiggle—

The door swings open, and I practically fall inside. A small yelp rushes out of me as I fall onto my hands and knees. Then, quickly, I turn and close the door, just after I spot Mrs Kaminski peering around her door.

My heart is pounding in my ears as I rest against the door. The guilt and shame feel like a layer of dirt over me. Pushing to my feet, I flick the lock into place. *I swear the door was locked...*

I push the thought from my mind. With everything going on, it wouldn't surprise me if I *thought* I locked the door, but in my haste, I had actually forgotten. It also wouldn't be the first time that's happened.

There is just something about showering in your own home. You're used to the water pressure and know exactly where the perfect temperature is. I thought I heard the front door before, but I think it was just my mind playing tricks on me. I had shut off the shower to listen but couldn't hear anything.

Gods, I can't even remember if I have a bottle of gin here. I'll need to find some cash and run to the Bottle-O.

I wrap a towel around my body as I enter the bedroom. It's so quiet. I can faintly hear the hustle and bustle of people in the street below, but... my heart aches. Guilt finds me. I ran away from Mallrie when he's done nothing but support and help me. I bite my lip as I sit on the edge of my bed, pulling my shirt over my head. *That level of intimacy...*

I think it would have been better if he had just walked away after we had sex. But, instead, it all just felt like... more. And I don't know how to take that. My words to Mallrie echo back to me. *"It's not like we're together or anything."*

"We could change that though," Mallrie said. And gods, I wanted that.

It's just happening so—

My head snaps to the bedroom door as I swear I hear a cupboard shutting. Pushing to my feet, I stalk to the door and peer around it.

My heart beats wildly, and I think I've stopped breathing. Cyan is leaning against the island bench, his long blonde hair half pulled into a bun. He's forgone his usual black suit for something a little more casual from what I can see, the black, collared shirt rolled up to his elbows as he lifts a glass to his lips.

What is he doing here? Does he know I am here? I cringe. *Of course he knows I am here.* He probably heard the shower. I curse myself for not getting out and checking the apartment properly when I thought I heard the door shut.

How did he even get in?

"It's rude to stare, don't you know?" Cyan drawls from the kitchen.

"It's also illegal to break and enter. Maybe I should call the GDO?" I rebut, pushing open the door but not leaving the safety of the bedroom. Instead, I eye the best possible path to the front door. But he is closer to the exit He'd easily catch me.

Cyan laughs, a deep, throaty sound that has all the tiny hairs on my body raising with awareness. "Oh, I'd take such pleasure in seeing you call the GDO, love." He turns to face me, sliding the other glass of gin across the island bench in offering. My eyes narrow as I see he's even got my favourite mixer. My fingers itch for that glass.

It has been so long since I had a drink. Mallrie really wants me to kick the habit, but...

I storm across the room and snatch the glass. "What did you do to it?" I ask, lifting my brows.

Cyan's lips quirk to the side. "What makes you think I've done anything to it?"

I shake my head as I watch him take a swig from his own glass. Feeling bold, I reach across the bench and snatch his drink out of his hand, replacing it with my own. "Good to know," I say, taking a sip. The bright and zesty flavours slip across my tongue and warm my soul. My eyes flutter closed for a brief moment as I take another sip. "Thanks for the gin. Now you can leave," I demand, pointing to the door for extra emphasis.

"And why would I want to do that?" Cyan asks, still smirking at me as he takes a drink.

"How did you get in?" I ask, lowering the empty glass, panic quickly building in my chest again.

He leans across the bench, splashing more gin into my glass and then topping it with the mixer. It weirds me out. He must have brought these over because I don't have any left.

"How did you get in?" I repeat, folding my arms across my chest to stop myself from reaching for the glass.

Cyan reaches into this pocket and pulls out a set of keys. My eyes widen as I lunge across the island, almost knocking over the glass to snatch my keys from his hand. He pulls them away, clicking his tongue in disapproval. "You're going to have to try harder than that, love."

"They're *mine*," I seethe. "Give them back!"

He pockets my keys, and I am practically seeing red. My magic thrums to the surface, desperate to be unleashed. But I know I am unstable at the moment. With all the emotions raging about Chelsea and Mallrie... I close my eyes and focus on my breathing, even though it terrifies me to close my eyes around Cyan. It's like turning your back on a Kailadon and then being surprised when it attacks you. It can't help it. It's only in their nature to attack.

"Why are you here?" I ask through slow, measured breaths.

Cyan cocks a dark brow. "I could ask you the same, love."

"I live here." I bare my teeth. Something about him just makes me so angry.

"Hm. Interesting." He leans back against the bench and takes another sip of his drink. "How's old Mallrie going?"

I shake my head, completely dumbfounded. "I am *not* making small talk with you. Get *out*!" I seethe, making a move for the phone.

"You're really going to call the GDO?" The amusement in Cyan's voice has my fingers bashing into the numbers. I lift the phone to my ear and wait.

"General disciplinary office, how can I direct your call?" someone rasps on the other end of the line.

"Hi, someone's broken into my apartment. I need someone to come get rid of him."

"Is this person someone you know?"

"Well, kinda, yeah. But I've asked them to leave, and they won't." Suddenly, a wave of panic bubbles up in my chest as I remember when I called the GDO on Beckett, and they didn't believe me.

My voice must have given me away because the person on the other end of the phone asks me if I'm okay.

"Yes, he's dangerous," I answer their question while looking directly into Cyan's eyes and the smug look on his face.

"If you're in a safe place and can do so, could you please tell me their name and briefly describe them?"

I start rattling off Cyan's description. All the while, he's leaning against the bench, smirking at me like he knows something I don't. Anxiety prickles at my spine, making it feel like I am stepping into some sort of trap.

Before I can say anymore, he reaches into his pocket and pulls out a small, black device. Portable phones aren't common in Datura, so seeing him pull one out of his pocket and answer it leaves me slightly stunned.

"Speak," Cyan barks into the small device, his eyes never leaving mine. "Yes, I am at Miss Nightingale's resi-dence, but no, the GDO is not needed." He hangs up the phone as I stare at him in disbelief, the disconnected tone blasting in my ear like an alarm.

"They… hung up on me," I breathe. Panic is building in my chest.

"Did you seriously think they would come and arrest me, love?" Cyan drawls, returning the small device to his pocket. "I work for Edgar. I am *above* the GDO." His tone is laced with amusement.

"So, what, you're here to drag me back to the government building? To Edgar?" My fingers tremble as I hang up the phone. They tingle with the heat of my magic.

Cyan shrugs. "I was thinking about it, yeah." But his tone tells me otherwise. I know he can hold his liquor well, but something about his behaviour makes me think he's coming down from some other sort of high…

"How did you know I was here?" I ask, inching away from the island bench. I've got no shoes on, but that won't stop me from making a run for it if I need to.

Cyan smiles arrogantly. His eyes flick over my body as if sizing me up. Not that I'd ever be a threat to him. As he's already pointed out, I don't know how to control my magic. And no matter how much I train, I doubt I'll ever be able to handle it like him or Mallrie, who have had… Gods, they've had decades' worth of practise.

"A little birdie told me," he drawls, taking another sip of his drink.

"Hesper," I breathe.

Cyan simultaneously shakes and nods his head. "Yes, and no."

I frown, looking down at my bare feet. *Who else could he…* "Mrs Kaminski?" My eyes flash to his. Cyan winks. I don't think I've ever seen him wink before, and it sends a shiver through me. His striking eyes alight with a predatory instinct. My mouth opens and closes with disbelief as I try to grasp for words.

"Have you not figured out by now, love, that I've got eyes and ears all over this godsforsaken town?"

I inch away from him towards the door. Cyan settles himself against the bench top as he takes another swig of his drink.

"How... How long has Mrs Kaminski been—"

"Working for me?" he finishes. "Since you moved into this building." He's so casual in the way he destroys every-thing I thought I knew.

My mouth drops open, and my knees go weak. My magic hums in my blood, demanding to be unleashed. If I wasn't afraid that I'd burn down my entire apartment, I would throw a fireball right at Cyan's stupid smirk.

I open my mouth to yell at him, to demand why he'd have someone watching me all this time. But his stupid smirk kicks up a little more as he drawls, "I see you're still not in control of your magic. Maybe you should stay with me." He pushes off from the bench and stalks towards me. "I could show you how to really use your magic."

I recoil at his words. "I will *never* stay with you."

His eyes flash as he looks down at me, now within arm's reach, but he's backed me up against the couch. "We'll see, love. We'll just wait and see."

I heat my hands and push against his chest. Cyan curses as the fabric burns. "I will *never* willingly be with you," I hiss, taking another step forward and pushing him again with heated hands. The skin peeking through the burnt holes in his chest is turning pink as I push him again. Cyan catches my wrists, his thumbs pressing into the sensitive tendons until my hands splay and my magic fizzles. With his hands occupied, I swing my leg, not sure where I am aiming for but hoping for the best. He curses as I get him in the back of the knee, causing him to buckle enough for me to push out of his embrace.

I grab a fist full of his hair to drag him towards the door, but his hands—no, *vines*—extend to wrap around me to the point of pain. Tiny pin-prick thorns dig into my skin, and I can feel a wash of something cool tracing through my veins, nullifying my magic.

The sensation sweeps over me in such a rush that I am brought to my knees, my hand spasming and releasing its hold of his hair.

Cyan stands to his full height, looking down at me. "Fates, you have a lot to learn, love," he muses, holding both vines that are binding my wrists and wrapping down my arms, forcing them together in one hand as he fixes his hair with the other.

"Are you always this fucking"—I cry out at the pain, but this time, the grip his vines have on me doesn't loosen—"vain?" I finish on a breathy pant.

Cyan chuckles, but the sound is lost when the front door is kicked in. I whip my head around at the sound to see Mallrie stalking forward. There is a flash of lilac. Then, the vines loosen their grip, and I fall back onto my ass. Mallrie has Cyan around his throat, but those vines snake up around his arm.

Whatever the vines are doing, they instantly bring Mallrie to his knees, his skin turning pale. Cyan kicks him in the chest. "Do *not* fuck with me, Mallrie," he says through gritted teeth. Finally, the vines loosen, and the colour returns to Mallrie's face and neck. I go to crawl towards him, but he swings a leg, knocking Cyan over. Mallrie is instantly atop him, forcing his hands above his head.

"What are you doing here?" Mallrie growls.

"Just keeping an eye on things," Cyan shrugs as casually

as possible while Mallrie pins him to the floor. "You know, just doing my job working for Mayor MacQuoid." His voice is filled with mockery. Whether that is aimed towards Mallrie or the mayor, I don't know...

Mallrie's on his feet, dragging Cyan with him. "Get the fuck out, Cyan, before you make me do something I'll regret."

"Oh, I'm sure that's already a long list," Cyan purrs. He glances over to where I am still sitting on the floor, wide-eyed, before flicking his gaze back to Mallrie. "I'm all done here anyway." He turns and heads for the door.

Mallrie doesn't move for a long moment after Cyan shuts the door behind him. I have no idea what just happened, but I know I need another drink. The guilt of leaving his house without saying a word bubbles its way to the surface, bringing with it tears of trepidation. "Mallrie, I'm so sorry," I breathe.

His hands are on my face, gently wiping away the tears. "Oh, little doe, you've got nothing to be sorry for." His expression hardens. "Why did you leave without telling me?"

My chest seizes up. *How do I even begin to explain...*

"Did I do something... wrong?" Mallrie asks quietly, gently lifting my chin so I look him in the face. Gods, he sounds so concerned, making me feel all the worse.

I shake my head. "No. It... I'm sorry."

"You have nothing to be sorry for, Eliana. Well, maybe the whole running away thing. Who knows what could have happened..." He closes his eyes as if the thought of something happening to me is too much to bear.

"It was just too much," I whisper, unable to look him in the eye. I take a deep breath. "Just, no one's ever... cared for me like that after sex. And just everything with Chelsea... It was all too much, and I guess I just got scared and needed some space."

Mallrie gently squeezes my arms as if he wants to hold me, to do more, but is restraining himself for my sake. "I understand. Things are going to get a little... crowded." He chuckles slightly. "The house is already feeling a little overcrowded, right?" I nod, tears pricking behind my eyes. "If you need space or time, that's fine. You're allowed time to yourself. We all are. But..." His brows pinch together, a sadness twisting at his handsome face. "You can't just run away like that, okay?" Mallrie glances over towards the door. "I don't know what Cyan is playing at. He's... unpredictable at the moment. His *Timeline*..." Mallrie trails off, unable to finish that sentence. I bite my lip. It must be so hard for him to have his brother working against him.

I take a step forward, intertwining my fingers with his. "I'm sorry," I whisper. "I didn't think... I just needed to get out."

Mallrie's cerulean eyes meet mine. "We can find you a safe place, a place only for you." The tears finally break free, and Mallrie pulls me into his arms. The feeling of being pressed against his chest, tucked under his arms, feels... amazing. I feel *safe*.

CHAPTER THIRTY-SEVEN
ELIANA

Mallrie's taken us out into the Melsheim Forest to run us through the training circuit he's created. Cold sweat runs down my spine, and we haven't even started yet. Something feels wrong. I hate coming into the forest, even with him holding my hand, grounding me.

"This tree, you're to go under," Mallrie says, but I am only half listening. I thought I heard a twig snap off in the distance. "Little doe, are you listening?" he whispers into my ear.

"Mm, yeah. Over the tree," I reply absent-mindedly.

"Under," Mallrie says sternly. Tyler's trying to rein in his laughter.

I smile brightly at Mallrie's cerulean eyes, which look darker with the shadows thrown across his face from all the trees. "That's what I said."

He rolls his eyes, continues with his debrief and drops my hand. I turn my attention back to the forest. *I swear I heard something...*

Snap!

I whirl around, and my heart seizes in my chest. "M-mallrie..." I whisper as I spot something moving through the dense bush. He is at my side in a heartbeat.

"You okay?" His hand presses to the small of my back, his thumb stroking me reassuringly. I point to where I thought I saw the creature. *It's gone.* "What did you see?"

"I-I don't know. Its eyes were *glowing*," I pant, panic trying to seep into my bones. Mallrie and I have worked hard over these last few days for me to get a better handle on my panic attacks. I don't think they'll ever go away completely, but I remind myself that I am in control. I know how to protect myself, and I will not let anyone hurt me. I focus on my breathing, and Mallrie praises me quietly.

It moved again! "There!" I point off in the distance at the seven-foot-tall creature. Its eyes are an ominous, golden glow in the tree's gloom. The shadows and thick brush obscure it from view, but I can clearly see great, pointed ears. It places a large hand on the tree in front of it. Long boney, pointed fingers wrap around it as it stares. The hairless body is perfectly stagnant, its beady eyes flickering between us, examining us, determining if we're a threat.

"Breathe, little doe. It will not hurt you," Mallrie whispers in my ear.

"What is that?" Chelsea asks. I steel myself at the sound of her voice, flicking a strand of blonde hair away from my face.

"An Ashga," Mallrie replies. "Don't worry, they don't usually like the taste of flesh."

"Usually?" Tyler remarks, with a snort of laughter. "That's really reassuring, man."

Mallrie looks down at him as if to say, *"Isn't it?"* The creature tilts its head over its shoulder before darting back into the forest. Mallrie's shoulders tense.

"What's wrong?" I whisper. He looks around. I try to

follow his gaze, but all I see are trees and bushes. "What's wrong?" I whisper-yell to him, panic setting in as the hairs on the back of my neck stand. Something is wrong. I know it.

"*Watch out,*" my grandmother's voice warns. My magic thrums in response.

"We've got a problem," Mallrie whispers to everyone. "We're being hunted."

"What?" Chelsea whispers, looking around us.

He shakes his head at her. "Stay quiet. Stay calm."

"Oh, yeah. You're superb at the ole pep talks today, mate," Tyler rebuts. "*Stay quiet. Stay calm,*" he mimics Mallrie. "You're just being hunted by some seven-foot-tall monster that only *occasionally* likes to eat meat. So he might eat you. But, on the other hand, he might just be hunting you for shits and gigs."

"Tyler. I swear to the Fates, if you don't shut your mouth—" A twig snaps above us, silencing Mallrie.

"What is it though? What's hunting us?" I whisper, trying to keep my breathing as even as possible.

"A Meshlynk."

We all stand there frozen in fear. Mallrie has gone over the creatures in the forest with us, debunking the myths we've been told as children. The Meshlynk are the only creatures within the Melsheim Forest that are a genuine threat. They hunt and attack for their own enjoyment. Then, my eyes fall on something behind Mallrie—a creature blending into the trees. Its tall body is covered in moss and shrubbery, long sharp claws extend from its fingertips and stag antlers protrude from its head. Its red eyes fixate on us from under its hood of shrubbery.

"I see it," I whisper, the icy chill from its stare paralysing me.

"Don't look at it," Mallrie hisses, but I can't help it. Its red eyes have me fixated. "Eliana. Look at me," he pleads. But it's no use. My brain screams to look away, but my body is lost to the Meshlynk.

My legs start ambling towards it. *Stop! Stop! Please!* I plead with my body, tears streaming down my face as I try everything I can to stop. To turn and run. The Meshlynk reaches its long arm towards me. Its sharp claws gently caress my face. The terrifying creature flicks back its head, dropping the hood of shrubberies and antlers to reveal a repulsive, greyed skull. Its red eyes are like glowing orbs burning into me, its lipless mouth exposing pink gums and yellowed teeth. I sob helplessly as the monster pulls me closer.

Something wraps around my waist, hoisting me high into the canopy of the trees. My arms thrash desperately, trying to free myself from whatever has me captive so I can return to the Meshlynk.

I scream as it falls onto its knees, water spilling from its mouth and eyes as it gasps for air. Mallrie's sword swings through the air, decapitating the beast. The pressure in my chest and head—that I didn't realise was the Meshlynk's grip—is suddenly gone. The pull the beast had over me is gone.

Tyler slowly lets me back down to the ground. The body of the Meshlynk decomposes into the earth as if it was merely made of black sludge. Small, white mushrooms sprout in its place. Mallrie runs his hands over my arms up to my face.

"Are you okay?" His voice is panicked but quiet. I nod, unable to look away from the mushrooms sprouting rapidly. "Burn them," Mallrie whispers, holding me close to his chest. "Otherwise, more will regenerate."

The tiny mushrooms ignite, letting off the pungent reek of death.

We're all sitting around the dining table eating breakfast when Mallrie walks in the front door, Winnie hot on his heels. The Misnac passes right by me and goes straight to Tyler, jumping to rest her large front paws on his knee. Winnie purrs loudly as he lovingly pats her head.

Throwing my hands up at the Misnac, I exclaim. "Wow! So much for Misnac loyalty." Winnie throws her large head my way, mewling loudly. That's when I see the piece of bacon hanging out of her mouth.

Tyler bursts into laughter from the other side of the table. "Loyalty can be bought," he announces, waving another piece of bacon in the air. Winnie lunges for it, and Tyler shrieks and counts his fingers animatedly as the Misnac chews happily.

I struggle to raise a single eyebrow. "That something Cyan taught you?" Chelsea shifts uncomfortably in her seat. She likes Cyan. Whatever she sees in him, I have no idea.

Mallrie's hand presses down on my shoulder in a reassuring squeeze. "No training today," he says before Tyler can speak.

My head snaps in his direction. "No training?" I parrot. We've trained ruthlessly for the last two weeks. *What's changed?*

"Thought you could do with a break," he whispers, kissing me on the top of the head, which makes me blush. I am not used to public displays of affection. "You've been working hard, and it's showing."

"What's that mean?" Tyler barks, dramatically swiping his thumbs under his eyes. "Don't tell me I've got bags under my eyes."

I bite down on my lip to stop myself from laughing. "Well, I didn't want to say anything…" I tease. Tyler tosses a bread roll at me, which I catch easily, subtly surprised. *Showing indeed.* My reflexes were not that good a month ago.

"You finished?" Mallrie whispers as he carefully pulls my chair out from the table. I nod. "Good. There's something I want to do with you today." That boyish glimmer in his eyes has my heart swelling and adrenaline coursing through my body.

"Aw, man, can I come?" Tyler laughs.

"No," Mallrie says coldly, not even looking up from me as he leads me out the front door.

"Where are we going?" I ask after a while. Mallrie lifts a branch out of my way, and I quickly duck under it.

"It's a surprise," he replies, grinning.

"Come on, you know I don't like surprises," I say. He knows I like to know exactly what's happening. After Beckett's unpredictable nature, I have always been anxious about what I don't know.

"Swimming," Mallrie offers, but that's all. I can't help the smile that tries to pull at my lips. *Swimming…* I've always dreamt of heading to the ocean. To see her crystal clear waters crash against the shore. I've tried so hard over the years to imagine how it would sound, what it'd smell like. But I never imagined actually *entering* the water.

I don't know how to swim. There isn't really any need to learn in Datura since there are no bodies of water around— apart from what apparently hides within the Melsheim Forest, but no one would be game enough to seek it out.

"I can't swim," I offer quietly, feeling the heat of embarrassment creep up my neck. I must seem so stupid to Mallrie. He's had years of experience and I... Well, don't. Sometimes, I don't know what he sees in me.

Mallrie's squeezes my hand. "Well, lucky for you, I do." He smiles at me with that boyish grin I can't help but fall a little more for. He's not like this around the others, and I don't think I will ever be able to tell him how much it means that he shares these little pieces of himself with me.

"The first thing you should know," Mallrie starts, snapping me out of my thoughts, "is that not every lake in the forest is safe to swim in. Actually, if you're ever caught out here alone, it's best to avoid them altogether."

"What if I need water?" I ask, fully knowing that I would never want to be in the forest without Mallrie by my side.

"Dig a hole, or collect it from the morning dew. Look, you don't need to stress, little doe. Just stay away from the lakes unless I tell you they're safe."

"Why? What's in them?" I ask, unable to stop my curiosity.

"Mermaids."

"Mermaids?" I exclaim. Suddenly, my curiosity explodes into childlike wonder. Never in my wildest dreams have I ever imagined that Mermaids could potentially be real, even with living in a town of flesh-eating monsters.

"Don't look so excited." Mallrie chuckles. "They're not as whimsical as you think. They're secretive and will lure anyone they can to their banks before dragging them to the bottom to eat."

My breakfast threatens to come back up. "They *eat* people?" I ask incredulously.

Mallrie nods as he pulls another branch out of my way. I

stop in my tracks. My breath is caught, and my mouth falls open as I take in the sight before me. Rocks pile up, creating a cliffside, a sparkling waterfall cascading down it. As much as this is like a dream come true, I can't help but think that this is a horrible idea. I would rather head back into Datura and deal with flesh-eating monsters and Cyan's psychotic mind games.

There is *no way* Mallrie will be able to convince me to get in *there*. No matter how deceiving and pretty it looks. Not when I don't know how to swim, let alone that a Mermaid is probably hiding in the depths, waiting to *eat me*.

Maybe the ocean isn't a dream I should be chasing after all?

Mallrie gently pushes me into the clearing. "It's okay, little doe. No Mermaids are in here."

"How do you know?" It's not like he can see into the depths of the lake. The water around the edges is crystal clear and a stunning blue, but the farther towards the waterfall, the deeper it gets. The water turns almost black and sinister.

"Because the Mer don't like the feel of the churning water." He nods towards the waterfall as he pulls off his boots and tosses them aside. "They have heightened senses, and the disruptive water hinders that." Mallrie is quiet momentarily, clearly trying to think how to best explain it before continuing. "You know how bats use sonar to help them see at night?" I nod, but I think I already know where this is going. "The Mer—*Fates*, if any of them heard me comparing them to bats, they'd kill me slowly." He laughs to himself, but that just has me more on edge. "They have heightened senses that *kind of* work in similar ways. Look, I don't know many Mer, so I'm no expert on the matter. Cyan, on—" Mallrie cuts himself off, his face turning sombre at the mention of his brother. "Doesn't matter," he says, clearing his throat and slightly shaking his head. "The disruption to the water can affect their senses, and they tend to avoid it. That's all you need to know."

He pulls his shirt off over his head. I bite my lip at how his muscles tense and shift with the motion. Heat floods between my thighs. I will never get used to the sight of him, of the muscles that just show years of dedication and training.

Mallrie looks over his shoulder to where I am still standing at the edge of the tree line. "Some say it's rude to stare," he says with that boyish grin.

I roll my eyes. "Like you care?" I take a cautious step forward, keeping a watchful eye on the lake, even though it's a good few feet away. "I think you like it when I stare." My voice has turned raspy as I gaze over his half-naked body.

Mallrie steps towards me, placing a finger under my chin and tilting my head up. "Oh, I really do, little doe," he purrs, kissing me lightly. His hands trail down my body as he deepens the kiss, his tongue coaxing my lips open. Mallrie's fingers toy with the hem of my shirt teasingly. The gentle swipes of his fingers against my bare skin have my body tingling with need.

Unable to bear it any longer, I pull the shirt over my head. Mallrie's hands move quickly, undoing my pants, then his own.

I look around, nervous that we could be seen. *But who would possibly be out in the middle of the Melsheim Forest?*

"Come," Mallrie says, taking my hand and leading me towards the lake.

"Do we have to?" I pull against his grip, afraid of entering man-eating, Mermaid-infested waters—well, potentially Mermaid-infested waters. "Can't we just sit on the bank?"

Mallrie raises an eyebrow. "I promise I will not let anything hurt you." My heart squeezes at the proclamation. Even though I know he cannot promise that.

"You're still making promises you can't keep," I mutter. His hand squeezes around my own. I look at him through my lashes as he coaxes me into the water.

"I will not let anything hurt you," he repeats as the water caresses my toes. I take another step forward.

Trust has always been something I have struggled with, but I *want* to trust Mallrie. How can you love someone wholly if you don't trust them? I close my eyes, inhaling the scent of the forest, letting it fill my lungs. *Trust,* I tell myself. I can trust him. I *should* trust him. I take another step forward.

Mallrie's rough, calloused hand grazes my hip. "That's my good girl," he encourages. The water licks up my legs to my thighs. Panic builds in my chest. "Breathe, little doe."

Breathe in. Hold. His cerulean eyes meet mine. The water of the lake is *almost* as stunning as them. *Breathe out.*

The panic still squeezes at my heart and the nape of my neck, but it's tolerable. The cool water slips over my waist, and I feel briefly weightless. Mallrie scoops me into his arms, wrapping my legs around his waist. "How are you feeling?" he asks.

A bubble of laughter erupts from me. "Nervous," I admit.

"Hold your breath," he says. As soon as I suck in a lungful of air, he dips us under the water. It's still so clear. My eyes sting and are blurry under the surface, but I can make out small, colourful fish swimming in the weeds.

We break the surface, the bright sun blinding and glistening off Mallrie's tanned shoulders. I run my hands along the stubble on his jaw. I drop my gaze to his lips and press myself closer. *Maybe dreaming of the ocean isn't such a bad thing after all.* I kiss him softly, my tongue sliding over his. I nip at his bottom lip and whisper, "I trust you."

CHAPTER THIRTY-EIGHT
ELIANA

The past two and a half weeks have been painfully slow, although Mallrie insists he is not responsible. I've spent countless hours meditating, working on honing my emotions and my concentration. Reading books and scriptures on spellcraft late into the night. Some nights, when Mallrie would leave to return to Datura, I'd stay awake, sitting on the small balcony jutting out from his bedroom surrounded by the sweet scent of the flowers wrapping themselves around the iron railings, reading my grandmother's grimoire by the light of my magic. When I wasn't meditating, practising my magic or having my nose buried in dust-covered books, I joined Tyler and Chelsea in the forest, running laps through the obstacle course Mallrie prepared.

I was pushing myself hard. I couldn't remember the last time I was this focused, determined not to fail. Not to let Mallrie down.

Tyler didn't find the training exhausting. But given what Mallrie said about his past and elemental magic, it didn't surprise me how he effortlessly bounced over fallen trees and floated over large pitfalls.

Then, there was the one-on-one combat training. It wasn't too bad, thanks to Mallrie being my partner. I often wondered when we trained one-on-one if he took it easier on me than the others. Tyler was my next favourite to spar with. His quick wit and humour made the hours of sword training bearable. My arms would be heavy with exhaustion, feeling a second away from falling off my body. Then, he would make a joke that would make me laugh so hard I would clutch my stomach. Mallrie always threw scathing looks our way, demanding we got back to work and to stop playing around. "Remember, Eliana, we're preparing for WAR!" Tyler would exclaim in his best Mallrie impersonation, and I would lose it all over again.

But my preferred weapon to practise with was the bow and arrow. Yielding the beautifully crafted longbow made me feel like I was living out all my fantasy dreams.

Then, Mallrie had us in three-on-one combat training. "You won't always have the privilege of fighting one enemy at a time. No one is just going to stand off to the side and wait their turn," he told us as we surrounded him. "You'll need to watch your own back because you won't always have someone watching it for you."

The worst training experience was the one where it was three against one. The thought of more than one person striking me always sent a cold sweat running down my spine. I never thought myself well coordinated, so having to wield a weapon—whether it be physical steel or my magic—and defend myself always felt overwhelming. It didn't matter how many times Mallrie pulled me aside after training and comforted me, telling me that if the situation ever arose and we were, in fact, in a battle, he would always watch my back. We were a team, and we all watched out for one another.

Or Tyler's attempt at reassurance, "Don't worry, E." He seemed to have a particular affection for abbreviating your name down to the first letter. "When thrust into that moment, you can do it. Kinda like how mothers get, like, superhuman strength when their child is in danger." He shrugs, the action seeming so effortless despite never knowing his mother. I guess we've been able to bond over that, even if neither of us talks about it much.

Chelsea and I have tried to keep our distance, but it's difficult in a small house with one bathroom and shared training partners.

Two and a half weeks has felt like an eternity.

Chelsea and Tyler have been camping out in the lounge room, though there have been nights when Tyler has taken to sleeping in the garden. It was tempting to join him, but the fear of a Kailadon or something from within the Melsheim Forest finding me always had me staying in the safety of the little house.

Then, there were the hours upon hours of reading and studying Mallrie's extensive library of personal grimoires and various other spell books. I feel as though my eyes are ready to fall out of my head.

Tyler would hover—literally, as if he was sitting on a cloud—over my shoulder as I read through my grimoire. He'd question bits and pieces of what my grandmother had written, trying to understand my relationship with her. Every time he read a little memory my grandmother had jotted down in the margin, he'd sigh, tilting his head to the side, and I'd feel a pang in my chest. Tyler never knew his family. They abandoned him as a newborn, left at the government building to be adopted. He never stayed with one family for long, and by the time he was thirteen, he had run away for good. He'd steal clothes and food, sleep on the rooftops or break into the commercial buildings if the weather turned. I asked him once if he was ever afraid of getting caught by the Kailadons, to which he replied, "When you have nothing and no one, death doesn't seem so bad." My heart cracked, and I pulled him into an embrace, biting back the tears. He laughed it off, claiming the perks were that he could do whatever he wanted, whenever he wanted—something he struggled a bit with once Chelsea and Cyan found him and he was forced into hiding. He wouldn't tell me where they made him stay or much about his relationship with Cyan, and I wasn't about to ask Chelsea.

CHAPTER THIRTY-NINE
ELIANA

I watch from the balcony, the cool night air kissing my bare legs as I fiddle with the hem of Mallrie's shirt I'm wearing. Finally, he turns to look at me from the barrier. He lifts a hand in farewell. My heart squeezes. I told him I could come with him on his patrol of Datura. That surely, two sets of eyes are better than one. That I could use that chance to practise my magic.

Mallrie refused.

He told me I needed to rest and didn't want to put me in any unnecessary danger. Mallrie was also going to go meet with Cyan again. Not that he told me outright. I kind of figured out that he's been meeting with his brother on these patrols on my own.

I overheard Mallrie and Chelsea speaking about it one morning . They both seemed nervous, but as soon as the bloody stair squeaked under my weight, their conversation shifted, and Mallrie looked up at me with a warm smile.

They seem to be getting along really well. Which irks me a little.

I settle into bed. It's late, and I am exhausted. My head

hits the pillow with a soft thump, and Winnie jumps onto the bed. The large Misnac has taken it upon herself to sleep on the end of the bed when Mallrie leaves. Apparently, he had never allowed her to sleep on the bed before. Yet, when he returned home after the first time he left me to go on his patrol, he found Winifred snuggled up under the blankets and a smile on my face. So he's allowed it. But only when he's not around.

Lifting the blankets, I let her crawl under and curl against my side. It's not long before I fall into a blissful, dreamless sleep.

Something startles me from my slumber. Winnie is nowhere to be seen, which is unusual for her. She usually only leaves the bed once—

I glance at the clock. It's only two a.m., and Mallrie doesn't usually get home till about four-thirty. Then, he does his weird little Hypreslep thing and is up by five a.m.. A thump on the stairs has me running for the door. Mallrie stumbles up the stairs, a bloody mess.

"Wh-what?" I stumble over my words as I rush to help him. "What happened?" Helping him onto the edge of the bed, he drops his sword on the floor. It falls with a soft thud against the carpet, black Kailadon blood splattering.

"*Cursed Fates*," he growls as he reaches behind his head, wincing as he pulls his shirt off. He is covered in so much blood. And hardly any of it is from the Kailadon.

"Don't move." I run towards the door, glancing over my shoulder as he flops back on the bed, flinging a muscled arm over his eyes. I roll my eyes. *Well, okay then,* I think as I rush downstairs to get a bowl of water and a cloth.

"Is everything okay?" Chelsea asks when I reach the bottom steps. Tyler is still passed out in front of the fire.

"Yep," I clip. *Why can't she be a heavy sleeper?*

"There's blood on the balustrade. Is Mallrie okay?" She follows me into the kitchen as I gather my supplies.

"He'll be fine, Chelsea. Go back to sleep." I turn on my heel and stomp back up the stairs, slamming the door a little more forcefully than I meant to.

Sitting on the bed beside Mallrie, I start to clean his wounds. He doesn't move, breathing steadily, even as Winnie lies on the bed beside him, her large head inches from his leg. "Mallrie?" I speak softly.

"Mm," he groans.

"What were you thinking?" I must have put a little too much pressure on the wound because he sucks in a sharp breath and sits up. "Fighting a mutant?" I assume that's why he is covered in so much blood.

His eyes turn cold, and his brows press together. "I wasn't fighting a mutant. I was fighting Cyan," he growls, placing his hand around mine to stop me.

I tilt my head to the side. "Wait, what?" I ask, snatching my arm out of his grip.

Mallrie looks down at our hands, at the distance I've put between us. "I'm sorry," he whispers.

"I know," I reply, lifting my hand over the wound. My magic hums within my chest as I press my heated palm to his side. We discovered that, along with my fire magic, the traces of Fae within me have given me a kernel of their healing ability. Something that has come in handy with training—no matter how careful we are, accidents happen. I guess it's a good thing because I can practise channelling that healing Fae magic.

"I found someone," Mallrie continues. "A Mortal. One Edgar and Cyan have been experimenting on." Apparently, Cyan's been assisting in the experimentations. Not that he wants to be—or so he claimed. Edgar has something over

Cyan that we can't quite figure out. Cyan doesn't know either. Which is strange. So, he's lying to Mallrie or, as I suggested, being drugged.

"Well, what was left of them, anyway," Mallrie continues. "Cyan appeared out of nowhere. I tried to talk to him. To ask him what was going on but..."

"But what?" I ask, gently running my fingers through his hair.

"*Fates*, Eliana, you have to understand that the Cyan you've seen isn't the Cyan I know. I love my brother, even if we don't see eye-to-eye. Even if every time we see each other, we're at each other's throats. I don't want to hurt him, and deep down, he doesn't want to hurt me either." Mallrie looks up at me, his eyes lined with silver as he finds the words to make me believe that there could be a *better* side to Cyan. Mallrie shakes his head. "He attacked me like I was the enemy. Like he'd do anything to kill me."

"Mallrie..."

"No, Eliana," Mallrie says. He takes my hands in his and gently squeezes. "You don't understand. Edgar did *something* to him." He pushes to his feet and sways a little. "I need to go help him. I need to save him."

I push him back down. "Okay, we will. But not tonight. You're..." I shake my head, tracking his wounds. "Not tonight. We'll do it together. Soon, I promise." Tears threaten to break free from behind my composed expression at the love and devotion Mallrie has for Cyan, even if I believe he doesn't deserve it. "Please, I don't think I could stand seeing you go after Edgar like this. You'll get yourself killed, and that—" My voice breaks at the thought of losing him.

Mallrie kisses my forehead. "As you wish."

"What's wrong, Win?" I yawn. My muscles ache in protest as I shift under the covers, trying to find her. "Win, stop!" I groan as she continues to nuzzle at my face and mewl incisively. "Go back to sleep." I rub behind her ears where I know she likes—

"OW!" I sit up. "What the hell, Win?" I clutch my hand against my chest that she just nipped, which is very out of character. The sleepiness instantly goes from my head as I inspect my hand to make sure her large teeth didn't puncture the skin. Winnie runs over to the balcony, mewling and flicking her tail impatiently until I drag myself out of bed and follow her. I rub my eyes, but it's still dark. With a flick of my wrist, a small flame takes flight, floating in front of me, lighting the way. I open the glass doors, and the fresh night air wisps around us. Something is wrong. I can sense it now. With another flick of my wrist, a series of fireballs set out from the balcony, illuminating the front yard towards the barrier.

My heart sinks, and my knees give out.

I clutch onto the rail, crushing the soft flowers underneath. Lying half through the barrier is Mallrie. Not that it looks like him at all. Blood has covered every inch of his skin. It seems like someone has just dumped a bucket of blood on top of him. I jump over the railing and fall gracefully. As soon as my feet hit the ground, I sprint across the pathway. "Mallrie!" I shout as I fall to my knees, sliding to a halt at his side. I don't even feel the scrape of the stones against my bare knees. He's unconscious but still breathing.

Just.

"El?" Tyler calls from the doorway, still half asleep.

"Tyler! Help me. Please!" I shout back, the panic rising in my voice. Before I can blink, he is at my side.

"Oh, shit!" he curses as he registers the bloody mess in my arms is Mallrie. "Is... Is he...?"

"No. But we need to get him inside now!"

"Yeah, yeah. Of course. Stand back." I take a tentative step back, not wanting to leave Mallrie's side. His breathing is shallow. Tyler waves his hands, summoning the wind, and it carefully lifts Mallrie, rolling him over onto his back. His shirt is ripped open, and the smell from the wound makes me want to gag. Tyler scrunches his nose as he holds his hands out as if he's holding up Mallrie, and we rush back inside.

Chelsea must have seen what is happening and has already cleared off the island bench and prepared a bowl of water and herbs for cleaning the wounds.

Tyler carefully sets Mallrie on the bench. A small flame encircles his shirt, incinerating it but not harming him. We all stand around his body, in shock at the bloody mess of what remains of Mallrie on the bench. I don't think I have seen so much blood in all my life, not even in my two days studying to be a medic. How he got back here at all is a miracle. My heart is in my throat, the beating so loud in my ears.

Tears well up in my eyes, and I do everything I can to not fall apart. The last few weeks have not just consisted of learning the art of our craft, how to fight, writing our own spells...

I have fallen completely and irrevocably in love with Mallrie. We would sneak away to the lake deep in the Melsheim Forest for picnics and swimming. The sex... Oh, gods. I have entirely let Mallrie into my heart. He knows every deepest desire of mine. I have shared my every worry and triumph with him. Mallrie is more than a lover; he is my best friend.

And now, watching as he bleeds out on the bench in front of me, feeling utterly useless... It's more than I can take.

Chelsea works away, trying to clear the blood on the massive wound across his chest. Tiny water beads run over the rest of his body, turning red as they magically clean the blood, then head over to the sink. She's talking quickly and quietly, giving Tyler orders on how to take care of his head. She's so efficient and thorough in her demands to Tyler that she hardly has to look at what he's doing. Finally, Chelsea meets my gaze, looking up for the first time since she started working. Her hands are covered in blood. "You okay, El?"

I'm not. I'm really not.

But how can I say that there's no way I can help? That my heart is about to jump out of my throat? I lasted all of two days studying to be a medic. Even though I have gotten better at being surrounded by blood, there is something entirely different in patching up a small wound and seeing the man you care so much about bleed out before you. I nod frantically and unconvincingly. "Wha-what do you want me to do?" My voice shakes more than I would like.

"Get the bath started with some valerian, calendula and lilac," Chelsea says gently yet sternly, somewhere between a mother's kindness and the demand of a practitioner.

My brain finally kicks into gear—garden apothecary was one topic Mallrie had us study. It is also my favourite, since it reminds me so much of my grandmother. "No, valerian is soporific. Vervain would be better," I say more to myself as I walk over to the sink to wash the blood off my hands.

I glance back at Chelsea… We have hardly spoken since our altercation in the forest. Both keeping a respectable distance from the other. "Hey," I call back to her from the front door. She looks up, but her water droplets take over, cleaning her hands. "Thanks. For everything." I glance down at Mallrie, then back at her. Despite our differences, I really appreciate her taking charge of this. The gods know I wouldn't have been able to keep my cool enough to help Mallrie. And as much as I am sure she is helping him because, well, we all need his help to restore the magic to the Enkanti Tree, a small part of me hopes that she is helping out because she knows how much he means to me.

"Don't mention it." She smiles, and the tension in my shoulders from holding onto my anger eases a little.

I flick a fireball from my fingertips, and it breaks off into three smaller orbs and flies in front of me, only stopping to hover over the plants I need. I rush over to them, plucking handfuls of what I need before sprinting back inside. The balls of fire follow me, then disintegrate at the front door. Winnie sits at the top of the stairs, whining sadly. My heart breaks for her too. "Win. Come here, darling," I call, jerking my head for her to follow. She's at my side before I can even get into the kitchen.

"I've already filled the bath. Can you just heat it?" Chelsea calls as I pluck the leaves from the stems and dump them into a bowl.

"Yeah, no worries," I reply, glancing over my shoulder. She's got Mallrie partially stitched up. That will take too long to heal. I should have done it. I should have been stronger for him. I give Winnie an apologetic look before heading off into the bathroom, tossing the florals into the bath. Pressing my hands together, slowly pulling them apart, the tension forms a flickering blue orb. I carefully submerge it into the water and briefly watch it bobble under the surface. The water will heat to 32º celsius before the orb extinguishes at the perfect temperature.

I run my hand through the water just to double-check. It's perfect. I turn to check on Mallrie, but Tyler has him propped up under his arm. Chelsea gives me a look, and I know she's done her best.

Mallrie's eyes keep fluttering open, but his iris' are white and cloudy. Tyler quickly helps me undress him and get him in the bath before turning to me. He suddenly looks so much older than he did yesterday. I guess experiencing your friend nearly dying can do that to someone.

"Do you want anything?" he asks quietly.

I shake my head and sit beside the bath, carefully cupping the water and pouring it through Mallrie's hair to clean it. Winnie comes and lays next to me, her head in my lap. Tyler nods lugubriously and walks out, shutting the door behind him.

I wake up late the next day... or maybe the day after. Someone put a blanket around me and refilled the bath with warm water and fresh botanicals. There's a glass of water and a bowl for Winnie and me. Both haven't been touched.

Winnie stirs as I straighten up. My body is stiff from sitting in an awkward position for too long. I apply some heat to my neck to ease out the knot. Mallrie looks better, but there's something wrong with the dark black/green circles under his eyes. They don't look like the other purplish-black bruises that pepper his body. I run my fingers through his hair, and he leans into my touch. "Mallrie?" I whisper, my voice cracking. He groans, responding to his name. "Hey, you're okay. I'm here." I run my fingers through his hair, and my other hand slips into the warm water, checking his wound. It's not healing correctly. It feels unnaturally warm—most likely an infection. "Tyler!" I shout as he bounces into the room.

"Yo?"

"Something's wrong. We need to get him into bed so I can seal his wound properly." My voice comes out stronger than I expected, even though my head spins as I stand up. Winnie growls softly at the rude awakening. I run my fingers through her fur as Tyler uses his magic, carefully lifting Mallrie out of the tub and taking him upstairs. I follow him out. Chelsea walks back inside, a dead chicken and some vegetables in her arm. She looks between Tyler and me, following Mallrie's body upstairs.

"What's happened?" She drops everything on the table and wipes her hands on her clothes.

"His wound isn't healing. I think there might be an infection."

"Impossible. That wound was practically sparkling when I was done with it." I shrug my shoulders, not wanting to get into a fight with her over this. Especially when things are just starting to feel a little better... Well, for me, anyway. I still haven't had a chance to talk to Chelsea about everything, but I think I am ready to finally sit down with her. To try and potentially patch things between us. I don't know if we'll ever be the friends we once were. Too much has happened since then, and we've grown in two completely different environments. We're just such different people. But if we can at least put our differences aside—well, if *I* can—then maybe we can make this whole living together situation a little less awkward.

But I know something is wrong with Mallrie. It's as if I can *sense* it. Like my magic can feel it.

I quickly look over his wounds, the first proper look I have had. The gash on his head looks good. It's joined back together nicely. He'll likely have a scar from his left eye to his jaw. But what worries me is the massive slash from his chest to his stomach. Chelsea has about—from a rough count—fifty-two stitches in there. It's a wonder Mallrie didn't die right where he stood, that he wasn't carrying his intestines in his arms as he stumbled home. He would have had to use his time elemental magic, which would have been taxing on his body.

The skin has come together effectively, but there's a greenish tinge where the flesh has joined back together. The look of it makes my stomach churn. *I don't understand.* Mallrie explained how the Kailadons can carry infections, and when cut by them, those infections can be... I bite my lip hard, forcing the bile back down my throat. *I don't understand.* We did *everything* we were taught to effectively clean a Kailadon wound.

"Duuude..." Tyler looks almost as green as the wound. "Something's messing with him."

"You don't need to stay, Ty," I say calmly. I know that whatever's happening, those stitches need to come out as soon as possible. And the pungent smell is only going to get worse.

"Yeah, nah. Whatever you need, I've got your back."

I look back over at Chelsea leaning against the doorframe, chewing her thumbnail as she gives me a nod as if to say, *"go ahead."* I take a deep breath, heat my hands, disinfecting them, and then give them a quick shake to dispel some of the heat. Then, I carefully run my fingernail along the stitches, singeing them away. The sound of the stitches snapping and burning into oblivion is the only sound before the sickening smell of decay emanates from the wound on Mallrie's chest. I scrunch up my nose. I can hear Chelsea make a run for it and Tyler gagging.

"Not helping, Ty!" I shout at him.

"Sorry—" He gags again. "I'm good."

I shake my head and take a deep breath before returning to the wound. I run my fingers over it, trying to figure out what happened. Mallrie groans at my touch.

"I'm sorry," I whisper, my face close to his.

"Magic..." he whispers in my ear. It's the first word he's said since we found him.

"What?" I look at him, bewildered.

"Needs magic..." His voice is weak, and I can see his eyes searching behind closed lids.

"We've used magic. Chelsea has cleaned it, and we've used some—"

"Faerie magic," Mallrie whispers weakly. "The mutant Kailadon is part faerie..."

"Fuck, man. Where are we going to get a Fae to help us?" Tyler groans.

I stand up. I don't know what to do. We have never seen a faerie before. Mallrie has told us stories about them, but he had hardly any scriptures on their magical abilities. I run my fingers through my hair, interlocking them at the back of my head. "Think, Eli. Think," I mutter to myself, trying to rack my brain.

My head feels like it's on fire, an inexplicable sensation; a memory burns to life before my eyes...

I'm a child, running around the oak tree in the town

centre. The small Fae—about the size of my hand—are dancing under my feet, singing a merry song. Their voices are too high and squeaky to make out the words, but the tune makes me happy. If people can see them or if they're just a figment of my imagination, I don't know—or care in this rare moment of peace.

I pick a lonely flower that's pushed through the cracks and lean against the tree. The white flower with a sunny yellow centre reminds me of a daisy. I smile down at it, twisting it between my fingers, and sit at the tree's base. A small faerie jumps up onto my knee. She's so light I wouldn't have known she was there if I didn't see her. Her bright green eyes glow up at me as she blinks curiously.

When you think of faeries, you think of something cute and whimsical, but there's something dark and mischievous about them. They dress to blend into their surroundings and can change the pigment of their skin like a chameleon.

My grandmother always told me that there's an unspoken rule. *Never piss off the Fae.* She'd tell me bedtime stories of the tiny creatures. How they have generous hearts but vicious natures. That if I ever encountered one, to always be polite and courteous. Even if they look sweet and innocent to keep my wits about me, for they can easily take down a fully grown man despite their size.

The Fae squeaks and points at the flower twirling around on my knee. I giggle, turn the flower upside down and spin it above her as she dances. Suddenly, there's a thump and crash. We look over, and a large black crow with milky white eyes has crashed into the tree. It gets up totteringly, shaking its head. *It must be blind,* I think, noticing its eyes. My heart sinks when the bird holds its wing at an awkward angle.

"Oh, no, it's hurt," I tell the faerie. Some of the Fae have backed away from the crow, looking uneasy, like they don't trust it. Others are tentatively approaching it, trying to calm it down. I hold out my hand. "Hey... you're okay," I whisper. "Relax. They're not going to hurt you." *I hope.*

The Fae on my knee looks up at me and points to the flower and then to the crow, squeaking in its high-pitched voice.

"Oh. You want the flower?" I pass it over carefully. She lifts it above her head. It looks like she's holding a little flower umbrella. She passes it off to another faerie, who pulls the petals off and rubs them over the pistil before feeding the crow. The sweet, apple-like scent drifts up to me, and I take a deep breath. The faerie returns to my knee as I watch her feed the crow carefully. She unfolds her wings, tucked close to her back, and flutters to my shoulder. Leaning in close to talk into my ear, the squeaks melt into words as I strain to listen to her soft voice talk. "That was a camomile flower. They're great for dissolving belly pains. However, mixed with a little Fae magic, it can heal almost any ailment."

That's it! I jolt from my daydream. Mallrie's pale face comes back into focus. *We're losing him.* I need to make haste. "Tyler, I know what I've got to do!" He looks at me, shocked. A wave of amazement rushes through me as the Fae healing spell burns to life in my mind like I always knew it. Like it was hidden deep in my memory.

"Okay. What do you need?" Tyler's ready to help in any way possible. I love that about him. Even if sometimes he is a bit juvenile and his jokes are dry, he's always ready to help anyone whenever they need it. My heart freezes.

"I need the mutant Kailadon's blood... and a camomile flower," I add, trying to lighten my tone.

Tyler's head nods quickly, clearly thinking of what to do. "Okay. You and I will go get the blood. Chels can stay here and watch Mallrie. Her magic is probably the best to keep the infection away from his heart." I can't help but smile. Despite the jokes and mischief, Tyler can be an excellent leader when he wants to be.

"Good plan. But you got to do what I say. This isn't like the Kailadons we've faced before." Tyler nods, and we head for the door. He explains to Chelsea what's happening, his arm holding her elbow as he speaks quickly while I lace up my boots.

Tyler and I rush through the Melsheim Forest. As much as I complained about Mallrie's circuit, he really did set us up for situations like this. Tyler uses his magic to clear branches on our path, and we're so used to climbing over fallen trees that it feels like second nature. I'm on edge. After our encounter with the Meshlynk, we'd be stupid not to be on high alert. I glance over at Tyler. I can see the small, black piercing below his lip flicking from side to side as he fidgets. "We've got this," I whisper to him.

"Of course we do," Tyler replies, but his usual confidence that I admire so much has been shaken.

We're almost at the forest's edge when I get a tingle up my spine. We're being followed. I push Tyler against a tree, my finger pressed to my lips. He carefully uncurls his long stock whip from his belt and holds it. He must have sensed it too. The forest is still and quiet. For the briefest moment, I wonder if I imagined it, but Tyler gives me a look, and I know I didn't.

In the two and a half weeks we have been training with Mallrie, we encountered some truly horrifying creatures in the Melsheim Forest. I try not to let the memory of the Meshlynk wash over me. How its eyes connected with mine and it could take complete control over my body.

Snap!

A twig breaks underfoot, snapping the memory away. I glance back at Tyler, who shakes his head. It wasn't us. I looked cautiously around the tree, my heart loud in my ears. No matter how often we've encountered the different creatures in the forest and how well I can protect myself now, I am still not used to being greeted with my worst nightmares.

Living, breathing nightmares.

Nightmares that will stop at nothing to kill me.

That's what my life consists of now. I take a deep breath, and the weight of a fireball in my hand eases a little of my anxiety. I poke my head around the corner and let out a relieved sigh. The fireball disbands back into my hand.

"It's okay, Ty," I say calmly, Winnie trotting over for pats.

"Win! Girl! I almost killed you!" Tyler says breathlessly as he wraps his whip back up. He must have been holding his breath too. Maybe it wasn't a good idea to bring him with me. He hasn't encountered the mutant Kailadon before.

"We've got to go," I say sternly. Tyler runs his hand through the Misnac's fur, and the three of us chase the setting sun in search of the mutant Kailadon.

CHAPTER FORTY
ELIANA

The silver moonlight illuminates the dark streets of Datura, the rancid smell of death and decay pungent in their tight meandering alleyways. As much as I would have preferred Winnie to return home, she was insistent on following us. Tyler pokes his head carefully around a corner. "You sure we can't just search for it from the rooftops?" he asks for the hundredth time since we entered the sleepy town.

"Tell me again how you'd get a sixty-four-kilogram Misnac onto the roof?"

Tyler's eyes light up with mischievous glee. Then, with a wave of his hand, a slight wind rushes around me, blowing my hair into my face. "Maaggiicc," he says with quiet reverence.

I scoff. "And how's your hand?"

Tyler rolls his eyes, muttering under his breath. He initially suggested we take to the rooftops when we got into town. Winnie almost bit off his hand when the gust of wind he created drifted under her belly. Apparently, Misnacs prefer to keep their paws firmly on the ground.

We sneak through the streets, water splashing against our boots, trying to keep to the shadows as much as possible, wanting to avoid drawing the attention of anyone who may contact the GDO in the morning. The garbage scent of death gets stronger the closer we get to the centre of town, so we keep following it. There is an eerie stillness to the night that has us all on edge. Winnie's hackles suddenly stand up, and she's hissing menacingly—a warning.

Tyler wraps his arm around my waist, pulling me against the wall. He presses a white-tipped finger to his lips, and I run my hand down Winnie's back, shushing her. Tyler jerks his chin towards the opening. His face is as white as the tips of his fingers. Pushing past the large Misnac, peering around the corner, I spot the mutant Kailadon at the base of the Enkanti Tree, its jaw dislocated as it ripped apart the body of another Kailadon.

"What the fuck?" Tyler whispers as I tuck myself safely out of view of this new nightmare. "It's... eating its own kind. Well, *sort of* its own kind. Can we still class them as the same—"

"*Tyler!*" I hiss, my stomach twisting uncomfortable.

This doesn't make sense.

"Surely there's nothing it can get from that—" I press my blackened finger to my lips, my glare silencing Tyler's thoughts. He's right though. Kailadons are practically skin and bones. There can't possibly be anything of nutritional value from eating one of its own.

Unless...

The thought makes my stomach stir unpleasantly. *Unless it is hunting for sport.* Since no mortal would dare wander the streets after dark, its only next prey would be a Kailadon.

The sound of bones cracking as the mutant breaks off

an arm reverberates through the streets and down my spine. I back up a bit, putting more space between the mutant and us.

"Okay, Tyler." My voice is shaky. The last time I encountered this Kailadon, I was with Cyan, and we barely made it out alive. Mallrie is fighting for his life.

"We've got this, E." Tyler smiles at me, but I can tell he's just as scared. There's no way he wouldn't have noticed the hole in the Kailadon's chest and head.

"Look, there's no way we're actually going to kill it with just the two of us." Winnie mews attentively. I roll my eyes. "Win. No. If anything happened to you, Mallrie would kill me. And honestly, you're not even meant to be here." I give her a stern look, and she shakes her head, pretending she doesn't understand me when I know she does. I pull a vial from my back pocket. "We just need a bit of its blood. One good hit, and then—"

"Get the blood," Tyler finishes my sentence. "Really wish Mal or Cyan were here," he says thoughtfully. I sigh. He's not wrong. They'd definitely have a better plan than... whatever this is.

"Me too, Ty. Me too."

He silently claps his hands together. "Great, so it's decided. Let's go to Uncle C and get him." I roll my eyes.

"No. Absolutely not." *There's no way I'm going to him for help.* "Besides, there's more chance of the mutant Kailadon giving us a blood donation than Cyan willingly helping us."

"Don't know until you ask." Tyler turns and jogs down the alleyway.

"*Tyler!*" I whisper-yell after him, but he's already gone.

Winnie's growling gets louder and louder. I look down. Her hackles are raised again, and she crouches as if she's about to strike.

Fuck.

My heart sinks into liquid goop in my stomach. I slowly turn. The silence is deafening. The sound of breaking bones is gone. I swallow hard. Standing at the entrance of the alleyway is the mutant Kailadon. Its jaw hangs limply, revealing rows of sharp teeth, and its long, forked tongue dangles from its mouth, thick mucus dripping onto the cobblestone.

I slowly bend down and grab a handful of Winnie's fur, hushing her quietly. The mutant looks around as if it heard something, but is unsure where the sound came from. I notice a thick gash across its face where the two nasal slits are.

Mallrie.

Instantly, I knew it was him who landed that blow. It looks like the laceration cut deep enough to affect the mutant's olfaction. It also isn't putting any pressure on its right leg. I can't see any wound from this angle though. Maybe Mallrie got it from behind. He taught us to find our opponent's weaknesses and use them to our advantage.

The mutant clicks its head to the side, a jarring, almost painful-looking motion. Its head hangs at a sickening angle, deep clicking sounds from the back of its throat, filling the space between us. I glance over my shoulder, quickly ensuring Tyler hasn't changed his mind.

When I turn around, the mutant Kailadon stands right before me. My hands sweat under Winnie's soft, spotted fur as I try to silently quiet her. I swear she's stopped breathing, as have I. The mutant's long tongue licks at the air but doesn't touch my face. Thick secretion drips onto my shoulders, and then, unexpectedly, I am flung through the air. My body crashes against the building at the end of the alleyway. The air is knocked out of me completely, my vision blurred.

I hear Winnie yowl painfully, and the mutant Kailadon's scream is so animalistic it feels almost other-worldly. My bones chill at the sound of impending doom. I struggle to my feet, steadying myself against the wall I was thrown into. The pain in my head is unbearable, but I can't leave Winnie.

I breathe through the pain as Winnie lunges at the beast again, the side of her face covered in blue blood. Her teeth sink into the mutant Kailadon's shoulder, and it swings an arm, slicing the tip of her ear. Winnie yelps, letting go and falling to the cobblestone, landing on her feet.

I draw a flaming arrow and fire it at the monster. My arrow finds its mark in the shoulder Winnie was just attacking, yet the mutant pays it no attention. It advances towards me, but my back is pressed against the wall. Panic seeps into my veins as I lunge out of the way of its arm. I roll against the cobblestone, water soaking into my clothes, sending a chill through me.

Winnie instantly leaps through the air, claws and fangs bared as her body slams into the Kailadon. It swings a sharp arm, making contact with her hind legs. Winnie shrieks but lunges at the monster's leg. She doesn't attack. Instead, she draws the mutant away from me.

Pushing to my feet, I chase after them. I won't allow that monster to hurt her. As soon as I round the corner, the mutant Kailadon is pressing its large body against me, forcing me back into a wall. The back of its arm presses against my throat, dragging me up the wall.

Fuck. Fuck. Shit!

I focus on breathing. The pressure against my throat is

enough to hold me up, but not tight enough to compromise my air supply. The smell of decay fills my lungs as the mutant Kailadon clicks wrathfully in my face.

Shit. Does it remember me?

I try to shake the terrifying thought from my mind. I heat my whole body. The flesh of the mutant Kailadon's arm sizzles as it presses me against the wall. It doesn't even flinch. I want to gag because of the smell of burning, rotten flesh that's assaulting my senses. The monster just continues to click aggressively in my face. I thrust my hips forward forcefully, causing the mutant to stumble back enough for me to free my arms. I grab onto its arm, pushing my legs up high against its chest. The mutant's clicking is getting more impatient, morphing into that blood-curdling screech. I let it bring itself closer, my knees pressing against my chest.

Waiting. Breathing. *Trying* to stay calm.

The mutant Kailadon presses its hot tongue against the side of my face and slowly licks its way up. Tasting me. In an instant, my body is white-hot. I thrust my legs out, using all of my upper body strength to grip the arm in place. The mutant screeches in pain as its body sizzles at my touch. I feel a snap, and then the arm falls limp at its side, dropping me hard onto the ground. I scurry between its legs and out the other side. Mallrie took a decent shot at its back leg. I stand and jerk my arm downward, producing a long, flaming sword.

I can't see Winnie, and my heart sinks. A part of me hopes she just bolted, but she isn't a coward. I know the loyalty Mallrie spoke of that the Misnacs possess. Winnie would never just abandon me. Her devotion has led her here. Her loyalty was to Mallrie to see this mission through, to save his life. But I fear that if I can't hear her...

The worst likely scenarios play through my mind. I can't think about the what-ifs. Right now, I just got to get a vial of blood. Kill the mutant before it kills me. Best-case scenario.

The Kailadon charges towards me. I grip my sword tighter, the flames licking at my hands. The mutant raises its sharp-bladed arm and strikes down at me. Raising my flaming sword, I meet its attack and block it. The sound of bone cracking against steel is like nothing I've ever heard before. The flames crackle and pop around the bone.

Its top jaw flexes and tightens, but its bottom jaw hangs slack.

Broken.

I take a quick step back and swiftly spin, getting more speed and force as I kick the broken jaw clean off the mutant Kailadon's face. Blood splatters across me and the ground as the jaw slides into the wall. The vulgar sound coming from the mutant Kailadon as it tries to scream has me instinctively dropping my sword to cover my ears. The weapon simmers out as it clangs against the cobblestone, leaving only an ashy imprint.

Fuck.

I am flung out of the alleyway and into the Enkanti Tree. My head spins as I try to push to my feet.

It's fine. I'm fine, I unconvincingly tell myself, even though I know that bit of Fae in me will try to heal my wounds. Even though I've never been in a situation that has called for it to work so quickly, I am conscious of the toll it may leave on my body.

If Tyler did manage to get Cyan to come, they could find the jaw and extract the blood. I just have to keep it distracted until then. "*Yes, but Mallrie needs you to perform the spell,*" whispers my grandmother's voice around me.

My eyes feel like they're going to fall out of my head. The pressure is too much. I blink hard, trying to focus. I toss a fireball. The mutant deflects it with a wave of its bladed arm. It throws me across the square again, my body cracking into the library stairs. My bones ache in protest as I try to push myself to my feet. The mutant Kailadon is upon me in a heartbeat. Its bladed arm threatens to turn me into bloody ribbons. I kick my leg out, sending the beast falling, but it lunges towards me. The remaining top jaw springs forward, sending its needle-like teeth into my flesh. I roll out of the way, but not fast enough. A searing pain laces down my leg as the creature drags its teeth through my jeans and flesh. I scream, unable to hold it in against the pain. Tears pour from my eyes as I crawl away from the monster.

Every move I make needs to be faster. Every time I move, the mutant has already got a counterattack ready.

The mutant Kailadon is tossing me around the town square like a fucking rag doll. The taste of iron fills my mouth as I spit a mouthful of blood onto the cobblestone. But I won't let Mallrie down. I will get that vial of blood and perform the spell to heal him. *And* I will kill this mutant in the process.

I push to my feet, a fresh wave of determination washing through me. I lick my lips deliberately—the blood mixed with my saliva will send it into a frenzy. I cross my arms before me, bracing for impact, creating a flaming shield. The mutant charges forward, crashing into me with such force that it pushes me backwards a few metres before it's pulled off of me, sending me falling onto my ass.

I open my eyes. The mutant Kailadon is on its back, vines rapidly wrapping around its body, pressing it hard into the cobblestone. The ground looks ready to open up and swallow it whole. Instead, Tyler's stock whip flies through the air and wraps around the monster's throat. I look to where Tyler stands, his biceps bulging against his shirt as he slowly pulls the whip tighter, wrapping it around his arms. A hard line is pressed between his brows. The look on his face is not just from the strain of holding down the mutant Kailadon.

Something is wrong.

I try to push to my feet, but feel sluggish and weak. An inescapable urge to just lay back down and fall asleep washes over me like the tide. My brows press together as I look over at Tyler, unable to bring myself to his aid. His muscles are tight, and his arms turn slightly reddish/purple as he loses blood flow from wrapping the whip tighter and tighter around his arms. Pushing to my feet, I try to summon my magic, but I'm too weak to call even a spark.

The mutant roars a muffled, gurgling sound around the embrace of the whip. Cracking and popping reverberates through the empty town centre before one final crack. The mutant Kailadon's head flies from its body.

Tyler falls to his knees, quickly unravelling the whip from his arms. Rushing to his side, I collapse beside him, helping pull the whip away to get his blood flowing again.

"Ty! Tyler, you did it! Are you okay?" Red rope burns snake up his arms.

His voice is quiet and shaky. "It... E... It doesn't breathe."

I look up at him, shocked. "What?"

"I tried removing the air from its lungs. All of it," Tyler says, falling back on his ass. He draws one knee up to his chest and rests his rope-burnt arms on it. "There was nothing. It's... empty." I look over my shoulder at the decapitated Kailadon, then look around.

"Where the fuck is Cyan?" I seethe, anger bubbling

inside of me. Tyler went to ask for his help, and he had the audacity to *refuse*? His brother is *dying*, and he would sit by and let him die because of their past—something that was out of Mallrie's control.

Tyler frowns, but there's sadness in his eyes. He looks over at the mutant Kailadon like he's seen a ghost.

"He didn't come." My voice sounds hollow. I knew he wouldn't, but—I follow Tyler's gaze to where the mutant Kailadon lies, its body slowly decomposing. The vines continue to crush its body. I jerk my head to the rooftops. He's here. I know it. Who else would have controlled the vines to help save me?

Tyler notices me searching. "He's not here, E." My head snaps to him at the panic in his voice, the movement sending a sharp jolt of pain down my spine.

"What do you mean, he's not here?" My voice sounds panicky.

"He wasn't at the apartment... It looked." Tyler sighs and scrubs a hand over his face, trying to calm himself. "Shit, E, I am *so* sorry. I shouldn't have left you. I-I was just so... I'm so sorry. I was too scared. You saw that *thing*." His voice breaks as shame and tears fill his eyes. Mallrie has drilled it into us that we stick together. Work as a team. And tonight, we did the complete opposite.

I pull Tyler against me, disregarding the aches in my body. "You're okay, Ty. You're okay," I whisper as he sobs into my blood-soaked shirt.

"There was a struggle," he whispers. "I came back as fast as I could."

"Then how?" I point to the body—or what's left of it. Tyler shrugs, shaking his head. He runs his white-tipped fingers through his dark hair. He's fidgeting with the black piercing with his tongue on the inside of his mouth like he always does when he's nervous. I watch as it wriggles from side to side.

"I don't know," Tyler says finally. "Let's just get the blood to Mallrie, then sort out what's happened to Cyan."

A sudden shock washes through me, panic filling my veins, causing me to scramble to my feet. "Winnie!" I shout, looking around, not caring if someone will hear. I can still hear her pained yelps reverberating in my head, the splattering of blue blood.

"Winifred? Come here! Winnie?" Tears pour down my face. *No. No. NO!* "Win!" I call her name over and over as I search for her, pausing only to toss the vial to Tyler, which, remarkably, didn't shatter.

"Get the—"

"Yep," Tyler cuts me off, already uncorking the bottle and filling it with the black liquid oozing from the neck of the rapidly decomposing Kailadon, another strange attribute of this mutation.

"Winnie!" I scream. "Godsdamnit! Just make a sound! *Please!*" I stumble past the Enkanti Tree, reaching out my hand to steady myself. She doesn't make a sound, and the panic pressing at my chest turns into terror. Tears blur my vision as I stumble forward before my knees give out and I collapse. I smash my fist into the unforgiving ground and scream. I need to find her. *I have to find her!* Then, through tear-blurred eyes, I spot a trail of blue blood. "Winnie?" I shout, my nails scraping against the stone as I push myself to my feet and race towards the blood.

It doesn't take me long to find Winnie. She's curled up on the doorstep of the Bottle-O in an adjacent alleyway. Blood trickles down her face and over most of her body. "Oh, Win!" I exclaim as I fall to my knees at her side. I run my hand carefully over her body. She snaps at me, hissing wildly. Yanking my hand away from her sharp teeth, my heart aches for her. The large Misnac struggles to open her eyes, realising it is only me. Winnie mewls sadly and licks where she just nipped at my hand.

I curse under my breath. Winnie didn't realise I was approaching her. Her left ear has been ripped off, and there's bleeding from the other. Her face is also swollen, one eye barely open. Tyler's hand is on my shoulder. "She'll be okay. Her breathing is steady, and she's starting to heal."

"How do you know?" I sniffle, looking up at him.

Tyler smiles sweetly at me, all humour gone on a rare occurrence. "Because the bleeding has stopped. Look," he says, pointing to her missing ear, and my heart cracks a little. *I should have told her to go back. I shouldn't have let her come. Winnie is hurt now because of me!* "Let's get you two home," Tyler whispers, carefully placing his hand under my elbow to help me stand. That's when I realise how much pain I am actually in. All the adrenaline finally wears off. There's a sharp pain in my ribs, my left leg, my right arm, my head... Pretty much every part of my body I examine is in some degree of pain. Tyler hands me the vial of blood and lifts Winnie effortlessly and carefully into his arms. She rubs her bloody face against his affectionately as he tries to pull his head away.

"Love you too, but don't love your bloody face in mine," he says, even though she can't hear him. I don't have the heart to admit that out loud without the fear of breaking down into a sobbing mess. Instead, Tyler wraps his free arm around my waist, pulling me close against his side. Even though I am seven years older, he towers over me.

"I'm okay," I say. He's got enough weight to carry with Winnie on his shoulders. He doesn't need to support me too.

"You're fine, E? Come on," Tyler replies sceptically, pulling me close to his side, supporting some of my weight, which I am grateful for. I quietly thank him, to which he makes a smart comment.

We head off back towards the Melsheim Forest. I try to get Tyler to run ahead with the vial, offering to take Winnie, but he insists that neither of us will return if he leaves. He is probably right, and I hate that. I look back towards the Enkanti Tree. The mutant Kailadon is all but decomposed, its remains seeping into the ground. *If Cyan didn't save me... then who was controlling the vines?* The thought rattles around in my mind like a loose bolt. Just as we start to round the corner, I get one final glance at the Enkanti Tree. Two tiny but bright green eyes blink at me, then, as quickly as they appeared, they're gone.

CHAPTER FORTY-ONE

ELIANA

"Are you *sure* that doesn't hurt?" Tyler questions, raising an eyebrow as he tends to Winnie's injuries.

I give him a stern look. "For the hundredth time... No." I'm sitting at the bottom of Mallrie's bed, a cast iron bowl bubbling away on my knee as I create the potion to help Mallrie heal from his encounter with the mutant Kailadon.

"Really?" Tyler drawls, still unconvinced.

"Oh, shit!" I exclaim, picking the bowl up off my knee. "Fuck, it's burning! Ow!" I bellow dramatically, then laugh darkly with Chelsea. "Now, quiet. I need to focus." I carefully pluck the petals off the camomile flower she retrieved from the garden. I cautiously rub them over the pistil before placing them into the pot. The warm, herbaceous, apple-like aroma fills the room. When all the petals have been infused in the boiling water, I carefully uncork the vial and add the black blood from the mutant Kailadon. It oozes into the pot and briefly engulfs the room in a malodorous aroma.

"E! I think you did something—"

"Tyler. Shush!" Chelsea says in her stern "mother reprimanding a child for not eating their vegetables" voice. But she gives me a careful look as if to say, *"you must have done something wrong."* When I move the pot to my other knee, the boiling water goes down to a gentle simmer. I stir it three times to the left and then put my hands over the pot. I shut my eyes, focusing on my energy.

Tyler gasps loudly. Chelsea must have thrown a pillow at him because there's a soft thud against the floor. I peek out of the corner of my eye and almost gasp just as loudly. A gold liquid is now swirling around in the pot. The smell is sweet and woody, like lily blossoms and black amber. I look around the room. Everyone's holding their breath. I crawl over to Mallrie and run my fingers through his hair, pushing the dark strands out of his face.

"Please work," I whisper, carefully opening his mouth and pouring a tiny bit in.

It takes a moment for him to swallow, and I shoot a look at Chelsea. "He's still holding on," she breathes. I let out a sigh. The weight on my heart is suffocating. I pour a little more into his mouth, and he drinks it, groaning.

A smile tugs at the corners of my lips, and tears burn my eyes as Chelsea's hand grips my shoulder gently. "It's working. He'll be okay."

I look at Mallrie, from the dark green circles that clung to his eyes that are fading, to Chelsea. "Thank you," I breathe. "Seriously, Chels." I take her hand in mine and press a kiss to her knuckles. "Thank you for *everything.*"

Chelsea blinks at me as if trying to hold her emotions in. She gives me a single nod before clearing her throat. "Tyler and I will give you two some privacy and help Winnie." I can hear her fighting the emotion in her voice. Softly smiling, I nod and watch her leave the room.

The putrid smell from the wound on his chest is gone,

and so has the discolouration. Mallrie's brows press together, a small line forming in the middle. He lets out a small groan. "El…" I smile from ear to ear. My left ear has a sharp pain from smiling, but I ignore it. Like I have ignored every single ache and pain in my body since returning home. I didn't care about my body screaming for help, or Chelsea voicing her concerns about my well-being. I just knew I had to save Mallrie. I had to help him. He opens his eyes groggily as I give him a bit more potion.

"What's happened?" His eyes fixate on my face, taking it in, the crease between his brows deepening. Horror flashes behind his eyes. He tries to push himself up, but I press my bloody hand firmly on his chest.

"Shh, I'm okay. I promise." A lie, but as soon as I know the infection is gone and Mallrie is going to be okay, I will go clean myself up. I pour a bit of the potion over the wound on his chest. He hardly winces at the pain.

"I'm sorry, I've got to—"

"I know," Mallrie says, closing his eyes. His fingertips brush against me as I seal his wound with my magic.

When I walk into the bathroom, the reflection greeting me looks like a completely different person. My face is covered in blood, my hair is messed up and my clothes are torn. But it is not just the dishevelled look that has my head tilted to the side to stare a little longer at the woman looking back at me. After all, I have been greeted with similar appearances before—not to this extreme, but a bruised eye or busted lip. *I* look different. Underneath the bloody mess… My eyes. There is a spark in them. *Life.* I hadn't realised how long I have been living in survival mode, just getting through each day. Not really caring about anyone—myself included—just living for the next sunrise.

I realise now that I have something to live for, someone to live for. Well, maybe more than just *one*. My heart aches with how much happiness is pouring through it. My eyes twinkle with tears, demanding to be let out. I have a family now. I close my eyes, letting them fall, no longer afraid to cry or if someone was to see me.

I am happy.

I have friends who've become family. Opening my eyes, I look back at my reflection. The first ever faerie-witch hybrid staring back, but there is more to me than just that label.

I carefully strip out of my bloodied clothes but can't lift my left arm above my head. I grit my teeth, press my good hand firmly on my shoulder and—*Crack.*

Instant relief.

Leaning against the wall, I catch my breath. As the room fills with the steam from the shower, I inhale the sweet scent of lavender from the salts I threw onto the shower floor. Then, stepping into the hot stream, I fall to my knees. I don't feel the crack of them against the tiled floor as more tears flood my face. The emotional release from all the tension and stress of the last few hours finally washes away under the hot spray. Watching Mallrie lie bloody and unconscious, the fear that consumed me.

If I lost him... I shake my head, dislodging that thought.

I didn't. That's what counts. He's lying in bed, resting. He is going to be okay. I shut my eyes and let the water pour over my body as the water runs brownish red down the drain.

The door creaks open, then clicks shut again. I open my

eyes, and my jaw practically hits the floor. Mallrie is standing in the doorway. *He's* standing! He still looks like hell, but he's up and moving. The wound on his face has knitted itself back together, leaving an angry red slash from his eyebrow to jaw—similar to the wound on his chest. The skin surrounding it is all aggravated by my magic, but at least it doesn't reek of death.

Mallrie silently drops his pants, and my breath catches in my throat. Every time I see him, it takes my breath away. He's probably the most handsome man I've ever seen. It shouldn't be possible to be that attractive, or this attracted to someone. My thighs tighten as he comes close, my desire burning through every inch of my body.

He extends his hand for me to take. I don't hesitate to place my hand in his as he carefully pulls me to my feet. Our bodies press together—*complete*. I let out a content sigh as Mallrie cups water and pours it over my back.

"You do know this is ridiculously hot, right?" I smile up at him. I can't help it. He's starting to sound like himself again. Tears roll down my cheeks—happy tears. Mallrie runs his thumb over my cheek, catching one. "Little doe..." He sighs.

"I'm fine, really. I-I'm just happy." Mallrie presses his lips against mine, and I hold him tight as I bite through the pain lacing my body. Determined to never let him go. "I was so scared," I whisper between kisses.

"I know, little doe. I'm sorry."

I reluctantly pull away. "What happened? I told you not to go after it again." I don't want to know, but I *need* to. Not that it matters. The mutant Kailadon is dead.

Mallrie sighs and gives me a heated look. "Now?" He looks me up and down. "You want to talk about it now?"

I give him a firm look and a single nod. "I need to know."

Mallrie sighs again and turns the water off, grabbing a towel and wrapping it around my shoulder before pulling me into his lap as he sits on the edge of the bath. The room suddenly feels cold, and a shiver runs down my spine. There's a knot in the pit of my stomach.

"Edgar has been arresting people." I turn to look at him. Crime isn't a big issue in Datura. When you've got bigger problems like flesh-eating monsters lurking in the streets, I've found that everyone wants to keep out of trouble as much as possible. If people getting arrested have caught Mallrie's attention—

I shake my head, confused. "He's arresting them for the pettiest of reasons. Littering, petty theft, vandalism. Offences that, under any other circumstances, you'd be let off with a warning or a small fine. Not imprisonment." I crane my neck to look up at him and notice he's frowning, too. There have been no reports in the news that I was aware of about increased crime or imprisonments. Not that I've really had access to the Datura Chronicle or a TV. Mallrie continues, not meeting my gaze. He's looking off into the distance. Staring into another dimension. "One wrongdoing doesn't justify death," Mallrie whispers.

"Death?" I repeat. There definitely have been no reports of the death penalty. That was phased out years ago. The only reason someone would still get the death penalty in Datura is if they were... I don't know, a serial killer?

Even then, I reckon they'd more likely do imprisonment for life. Mallrie nods somberly. "Edgar has it all hush-hush. It appears he's got quite a few *side projects* on at the moment, and not just experimenting on people." He scrubs his hand over his face. "Are you sure you want to hear about this?" he asks. I take his hand in mine and nod. Mallrie looks down at our entwined hands, his face pinched as he wars with himself. "Edgar is tying people to the Enkanti Tree just after sunset, slitting their wrists to attract the Kailadons. Then, Edgar gets..." He clears his throat awkwardly.

"Gets Cyan to trap the Kailadons?" I offer quietly so he doesn't have to.

Mallrie nods woefully before looking me dead in the eyes, a flicker of protection in his gaze. "He doesn't know what's happening. Well, not in its entirety." Another woeful sigh, and Mallrie runs his hand down his face. "Edgar's been busy, and I've been negligent. I should have been keeping a better watch on him. I should have been in town all along. I should not have left Cyan after Morana was murdered. That broke him more than I think either of us would admit. Instead, I left him in Edgar's clutches in search of dead ends—"

"Mallrie. Stop." My hand runs down his face to rest on his jaw, pulling it towards me so I can look into his eyes. His grip around my waist loosens a little as he meets my stare.

"What's Edgar done to Cyan?"

Mallrie closes his eyes, tension between his brows as he thinks. "He's created a new drug. Faerie venom mixed with lidocaine and erythroxylum coca. The small dose of faerie venom temporarily restricts an elemental's magic. The lidocaine and erythroxylum coca speed up messages between the brain and body. When mixed with subliminal messaging, Edgar can temporarily confuse Cyan—or any elemental —into doing whatever he wants. I guess that's how Edgar kept Cyan under his thumb all these years." My shoulders slump, and I rest in Mallrie's arms a little more.

The weight of his words is heavy and terrifying. "Like, mind control?" I breathe, dumbfounded.

Mallrie nods sadly. "I knew something was wrong with him," he hisses to himself, and all my anger towards Cyan is suddenly gone, replaced with sadness and a sense of help-lessness. *How many of our encounters was Cyan under the influence of Edgar's drug?* I can feel Mallrie's tense body behind me.

"What can we do? We've got to get Cyan out. Now," I say, pushing to my feet. He smiles up at me.

"We will, beautiful girl." He pulls me back down onto him, pressing a kiss to my temple.

"Tyler and I went into town and killed the mutant—well, Tyler killed it. So we don't need to worry about that anymore. We'll get Cyan, the grimoire and restore the magic in the Enkanti Tree." I can feel Mallrie's smile against my neck where his face is buried, the little kisses he's been placing there since he pulled me back down turn into small nibbles.

"Impressive. Really. Maybe I should give Tyler more credit," he says between kisses and gentle grazes of his teeth.

"Yeah, he really held his own," I voice. "I should make sure his arms are okay. Oh, we should probably do it during the day. You know, save Cyan and get the grimoire. Since Edgar won't be at home, I'm sure that's where he's most likely got the grimoire. That's where I'd keep it anyway. I wonder if he's got it in a safe or something—it doesn't matter. I can melt the hinges." I'm rambling. My brain is running a hundred miles a minute, trying to devise a work-able plan that will be simple enough to carry out, but not simple enough that anyone gets caught or injured. I roll my shoulder, which is still tender, and rub my hand against my ribs, which I notice are protruding a little.

"Sounds like you don't need my plan then," Mallrie says, looking up at me.

"You've got a plan?" He frowns down at my hand, clearly noticing the protrusion. Mallrie carefully slides my hand away. His eyes widen slightly before scanning the rest of my body.

"Have you not healed yourself yet?" His voice is firm and a little angry. Honestly, I didn't pay too much attention to my injuries. I was too preoccupied with saving his life. I gathered the more I looked at it before washing off all the blood, the worse I would feel, and it was a good thought because I practically didn't feel a thing. But now? The pain is getting uncomfortable.

"I'm fine," I say unconvincingly. "You needed my help. I was just—"

"Eliana. Seriously." Mallrie pushes to his feet, snatching another towel from the rail and wrapping it around his waist. As he heads for the door, a small whimper makes its way out of me.

"Really, I'm fine." He storms out of the bathroom before I can convince him otherwise. Sighing, I wrap the towel around my midsection, wincing at the pain in my side and shoulder. Following behind him, I call weakly, "Mallrie... come back." I stand in the bathroom doorway, looking into the kitchen. Tyler is sitting at the island bench, eating a sandwich that has my mouth practically drooling.

Typical. Tyler always seems to pop up at the most inconvenient times with a quick-witted remark. I prop a hand on my hip, trying not to wince at the movement, and wait for it.

Chelsea is cleaning up after the mess we've all made,

and has made the plate of sandwiches Tyler is helping himself to. Winnie is sitting at the bottom of the stairs, her ears wrapped up. There's a pain in my chest and guilt in my stomach at the sight of her. Mallrie doesn't acknowledge the others. Chelsea and Mallrie work around each other effortlessly as if performing a choreographed dance. Tyler and I exchange a long look before he looks me up and down and raises his eyebrows quickly.

"Playtime over already, Mal?" he jokes. I can't help but giggle. I've quickly grown to love Tyler's playful teasing of Mallrie... and what I imagine him doing to Cyan too.

Instead, Mallrie shoots him an irritated look. "Have you not seen the state Eliana is in?" he growls. A mischievous smile spreads across Tyler's face as he looks back at me, his eyes raking from my head to my toes. I clutch the towel tighter to my body. Tyler is like a brother to me, and I a sister to him. He's remarked how much he would have loved to have known me growing up. Still, how he deliberately drags his eyes over my body is awkward.

Tyler winks at me before he rolls his head in Mallrie's direction. "She looks tastier than this sandwich, man. If you're not going to gobble her up—"

"Tyler!" Mallrie growls. Tyler winks at me again as if to say he's won. He got the reaction he wanted from Mallrie—he successfully broke some of the tension that was thick in the air. That's what I love about Tyler; he can ease the tension in a room with just a comment, and he is just so easygoing and fun.

My quiet giggles turn into belly-aching laughs. They hurt so much, but I've missed this. The playful banter between the two of them. How Tyler knows exactly what buttons to push to trigger a reaction. Mallrie shoots me a glare.

"Do not encourage him. Do you not realise how important you are, Eliana?" he asks, pointing a finger at me. I raise my hands defensively, then double over, clutching my ribs.

"Stop it, the both of you," Chelsea interjects evenly. "Ty, you're not helping. Your *jokes*," she says as if she doesn't think he's funny. Maybe he isn't. Perhaps I just have a sick sense of humour like him. "They're clearly causing El pain. She's got three broken ribs, a—" She looks over me.

I can feel a cool wash run under my skin, and I take a step back. "Stop that," I say, but Chelsea ignores me, continuing her examination. It still baffles me that her magic can determine someone's injuries or illnesses.

"A dislocated shoulder. You really should have got me to pop that back into place. You've done it all wrong." Chelsea has surprised me with her extensive knowledge of healing. I wonder how many times she's had to heal Cyan after these supposed *consequences* for him looking out for me. A small wave of guilt washes over me, but I try to push it out of my mind.

"I didn't think there was a right or wrong way," I say, and Tyler chuckles quietly. Chelsea opens her mouth to continue, but I hold my hand up. "Okay, okay, WebMD, we get it. There are some broken bones, but I feel fine. Mallrie needed the attention more, yes?" Mallrie walks over to me, handing me a steaming cup. I sip it tentatively as he carefully turns me to step back into the bathroom.

"Don't forget protection!" Tyler calls after us, and Mallrie glares at him. *Oh, if looks could kill.* I can't help but laugh again. Chelsea starts reprimanding Tyler as Mallrie shuts the door behind us.

He waits for me to take another sip before taking the cup from my hand and placing it on the edge of the bath.

"Mallrie, you really were in—" He gives me a stern look, and I fall silent. I know when to shut up, even when Tyler doesn't. Mallrie carefully takes the towel off of me and examines my body. The way his eyes drift over my body makes me feel a little uncomfortable because of the way he's frowning.

He sighs before meeting my eyes. "I'm sorry, little doe," he whispers, taking a step closer. My mouth parts slightly as if to speak, but his hands are already wrapping around my body, one hand pressing against my broken ribs, the other at my back. "Take a deep breath..." I breathe in deeply. The sting in my side makes it difficult. "Breathe out," Mallrie says calmly. I let it out. His hands move quickly, snapping my ribs back into place. A blood-chilling scream leaves my body, and my knees go weak. Mallrie's arms move quickly, catching me before I fall. "Good girl," he whispers in my ear as his fingers lace through my hair, gently pulling my head back so I look up at him. I give him a weak smile. "One more. Ready?" My eyes widen as he steadies me back onto my feet. His hands adjusted to my shoulder. "Deep breath, beautiful girl..." I breathe in, and the pain in my side is significantly less. "One... two..." I breathe out, unable to hold it any longer. Mallrie pops my shoulder into place. A loud, popping sound reverberates in my head. He quickly scoops me into his arms and sits on the side of the bath. He hands me the cup of tea. "Drink. You did so well."

I struggle to catch my breath, but something pops into my head with a wave of panic. "The mutant bit my leg!" I blurt out, almost choking on the herbal medicinal tea. I lift my leg to inspect the mark—

"It bit me, look. Right there!" I run my fingers over my calf, over raised and sensitive flesh, where the mutant tried to bite me with half a jaw. My eyes fall to my fingers. The skin has closed up, leaving only a red, jagged scar.

Mallrie runs a hand through his hair, "Mm," he murmurs thoughtfully.

I shake my head at him, dumbfounded. "*Mm?* That's all you have to say? You almost *died* from the infection, and my leg..." I look back down at it again. "What even is that?"

Mallrie shrugs a shoulder. "The Fae can heal themselves quickly," he says, as if that makes all the sense in the world. "We know the mutant Kailadons have traces of faerie venom in them. Which probably caused the infection in me, but for you, being part Fae." Another shrug. I want to shake him. I look at him with wide eyes. *Gods, they feel like they might just fall out of my head.* "You're part Fae, Eliana. The faerie venom wouldn't affect you as much. You also heal faster. Clearly."

I shake my head in disbelief. "But I've been hurt before. A *lot* of befores, actually. I've never..." my voice trails off.

"And we've tended to those wounds right away, yes?" I nod in agreement. "And all those *befores*," Mallrie's voice softens as he carefully treads this painful topic. "How long did you have the black eyes? The busted lips?" I shake my head. Not long, but that doesn't explain the large scar running down my inner thigh. As if Mallrie plucked the thought out of my head, his hand gently intertwines with mine. "You're only part Fae, Eliana. Not every injury is going to heal quickly, or the same. Plus, you're the first of your kind. We don't know how much Fae is in you, so it would make sense for some injuries to heal faster or better than others. So try not to worry too much about it, okay?"

Mallrie turns the shower on as I finish the rest of my tea. He jerks his hand out of the water and looks sternly at me. "You really shouldn't have the water that hot, you know." I roll my eyes playfully. "It'll damage your keratin cells," Mallrie adds matter-of-factly.

I raise my eyebrows innocently. "But the heat doesn't bother me." He pulls me onto my feet before the last word leaves my lips. Something dark and playful flickers behind his eyes, which sends my heart racing and my thighs clenching in anticipation. A sly smile twitches at the corners of his lips under his stubble. "Well, let's see how much heat you can really handle." I'm still cupping the teacup with both my hands when Mallrie wraps a large hand around my wrists, taking the cup away with the other. He walks backwards, leading me into the shower. The cool water runs down the side of my body as he raises my arms above my head, pinning them against the cool, tiled walls. He steps between my legs, pushing them further apart. The water cascades down, pooling and spilling over where our bodies meet.

The cool water sends a shiver through me. It is way colder than I prefer, but the heat in my veins prevents the goosebumps from breaking out over my skin. Mallrie grips my wrists tightly above my head in one hand while the other teasingly trails down my neck until his fingers gently caress my peaked nipple. "I don't think I have properly thanked you for everything you did," he murmurs against the side of my neck, his fingers tightening on my nipple, causing a little squeak to rush out of me. "Or should I be punishing you for not taking better care of yourself?" He twists his fingers, rolling the taut bud between them to the point of pain. His mouth is on my neck, kissing and licking up the side of my ear. My brain struggles to focus on one sensation, the pain or the pleasure. Mallrie squeezes my breast in his hand as his teeth clamp down on my neck, switching the pain and pleasure.

My back arches at the sensation, and his name is a moan on my lips.

"Sounds like you want to be punished, little doe," Mallrie says, lifting his gaze to meet mine, which is a struggle since my eyes want nothing more than to just close and enjoy his touch. I scream as Mallrie's hand slaps my pussy. The pain has it clenching, desperate for more.

The scream blurs into a moan. "Yes," I moan again, and his hand falls hard against my pussy again. My hips jerk, the cool water rushing over the sting, soothing it. Our lips crash together, and Mallrie's tongue slips across my own, claiming me. His hands move quickly under my knees, lifting and pressing me against the tiles. My arms fall to his neck, and my fingers lace between the thick, tangled mess of his hair. Our kisses become wild. I nip at his lip as I reach between us, desperate to feel him inside me.

Mallrie groans into my mouth, "Fuck, little doe, I had a whole thing in mind..." His voice trails off as I position the head of his cock at my entrance. "You have no patience, do you?" he growls as he drops me down onto his length.

"When it comes to your cock inside me?" I moan, my nails digging into his shoulders as he slowly stretches me. "Never."

CHAPTER FORTY-TWO
MALLRIE

Leaning against the kitchen bench with my arms crossed over my chest, I glance over my shoulder out the small window in the kitchen. I watch Eliana and Tyler chasing Winnie around the garden. The Misnac pounces through the flowers, careful not to crush them under her large paws as she tracks Tyler and Eliana. The former sends small gusts of wind around Winnie, and the latter... Eliana laughs. Her face is lit up with such joy that I momentarily forget what I was doing.

"Mallrie!" Chelsea's voice is irate as her hand slaps against my bicep. I turn my attention back to the young water elemental standing in my kitchen, a dusting of flour over her dress as she turns back to the apple pastries she's folding for dessert. "Do the spell," she demands.

I raise a single eyebrow at her. "It's not that simple—"

"We need to know. She's busy." Chelsea waves a flour-covered hand towards the window. "So do it now."

I narrow my eyes at her. "Last time I checked, *you* weren't the boss of me, little witch." My voice drops into a deadly octave, but Chelsea just closes the distance between us, pointing a long, blue-tipped finger in my face.

"Last time *I* checked, *you* were the one living a free and easy life here in your little slice of paradise while your brother is being tortured."

My magic thrums in my veins, and I snap out my hand, gripping her wrist and pressing my thumb into her tendons. "You know *nothing* of Cyan's and my relationship. Of what I have *sacrificed* for him." *Of the secrets I've kept to protect him.* Chelsea looks up at me, her dark eyes wide. "I'll do the spell, but not because you're demanding me." Roughly, I let her go. "Remember your manners, little witch. You've still got a lot to learn."

Chelsea quickly checks the chicken pies in the oven before keeping an eye on Eliana and Tyler—who are sprawled out on the lawn, watching the sunset—making sure they don't come in and interrupt us. I sit on the old leather couch, close my eyes and focus on my breathing. The air shifts around me as my magic gathers. Vaguely, I can feel the air around me getting cooler. Moving my hands, I can feel the weight of the *Timeline* forming into a glittery orb. Though I'm not physically holding the globe, I can sense the pressure of it between my hands. My eyes snap open. I don't need to see the orb itself. Honestly, I only produced it for Chelsea's benefit. I can do this spell without the globe and still see this fragment of the *Timeline*.

I can sense Chelsea moving closer from the kitchen to watch what's happening in the glittery orb, even if I can no longer see her myself.

Instead, I quickly flick through all the different variations of tomorrow's *Timeline*. Snippets of Tyler and Eliana flash before my eyes as I swipe to find the best possible outcome.

Blinking, the visions blur back into reality. Chelsea looks a little pale as she stands before me with her arms crossed over her chest. "Well..." she breathes.

"Are you happy now?" I feel a little sick myself. I have tried *very* hard to keep Eliana safe all these years. Initially, it was for purely selfish reasons, but after that first night I saved her in the alleyway from the Kailadon, my sense of morals shifted. Cyan and I decided when Eliana was born that we would protect her, but I still had a promise to keep. Not only to my mother, but to my little sisters too. They died because a scared man let his false sense of power go to his head. I *should* have been able to save them. Instead, they were ripped from Cyan's and my arms and beheaded before us. I can still hear their screams. Now, I will not let my fear of losing Eliana rip her away from me, too.

I close my eyes and focus on my breathing. "Eliana will be fine," I whisper before opening my eyes to find Chelsea chewing at her nail, her face pinched with concern. "They both will be fine as long as they follow the plan."

CHAPTER FORTY-THREE
ELIANA

The cool, crisp air, mixed with the smell of the forest and the campfire, fills my lungs. Tyler and I look up at the stars in the soft grass. My stomach is so gloriously filled with dinner. The chicken pies Mallrie and Chelsea made could be my favourite food—apart from waffles. Waffles will always be my favourite thing in the world. I'm not ashamed to admit that Mallrie is a better cook than me. I tried making him dinner one night. It didn't end well.

"Pity you don't have any neighbours we can just steal a lasagna from," I joked.

Mallrie laughed, replying, "You're never going to let me live that down, are you?"

I pushed up onto my toes and kissed him, whispering, "Never."

It still baffles me that we can relax and take in the millions of twinkling lights above us without the fear of getting attacked. I roll my head to the side. Mallrie and Chelsea are talking quickly in hushed tones. Winnie's got her bandaged head in Mallrie's lap, and he gently strokes her head. She's got a bit of healing to do, but he was happy that she was chasing us around the garden before. He reassured me that it was a good sign, that her magic was healing her wounds. But her ears make me nervous. I was certain Mallrie would kill me when he saw her, but he was surprisingly calm. I still can't help but feel responsible for what happened to her though.

I should have sent her home. I should have made sure she was safe.

Mallrie looks over at me as if he senses where my thoughts have gone—Chelsea still talking—and smiles. He gives me a cautious look as if to say, *"you okay?"* I nod, letting out a content sigh.

I wish we could stay like this forever.

I look back up at the sky. I've read about the aurora borealis before, but I never thought I'd be able to see it for myself. The striking green and purple ribbons slowly flicker above the trees and around the twinkling stars. I close my eyes and take a deep breath. Savouring this moment. Locking this away so I'll never forget it.

Mallrie clears his throat. I don't know how long I've been lying in the grass with Tyler, but I feel groggy, as if I may have fallen asleep at some point. Tyler and I turn to look at Mallrie and Chelsea. A small line has formed between his dark brows, and my heart shatters into a million tiny pieces.

Mallrie jerks his head for Tyler and me to join them. "Good feeling gone," Tyler sings as if he read my mind, helping me to my feet. He must also sense the looming darkness of Mallrie's gesture because he says nothing as we walk over to where Chelsea, Mallrie and Winnie are sitting. I sit on the other side of Mallrie, and he wraps his arm around me, pulling me closer. His body is tense, and I brace myself for what's coming. Mallrie and Chelsea exchange a long look.

"No, don't tell me the Spring Equinox is cancelled! I wanted to show you the best view from the rooftops," Tyler jokes, yet my heart squeezes with anticipation as I look over at him. To see the town centre all decorated with the twinkling lights and pastel ribbons from above would be stunning.

"We're going for Cyan." Mallrie's voice is low and rough, and my body tenses. Tyler's eyes drop to the grass, all humour forgotten. But I don't voice my concerns about rescuing Mallrie's brother. As much as I am sure he still wants me dead, he has also saved my life. "We're going to get Cyan and the High Witchess' grimoire. In and out with the both of them." I look at Tyler, who is plucking at the grass before him, then to Chelsea, who's watching Mallrie intently. Then, finally, back to Mallrie, whose expression is calm and even. When no one speaks, Mallrie continues, "Tomorrow morning. We go into town. Chelsea is going to take me in as a distraction for Edgar. He wants me so he can..." He swallows hard. I try not to notice his jaw as it clenches and unclenches at the thought of being forced to make Edgar immortal. Mallrie clears his throat and continues, "We still hope that Edgar doesn't know about Tyler." He nods in Tyler's direction. "Cyan and Chels were very systematic in keeping you out of sight." I shudder internally at how casually he abbreviates her name.

I know there is no need for jealousy, but this is the first time I have truly felt in love. And some selfish, wounded part of myself is afraid of it. So the need to defend it bubbles to the surface. I take a steadying breath to calm the rage of emotion and magic bubbling beneath the surface. Now is not the time to cause a scene.

"So, while we're distracting Edgar—preferably in the lobby of the government building—the two of you are going to break into the penthouse. Now, the windows are made of fibreglass, which is resistant to extreme temperatures." Mallrie looks down at me, his thumb caressing the nape of my neck. "I know you'll be able to break in still, but it'll take time, which is something we don't have, so go through the door on the roof. Edgar now has two guards there around the clock. You'll need to take them out first." Suddenly, Tyler jerks his head up, and a flash of fear crosses his face.

"You don't have to kill them. Just knock them out," Chelsea clarifies, putting a comforting hand onto Tyler's arm, and his shoulders relax. With everything going on, sometimes it is easy to forget just how young he actually is.

"We want you two to get the grimoire and get out of there. That's it. We will find Cyan. Got it?" Mallrie's voice is stern as he looks between Tyler and me. We nod without saying anything. We knew this day was going to come; when we had to get the High Witchess' grimoire, resurrecting the magic within the Enkanti Tree so the Kailadons are banished from the town. It just feels so surreal that the moment is almost here.

Are we ready for it?

I look up at the stars. A sickening feeling washes around in the pit of my stomach. I can't help but wonder if this could be the last time I will get to see the stars.

We don't hang around much after Mallrie carefully goes over the plan again in painstaking detail. I lie on the bed staring blankly at the ceiling, that feeling of dread from before still lingering in my gut. He looks through the papers on his desk as I roll onto my side. I still do not know how he knows where anything is. The mess on the desk has gotten worse since I first stepped foot in Mallrie's bedroom.

A pile of books sits beside the desk. Papers are pinned to the walls, some held there with small throwing knives, and more books and paper litter the desk in piles of shambolic chaos. Mallrie runs a hand through his dark hair, the muscles in his back flex and it takes all my self-control not to go to him, run my fingers down his back and beg him to come to bed.

I know he's trying to piece together as much of the ritual to reincarnate the magic to the Enkanti Tree without the grimoire. In case we can't retrieve it. *"We know Edgar has it, but we're not sure where. If, by chance, we cannot find it, we will need a contingency plan,"* he told me once. Mallrie's been working on this *a lot.* He locks himself away up here while the rest of us train. When I return, he's flustered and angry. Mallrie has got so many books, yet they don't seem to give him the answers he's looking for. He won't let us help him—not that we'd be much help when we can't read the languages as well as him, but I just feel so helpless sitting by while he carries all this weight on his shoulders.

My stomach twists at the memory, and I walk over to him, thinking, *If they're sending us to collect the grimoire, then why's he still fussing over these old scriptures?* I silently step to his side, running my hand over his shoulders. Mallrie quickly moves the papers as if he's trying to hide something. He picks the pile up and taps it on the desk, quickly discarding it onto another stack.

Maybe he's just cleaning up. Perhaps I'm just nervous and paranoid. Not everyone keeps secrets.

Mallrie twists in his chair to face me. The briefest flicker of fear flashes behind his cerulean eyes at the sight of me. It's gone with a blink before I can read too much into it. His expression evens out as he wraps his arm around my waist, pulling me closer.

"Nervous?" he asks calmly, as if tomorrow I will just be sitting an exam and not breaking and entering the most dangerous mortal's penthouse to recover a century-old grimoire that may or may not even be there. I try to smile reassuringly down at him, but my smile doesn't meet my eyes, and I know I am not fooling him. "I am doing everything I can to keep you safe." His words cut through me like a hot knife through butter.

Always about my safety and well-being. But who's watching out for him?

"What about you though?" My voice comes out barely louder than a whisper as I trace my fingers along the still-healing scar on his face. "Your body still needs time to heal."

Mallrie pulls me into his lap. He runs his hand up my shirt and caresses my bare skin. "There's nothing Edgar can do to me that I can't handle."

I cock my head to the side. "What about the drugs?" I ask flatly.

Mallrie smiles, cupping my face in his big hands and kissing my forehead. "Everything is going to be fine, little doe. Come on. Let's go to bed."

I push to my feet. My hand intertwines with his as he leads me back into the bed. He glances over his shoulder at the papers he put away with a hint of apprehension.

Mallrie would tell me if there was something I needed to know, I reassure myself. He speaks about me trusting him, and now that's precisely what I must do. *Trust.*

Trust that he knows what he is doing.

Trust that everything will be fine if we do what we are meant to do.

Trust. The word hangs around me like a weight slowly, pressing down on my chest as I climb into bed and fall asleep.

The walk from Mallrie's home in the forest to the edge of Datura is solemn. No one dawdles, but there is no rush. It feels as if everyone understands that this is the first step we're taking in this *quest* we've embarked on.

Mallrie has gone over the plan multiple times on the walkover, reiterating that Tyler and I are only to get the grimoire and leave. We're not to look for Cyan or Edgar, and under no circumstances will we help Mallrie and Chelsea if we hear them in distress. The look exchanged between Tyler and me when both Mallrie and Chelsea drummed that into us was concerning. "Why does this sound more like a suicide mission than a simple extraction?" Tyler whispers to me as Mallrie and Chelsea lead us through the forest, whispering quietly to one another. Chelsea is on edge. Something about her posture and how she keeps glancing over her shoulder at Tyler and me has that feeling of impending doom settling in my stomach. Tyler squeezes my wrist reassuringly and gives me one of his lopsided grins.

My heart is beating too loudly in my ears when we stop at the edge of Datura in the shade of the buildings. "Okay. Tyler, Eliana, remember, don't worry about anything other than finding the grimoire and getting out," Mallrie says for what feels like the hundredth time.

"Yeah, man. We know," Tyler says seriously. There is a hint of a threat in his tone that has me hoping Mallrie will not tell us again. What does he think will happen if we don't follow his plan to the letter?

The metal clink is like a warning klaxon, sending a shiver down my spine as Chelsea pulls a set of handcuffs out. I glance over at Tyler, who's fidgeting with his piercing and thumbing his stock whip. Mallrie removes his sword from his back and hands it over to Chelsea. *This looks so wrong.* I have to fight back the lump in my throat as the fear that something isn't right pushes its way up.

Mallrie's hand catches my wrist, pulling me away from the group. "Whatever happens," he says in a low, hushed voice, "*stick to the plan.*" I look up at him, at those stunning cerulean eyes that remind me of the ocean I long to find. My mouth parts to speak...

"Promise me you'll get the grimoire and get out," he says urgently, his hand squeezing mine. "If you can't find it, forget it."

This uneasy feeling I've had since last night feels like an admonition, and I can't keep it in anymore. "Mallrie, I really don't think we should be doing this." The words are like fire in my throat. "I-I feel like something horrible is going to happen."

Mallrie smooths my hair as the wind picks up. "I know," he says gravely.

Panic bubbles in my chest, even as I remind myself to trust him. I can't help but blurt, "Then let's go home. We'll go home and figure out a better plan. Surely there is—"

"There's no other plan, Eliana." Mallrie looks down at our feet, and my heart lurches into my throat.

"You... You've looked, haven't you?"

He finally meets my gaze, his expression soft and sad. "Yes."

I lick my lips, and suddenly, I feel as if all the blood in

my body has left, and I am just a shell of a person. "What happens?" I manage to say after a long silence. Mallrie smiles at me, a genuine smile, easing that pending doom impression in my stomach.

"As always, there are a myriad of outcomes. Best case, if we follow the plan, everything turns out in our favour." I reach up for his face, his stubble prickling my fingertips.

"And... worst case?"

Mallrie smiles, but it looks forced. His lips quiver to stay up. "No need to worry yourself any more than you already are with the what ifs, little doe." His hands wrap around mine as he pulls me closer. However, the way he kisses me reanimates that feeling of impending doom. Not that he hasn't kissed me like this before—a desperate kiss filled with lust and desire to consume. He bites down gently on my bottom lip as his hands slip down to my waist, closing the last distance between us. The pressure on my lower back is almost painful as he holds me against him. Suddenly, our kiss turns wet. Mallrie pulls away and wipes the tears from my cheeks.

"Stick to the plan. I'll see you at home for dinner." Another long kiss that feels like it could be our last, and Chelsea has him in cuffs. Not something I ever want to see again. She leads Mallrie off through the alleyways of Datura. Mallrie looks over his shoulder one last time before they disappear around a corner.

Tyler silently steps to my side. "You okay, E?" I can tell he's trying to keep his voice as even as possible. But his voice cracks a little on the word, "*okay*," as if he knows, too, that nothing about this is okay.

I give him as much of a convincing smile as I can muster. I know I never need to pretend to be okay or put on a brave face for Ty, but this feels different. His mouth presses into a hard line, and his arms fling around my neck, pulling me in for a hug.

"Come on," I say, patting his back. Tyler pulls away, his expression composed as he uncurls his stock whip from his belt. He runs the braided thong through his fingertips nervously. I try to repress a sigh. "It'll be okay, Ty. Let's just get in, get the book and get out."

His eyes study me for a long moment. "I know you've got a bad feeling about this, too, E. You haven't been able to breathe steadily since Mallrie told us the plan last night."

I fold my arms across my chest, suddenly feeling a little vulnerable. I raise my eyebrows. "Don't analyse my breathing patterns, please. It's creepy."

Tyler lets out a forced laugh. But it's short and sharp. "It's a little hard when you practically stopped breathing and haven't taken a full breath since. It disrupts *my* breathing pattern. I feel like I'm suffocating."

I purposefully take a steady, deep breath. "Happy?"

Tyler rolls his eyes, still fidgeting with the whip. "You realise that your breathing and heart rate go hand-in-hand?" He looks down, his tongue playing with the back of the piercing below his lip, moving it from side to side. As much of a shit-talker as Tyler is, admitting that he has sensed every flutter my heart has made makes for an uncomfortable silence between us. He clears his throat tensely. "Like, I mean, you haven't been able to rest since last night." He winces at his words, and I try to diffuse this conversation for both our sakes.

"It's fine. I'm just nervous. I don't like going into this separated," I say. It's not a complete lie. "I just feel like we would have been stronger together. As a team, you know?" Tyler nods and then looks down the path Chelsea and Mallrie went.

"Yeah, I know," he says, his voice wandering down the path as if to catch up with the others. "The wind is whispering too. It's nervous," Tyler adds quietly.

I cock my head to the side, examining his features. He's serious. I didn't know the wind *spoke* to him. "I'm sure it'll all be fine," I lie again. "Come on. Let's go," I say, tugging his arm.

CHAPTER FORTY-FOUR
ELIANA

The midmorning sun and the brisk breeze hits me in the face as Tyler holds the door to the rooftop open for me. Stepping out onto the exposed flat roof, my eyes instantly fall to the roof of the neighbouring structure. The government building. The branches and leaves of the Enkanti Tree fill in my peripheral vision, desperate for attention, but I cannot drag my gaze away from the identical structure that we're standing on, except where this building is all department stores and high-end restaurants, the one staring back at me is heavy with secrets and a weight of impending doom.

We agreed it would be smarter to get a vantage point where we could inspect the guards on the government building. Somewhere they wouldn't see the attack coming.

We peek our heads over the side, and, to my surprise, only one beast of a man is standing by the door with his arms folded across his chest.

Where does Edgar get these enormous men? I wonder to myself. They'd easily stand out in a crowd.

"Ready?" I ask Tyler quietly, though there's no way that

the brute on the other building could hear. The wind has picked up around us, which I am almost certain is Tyler's doing. However, Tyler's words from earlier, *"The wind is whispering too. It's nervous,"* still send a shiver through me. I'm still unsure if he was being literal when he said that the wind was whispering or if it was just a feeling he was getting. Either way, it's unnerving as hell.

"You?" Tyler retorts.

I give him a slight jerk of my chin. "As ready as I think I'll ever be." Tyler is fussing with his piercing again. "You realise you haven't taken a complete breath since we got up here?" I say mockingly, repeating his earlier remark, trying to calm his nerves in typical Tyler-style.

He laughs roughly. "Yeah, yeah. Good one." But the tension in his shoulders has relaxed significantly. He takes a deep breath, his eyes narrowing as he focuses on the man standing between the door and us. The beast of a man sways a little and presses his palms to his eyes, rubbing aggressively before moving a hand to his chest. Suddenly, he collapses into a heap on the ground, unconscious. Tyler stands up abruptly to get a better view and then sighs with relief.

"Okay, let's go," he says, reaching his hand out to help me up. He jumps effortlessly across to the government building, whereas I need a running start. Even then, I fall clumsily onto the other roof. Tyler catches me under my arm before I finish my embarrassing landing, which would have resulted in me face-planting into the ground.

"You good?"

The butterflies in my stomach make it hard to keep my voice straight. "Yeah," I manage quietly, swiping my wind-blown hair from my face.

The door's locked—not that I expected it to open. Tyler

ruffles through the pockets of the unconscious guard and pulls out the keys before turning on his heel, tossing a gun onto the other roof. I give him a look of horror. "What did you do that for?" I hiss, swiping my hair from my face *again*.

Tyler looks at me, confused. "What?"

"Get rid of the gun?" We're both whispering frantically. Afraid someone might hear, even though there's no one else around and the wind is howling, muffling our voices even more. He glances down at the body, then back to me, and again as if to reiterate his point.

"Do you *want* him to come after us, armed?" Tyler asks, handing me a hair tie from around his wrist.

"Obviously not," I say, nodding my thanks and pulling the top section of my hair back. "But *we* could have used that," I say, securing the band and running my hands over my hair to make sure it's okay.

"Oh, because we can't just use our *magic*?" Tyler rolls his eyes as if I just told him we can't breathe without an oxygen tank. And he holds his palm up—the contrast of his whitened fingertips against his tan-kissed skin—a small tornado spiralling up and dispersing into the wind.

I decide now isn't the time to bicker. Who knows where Mallrie and Chelsea are. Or Cyan. Or Edgar. My stomach twists as we head down the few steps from the rooftop into the building. There is a long hallway with only two doors. The one we just walked through and the one to the mayor's penthouse.

"Something doesn't feel right," Tyler whispers. I nod, looking around, agreeing. I would have expected more guards. Especially someone guarding the penthouse's front door. My mind drifts, telling me we're about to fall into a trap. Still, my heart is fighting, telling my mind that Mallrie would have known if there was going to be a trap and not let us walk headfirst into it.

Wouldn't he?

After all, how well do I really know him?

The small, helpless girl of my past starts listing all of my fears and vulnerabilities. I try to push those melancholy thoughts from my mind.

Trust. Trust. Trust.

I repeat the word in my mind like a mantra, hoping it'll override that voice filled with my past fears and vulnerabilities.

After trying all the keys we took from the guard, I press my hands to the hinges of the penthouse's front door. A shimmer of realisation rushes through me. Slowly, I straighten up and turn to face Tyler. Crossing my arms over my chest, I ask him, "How are we going to get in?" He raises an eyebrow, waiting for me to continue. *"Get in and out undetected."* Those were Mallrie's exact words. If I melt the hinges and knock down the door, Edgar and his men will know we were here. That *I* was here."

Tyler runs his hand down his face, then pushes me out of the way. "Let me try something... I doubt it'll work." He crouches down, feeding the cracker, then, the fall of his whip through the gap between the door and the ground. He rocks back onto his knees and gives the handle a gentle flick. The rest of the whip snakes under the door and out of sight. I open my mouth in shock, wanting to ask him how —*what*—he's doing. But the way he closes his eyes, one hand holding the whip's handle, the other pressed against the door. I decide it is better to let him focus. I hold my breath, and then—

Click!

Tyler's eyes snap open, and his head jerks to look up at

me. He pushes to his feet and casually twists the handle, opening the door.

I let out a small shriek. "Oh my gods! Ty!"

His laughter unknots the sickening feeling in my stomach, and we step into the lavish penthouse. Tyler lets out a long, slow whistle as we look around.

Everything is white and modern after Edgar's extensive renovations. Large floor-to-ceiling windows look out onto the centre of town. We tentatively step into the ample space, and I subconsciously wipe my feet. Tyler gives me one of those firm looks that makes him age about ten years. "I know you don't want to, but let's split up." Tyler's voice is calm and balanced, jokes and frivolity pushed aside for the leader within him. I can't help but smile at him. I am proud of how he's grown these last few weeks. *Gods, I guess I've grown too.* After all, if someone told me I'd find a group of people to trust with my life and hold their lives in my own hands, I probably would have laughed in their face. *And yet here I am, breaking into the mayor's penthouse, putting my faith in Mallrie and Tyler. Hell, even Chelsea.* I shake the thought from my mind. We're on a mission. It's not the time for deep and meaningful revelations. "Get in and out," I finish, and we head off in different directions.

I stumble into the master bedroom. The lavish king-size bed sits in the centre of the room, looking out the enormous windows. Its plush silk sheets look good enough to curl up into. I blink hard as I move around it into the walk-in wardrobe and ruffle through the array of suits and dress shirts, all neatly stacked and organised by colour. I've watched enough movies to know there's usually a secret safe somewhere in the wardrobe.

Crash!

Something sounds like a vase breaking outside in the

main living area. I race back into the living room, my heart pounding. All the blood drains from my face, and a loud ringing starts in my head as Tyler lies unconscious in the hallway over a million shattered fragments of a vase.

A tall figure steps over his lifeless body, and the last thing I see is the flash of the gun before a sharp pain hits me in my neck.

CHAPTER FORTY-FIVE
MALLRIE

"You better know what you're doing, *witch*," Chelsea hisses behind me as she pushes me through the streets of Datura. We've been fighting all morning, careful not to let Tyler or Eliana catch wind of the tension brewing. I scoff, jerking my bound hands out of her grip and spinning on her. Then, using my weight, I push her against the wall. Thank the Fates, we're still close to the outer rims of town that there are scarcely any people. "Don't use that tone with me, Chelsea," I growl. "You know I don't want any harm to come to Eliana."

"You have a funny way of showing it," she huffs.

I glance down at her before snapping my attention back to her eyes—something I've seen Cyan do multiple times when he's intimidating people. "You know *nothing* of what I'll do to keep her safe," I say, stepping away. "Even going along with this ridiculous plan that will get me captured. You just better hope you follow through with the rest of the plan."

We walk in silence the rest of the way towards the government building. Chelsea pulls her GDO badge out from her back pocket and hangs it from her jeans. I feel anxious about this. One wrong move and it all goes up in flames, and Eliana's head is the one on the line. "It'll work," Chelsea whispers, even as she pushes me forward with the pommel of my sword. It also has me anxious that she is holding my weapon. *If that got into Edgar's hands...* I repress the shudder that wants to shock through me at the thought of Edgar wielding a sword that can trap the souls of those it slays. We round the back of the government building, and Chelsea punches in the code for the back door.

It buzzes, and we step inside. My heart sinks a little. Cyan stands at the bottom of the stairs in his tailor-made black suit with his arms folded across his chest. I notice the same glaze over his eyes that haunted him the night the Kailadon attacked.

"Cyan," I drawl. He doesn't even notice me. I am a ghost to him.

"Officer Huang," Cyan says stiffly. "Congratulations on bringing in the *witch*," he spits the word like it's an insult, like he's completely forgotten his heritage. His people.

Chelsea smiles sweetly back at him, but I feel her tense behind me. Her hand grips my arm a little tighter. "Thank you, sir. I'd like to take him straight to Mayor MacQuoid. Can you point me in the right direction?"

Cyan pushes off from where he's leaning against the wall. His eyes scan down our bodies before snapping back up to Chelsea's eyes. *Fuck. This can't be good.* I can smell the tang of magic in the air—the first sign before I feel a ripple in the *Timeline*.

No. No. NO!

"Sorry, Officer Huang," Cyan drawls as he walks over to where we stand. "There's been a change of plans." He reaches inside his jacket and pulls out a syringe.

"Chelsea, run!" I shout. Pushing her away, I jump and get my hands in front of my body. But it's too late. Cyan has wrapped a hand around her throat, pressing the syringe into the base and injecting the yellow serum. Chelsea's body falls to the ground, unconscious.

Cyan stretches his neck, turning his attention to me. "Hello, brother," he says smoothly, his voice like honeyed death.

"Cyan, you don't want to do this. This isn't you," I plead. Cyan laughs in my face. His laughter is stiff and filled with darkness. "Brother," I try again.

"Shut the fuck up!" Cyan shouts, backhanding me across my face. I stumble into the wall, catching myself before lunging at him. I'm at a disadvantage, being hand-cuffed, but I am bigger and stronger than him. I've always been able to take him down a peg or two.

Cyan falls backwards into the staircase, cursing as I raise my hands and bring them down on his face. He twists at the last moment, and my hands crack against the marble stairs. Pain shoots up from my left hand to my wrist. I think I might have just broken a finger. Cyan punches me hard, my nose crumpling under the impact, blood sprayed across his face. He pushes me away from him, and I stumble onto the cool marble back entrance of the government building.

Cyan straightens up, fixing the cuffs of his jacket. "It didn't have to go this way, *brother*," he spits, as if it's an insult to be related. Maybe he's right, even in his drugged state. I've been beginning to wonder if I am the problem. I've been so busy trying to protect those I love out of fear of losing them, like I lost my mother and sisters. Maybe Cyan would be better off without me. Maybe Eliana would be better off without me. "And to think, you just walked right into our trap." Cyan pulls out another syringe, flicking off the cap and tapping the side. "Now, Edgar has the hybrid bitch. He will restore the magic to the Enkanti Tree, and the people of Datura will treat him like a god." Before I can say anything, before I can move, vines have pushed through the marble floor and wrapped around my body. Cyan's toxins seep into my veins as he leans over me.

I try to move, but the vines tighten their grip until they're crushing my bones. My magic tries to rally to the cause to slow down the toxins, to ease the pressure of my bones breaking. Cyan taps the tip of the needle on the end of my nose. "Sweet dreams, Mallrie."

"Fuucck," I groan as I come to. The scent of slightly rotten eggs and death hangs in the air. It is cold and damp. This must be what Cyan was talking about. The underground tunnels where Edgar has been experimenting on people—and worse, the Kailadons.

I go to rub my eyes, but my hands are bound behind my back, for being underground in a sewer. The room is so white and sterile it's almost blinding. To my right is a shiny metal workbench with leather straps to bind a person—no, it's big enough to secure a Kailadon. A shiver runs down my spine as a docile clicking sound comes from behind me. Twisting as much as I can in my chair, my heart almost leaps out of my throat.

Chained to the wall is a Kailadon. It snores, clicking softly as it exhales.

The door clicks, metal hinges squeal as the door is pushed open, and Edgar, with a now clear-visioned Cyan, steps into the room. The haze of the drug is replaced with a pinched expression reeking of regret. My hands ball into fists behind my back, and my jaw clenches angrily. He has *no* idea how much he's fucked up the *Timeline* and Chelsea's and my careful plans. *Where the fuck* is *Chelsea?* Concern for her well-being pushes at my chest, and I can feel the faint flicker of my magic deep within my core struggling to wiggle its way to the surface. Cyan looks at me with pleading eyes, but I avoid his gaze, unable to look at him with my anger right now. Even if he wasn't in his right mind. I steel myself for whatever shitstorm is about to blow in. Cyan gives up trying to catch my attention. Instead, his focus has fallen on the Kailadon behind me. There is the start of some dark bruising gathering around his right eye. As much as I wish that blow was from me, it wasn't.

"Hello, Mallrie. Long time no see," drawls Edgar in his pristine olive-green suit, which reminds me of the colour of baby vomit. He's paired it with a soft blue dress shirt. Edgar's grey eyes bore into mine, waiting for a response. *Fuck him.* When I get out of here, I'll lock him in this fucking room to rot with the Kailadon. "Not in the mood to talk?" Edgar removes his jacket and tosses it onto the table. He looks exactly how I remember him, all sharp cheekbones and jaw and those eyes that look at you with a haunting presence. They say eyes are the window to the soul. If that is the case looking into Edgar's eyes, you can see how black his soul has become. They are haunting, and yet he is handsome and unearthly charismatic.

"That's fine. You can listen then." Running his long fingers through his brown hair, Edgar leans against the table and folds his arms across his chest. I glance at Cyan out of the corner of my eye. He's still intent on staring at the Kailadon in the corner. "I'm in a generous mood today, *witch*. Want to know why?"

I slide my eyes away from my brother and back to Edgar. A dark eyebrow is arched in anticipation. "Why are you in a good mood today?" I growl. My throat is rough and sore from the serum, knocking my magic out. I search inside myself for the source but can't find it. *Fuck. They must have upped the concentration of faerie venom.*

"I'm so glad you asked." He winks at me. *The fucker has the audacity to wink at me right now.* I'd like to see him have the gall when I'm not restrained in a fucking chair. Even without my magic, I could kill the bastard with my bare hands. Edgar clears his throat. "I'm sure you're more than aware by now"—he glances over to Cyan with disdain—"that I've got a little... side hustle going on."

"You're experimenting on innocent people and Kailadons," I spit.

Edgar tsks. "I'd hardly call them *innocent*. It's not like I'm plucking babes from their beds. These people are knowingly doing the wrong thing."

"Still doesn't give you the right to experiment on them against their will."

Edgar shrugs as if this is all just a bunch of moral indifferences. "Agree to disagree, shall we, *witch*? Anyway, your *brother* here"—he chuckles—"has a bit of a loose tongue, it seems. If he wasn't so good at what he does, I'd have cut it out long ago." Edgar turns to Cyan, crooks a finger at him and coos, "Come here, Cyan."

Cyan unfurls his arms from across his chest and finally takes his eyes off the Kailadon and walks over to Edgar like a good fucking toy. I was too distracted, too focused on Cyan. And him on the Kailadon. Neither of us saw Edgar reach into his pocket and pull out a syringe. "NO!" I shout. Chains rattle behind me as the Kailadon stirs from its sleep. The needle pierces Cyan's chest, his eyes blowing wide as he clutches Edgar's hand. The Kailadon clicks angrily and thrashes against its restraints, trying to get free.

Cyan falls onto his knees before Edgar. "Mm, just the way I like to see you," Edgar drawls, lifting his chin so he's looking up at him. "On your knees." Edgar kicks him in the chest, and Cyan falls backwards. "Now, Mallrie, I have a proposition for you."

"I will do *nothing* for you, ever!"

"Is that so..." Edgar grabs Cyan by the scruff of his shirt and hauls him onto the table. Cyan curses and tries to fight back, but he's weak from the serum. I try to free my hands to save my brother as Edgar quickly ties him down. Finally, Edgar moves to the cupboards along the wall and pulls out a scalpel. "Maybe you just need a little *persuasion*."

CHAPTER FORTY-SIX
ELIANA

"You don't need her. She's practically useless." Mallrie's voice laughs humourlessly off in the distance. My brain is foggy, and I am not entirely sure if I am dreaming or not. "I really don't think the faerie venom did anything to her. She doesn't have any special abilities. Her magic is subpar," he continues, and it takes every ounce of my self-control not to force my eyes open to prove that this is just a horrible nightmare. That Mallrie really isn't talking shit about me to...

My heart sinks as Edgar's deep, calm voice speaks. "Hmm, useless, you say?" My body shudders at the way he's speaking. I can feel the heat from him as he circles around me, his footsteps ringing in my ears. Long fingers run through the back of my hair and jerk my head backwards. My eyes fling open, focusing on the man before me. Mayor Edgar MacQuoid, in his impeccable olive-green suit with a powder blue dress shirt. He's a good-looking guy with an athletic body. His bright brown hair parted off to the side. His grey eyes narrow as he looks me up and down, and my skin crawls, screaming to get out of his embrace. The smell of his cologne is pungent, but it isn't enough to mask the stench of death and decay. I try to glance around, but Edgar's got my hair in a punishing grip. Tears prick at my eyes from the pain. All I can see is his cold, grey eyes. The little room I can see around him is white and sterile, like a morgue.

How his full lips curl into a snarl doesn't match how charming his face is. Edgar cocks his head to the side, still examining me. "Well... if she's as useless as you say, then I guess we've got no actual use for her anymore." He roughly lets go of my head, and I look over to Mallrie. Two enormous men are standing on either side of him, their hands behind their backs. I give him a pleading look, mentally screaming, *"HELP ME!"* But his face is cold, expressionless.

My heart shatters into a million tiny pieces. *What is going on? Why is Mallrie with Edgar?*

I look back at Edgar, who waves his hand dismissively. Footsteps recede, and the door closes. When I look back, Mallrie is gone. *Why would he say those things? I-I thought he cared about me. Was he just using me all this time? Just a pawn in Edgar's game?*

Edgar circles back to stand before me, one arm folded across his chest, the other rubbing his chin thoughtfully. His thumb traces the curves of his lips as he examines me. I can't hold it in any longer. The lump in my throat suffocates me, and the tears prick behind my eyes.

Edgar clicks his tongue. "Oh, darling, save your tears for someone who honestly cares." His voice is so composed it's terrifying. I've never seen someone who can be as frightening as Edgar but also be so charismatic. He could stab you, and you'd thank him as you bleed out.

I try to speak, but nothing comes out. It's as if my voice has been stolen. Edgar's lips curl at the corners of that sickening, sinister smile as he closes the distance between us. He jerks my chin so I look into his stormy grey eyes. "The time *witch* may say you're useless, but I know what you are. I know you've got *some* of that *Fae* in your blood, so you'll do just fine." His words are like a bucket of icy water, how he spits the word Fae as if it is poison on his tongue to how he looks at me as if I am some abomination. *What is he going to do to me?* My body shakes with fear, and I mentally claw for my magic, which is nowhere to be found.

Edgar heads towards the door. Something sharp stabs me in my throat from behind. He looks over his shoulder back at me. Everything is going blurry again as if in slow motion. His words slur, and I know he's talking to whoever is behind me.

"Get her ready. We're doing this tonight." His eyes fall onto me as everything fades out. He says, "Be a good girl now and go to sleep."

My feet drag behind me as I stumble to gain control of them. Two of Edgar's men carry me through a long, damp tunnel. The only light comes from the bunker cage lights attached to the wall every two metres or so. "I hate it down here," grumbles the man on my left, and the other grunts in agreement. "Those fucking *things* are down here, I swear," he continues.

"Shut up, Fredriks," says the second man, and I can feel his grip tighten as he looks around.

"It smells like death," grumbles Fredriks, and he's not wrong. The smell of death and decay hangs heavily in the damp air. My feet thump limply against some stairs as we make our ascent. There is a door at the top of the stairs. A metal plaque in the middle of the heavily stained door reads—

My heart has somehow lurched itself out of my chest and into my throat. I choke on a sob as Fredriks pushes open the door. The two men lift me effortlessly. I thrash wildly in their embrace as they toss me onto a round table in the centre of the room. I whip my head up, my eyes meeting the bookshelf with the label BANNED BOOKS printed on the side. It feels like I was in the library's basement only yesterday, contemplating how to get in here undetected and riffle through that shelf. Yet here I am. I managed to enter the library's basement undetected, just as I wanted. Except now, I don't want to be here. I guess the Fates Mallrie always talks about have a sick sense of humour.

The other man steps behind me, forcing my head back against the table. It cracks against the wood, sending a shooting pain through my entire skull. He grabs my wrists and holds them above my head. Fredriks is at the other end of the table. He's a tall, bull-necked brute. I try not to look at him as he grips my ankles, and they hold me to the table.

I manage to turn my head towards the nauseating sound of a knife being sharpened. Five hooded figures stand huddled around the small kitchen.

I squeeze my eyes shut, willing my magic to come the fuck out of wherever it has been sent. *What good is being half-faerie when that bloody serum can still affect my magic?* I thrash against my captor's hold. Praying for help.

I pray to the gods of life and death. *Screech.*

I pray to my father and mother. *Screech.*

I pray to my grandmother. *Screech.*

The only response is the scraping sound of a blade being sharpened. My body thrashes, desperate to fight my way out, bloody tooth and nail if need be. "Sort her out!" seethes one of the hooded figures. Fredriks lets go of one of my legs to pull a syringe from his pocket. I kick wildly. My foot makes contact with his chin before he curses, and a sharp pain shoots into my thigh.

But I don't black out. Instead, my heartbeat slows, and I feel drowsy, but I don't sleep. Rather, my body slowly seizes up like someone has poured cement all over me, my body is paralysed from the neck down.

The five librarians turn to face me.

Each has their hands outstretched. One hooded figure holds a ceremonial-looking knife. The others hold a bowl of water, crushed herbs that smell strong and bitter, a candle and, finally, a large, brown feather with white spots.

The muffled sound of thunder rumbles through the quiet room. The librarians circle around me, and I open my mouth to speak. It takes me two reasonable attempts before I can form words. "Help."

Selma, the librarian with the long silver hair, lifts the knife and carefully cuts open my shirt. "Shh," she whispers, gently caressing my cheek. "You do not need help. You *are* the help." She speaks slowly, as if I need to savour her every word. Her pale eyes glisten in the light, and she starts chanting in another language. I assume she's speaking Enkantian.

When Selma finishes her chant, the others reply, also in Enkantian. I have no idea what they're saying. My eyes dart around the table to the other familiar faces. The hoods of the four remaining librarians hang low, trying to hide their identities, but I know who they are. One librarian starts to wash my body. They carefully wipe down my arms, face and then my exposed chest and stomach. I try not to shudder at the invasive touch. When they're finished, they mutter something in Enkantian before stepping back. The librarian with the feather then steps forward, gently sweeping away the droplets and murmuring. Once they're finished, Selma once again steps forward, the ceremonial knife in the palms of her hands. She holds it high above her head. "Oh, High Witchess, grant me your power and wisdom. Grant me the honour of taking this life—"

"STOP!" I shriek, demanding my body to move for my magic to help me. For fuck's sake, I even pray that Mallrie or even Cyan will come to save me. Even though I know Mallrie's turned his back on me. Played me like a damn fool.

Selma doesn't pay me any attention. "For this life, the soul of both witch and Fae will restore the magic of the Enkanti Tree."

"W-what?" I breathe to no one in particular because no one is listening to me anyway. My mind is reeling. The ringing in my ears blocks out what Selma says next. *I need to be sacrificed so they can restore the magic to the Enkanti Tree?*

WHAT THE FUCK?

Did Mallrie know—

Of course he knew! He's been planning this for decades.

Selma lowers the knife, turning her attention to me. Gently stroking the hair out of my face, her voice drops to a kind, reassuring whisper. "Eliana, dear, there's no need to struggle. Your sacrifice will help us all. You have done so well. You should be *honoured.*"

I try to shake her hand away from my face. "Fuck you," I spit, but it doesn't come off as menacing as I hoped.

Selma's expression goes cold as she straightens up. "Fine." Her voice is cold and calculated. "The more you struggle, the worse it'll be for *you*. Doesn't bother us either way. We have had to sacrifice people on the run before. So don't think your weak attempts at escaping will stop us from completing the ritual." The horrifying scene of someone being chased through the streets plays on repeat in my head. It's only when I feel the sharp sting of the knife as the librarian carves the first rune into my chest that my eyes snap shut. The cool blade drags along my skin, goosebumps spreading all over my body as I shudder. The man behind me, holding my wrists, chuckles at the reaction.

The knife's tip briefly dances around the next spot before Selma plunges it into my flesh, carving again. I hold my breath. My head is going light and dizzy as I try to block out the pain, not wanting to give them the satisfaction of seeing me weep. I bite down hard on my lip. Hard enough to draw blood. The coppery taste fills my mouth, and my lip tingles. Instead, I try to focus on something—anything—other than the rough burning sensation of being methodically cut open.

Selma steps back, cocking her head to the side, taking in her handiwork of adorning my body with runes. She twists the bloody knife in her hand and then gives a final nod. The last two librarians step forward. They work in unison. One pours wax into the runes, and the other rubs the herbs into the alternate markings. It hurts so much worse than actually getting the runes carved. I squirm and scream. *To be dammed with sitting in silence. Fuck them! Let them know how*

badly this hurts. Maybe then they might have to live with a sliver of guilt, though I very much doubt they feel anything anymore.

Thankfully, they work quickly, and I am hauled back onto my feet. Edgar's brutes hold me up under my arms. If they weren't there helping to support my weight, I think I would just collapse onto the floor. They rip the rest of my shirt from my body and replace it with a black button-down blouse covering the harsh lines and runes of a sacrificial offering. All the wax and herbs they stuffed into them have helped clot the bleeding. It will totally give me an infection, but I guess that doesn't matter since they're going to kill me.

It looks as if the whole town has gathered around the large oak in the centre of Datura, utterly unaware of the dormant magic it possesses. Of the Fae who dance around its roots and in its high branches. Of their deranged mayor, who believes he will weaponise the monsters that have us living in fear, that he'll be able to grant mere mortals the gift of *magic.* My stomach twists into knots. I am led towards a small stage placed at the tree's base. Edgar steps onto the small platform, smoothing one hand down his suit jacket. My brows press together as I notice the dark stain of blood under his nail. He can try to scrub away his crimes, but the blood still stains his hands.

"The good people of Datura!" his voice extends over the rumbling thunder in the distance and the murmuring crowd, silencing them. I crane my neck, looking amongst the masses for Mallrie, Chelsea and Tyler. Gods, even Cyan. The latter, I spot first. Standing between two of Edgar's thugs, the sleeves of his black button-down, rolled up to his elbows and his arms folded tightly across his chest. His eyes flicker to one of the men by his side, and his mouth moves rapidly. He looks... horrible. He's got a cut on his lip and a bruised eye. One of his hands has been bandaged.

The thunder rumbles around us as the enormous men lead me onto the stage, where Edgar waits. The two men are still gripping my arms, even though my hands are tied behind my back. My body aches from the sacrificial runes on my chest and the drug injected into my neck, immobilising my magic. "It's with a heavy heart that I bring you all here today." He looks around the crowd. Edgar genuinely looks sincere. It makes me want to puke. The people of Datura are utterly enraptured by his every word. Some are nodding sombrely with their hands over their hearts. Others are watching on with smiles, just happy to be in his presence.

"We have caught the citizen who's been sacrificing our friends, family and neighbours to the Flesh-Hunters." There is an eruption of shocked gasps and murmurs throughout the crowd. That's when I see him.

Mallrie.

My heart stops, and I stare at him. The wound on his head has split open again, and blood has been smeared across his forehead. His shirt clings to his shoulder with an obscene amount of blood that has my breath catching in my throat. And no matter the anger that's got my jaw clenching. The sight of him wounded like that has tears pricking at my eyes. I should *want* to see him hurt like this, but I find myself fearful for his well-being. My heart sinks, and my head reels at what I am seeing. Chelsea and Tyler stand beside him. Chelsea's face is cut up, and she's talking quickly, tugging Mallrie's arm. But his eyes are wholly focused on me. My friends... my *family*. Edgar has hurt them. Tyler looks like he's about to lose it at any moment. His mouth moves a hundred miles a minute, and Chelsea nods with him.

Mallrie... Mallrie's face is a picture of melancholy.

As much as I want to hate him now for what he said to Edgar about me, for working *with* Edgar all this time... Mallrie's eyes glisten with tears as he mouths two words that shatter my heart.

"I'm sorry."

A shuddering sigh leaves my chest. There is no way Mallrie could have been working with Edgar and be standing there now, apologising, bloody and bruised, looking like he is a second away from losing it. That is the look of regret plastered over his face.

He must have tried to persuade Edgar that I wasn't worth the sacrifice. That they'd need to find someone else. My heart spins happily in my chest. If I am to die, I want to die knowing my heart didn't fail me once again.

The lump in my throat returns, but I swallow hard. If Edgar wants to make me the bad guy, I'll be the bad guy. I can feel my magic deep, deep within me. Sluggish and dormant. If I can just bring it back to the surface... Closing my eyes, I try to summon it. Try to call it back to me.

"Today, my friends," Edgar continues, his eerily calm persona making it hard to concentrate. "Today we get closure. Eliana Nightingale will be hanged by the neck until dead for the murder of"—Edgar pulls a list from his pocket —"Susan Miller." That name hits a nerve. I snap my head to where Edgar is standing. *Fucker! You killed her!* I want to scream, but something presses into my lower back. I turn my head and see a small pistol pressed against my side. Biting my tongue, I return my attention to the crowd. Edgar continues to read out name after name. "Kyle Jensen, Morana Walton—" My head jerks to where I saw Cyan standing in the crowd. His hands are clenched at his sides, knuckles going white. He looks a second away from ripping Edgar's head from his body. I have a feeling deep in my gut that Edgar will regret falsely accusing me of Morana's murder when her blood is on his hands.

Edgar continues reading name after name, falsely accusing me of senseless murder. "Miles Maloney, Ethan Larsen, Beckett Peiris." My head snaps up again, a loud ringing in my ears blocking out the rest of the names Edgar continues to read.

I glare at him. I feel as if my eyes might fall out of my head at the mention of Beckett. Edgar turns to me, the corner of his lips curling. "How do you, Eliana Nightingale, plea?"

I raise my eyebrows at him. It takes a moment to register that he asked me a question. Even though someone has already secured a noose snugly around my neck, Edgar is going to deliver one last blow. He wants me to beg for my freedom.

A rough laugh escapes my lips, the sound almost hysterical. I roll my eyes. *As if I get a say,* I think to myself. I know only Edgar understands the meaning behind my laugh. The crowd, however, once again erupts in shocked gasps and whispers. The curve of Edgar's full lips twists even further into that sickening smile, as if knowing that I have just sealed my fate. He turns back to the crowd, arms outstretched like a cult leader, preaching to his followers. "Ladies and Gentlemen, we will now hang Miss Nightin-gale. If you have small children or choose not to bear witness on this monumental occasion, please leave now."

It begins to rain. Not an outright downpour, but more

of a steady, misty drizzle. Nobody seems to notice or leave, exposing the genuinely horrific side of human nature. Even as the building burns, killing hundreds, they will all still stand by to watch. Doing nothing. Feeling nothing. A side to human nature where they will disconnect from their humanity to fill their own morbid curiosity.

I shiver against the cool rain and wind. The noose gets pulled tighter around my throat, and I frantically try to wriggle my wrists free. I plead with every fibre of my being, magical and mortal, to be set free.

I search the crowd for Mallrie again, this time unable to contain the tears. Chelsea is pushing through the crowd after Tyler, whose eyes are red and puffy. She gets to him before he gets far, wrapping her arms around him, holding him tightly against her as he thrashes, trying to break free. Causing several onlookers around them to turn away from me towards the scene Tyler is making. I meet her eyes, and she whispers, "I love you, El. I'm sorry."

I give her a slight nod as she pulls Tyler away. Whatever she says to those around them seems to work because all eyes are back on me. I don't need to be mouthing my last goodbyes in front of everyone, putting targets on the other's backs. I look back at Mallrie. He's just staring at me in shock. Tears run down his cheeks, and my whole body shakes. Not with fear of dying, but having to leave him.

Fuck it, I think, and mouth the three words I've been dying to tell him but have been too afraid. These are the three words I haven't uttered to anyone for so long. *"I love you."*

His expression changes, his eyes going dark and ravenous. *"I love you too, Eliana,"* he mouths, and then he's belligerently pushing through the crowd. Suddenly, my feet fall out from underneath me. *No, not yet,* I think. My body jerks back upwards. I hear a sickening crack in my skull, knowing my neck has just been broken. But it doesn't hurt. My legs spasm as they hang in the air. My vision blurs as Mallrie frantically pushes people out of the way. I gasp for air, unable to fill my lungs. Everything fades in and out, and then—

CHAPTER FORTY-SEVEN
MALLRIE

Cyan lies on the cold metal table, unconscious. The Kailadon chained to the wall behind me is in a frenzy, trying to get to the source of all the blood. The coppery scent hangs heavily in the air. Edgar has stripped my magic from me with another injection of faerie venom so I can't do anything to help except thrash in my bindings.

The Kailadon's hot breath breathes down my back, which has my whole body on high alert. *How long will it take until it breaks free of its restraints?*

My lip quivers as Edgar flips the scalpel in his fingers, examining how Cyan's blood glistens under the fluorescent lights. Stalking around the table, he stabs the scalpel into my brother's stomach instead of just putting it on the fucking bench. Cyan groans, his bloody and broken fingers twitching. Or attempting to. I try to growl at Edgar as he stalks towards me, wiping my brother's blood from his hands. But my voice is hoarse from screaming and demanding Edgar to stop.

Of course he didn't.

Edgar won't stop until he burns everything around him.

My stupidity and short-sightedness have caused this. All those years ago, when we watched as Edgar murdered his father in cold blood and took his place as mayor. That is when I started fucking everything up. I shouldn't have allowed Cyan to stay in town. When he met Morana, I should have forced them both to leave. It should have been me who stayed. I should have kept a closer eye on Edgar myself. I never should have let Cyan get into this position. He lost the love of his life because of me, and now Edgar will kill him.

Tucking the bloodied handkerchief back into his pocket, Edgar glances over my head, where the Kailadon thrashes against its restraints. Its hot breath reeks of death and breathes heavily down my back. "Are you ready to listen to me?" he coos as he places a hand on my shoulder. "We both know how to restore the magic to your little tree and what restoring the magic will do for the people of Datura." His fingers dig into my flesh, pushing the chair back on its hind legs. The Kailadon's teeth sink deep into my shoulder. I roar in pain as the monster's teeth shred into my flesh. It opens its mouth and clamps down again, twisting its head from side to side, trying to sever the bone. The monster's tongue laps at the blood, a frantic clicking sound resonating deep within its throat.

Edgar releases his grip, letting the chair flop back onto all fours, causing the Kailadon's teeth to rip through my shoulder. It shrieks at its lost meal, and I echo its scream as my flesh is shredded. "Eliana must die," Edgar says, stepping away, his voice even and calm. The voice of a psychopath.

"You're fucking delusional if you think I will let you kill her!" I spit a mouthful of blood towards him.

Edgar picks a piece of lint off his light blue shirt and

fixes his rolled-up sleeves, completely unfazed. "Ah, see, I thought you would say that." Turning, he heads over to the cabinetry. The click of his shoes is like the ticking of a bomb about to explode. Unlocking and opening the door, he pulls out a small vial. "Do you know what this is, *witch*?" I frown at the vial in his hand. Inside is a shimmery purple liquid that almost sparkles in the light.

"Faerie venom," I spit.

"Mm." Edgar returns it to the shelf and pulls out another vial. This one is black, but it still shimmers the same as the venom. "Now, you know that I've been doing a little experimentation. I've been trying to use the faerie venom to help extract whatever it is you *witches* possess that gives you your elemental magic." He starts pacing the room like a wild animal caught in a cage. The Kailadon continues to breathe down my back and snap its jaws. Surely its restraints can't last much longer, and when they break, I am well and truly fucked. Edgar is just buying his time. "Whatever gives you that magic cannot be reproduced or manufactured."

"I could have told you that, asshole," I growl.

"Mm, don't worry. Your brother also tried to tell me. But, you see, I am a man of my word. And when I want something, I get it." Edgar pulls the handkerchief back out and polishes the ring on his finger. "If I cannot grant the people magic, then I need to do something else. I bet you didn't know I've been in contact with the cities beyond the Melsheim Forest, did you?"

My brows press together, and my jaw tightens. *No, I didn't know that.* "Ah, your brother's been keeping secrets from you too. Well, his little *pet* turns out to be quite obedient to its master. Especially when its master's life is at stake. The king on the other side of the Melsheim Forest wants to start a war with a neighbouring kingdom. Details I am not concerned with. We're safe where we are. Their trivial dispute won't affect us. However, he will pay me handsomely to have an army of Kailadons to be the brute force of his militia." Edgar turns back to the cupboard and retrieves a syringe. "Of course, as we know, we cannot control the Kailadons. But I am *almost* there. I am so close. I can feel it." Edgar's eyes are wild with mania. He injects the needle into the vial, drawing the liquid into it. "You see this?" He holds up the syringe, tossing the vial aside. It shatters against the tiled floor. Edgar turns it as he holds it up to the light, admiring it. "*This* is what turns the Kailadons into real killing machines. I just need to tweak it a little more, and then..." He stalks over to me and kicks my chair over. The Kailadon lunges for me, its teeth sinking into my side. "Then I will be able to *control* them as well," he calls over my roars and the Kailadon trying to rip me to pieces.

Edgar moves quickly, injecting the serum into the distracted Kailadon. He grabs the chair's leg, dragging me out of the way. The monster falls to the floor, its body convulsing. "Listen to me, Mallrie, and listen well. That serum takes about five minutes to completely run its course. Another two for it to start mutating. When it does, it'll smash through those chains. You'll only survive if you join me on the other side of that blast door." Edgar points over his shoulder to the door. "I am not a cruel man. I know you've developed feelings for our little hybrid, but you now have a choice to make. Either die here with your brother *or* join me. I'll even let you spare his pathetic life. First, we will restore the magic to the Enkanti Tree. Then, you can do your little spell to protect my town. Together, we will bring in a new era. We will put Datura on the map!"

CHAPTER FORTY-EIGHT

ELIANA

The darkness surrounds me. Death is peaceful but lonely. *Where is the white light? Where are my loved ones waiting for me?* An ache pierces through my chest as I realise I am alone. This isn't the Afterlife my grandmother spoke of. This is something else.

The darkness is consuming. I can't tell which way is up or down. If there even is an up or down. Panic starts to sink in, my breathing becomes laboured and there is a sharp pain in my neck. Lifting a trembling hand in the darkness, I tentatively touch my neck. My hand jerks away from the break in my spine. I can *feel* my broken spinal cord protruding from my neck, yet somehow, I can still hold it up.

Maybe this place is cursed.

I am to live with my sins. To know that my depravities have caused this and that now I am stuck in this... limbo between life and death.

Maybe this is the gods Vid and Achel's revenge on me for turning my back on my faith.

Feeling desolate, I pull my knees up to my chest and

sob. There is nothing else for me to do. *Did Mallrie betray me? Did he sell me out to Edgar?* I don't want to believe he did, but his words still hurt. I don't want to consider it. Mallrie looked at me with such regret and pleading. Unless he betrayed me and wanted my forgiveness before I died, so he could sleep easily at night. I scoff. Mallrie doesn't even need to have a clear conscience to sleep easily at night. He can just take his stupid little potion. Once again, I let someone in, and they have hurt and betrayed me.

"Sweet girl, Mallrie didn't betray you." I snap my head up, looking around for the source of the voice. My grandmother's voice. There she is, standing before me. My heart cracks, and my chest feels like it will open up for my heart to leap into her open arms. I never thought I'd ever see her again. I struggle to breathe around the sobs. *This can't be real.* My vision blurs around the tears, her short grey hair in a perfect perm. Her eyes still twinkle with that gentle kindness.

Those are my undoing.

I scramble to my feet as I rush forward, trying to close the distance between us. But no matter how fast I run or how hard I push my legs, I cannot get to her.

My grandmother lifts a hand, and her sapphire rings sparkle in the non-existent light. "Calm down, Eliana. Relax and focus." She steps forward, and suddenly, she's kneeling before me. Knee to knee. I throw my arms around her shoulders.

I can *feel* her.

I sob harder. "I-I never thought I'd ever see you again. H-how are y-you here? Where are w-we?"

A gentle hand lifts my head. "We're in the in-between, my darling. Vraska."

"Vraska?" I breathe. Mallrie had mentioned it briefly.

It's the place between life and death. The place where the Fae help guide the souls into the Afterlife. I look around. It's not really what I had imagined. "H-how?" I ask again. To think that my grandmother has been stuck here for so long has my heart aching. My magic feels distant here, but I can feel it thrum with my anger at the Fae. *How could they let her stay here?* She had done nothing wrong in her whole life. My grandmother was so selfless, always willing to help others when she could. *How could they let her soul rot here in this empty darkness?*

"Child, calm yourself," my grandmother whispers, running her fingers through my hair. "I chose to stay here. This is how I've been able to communicate with you."

I snap my head up to meet her eyes. "You stayed here... for me?" *Even in death, she's been looking out for me.*

"You're part, Fae. I knew if I stayed here, I could communicate with you. It did not impress the Fae, naturally. Since their job is to help souls into the Afterlife and to protect Vraska. But..." A sly smile stretches across her face. "Your old grandmother can be persuasive when need be."

I laugh, the sound echoing around us endlessly. *Don't I know that!* The way she could persuade me to do anything... I used to think it was her magical talent.

Now that I know she's a witch, maybe that thought isn't so far from the truth.

"You... You never told me..."

Her eyes turn sympathetic. "I'm so sorry, child. You have been through so much. I never wanted to keep it from you, but I knew you'd blame yourself for Nina's death. That staining your soul was not something I could allow. You've always taken on too much, child. Taken on other people's perceptions and feelings towards you. Whether they are real or just your own projections of yourself. I couldn't allow this to be another strain on you." I open my mouth, but before even a sound comes out, my grandmother says, "You didn't kill her, Eliana. Edgar did."

Knowing that tone, I keep my mouth shut and nod. "So, what now?" I ask, looking up at her. Her gentle eyes turn hard. I know that expression, and I know I will not like what comes out of her mouth next. "I-I don't get to stay with you. Do I?" I breathe.

"No, child. Your time is not up just yet." Her words pierce through my chest. *No. I can't lose her again.* My grandmother laughs, the sound rough and humourless. "I am never lost, child. Are the stars lost when the sun comes out? Or the sun when the moon returns?"

I shake my head. "This is different."

"How? Just because you can't see me doesn't mean you stop loving me, does it?"

"Of course not."

"Then I am never lost. I will always be with you"—she presses her hand against my chest, over my heart—"in here."

I suck in a startled breath.

Under her hand, I can feel my heart beating. I reach out to her chest. It is cold and empty. "I told you, child. Your time isn't up yet. We will be together again. When the time is right. But now, you need to return."

"I don't know if I can."

My grandmother's brows pinch together. "Whatever do you mean?"

"Mallrie... He... I..." I squeeze my eyes together. "I messed everything up."

"Messed everything up?" My grandmother's laugh echoes around us. "Mallrie helped you learn to open your heart back up. To stop closing yourself off from everyone around you."

My eyes snap open. "And he got me killed!" I shout, pressing a hand to the back of my neck. The break... It's gone.

"Maybe so. But you can't keep yourself closed off. Mallrie has made you happy, no?" I roll my eyes. My grandmother smiles back at me knowingly. "Then it was worth it. Hear him out, then decide if you're willing to forgive him and move forward."

The sound of fluttering wings echoes around us. It sounds like they're coming from every direction. My grandmother pulls me into her. "I love you so much, and I am so proud of you."

CHAPTER FORTY-NINE
MALLRIE

I sit on the chair in the corner of my room. I haven't slept for five days. *Five days have passed since Eliana's—*

I can't even bring myself to think the word. I look at the bed, a vast and barren landscape. Eliana's scent still lingers on the empty sheets. I have nowhere to sleep. Looking at the space before me—two lamps, two bedside tables, one heart—the sound of it breaking echoes in the darkness.

I roll my head along the back of the chair over to my desk. Where there once was organised chaos has now been reduced to a pile of books, papers, and splintered furniture. Winifred walks into the room. Her mutilated ear has healed up, the other wholly gone. But at least she can still hear. The large Misnac lies at my feet, purring.

I feel empty.

There's a hole in my chest that will never be filled, and I will be dammed if I help anyone ever again. The town of Datura can have these few days where I am too numb to move, to think before I burn them all. Before I stand by and watch as the Kailadons murder every single one of them.

Then, I am officially done.

My promise to my mother be damned. Damned like my soul. I'll move to the seaside. Where I should have taken Eliana that first night after I saved her from the Kailadon. The painting in the antique shop that she loved so much; that's where I will go. I'll rip the artwork from the wall, a reminder of what I've done, and I'll search every inch of this lonely planet until I find where it was painted. And there I'll stay.

That's what I should have done the first chance I got. I should have saved Eliana from this horrible fate. After everything she's been through, she deserved to find peace and happiness.

I always knew that this was what needed to happen. No matter how hard I tried to find another way. A loophole—*something*. She still had so much life left in her, so much more that she needed to experience. I can't get those beautiful brown eyes out of my head. Her handprints burnt into the bed frame are a stark reminder of all I have lost.

"What the fuck is he doing here?" I hear Tyler shout from downstairs somewhere. Winnie stalks over to the balcony. Hackles raised, my eyes follow her lazily. *It doesn't matter anymore.* Winnie's body language changes as if she's just seen a ghost, and she bolts for the door, her sharp claws clacking against the stairs.

It doesn't matter.

Nothing matters anymore.

"Mallrie!" Chelsea calls from the bottom of the stairs as the front door shuts. "I think you should come down here."

Why? I think. *Nothing will bring my Eliana back. I have failed her, and deserve every inch of this painful torture. I deserve to slowly rot in this chair.*

Footsteps ascend the stairs, but they're not Chelsea's or Tyler's.

Whatever.

It doesn't matter.

I roll my head back and close my eyes. Maybe whoever it is will come and end my suffering. Not that I am deserving of such a quick end.

"Mallrie?" a familiar voice calls from the door. I run my hand over my face, stifling a groan.

"What are you doing here, Cyan?" My voice is gravelly from not talking or drinking for the last few days. Chelsea has tried bringing up food and water for me, but it always remains untouched, where she leaves it beside the chair until she takes it away.

When he doesn't reply, I force myself to look at him. Cyan is standing in the doorway to my bedroom, his hair bound at the nape of his neck. One braid on the side of his head has slipped away, and hangs by his shoulder. Flecks of blood stain his hair and his face... Almost every inch of his body has a splattering of blood on it. His black business shirt has been torn, and the sleeves rolled up to his elbows. I try not to look too closely at his exposed skin, afraid to find any evidence of Edgar's torture. If the blood and his dishevelled hair weren't enough of a giveaway, the state of his clothes clearly indicates that he's been doing a *lot* of killing. My eyes fall onto the lilac glow of my sword. My stomach churns as if I have consumed sour milk at the sight of it.

"Get that out of here. I have no use for it anymore," I say, letting my head flop back against the head of the chair and closing my eyes again. Cyan's footsteps echo as he comes closer. "Don't," I say simply. Peeking through one eye, he is about to sit on the bed. He straightens up and looks over the bed. His eyes finally fell on the handprints on the bed frame. The handprints Eliana burnt into the wooden frame the first time we... I can't even bring myself to remember how her body felt pressed against mine, how her scent filled me with something I hadn't felt in such a long time.

His body tenses, and his ears glow red as he flushes. "I'm sorry," he mumbles, not meeting my eyes but unable to look at the bed either. Instead, he walks across the room and leans against the wall, resting my sword beside him.

"What do you want, Cyan? It's over. I'm not..."

He raises his hand to stop me. "I'm only here to return —" His voice cracks. I narrow my eyes at him. *I don't want that fucking sword back,* I think angrily. Cyan clears his throat. "She's downstairs."

My eyes snap up to meet his. There's something behind his expression—something he's trying to hide from me. I narrow my eyes. As much as I want to rush downstairs and hold my girl in my arms, there's something about how Cyan looks at me that I don't trust.

"Why—" My mouth keeps working, but I can't bring any more words into existence.

Cyan looks away, unable to meet my gaze. "She deserves a proper burial." That is all he says. The empty cavity in my chest where my heart used to be implodes. I look up at my younger brother. A lump forms in my throat, tears stinging my eyes. My mouth opens to speak, to apologise for not being able to do the same for him. The incessant pain in my chest I've felt since I watched Eliana's lifeless body sway against the noose flares with guilt for how Cyan felt when I left Morana's body to save him. I should have done *more.* I should have killed Edgar, even if it was the last thing I did. At least then, Cyan could have given Morana the proper burial she deserved. He folds and unfolds his arms awkwardly. "You would have done the same for Morana..." he says finally, as if understanding. As if reading the apology from my gaping mouth.

"I really am sorry about that," I manage after a moment of silence.

I meet his stare, and he nods. "I know." Cyan clears his throat uncomfortably, "Well... I'll... I guess." He gestures with his thumb back towards the door.

"What happened?" I ask, nodding towards his bloody and torn clothes. Even though I'm sure I already know the answer. Cyan rubs the base of his neck, unable to meet my eyes again. His face colours slightly as if he's embarrassed to admit what's happened. I push to my feet, standing at my full height, my back aching. My knees buckle somewhat under my weight, and a wave of pins and needles cascades through my legs from scarcely using them these past days. Stalking on weak legs over to where Cyan stands. I am not that much taller than him, but I use that little height to my advantage. I look down my nose at him, which I know always has him crumbling.

Cyan sighs in defeat. "I killed them all... It's over." He looks like he would give anything to not be here, talking to me about this. He rubs the back of his neck again, then folds his arms one way across his chest, then the other.

He's nervous. Cyan doesn't want to speak about this with me, which is strange considering he's never had a problem sharing his kills with me before, even if the details made me feel uneasy.

My brain feels foggy and slow. I am trying to comprehend what he just said. "*I killed them all. It's over.*" Blinking hard, looking from his bloody hands to his face. "Killed them—" I start.

"Edgar and all of his men are dead. Don't worry, brother. Edgar suffered. It was slow. Took the last three days. I healed him just to torture and maim him again."

My eyes feel like they might fall out of my head, and a pang of jealousy rolls in the pit of my stomach. Anger bubbles inside. "Why?" I growl, closing the last of the distance between us, my hand firmly pressed around Cyan's throat. "Why?" I repeat, clearly unable to say anything more.

Cyan reaches up, clutching at my arm. "Don't act like you wouldn't have done the same," he spits out.

"Exactly!" I growl. "Edgar was mine to kill! He took the only person I've ever loved. His blood was *mine* to spill!"

Cyan tries to break free from my grip, but only to talk better—we've sparred many times, fought many times. I know he's stronger than this. I know if he wanted to, he could overpower me.

But he doesn't.

It is as if he wants to be punished. He wants to feel my wrath for taking away the satisfaction of murdering Edgar myself.

I drop my hand, staring at him in disbelief. Cyan rubs his throat but doesn't say anything. We just stare at each other for a long moment. *If he's going to say nothing...* My fists clench at my side. Cyan gives me an apologetic look, but it doesn't reflect in his eye. I know he doesn't mean it. "I loved her too," he whispers, averting his eyes. That, he meant. I've only ever heard my brother confess his love once, and that was for Morana. He has had lovers in the past, but no one he has ever truly cared enough to admit his love to.

I feel as if all the blood has left my face. My head spins, and I feel a little faint from days without food. There is a long silence that stretches out between us. Neither wanting to look at the other, let alone speak. My mind spins. *How? How could he possibly love her?* Not that she's unlovable. She is very easy to love—*was. Eliana* was *very easy to love*, I correct myself somberly.

Eliana was so strong. She was stronger than she knew. She lived through more than anyone should have had to in such a short time. Experiencing so much death and darkness, and yet, even though she tried to push others away, she loved so freely. I think she pushed people away. Not to protect herself, but to protect others from her irrational fear of the darkness that follows her. She loved Tyler the moment she got to know him and loved him with fierce protectiveness. She was smart, picking up how to use her magic quickly and unlocking the mysteries of her Fae magic. And she was so damn beautiful, her curves and even her scars—which she was sometimes self-conscious of. I can't remember how many times I told her those scars were proof of her strength. My mind wanders down a dark path, knowing I'll never feel the warmth of those curves in my hands again. Or hear the quick wit of her words.

Cyan finally meets my eyes. He's no longer nervous. Instead, his body language exudes arrogant confidence. He really has grown—even if he physically hasn't aged—and he takes a deep breath. "I will not apologise or be made to feel bad for loving her."

"She thought you were a dick," I say dryly.

Cyan's mouth presses into a firm line, but he ignores the jab. "Like you, I have watched her for her entire life. I tried to protect her when no one else would. I threatened that piece of shit, Beckett, for a *month* before Eliana finally escaped. Then, *I* made sure no Kailadons got her that night. I only spared Beckett's miserable life so I could torture him myself. I knew she'd never feel the same for me, and honestly, I was happy that you found her, even if…" His voice trails off as he looks over to the bed, at her hand prints.

Cyan clears his throat as if he's envious of what Eliana and I shared. I don't blame him. I would envy any man who shared his heart, let alone his bed, with her. "Doesn't matter now. She's gone. So are Edgar and his men. I just thought she deserved to be back with you." Cyan turns to leave.

"Cyan, wait." He presses a dried, bloody hand to the doorframe, steadying himself. "You should stay. Say good-bye." His body shudders a little like he's trying not to cry. He straightens up slightly and gives a slight nod before leaving.

I follow him to the doorway. "I'll be back," he mumbles as he descends the stairs. I linger in the doorway, unable to move. The front door clicks shut, and Tyler moves to where Chelsea must be standing. I hear him talking quickly in a hushed tone, but my mind reels with what just happened.

Cyan killed Edgar out of revenge for Eliana's murder because he loved her. How did I not see it before? How long has he cared for her?

It takes me a few minutes to compose myself enough to head downstairs. When I finally go down, my heart lurches into my throat as Eliana's body is lying on the island bench. Cyan has clothed her in a stunning white dress, her hair has been brushed and he tucked small flowers into her hair, creating a crown. Of course, knowing Cyan, he would have carefully picked each flower. I take a step closer, drawing in a deep breath that feels like a thousand knives, dragging down my throat. At least Chelsea and Tyler had the courtesy of leaving the room when I came downstairs.

We're alone.

But that doesn't make this any easier.

Noticing the flowers delicately tucked into her hair. Hyacinthus, cupressus, gypsophila, asphodelus, galanthus and anemone.

My heart aches as my eyes linger on the black-eyed anemones, their soft, white petals and black centres staring up at me like soulless eyes. Cyan's written a love letter in the language of flowers on my dead girlfriend... To my surprise, I am not angry.

Please forgive me for your death. You were young and innocent. My regrets will follow you to the grave. Consolation. Your forsaken love.

I step closer and run my finger down her cold, grey, lifeless face, her lips painted blood red. She looks like an Enkantian Princess. Winnie rubs her body against my leg. I scoop her up into my arms, and she mews sadly at Eliana's body.

Tyler and Chelsea eventually make their way back inside and stand beside me. Chelsea wraps her arm around my shoulder in an attempt at a hug. "She's stunning," she whispers. The sound of wood being chopped snaps my attention to the window in the kitchen. Chelsea and Tyler follow me silently as I walk outside and around the side of the house, where Cyan has prepared for the cremation.

My jaw drops at what I see before me.

Cyan's prepped a funeral fit for a true Enkantian

Princess Warrior—the highest of honours, even though there hasn't been royalty in the Enkantian coven for centuries after the slaughter of the Misnacs. A pyre covered in runes and flowers. Cyan looks up at me, and I mouth, *"Thank you."*

He just nods once and keeps working. With painstaking care, he carves out each rune with a small blade. I silently help him finish the ritual before looking up at him. "You've still got some clothes in the back room. I had it sealed off after you left. Go get cleaned up." Cyan scoffs quietly, and I can almost hear him say, *"Of course you had my room sealed up."* But he gives me a firm jerk of his chin, unable to meet my gaze as he follows me back inside. I watch as he stands before the door beside the staircase and places his hand on the doorknob. My magic that sealed up his room leaks away like ink in water, allowing him to turn the doorknob. Only he could break my sealant spell. I watch as he takes a deep breath before stepping through the door into the darkened room.

Scooping Eliana's body up into my arms, her head rolls inertly into my chest, like a knife piercing my heart. Tears well up in my eyes as I carry her to the pyre Cyan built.

The gentle breeze blows around us, sweetly perfuming the air with the scent of the flowers in her hair.

I carefully place Eliana on the pyre and brush her hair out of her face. Straightening a stray flower and repositioning her hands under her chest, pressing one last kiss to her lips—they're cold, and my heartaches. I don't know if I can do this. I don't know if I can say goodbye.

Cyan's hand rests on my shoulder, giving it a firm squeeze. I step back, away from where Eliana lies on the pyre like an Enkantian Princess Warrior. Dressed in white with flowers in her hair, I try not to think too much about the meaning behind the flowers. Of Cyan's last plea for forgiveness.

Tyler, Chelsea and even Winnie are all standing by, waiting. I see Cyan looking longingly at Eliana's body. I give him a gentle nudge with my shoulder. He turns to look at me. I give him a slight nod. "It's okay," I whisper, just loud enough for him to hear. He takes a cautious step forward. His back is blocking Tyler and Chelsea's view. Still, I watch as he leans forward and kisses her forehead, whispering something in her ear before falling back in line. We stand in silence for a moment before Cyan gives me a nod.

Inhaling deeply, I try to calm my nerves and racing heart. I've performed many Enkantian burials before—one of the duties of a time elemental—but never have they been this hard. I didn't get the chance to give our mother or Alinta, Abeline and Adriana a proper send-off because of the iron fist Charleston laid down, so the weight of this moment is not just to provide Eliana with the send-off she deserves, but also to honour the family they robbed her of. The mother she never met, the sisters she never got to hold.

They'll all be together now.

She'll be with her family too.

Something warms inside me, knowing she'll finally meet her mother, see how proud she would be of the woman she became. Even in the end, she held herself with dignity and honour.

The ceremony took longer than it should have. I choked a few times and had to take a minute to recompose myself. We stand in silence as Eliana's bed is engulfed in flames. The fire licks up and around her body. My knees shake as our ultimate goodbye draws closer. I hear Chelsea quietly tell Tyler that they should go.

I have to give credit to Chelsea. She is very intuitive, but I guess all water elementals are. No doubt she suspects or has figured out Cyan's feelings towards Eliana. I think, in her mind, it's only fitting for the two men who loved her the most to stay with her in this final ascent to the Afterlife. As soon as they've returned to the house, the door closing behind them, I slump into the grass. Kicking my legs out in front of me, I lean back on my arms as I watch the flames rise. Cyan sighs and carefully sits next to me, cross-legged. A red tulip grows before him before wilting, dying and growing again—a cycle of life and death. It reminds me of those long, painstaking lessons on the languages of the flowers.

A younger Cyan sits cross-legged, leaning forward intently, listening to the lesson with such intensity it makes me tired.

"Why do I have to be here? This isn't my element," I groan to Cyan, who waves his hand in front of my face, shushing me. I swat his hand out of my face before resting my head on my knee and *trying* not to fall asleep.

Cyan shakes me awake. I must have dozed off and missed the end of the lesson. *Good riddance,* I think as Cyan pulls me to my feet. "Did you *really* fall asleep? *How* could you have fallen asleep?" he jabbers before giving me a stern look. "Mother won't be impressed when she finds out, you know." I wave a hand in the air, knowing I am our mother's favourite child. Apart from the triplets. Not just because I am the oldest, but because I possess the element of time—a rare magical gift. Mother won't mind if I fell asleep during a silly earth elemental lesson.

Even if she gets upset, I can always spin that I was up late practising my magic or reading some old scripture relating to my element.

Cyan is talking cursorily about the legend of Ferhad and Shirin. Two lovers who longed to be together but whose love was forbidden. I roll my eyes. "Ferhad heard Shirin had taken her life so he killed himself to be with her for eternity," Cyan says, sighing dramatically. "Tulips spring up where his blood spilled. A symbol of his love and devotion." He studies the palm of his hand as a small red tulip appears. "Could you imagine loving someone so much, knowing you'd never be together? Then they died before you could even confess your love?" Cyan says, wide-eyed.

I pluck the flower out of his hand, twist it between two fingers and examine it. "Brother," I say, flicking the bud into a nearby bush. "Don't bother yourself with such drivel. I'm sure you're not destined for some great love tragedy."

Cyan looks back at the bush I tossed his silly flower in. I drape an arm across his shoulders. "Why trouble yourself with something unlikely to happen?" I clap my hand on his chest. "Come, let's go train. I could do with a wake-up after that boring lesson."

I look over at Cyan, sitting cross-legged in the grass, watching that red tulip grow, wither and die. I know he's mourning just as much as I am, but she *didn't* love him. She loved me. His vexatious flower talk is getting on my nerves. I pluck the flower out of the ground before it can wilt and die and toss it into the fire. "Stop it," I growl. It comes out rougher than I intended. Cyan probably isn't just mourning Eliana's death, but also Morana and our sisters.

He doesn't meet my gaze. Instead, he just looks at where the tulip is now burning. "I'm sorry. I didn't—"

"Don't," I seethe. I should be more understanding of his pain and grief since I am riding that same dark wave. "She didn't love you, Cyan." I sigh. "You don't need to throw your Ferhad-Shirin tragedy in my face." That catches his attention.

He raises an eyebrow. "Ah, so you did listen to the lessons," he says, his tone dripping with condescending arrogance.

I narrow my eyes at him. "No. *You* wouldn't shut up about it for days after." I roll my eyes and mumble, "You practically pleaded with the Fates to give you your own tragedy."

Cyan's mouth presses into a hard line like he's trying to hold back what he wants to say. Finally, he opens his mouth to speak but decides better. *Good.* I'm not in the mood for his shit.

We turn to watch the flames again. I push to my feet, my mouth agape. Cyan must see the same thing because he's now standing beside me. Eliana's once-white dress has turned black—not from the smoke or soot. Her body is entirely unaffected by the flames. There's the soft crackling of the fire and a deeper cracking as if bones are breaking back into place.

Cyan and I look at each other, stunned.

Never in all our years have we seen—or heard—of something like this. The flames erupt into a ten-foot wall of fire around her, the force flinging Cyan and me backwards, into the side of the house.

CHAPTER FIFTY
MALLRIE

Neither Cyan nor I dare to breathe, let alone speak, as we carefully push to our feet. Chelsea and Tyler come running from the house. Cyan holds up a hand for them to stop.

"Um, is this meant to happen?" Tyler calls, waving his arms at the wall of flames. I open my mouth to speak but can't find the words.

Cyan looks at me, searching my face for any hint of an answer before turning to the others. "No. This is not meant to happen," he says darkly, his voice a deep rumble like rolling thunder, filled with warning.

The wall of fire drops suddenly into a small flicker around the base. Cyan takes a cautious step forward before I grab hold of his arm. Something in the back of my mind reminds me of an antediluvian scripture about reincarnation. But whenever I asked anyone about it, they all told me it was impossible. That one would have to possess more than one source of magic. I look at Cyan, my heart frantically leaping from my chest at the possibility.

"No," he says, staring back at me, his voice wavering

slightly with disbelief. On countless nights, Cyan stayed awake while I tried to decipher that scripture.

"She's got both Fae and witch magic in her," I say simply as I step forward. Eliana lies on the bed, the colour returning to her face, her lips parted slightly as her chest rises and falls with shallow breaths. I turn to face Cyan, tears pricking at my eyes as I nod towards him. His face falls into a frown as he takes a step back. I don't know what his problem is. You'd think he'd be happy she's alive.

Doesn't matter what his problem is. His problem is precisely that—*his* problem. I return to Eliana as the flames extinguish with a dramatic whoosh, and her eyes fly open.

She blinks a few times before her eyes meet mine.

"Ma-Mallrie?" she says quietly, groggy as if she's just awoken from a long sleep. I smile down at her as I reach out to help her sit up. She looks down at the now-black dress, her fingers gently touching the flowers in her hair. Her eyes flick around her and then back to me. "You've been crying," she whispers. Her hand reaches my face, and she gently runs her fingers down my cheek.

I grab her hand, pressing a kiss to the back of it. "What do you remember?" I ask, concerned. *Does she remember being hung? What happened to her consciousness in those moments after her neck snapped?*

Eliana blinks hard, her dark brows knitting together, and straightens up further, running the fabric of her dress between her fingers before she looks at me with horror. "I-I died."

It's as if an immense wave of relief washes over me, but I am not entirely relieved. I feel like I might wake up at any moment and realise this was all a dream.

"Is..." Eliana looks around. "Is this the Afterlife?" She looks around again, cautiously, and mumbles, *"I wasn't meant for the Afterlife."* Then, her eyes fall on something behind me, and her expression changes. I don't need to turn around to know she has spotted Cyan and the others. But I know it's the sight of him that causes her mouth to press into a hard line and a small line to form between her dark brows. She looks back at me, but her eyes can't help but flick back to Cyan. A sickening feeling rolls around in my stomach.

Surely, she doesn't reciprocate Cyan's feelings.

"Is this the Afterlife?" she repeats sceptically.

I shake my head. "No, little doe. You're alive." I run my fingers down her cheek. "You're safe." *Fates! How many times did I tell her that before?* My chest tightens at the memory of how many times I lied to her face. Promised her she was safe with me, even though I knew her blood needed to be spilt to restore the magic to the Enkanti Tree. No matter how long I spent stalling Edgar, keeping Eliana out of his clutches and keeping her as safe as possible, I still *knew.* And that knowledge never sat well with me. How was her life deemed insignificant enough to be born only to be sacrificed?

Through all my years, I made sure the lives I took were never taken readily, and yet, I was meant to turn a blind eye and just let her blood be spilt so we could return the magic to the Enkanti Tree? It was *wrong.* So, I spent *months* searching for a solution—*anything* to prevent what had happened. And I failed. I failed Eliana, and that is a burden I must carry for the rest of my life. Even if she stands before me now.

Her eyes meet mine. There's something different about them. A flicker of gold and red amongst the brown—her eyes burn like there is a fire within. She clears her throat awkwardly, carefully raising her hand to her throat. Her movements are stiff and slow. Eliana slowly twists her neck, testing her motion. "I'm alive? How?" she breathes, almost to herself.

Blinking up at her. I honestly don't have an answer. "I don't know. A gift from the Fates, maybe?" She looks around, and realisation sets in that she's sitting on top of a pyre.

Eliana scrambles onto her knees. "Get me down. Please, Mallrie. Now!" she panics, which I can't blame her for. I'm sure this is a lot for her to take in.

I scoop her up in my arms, and for a moment, I consider never letting her go again, but against my better judgement, I carefully set her on her feet. Her bare feet touching the soft grass causes her to gasp as if she's feeling it for the first time. She looks up at me, running a hand down my face. "Thank you," she whispers.

I frown down at her. "What for?"

"For everything. For teaching me to love again, for saving me from my destructive, mundane life." She pushes up and presses her soft, warm lips to mine. I wrap my arms around her, careful of holding her too tight. She smiles into my mouth and whispers between kisses, "I'm not going to break."

With that, I pull her to my chest and wrap my arms around her tighter as if I will never let her go. Our kiss grows deeper, and I wish everyone would leave so I could give her a proper reunion.

But a small part of her feels reserved. Her body is tense in my embrace. I push that thought out of my mind. *This is a gift from the Fates. Of course she probably feels reserved. Who knows what happened to her consciousness in the days that followed her death?*

Tyler clears his throat behind us, and we—reluctantly

—peel our bodies apart. Eliana smiles at Tyler, and then sprints over to him. He picks her up quickly, spinning her around. Her once-white dress flows out behind her before he kisses her forehead. "You had me so fucking depressed! Don't you *ever* do that again!"

"Oh, don't worry, I don't plan on it." She giggles.

"What was it like?" Tyler asks bluntly, and I groan at his insensitivity.

Not that he cares. And nor does Eliana, by the way she giggles and says playfully, "What being hung? Or... afterwards?"

Something happened in those moments after her hanging, then.

Tyler blinks, clearly surprised by her casualness. "Well, both." He shrugs, finally letting her go.

Chelsea pushes Tyler out of the way. "Ignore him. I'm so glad you're back." Her voice is shaky as if she's trying not to cry. Eliana flings her arms around Chelsea. This is the first time they've embraced since Eliana found out she was alive. Maybe in death, you forgive all your old grudges. Something like hope flutters in my chest. Hopefully, she'll forgive me and understand when I explain what she overheard before her hanging.

But I can't help but glance over to where Cyan leans against the house, his arms folded across his chest. *Will she forgive Cyan for his digressions as well?*

Eliana looks over Chelsea's shoulder and whispers to Tyler, "I'll tell you later."

"I heard that," Chelsea groans, and they all laugh.

I lean against the house, my arms folded across my chest, my heart is whole, and I'm smiling. Eliana has a new family who loves her unconditionally. Everyone is smiling and laughing. Winnie keeps prancing around Eliana's legs, tripping her over.

Well, almost everyone—Cyan has silently started to leave. Eliana has noticed and gives me a long look. I nod, silently telling her she should go after him. As much as I love her, I know how much my brother loves her too. Seeing her rise from the dead is not a simple thing—and for him? It must be almost impossible. Seeing her laughing and embracing those she loves, knowing that she *might* hate his guts. That Eliana gets a second chance at life, but Morana doesn't.

But seeing how she looked at him when she thought she had reached the Afterlife. I feel as if she might have some sort of feelings for him. Even if she doesn't quite know what those feelings are yet.

Eliana jogs after Cyan, lifting her long dress as it bellows around her. There is a pang in my chest. She reminds me of those trashy rom-coms she watches, where the heroine runs after the one she loves, and they wrap each other in a longing embrace and share *true love's kiss*.

"Cyan! Wait!" she calls after him, and they stand together at the edge of the barrier. My eyes linger on where she holds his wrist.

I stalk back inside with a reserved sigh. A part of me wants to stay and watch what happens, but a bigger— maybe a more mature part of me—knows they deserve privacy, and a small piece of me is afraid of what I might see.

CHAPTER FIFTY-ONE
ELIANA

I hold on to Cyan's wrist tightly, afraid that he might slip through my grasp before I can get what I need to say out. He looks down at where my hand holds onto him. He's dressed in black jeans, a shirt and combat boots. So different from the well-put-together Cyan I am used to in immaculate suits. His hair is in a messy bun; a few strands have fallen free and hang around his eyes. Their colour is so similar and yet so different to Mallrie's. I find myself resisting the urge to reach up and push those strands of dark blonde hair away from his face. Instead, I bite my lip, diverting my eyes to where I hold on to him. My hand feels hot, but he doesn't shy away from the heat. His tattoos are on full display, a patchwork of various little designs. Closing my eyes so I can focus, I whisper, "Why are you here?"

Seeing Cyan standing there when I awoke was a shock, but when I felt the flowers in my hair, I just knew he was the one who had brought me back to Mallrie.

Cyan scoffs quietly. "I was just returning you to Mallrie, that's all." His words cut like daggers, like I am just a piece of property to be returned. My hand heats with my anger. He rips his arm from my grip, a red handprint still gripping his wrist. "Don't start getting ideas in your head that—"

"Well, if that's all you were here for, then—"

"Mallrie asked me to stay," Cyan cuts me off, and I have to ball my hands into fists by my side to stop myself from snapping at him. *Gods, he can be annoying!* "For the…" his voice trails off as he looks towards the pyre. The anger inside me fizzles out as I watch Cyan's expression soften as he looks over my head.

Following the direction of his gaze, I whisper, "Did you do all of this?" My heart aches, desperate to know, but also slightly terrified. I don't even know *why* I am here talking to him in the first place.

Cyan's dark brows press together slightly as if he's putting up his own defensive walls. "I wasn't a part of your murder, if that's what you're asking," he spits.

I fold my arms across my chest. "No. I meant—" I wave a hand from my head to my toes, then over to the pyre. Like skeletons, you can still see the burnt remnants of flowers adorning it.

"Ah." Cyan's features soften slightly.

"Well…" I prompt. I need to hear it from him. Something my grandmother told me is floating around in my mind. *"Cyan isn't what he seems."*

"Don't flatter yourself, love…"

"Cyan!" I grit out, taking a step towards him. When he doesn't back away, I regret the decision instantly. I glare at him, our bodies so close I can feel the heat radiating from him. My magic can sense his pulse racing. "I don't want to play games. I *literally* just died!"

"Actually, love, you died five days ago."

My mouth falls open, and my heart races. I can feel a

panic attack coming on. No matter how many breathing exercises I try to run through, I can't catch my breath. Mallrie's little saying about rocks and storms is too far gone to remember correctly, and I-I...

Cyan's hands wrap around my arms, steadying me as I sway. "Breathe, love. You're stronger than this. Don't let your fear control you." Sucking in a deep breath, I look up at him. His eyes search mine for a moment before releasing me and stepping away. "Don't let the fear control you," he repeats as if it is something he has told himself time and time again.

Don't let the fear control you.

My grandmother said something similar in Vraska before I left. Such a simple statement, and yet it helps push away the panic. I *am* stronger than this. My fear *shouldn't* control me.

I look up at Cyan, eyes wide. He glances over to the pyre, muttering, "Yes, I did this." Then, clearing his throat, he adds, "Mallrie helped too."

I nod noncommittally. "Why? Why help? You *returned* me," I spit his words back at him, and I see them land like a physical blow. "So why do all of this?" I pluck a flower from my hair and twirl it between my blackened fingers. The black pistil is a stark contrast against the velvety soft, white petals.

"Do you forgive him?"

My attention snaps up to Cyan, shocked by the question. "What?"

"Do you forgive him? For lying to you? For not being able to save you?"

I look over my shoulder at Mallrie's home. The chimney lazily puffs smoke, and the flowers on the balcony sway in the gentle breeze. "No one could have saved me," I say, not pulling my attention away from the house. "Not from being hung anyway."

If I have learnt anything living with Mallrie, it's that some things are just meant to be. Ever since I met him, the goal has been to restore the magic to the Enkanti Tree. Which required my death. *No one could have saved me from that fate, but the dark and destructive path I was on before...*

"But Mallrie did save me." I look back at Cyan. His face is unreadable. There is an ache in my chest, even as I admit that. I did something I promised myself I would never do again.

I fell in love. I fell for Mallrie. Hard. It feels strange because I thought, after Beckett, that allowing myself to let another person into my life so readily would be impossible. But after years of refusing myself an ounce of human intimacy or even human interaction, when Mallrie came along, he wanted to help me, that he wanted to protect and care for me. I realised how much I missed that. How much I *needed* that. I think... At the base of it all, I was just a depressed, lonely and broken woman who fell for the first person who showed me a scrap of kindness and promised me safety.

Mallrie wanted to protect me, I think. He said it many times, promised me that nothing would happen. But *something* happened...

My throat burns with emotion, and I can't look at Cyan as I ask him, "So he knew all along that I needed to die to restore the magic?"

In my peripheral, I see Cyan nod. "We knew you were the key to restoring the magic." He looks at me through hooded eyes. "You were our salvation, Eliana."

For some reason, his words land like a lead weight in the pit of my stomach.

They both knew.

Chances are that Chelsea knew as well. *But that's in the past, I try to remind myself.* Even though it feels like someone has just shoved a hot branding iron through my chest. "I guess I will learn to move past it. I will learn to forgive him." Even as I am saying the words, they ring hollow, and my chest feels like it's being ripped apart from the inside out.

"Then I did it for Mallrie. He's my brother, even though we don't always see eye-to-eye. He loves you, Eliana."

My chest feels tight. I don't know why I expected him to say anything else.

CHAPTER FIFTY-TWO
MALLRIE

It's not long before Eliana and Cyan both walk inside. Eliana clears her throat to get everyone's attention. "We need to fix the tree," she says simply. Cyan leans against the doorframe, his arms folded across his chest. I look at him, and he silently sighs and nods. *She really wants this.* I run my hand over my face before pushing to my feet. "Mallrie, before you say anything." Eliana holds her hands up in front of her as if she knows I am not in the mood to help those who watched as she died for crimes that weren't hers to die for. She clasps her hands together in front of her as if she's unsure of what to do with them now. "The magic *needs* to be returned." Her hands start to shake a little, and she clutches them together tighter. "The Kailadons"—she swallows hard—"are the least of our worries. When I died, I awoke in Vraska." She explains, "The Fae showed me a dark, damp tunnel. It smelt of rotten flesh." Eliana shudders a little at the memory. "Edgar has an army of mutant Kailadons."

"Edgar is dead," I say simply, casting a dark look over to where Cyan stands.

Eliana stands frozen for a beat, blinking her big brown eyes, now with flecks of golden fire. "Doesn't matter," she says quietly, regaining her composure. "The Kailadon queen is pissed. Did you know that she spawns over a thousand eggs once a year? She is the mother of *all* Kailadons."

I frown, looking up at Cyan. "I didn't know the Kailadons had a queen. You?"

Tyler is blowing up in the background. "A thousand eggs? Fuck me!"

I try my best not to snap at him to shut the fuck up. I stare at Cyan. My stomach drops as he subtly nods his head. I stalk forward. "And you never thought to share that bit of information with me? How did you even find out?"

Eliana's hands are on my chest, stopping me from going to rip Cyan's head from his body. *What else has he not been telling me? What has he been doing for Edgar all these years?*

"That doesn't matter, Mallrie," Eliana pleads, trying to drag my attention away from Cyan. Carefully, I pull at the flowers in her hair, tossing them onto the bench. I can't stand it any longer. I want to rip them all from her head and throw them into the fire. My patience for Cyan's silent pining is getting on my last nerves. My careful extraction starts to get a little rougher with my anger as I try to quickly pull the flowers from her hair.

Eliana stops me mid-pull. "Mallrie, she's going to send for the mutant Kailadons. Then rage a war against everyone. Fae included." She looks off into the distance as if she can still see whatever it was she saw when her mind separated from her body. That dark tunnel, or something else? It has my chest squeezing. I wish I could take away that pain. I wish I could go back and fix my mistakes.

"They're pissed too," she says, returning her attention

to the rest of us. "The Fae. Edgar has made a lot of enemies."

The room falls into silence. No one can argue with that. The weight of Eliana's words hangs in the air. "We need to protect the town as best as we can, and the best way to do that is to restore the magic in the Enkanti Tree. Restoring the magic means the Kailadons won't go into town, protecting both the mortals and the Fae." She turns to face me. "There's a portal to the Fae realm in the Enkanti Tree?" she questions, but it sounds like she's just seeking clarification, like she already knows there is one.

I nod. "A small one. Only big enough for their scouts to slip through."

Eliana nods as if storing that information away for later. "With the magic restored to the tree, protecting the town and that small Fae portal, we can focus on destroying the mutants."

I can't help but smile. Eliana has risen from death stronger and with a determination burning in her eyes. She's absolutely remarkable. Running a hand over my face, I sigh. "Okay."

"Yeah! Let's do this!" Tyler adds enthusiastically.

"What do we need to do?" Chelsea says as she gets to her feet.

Eliana smiles at the support of her friends. My heart feels full. I've missed that smile. I give her hand a little squeeze. "I'll go get what I've gathered so far for the ritual to restore the magic."

"No need," Cyan says, pulling a small leather journal from the back pocket of his jeans. How I didn't notice it before, I have no idea. Five gemstones—carnelian, moss agate, aquamarine, tourmalated quartz and the sacred

Super Seven—are set into the cover. Each stone is engraved with the corresponding elemental's mark.

"Mother's grimoire," I breathe.

Cyan nods. "I took it after—" But he doesn't finish his sentence. *I wonder if he even told Eliana that he killed Edgar for her.* He holds it out for me, and I cautiously cross the room and take the grimoire from him. Cyan's eyes are dark as he glares at me. "We need to talk," he says, not letting me take it out of his hand.

I sigh, knowing he most likely already knows what I know. I nod, but he pulls the grimoire out of my grip. No one else follows us as Cyan leads the way outside.

"You knew?" he asks darkly, turning on his heels to scowl at me.

"You'll need to be more specific, Cyan," I say coldly, trying to keep calm. He throws the grimoire at me.

"You knew she was going to die! You kept her alive only to ensure she met her end at the right time! You watched her grow up, fully aware that she was destined to die like an animal! " Cyan's hands are balled up at his sides. I can feel the earth tremble under me. It has been a long time since he has been so incensed that he's lost control. I draw in a deep breath, keeping my voice even.

"Yes. I knew. But I was trying to find a way around it. A loophole. *Anything.*" My voice shakes, I suck in a deep, mollifying breath, trying to calm myself. "I didn't mean—"

"What?" Cyan spits. "You didn't mean to fall in love?" He dares to smirk.

That small smile threatens my calm composure. "No. I didn't mean to fall in love." I bite back. He's right. I didn't mean to fall in love. I had a promise to keep.

"You sick son of a bitch!" Cyan spits.

I raise an eyebrow. "Strong words coming from you," I mutter.

"After all she went through!" he seethes, ignoring me. "You were just willing to sacrifice her!" he shouts. I cringe internally, knowing Eliana can hear everything.

"No, I fucking wasn't!" I shout, taking a step forward. "I was trying to find another way!"

Cyan shakes his head wildly. "We both know ancient magic *doesn't have* loopholes—especially dark magic." He swings his fist. I block it. Then, he swings again.

"Really?" I say, blocking him again. I can see his rage is distracting him. I punch him in the stomach. He staggers back a step but regains quickly—the bastard always could take a punch—swinging again, making contact with my injured shoulder.

Fuck.

I forgot how well he could throw a punch. "Don't act all fucking innocent, Cyan. You knew what the ritual required." I swing a kick and get him in the side before hitting him square in the jaw, splitting it open.

He curses and kicks me in the side of my knee, causing me to lose my balance. "I wasn't *fucking* her!" Taking advantage of my position, Cyan drives his elbow into my collar bone. A snapping sound bounces around in my head as he breaks the bone. *Motherfucker!*

Eliana comes running from the house, shouting. "Stop it! Both of you! Stop!"

We both ignore her. *Stupid* fighting over a girl, but not willing to listen to her. A ball of wind pushes us apart as Tyler makes his way to Eliana's side. She picks up the grimoire. A pang of guilt strikes my heart as I watch her dust off the old book.

"Look," she says sternly, the picture of grace. Death

surely changed her in more ways than I think I am prepared to admit. "I'm alive. I don't completely understand how, but I am. The ritual asked for me to die. Technically, I did. So let's just move onto the next step and…" Her voice trails off as she looks between the two of us.

I've fucked up. Behind her eyes, I can see the pain. I know I have lost her trust, and if seeing how she handled Chelsea's betrayal is anything to go off, she will never forgive me.

"Eliana, I'm—"

She holds her hand out to stop me. "Mallrie, please." Eliana looks at me, and I can see the pain in her eyes. She looks at me as if I am a stranger.

I've fucked up.

"I'm sorry," I say, ignoring her plea.

Eliana gives me a sad smile that doesn't meet her beautiful brown eyes. Eyes that are filled with pain and sorrow. "I know." She inhales deeply. "I still love you though," she breathes, but somehow, I feel like that love has changed. It's different from what it was before.

Out of the corner of my eye, I see Cyan wipe his jaw with the back of his hand, resentment flickering in his eyes.

"Let's go to bed," Eliana says, taking my hand and pulling me off the couch. This small cottage was never meant for more than two people, so five under its roof feels awfully cramped, worse than the citizens of Datura cramming into their buildings like sardines in a can. Once dinner was over, Cyan retired to his room. He wanted to return to his apartment in Datura, but I persuaded him with his favourite bottle of whisky to stay the night. After he showed up covered in blood with Eliana's body, I didn't trust him not to do something incredibly stupid and hurt himself.

Chelsea is washing up—something I know she could have done in half the time, but I suspect she is trying to give us some privacy. And Tyler is curled up in a ball by the fire with Winnie, fast asleep and snoring loudly.

I smile at Eliana and let her lead me up the stairs and to the bedroom. I was half afraid she wouldn't want to be in the same room as me, let alone share a bed.

"Five days, huh?" she says as I close the door. Her eyes scan over the room, over the destroyed desk and the unslept bed.

"It was unbearable," I whisper, shame burning in my gut. I should have done *more*. I should have looked at the damned *Timeline* more closely and ensured there weren't any fragments I was missing.

Her death is solely on my hands.

I sink into the armchair that has been my home these past five days, hanging my head low and in my hands. I cannot look at her.

"Hey," Eliana gently pulls my hands away from my face. Through the tears, I see her on her knees before me. Those beautiful big brown eyes, now with flecks of gold and red, look up at me, filled with sympathy. Sympathy I don't deserve. "Whatever is going through your head, stop. You're not responsible for my..." Her voice trails off, and she very subtly twists her neck as if trying to work out a knot. "I don't blame you," she says, but it sounds like she's trying to convince herself too.

"Yes, I am. I should have—"

Eliana's lips crash against mine, silencing me. My arm wraps around her and pulls her closer.

I am not deserving of this woman. Not after all she has been through.

Her tongue caresses my lips, begging for me to open them. *How could I ever say no to her?* Her tongue slides across mine, but I don't kiss her back. Not like I would have in the past. Not like I did by the pyre.

"Mallrie," she whispers, her voice all soft and sultry, "I am not going to break."

"I know you won't, beautiful girl, but I don't deserve you. Not like this."

Eliana pulls away, her brows pressed together, and she looks... hurt.

Fuck. That was the last thing I wanted to do.

Of course I *want* her. There's nothing I want more than to rip that dress off her body and kiss and lick every inch of delicious pale skin. To reacquaint myself with the taste of her sweet cunt.

"Mallrie, I know you're blaming yourself for what happened. But there's nothing you could have done. If there's anything you've taught me, it's that the Fates just have some things set in stone."

I shake my head. "No, little doe, I could have looked deeper into your *Timeline*. I *should* have looked deeper. I should have found what it was that would have led to you—"

"Mallrie," Eliana's hands touch either side of my face. "Stop, you're just going to drive yourself crazy. Look at me." I look into her beautiful, unnerving eyes. "I don't blame you. I am hurt that you lied to me, but I want to move on. I want things to go back to the way they were before."

I cup her face in my hand and trace the curve of her jaw with my thumb. *Fates, I wish I could just look inside her mind and know what she's thinking. How she's truly feeling. But I* can't. I can only take what she says and act accordingly. She wants to move on. I can do that for her. It looks like we both could do with a little distraction.

"Well, then, I guess I have to show you precisely how much I missed you," I murmur, and Eliana's eyes light up, and her cheeks flush with desire.

"Oh, please do," she purrs.

A smile slips across my lips as I look her up and down, drinking in the flush on her cheeks, highlighting her freckles, her curves and the sweet way she presses her thighs together. "As you wish, little doe." My magic thrums in my body from sitting stagnant for so long, and I have her on the bed before she can take her next breath. She blinks up at me, a little confused about how she got here so quickly, but I don't give her an explanation. Eliana is smart. She'll figure it out. I can almost see when she realised that I used my magic because her teeth sink into her bottom lip, and she rubs her thighs together. My magic buzzes around us as I slow down time and rip her dress straight down the middle. Her eyes are filled with heat as she watches each thread be pulled taut and then snap. Once her breasts are exposed, I allow time to resume its pace and rip the rest of the fabric.

"That is so fucking hot," she moans as I take her breast in my mouth. I also make a mental note to punch Cyan in the face for not putting a bra on Eliana, and I wonder if he cleaned and changed her clothes, or if he paid someone to do it.

I bite down on her peaked nipple at the thought, but Eliana's moan has me doing it again for her pleasure. My tongue circles the hardened bud, easing away the sting. Her fingers tug at my hair, and it feels like she's tugging directly at my cock, returning my attention to her full lips and half-lidded gaze. She gives me a sultry smile before pushing my head towards her pussy. *Fuck yes!*

I rip the black lace of her thong and toss the scrap of fabric away. Somehow, the scandalous undergarment felt like an insult. I grip her thighs and push them apart before burying my face inside her sweet pussy. Eliana's body jerks at the first swipe of my tongue as I drag it from one end to the other, stopping at her needy little clit and gently biting down. The way she moans my name is like music to my ears, but it's not enough.

"I fucking love it when you say my name like that," I say, my voice vibrating against her entrance, and I can feel how wet she is already. "Now, let's hear you scream it," I growl.

Not that she needs it because her pussy is practically weeping for me to fill her. Still, I spit on her cunt and drag my fingers through it, slowly circling around her entrance. Eliana writhes under my touch, bucking her hips, desperate for any sort of contact.

"Say please, little doe." My cock presses against my jeans uncomfortably, and I reach down to readjust myself. *Not yet,* I think, *not until I have her coming on my face.*

"Please, Mallrie, please, please, *please*," she chants desperately.

I plunge two fingers inside her and curl them upwards. Eliana screams, and her back arches off the bed. Then, using my magic to move quickly before her back falls to the mattress, I grab a pillow and shove it under her hips, keeping them at an angle that'll give her the best pleasure.

Her eyes widen slightly, and her head lifts, and she's got the most beautiful smile on her face that has me weak at the knees.

My mouth is on her, my tongue circling her clit as my

fingers pump inside her. Soon, her pussy is clenching around my fingers, and I look up at her. Her head is flung back into the pillows, her breasts pushed forward as she arches herself into my touch. *She's close.* I drag my free hand up her thigh, her little shiver edging me on, and I feel impossibly tight in my jeans. My hand rests just above her pussy, and I stroke my thumb across the fine dusting of dark hair before I press down on her. *"Oh, fuck!"* Eliana moans loudly. Loud enough that the others downstairs surely heard her. *"Oh, Mallrie!"*

"That's my girl," I praise as her pussy clenches around my fingers. Then, I give her clit one quick nip. "You scream my name."

She convulses around me as she comes again, squirting and coating my tongue with her sweet taste. Eliana slumps into the bed, but I am not done with her yet.

I sit back on my knees and wipe her orgasm from my face, her eyes watching every movement with rapt attention.

"I'm not done with you just yet, little doe," I say as I undo my pants and free my cock. I sigh as I drag my hand down my length.

Eliana pushes up onto her elbows, eyes wide. "I want you," she breathes.

I smile down at her and remove my jeans, "Don't worry, little—"

"No," she says, cutting me off. "I want your cock... in my mouth."

I arch a brow. *I don't fucking deserve this woman.* "How could I say no to you?" I reply. She's moving, climbing off the bed and touching my hips. I arch a brow when she leads me away from the bed. The chair I had sat in for the past five days clashes against the back of my legs, and she pushes me down. I look up at Eliana, at this queen before me. *How could I have ever been so careless with her life?*

Gracefully, Eliana goes to her knees before me. Her delicate hand wraps around my cock and slowly works my length. I groan, my head falling back.

"I... I haven't done this in a while," she admits sheepishly.

I look down at her. "You can't do it wrong, little doe."

She smiles up at me, but it doesn't reach her eyes. It almost looks sad. So much so that my hand is reaching out to touch her cheek. She leans into my touch, and slowly, I trace my hand around the back of her head and grip her neck gently. "If you're not ready, you don't have to."

Eliana's eyes lock on my own as she lowers her mouth over me, her hot breath fanning across the head of my cock. She squeezes her hand around my length, and then her tongue darts out and licks at the beads of precum.

Then, she is sucking me down her throat. She gags a little at my size, which makes me smirk. "You can fit it, beautiful girl." I grip her hair reassuringly, and she moans around me until her lips caress my base. She feels so fucking incredible. I am glad I'm sitting, or my knees might have given out under me. Her little moan sends a jolt to my balls, and they feel warm and tingle like she sent a kernel of her magic straight down there with that little moan. I almost blow my load right there, but I bite my lip and tilt my head back.

I chuckle as Eliana's mouth works my length in a dance of teeth and tongue. *And she wasn't sure if she could please me.*

Eliana looks up at me, the gold and red flecks in her eyes dancing in the low light, "You're fucking incredible," I groan. "I'm so close. Are you going to take every drop like a good girl?" She nods eagerly, her hand working in unison with her mouth. Then, I am spilling inside her mouth, my hand tightens in her short blonde hair, and I watch as she drinks every last drop of my release.

Eliana leans back on her hunches and licks her lips. "How was that?" she taunts. My hand is still buried in her hair, and I tug her forward, crushing my lips against hers. My tongue slips across her own, tasting my release. "You're incredible," I say again, and I will tell her that every day until my last breath if it means she will believe it. "Do you want more?" I ask.

Her eyes fall, sadness washes over her face again, and she shakes her head. Holding her close, I pull her into my arms. "That's okay, beautiful girl. You ready for bed?"

She nods, and her silence rips at my heart.

"I really am sorry. For everything," I say for what feels like the millionth time.

Eliana pushes up onto her elbow. "You don't need to apologise."

I frown up at her. We should be sleeping, but we've been talking about everything that happened five days ago.

"What?" she asks, smiling, but that smile doesn't meet her eyes again. Instead, her bright eyes seem almost... haunted.

"What did you say to Cyan?" Her expression shifts at the question.

"Nothing. I just asked him why he was here, that's all." I can tell she's not telling me the whole truth, but I can't blame her for being reserved. I won't push her if she feels the need not to tell me her truths. I have lost any right I had to them.

"You were happy to see him," I say. Eliana looks towards the balcony. It's a clear, starry night.

She takes a deep breath before turning back to me. "I was." Determination fills her beautiful face. That she will not spare my feelings from lying to me.

I run my fingers through my hair, those two little words hitting me like a tonne of rocks. It bothers me that Eliana was happy to see Cyan, and for selfish reasons, I don't want to look too deeply into it. So I push that feeling aside. "Did he..." I don't know why this is so hard to ask. *Am I worried that she might actually feel the same way about him?* "Did he tell you why he brought you back?"

She looks at me curiously. "He said that he brought me back to make amends with you. That he was doing what you would have done for Morana."

I let out an internal sigh. He mustn't have told her that he loves her. I stare up at the ceiling and nod.

"Why?" she asks. "Was there something else?" Her tone is distrustful, and honestly, I can't blame her.

I shake my head. "If there was, he would have told you."

Eliana snuggles back down into me. "So everything is good between us?" she asks quietly.

I kiss the top of her head. "Of course, little doe."

Nothing changes. I have been given a second chance. By the grace of the Fates, I don't intend to fuck this up, but her happiness is the most important thing. If I am no longer the one who makes her truly happy. I sigh quietly into the darkness. *Then that is just the cross I must bear for my negligence.*

CHAPTER FIFTY-THREE
MALLRIE

It is organised chaos downstairs. Chelsea is cooking bacon and eggs for breakfast. The bacon is courtesy of Cyan, which even I am grateful for. Its meaty scent fills the air, the fat popping and crackling over Cyan and Tyler's bickering. It is nice to see that Cyan gets frustrated with Tyler's smart mouth just as much as I do.

Eliana is in the garden with Winnie and Hesper.

"I need a moment," she announced to the room. After descending the stairs, her eyes scanned the crowded room. They fell on a shirtless Cyan sitting on one stool at the island bench, heatedly discussing the ritual with Tyler, who sat on *top* of the bench like an untrained Misnac. To where I sit in the living room on the sofa, pages sprawled out on the coffee table before me, before walking out into the garden.

We talked for hours last night.

I explained to her how I knew the ritual to bring back the magic was an ancient blood ritual. That it asked for the blood of the Fae-witch hybrid, and that the prophecy called upon her. That I spent months searching for a loophole, for something, anything that could be done rather than a full sacrifice. Eliana was obviously hurt, and rightly so. I gave her the out she deserved. She shouldn't feel trapped in another relationship. I want only her happiness, even if that means we're no longer together romantically. She admitted that something had shifted in her heart, but she doesn't know yet what exactly that is. So, for now, she still wants things to return to how they were. At least until we sort out fixing the Enkanti Tree.

She spoke about how she'd like to stay here. How this house feels like a home to her, that she enjoys spending time in the garden and outside at night. But she also mentioned that she might return to her apartment or her grandmother's. Apparently, she feels like she's got some unresolved business there.

I let Eliana know that whatever she decides, I will support her in any way she needs. Even then, she slept restlessly on her side of the bed, facing away from me.

I'm double-checking that the Fates are not just tormenting us, that tonight actually is a full moon. Cyan walks over to where I am sitting on the lounge, rubbing the back of his neck. I can't help but chuckle at how exhausted he looks.

"Tyler?" I ask simply. Cyan grunts in acknowledgement as he flops down onto the lounge next to me.

"What are you doing?" he asks, pulling the charts across the coffee table for a better look.

"Just double-checking the trajectory of the moon for tonight."

"Mm. You got a bad feeling?" he says, lowering his voice. I look up at him as something flickers across his face.

"I didn't until now. What do you know?"

Cyan shakes his head. "Nothing. Just something doesn't feel right."

"What do you mean?" I push. Cyan has always been intuitive. Sometimes I wonder if he possessed the same intuition water elementals have but never asked.

Cyan looks around. "The earth is restless. It can't sit still. Like it knows something bad is coming." His voice is low. He jerks his chin to the windows where the trees are swaying in the wind. "Look," he whispers. I follow his gaze but then look back at him, frowning, not quite following. "Look at the trees, at Eliana's hair." That's when I see it. My stomach lurches. "There's no wind. The trees are just... restless." he says as if having to dumb it down for me. But I can see Eliana sitting amongst the wildflowers, looking out into the trees swaying as if being blown in a gentle breeze, but her hair remains firmly at her shoulders.

"It just feels as if the Fates are playing some kind of sick joke, doesn't it?" Cyan murmurs, lowering his voice even more. I can't help but agree silently.

Night comes. Everyone took the day to prepare. First, I made sure my sword was sharpened. Then, begrudgingly, I gave Eliana space while she practised her magic. Even that seems... different now. Cyan went over the ritual with Tyler and Chelsea a few times, ensuring they knew precisely what would happen. We're ready. Or as prepared as we're going to be.

Everyone is on edge. We've all got a lot riding on this to work. We all love and care for Eliana, and don't want to see her death being in vain.

The sky is clear, the stars dance in the sky, and the full moon lights our way as we cross the open field between the

Melsheim Forest and Datura. I'll be glad once this is over. I wrap my arm around Eliana's waist, pulling her close. "What do you say? When this is over, we take a trip?"

She looks up at me. The reflection of the stars in her eyes, those red and gold flecks shimmer in the moonlight, are still a little unnerving.

"A trip?" The joy in her voice sends a jolt of energy through me.

"Mm. To the seaside."

"I'd love that. Just the two of us." She smiles at me, but that smile doesn't reach her eyes. There is an emptiness in them.

I press a kiss on the top of her head. "As you wish."

Yet it doesn't feel like a perfect plan. I drop my arm from around her waist, and she takes a small step away. Small enough that one wouldn't notice, but I am so hyper-focused on her every move that it felt like she pushed herself away from me the moment she got the chance. The action sends a pain straight to my heart. Not that I'd let her know. If she needs time to sort out how she feels about everything that's happened, then that is what I will give her. A trip away from everything may help sort out the mess in her head.

The town is dark and quiet. Everything has stayed the same since we left less than a week ago. Cyan grips his twin Sai blades tighter. He hasn't touched them since he left for Datura. I left them on his bed, a protective enchantment around them to keep them sharp and safe, awaiting his return. Tyler has uncurled his whip. I draw my sword, too, the purple glow illuminating the path in front of us.

"It's really quiet," Chelsea observes.

"Too quiet," Cyan agrees.

"Let's just get this done, 'kay?" Tyler's voice is apprehensive, even though his body language screams confidence. Eliana is silent like a spirit moving through the streets beside me. If it wasn't for her arm brushing against mine now and then, I'd think I imagined her resurrection altogether.

We pick up the pace, moving through the meandering alleyways as silent as the night. So many nights, I'd look down onto these empty streets. It now feels surreal to be running through them with my fellow witches, about to restore the magic in the Enkanti Tree so long after I swore to my mother that I would make things right.

This is all coming to an end.

Cyan looks back at me as we enter the centre of town. He gives me a small smile. "Ready to fulfil your promise, brother?" My chest swells with pride, being able to share this moment with him.

I smile back at him and nod. "You?" I approach him, clasping his shoulder and giving it a slight squeeze.

Cyan returns the gesture. "For mother." His eyes shine brightly. "For Alinta, Abeline and Adriana." The others stand around the tree waiting for us.

"For Morana," I say. Cyan's brows twitch, and his eyes glisten with unshed tears as he nods.

Eliana stands to the east of the Enkanti Tree, Tyler to the west and Chelsea to the south. Cyan and I take our places on either side of Eliana. We all stand there waiting silently in the cool chill of the night.

I look over at Cyan, past Eliana. She turns to look at Cyan and back at me. I can sense something is wrong, too, but we're here. The moon is complete, and according to Eliana, if we don't do it now, we will have an even bigger Kailadon problem.

But that's what's got me feeling apprehensive.

We only ran into a single Kailadon on our way in. It was as if they'd already left town. It just felt *too* easy. Cyan looks at me as if he is thinking the same thing. Eliana looks back at me.

"What's wrong?" she whispers.

I frown slightly. "Does something feel off to you? There were far fewer Kailadons roaming the streets than usual."

She looks around before closing her eyes and taking a deep breath. "I don't know. Maybe it's just luck?" she replies, shrugging.

Luck. Ha. Luck and Kailadons rarely go together. I sigh and look up at the moon; it's almost in optimal position above the Enkanti Tree.

"Ready?" I call out, and everyone responds one by one.

"Ready."

"Do you all remember the incantation?" I ask, glancing up at the moon again. We've got one shot at this otherwise... I shudder, trying not to think of the consequences.

If we fail... *the sacrifice would have been for nothing,* a small voice says inside me. We would have to do it again.

There is no way any of us will ever let anything hurt Eliana again. This will all have been for nothing. Everyone has voiced his or her acknowledgement of remembering the incantation. It's a quiet affair. One needs to harness their elemental power from deep within their core and peel a fragment of that element away to offer to the tree. I'm nervous. Even though Cyan and I have years of practise with our craft, the others have had months. Eliana is the least experienced but also the most in tune with her powers. The part that concerns me the most is this incantation—this ritual—cannot be practised beforehand.

One cannot just keep detaching pieces of their element. If they do, they'll slowly tear out their soul. Ancient magic is dangerous and brutal in its consequences. I realise I am holding my breath as I extract a fragment of my magic. It is a painful process. I place one hand on my chest, creating a portal. The other is deep within—not within my physical body but the metaphysical body, kind of like reaching deep into my astral form, the body that contains my magic. There, I need to find my core.

There it is.

It is like a ball of heat and energy, pulsating like a clock ticking through the seconds.

I wonder what everyone else feels—assuming this is a deeply personal connection between you and your elemental power. I take a deep breath as I carefully grip a section of it and twist it off. The ball pulsates aggressively as it tries to pull back. It's as if it doesn't want to release a part of itself. Finally, I twist it free, but it feels like I have just broken a bone deep within my chest. I gasp for air as I quickly pull my arm from my chest.

The portal closes instantly, and I drop to my knees, parched for air. I look up and notice the others are in similar positions, each with a small, glowing orb in their fingertips; Eliana's is red, Cyan's green, Chelsea's blue, Tyler's white, and I look down at my fingertips, at the tiny purple orb shining brightly up at me. I can't help but smile.

The hardest part of this whole ritual has been done. *And quite successfully,* I think, looking around as everyone slowly pushes to their feet. Everyone smiles except for Cyan, who's looking around down the alleyways. I follow his gaze. Did he hear or see something? He looks over at me, noticing I was watching the same space he was. Cyan shakes his head.

False alarm.

We all place our hands before us, one palm under the

other. Our elemental fragments float above our hands. I clear my throat as I start the ritual.

Speaking in Enkantian. Besides Eliana's ascension into the Afterlife, I haven't spoken the language for decades. I frown a little at some of my pronunciation. I can practically feel my mother reprimanding me for it. But, once everyone was gone, there just felt no actual point in continuing to speak it. It was just Cyan and me, not including the librarians.

But some things you just don't forget.

This recitation is from a timeworn ritual. Some phrases haven't been spoken for centuries.

Never mind.

No point dwelling. I kick my mother's grimoire by my feet shut. We all take a step forward and offer our frag-ments. They float up towards the tree, and we all step back quickly.

"Nobody moves," I growl quietly, reminding them we need to keep our positions until it has completely finished, no matter what.

We watch as the orbs float towards the tree, and the quietest hum fills the air. Finally, the spheres start circling the tree three times before stopping back at their original starting point and slowly melting into the tree.

The humming stops.

I hadn't realised how loud it actually was. The night is quiet, and the faint sound of crickets echoes through from the Melsheim Forest. Then, suddenly, the ground shakes. I draw my sword and glance around. Eliana has a flaming arrow ready. Cyan's got his Sai blades, swinging them in his hands. Chelsea has two orbs of water. And Tyler's got his whip uncurled, his knuckles white around the handle.

Then, the shaking stops, and the tree starts to glow as if the bark is translucent and has been lit up from the inside.

I look at Cyan. My heart feels light. He smiles back at me and gives me a nod. I remember the monthly rituals. Where our mother would coordinate each elemental to offer their element to the tree—different from a fragment ashis was just a simple conjuring of the element, like a fireball or a small whirlwind. The tree would glow just like this for two days before it faded. I return my sword to its sheath attached to my back and sigh, relieved that it accepted Eliana's sacrifice, even though she is alive. I walk over to her, taking her face in my hands.

"Are you okay?" I ask quietly as the others join us. Chelsea and Tyler are talking quickly, and Cyan stands, arms folded across his chest. His blades are still gripped tightly in his hands.

But Eliana is all I can focus on.

"I'm fine, really. That extraction was painful."

I smile down at her and press a kiss on her forehead. "It's over now," I say, and she pulls me close.

I close my eyes, taking in this moment.

It is finally over. I have fulfilled my promise to my mother. We have restored the magic in the Enkanti tree. A wave of relief crashes into me so profoundly it almost knocks me to my knees.

Cyan has avenged our sisters, Morana and Eliana by killing Edgar. Eliana's scent fills my lungs like a drug.

"Uh—guys..." Tyler's voice shatters my bubble of serenity. "Not to ruin this happy, feel-good moment, but..." An ominous *whoosh* shoots out from the Enkanti Tree as the light fades from a bright white to black and then goes out completely. "Is that meant to happen?" Tyler looks from the tree to Cyan and me. We both shake our heads, and my mouth falls open.

Fuck. What if it didn't accept the sacrifice?

I look at Cyan, who is staring at Eliana. *Is he thinking the same thing?* His eyes scan her body protectively, ensuring no harm came to her.

There's a rumble from deep beneath the tree when a small faerie crawls out from under one of the large, protruding roots. It unfurls its wings and flies straight to Eliana, who holds her hands for it to land on. She smiles lovingly down at it, completely unaware of their mischievous nature. It chatters frantically at her, but something has caught my eye. I draw my sword as a dark figure emerges from the alleyway.

"Umm... guys. Who let the mutants out?" Tyler asks nervously. I look over my shoulder as the Fae takes flight. Eliana's face has turned deathly pale. She looks as if she's seen a ghost.

Past her, everyone is on high alert. There are mutant Kailadons at every entrance to the centre of town. We're entirely closed in. There are easily over a dozen—too many for us to fight alone. I look back at Eliana, who's still frozen. I put my hand on her shoulder, giving her a slight shake. "What did the scout say?"

She looks up at me, her eyes almost black with how dilated they are. "They... They've rejected our offering. The Fae queen refuses to accept it. She refuses to help."

"We're fucked!" Tyler calls out with a flick of his wrist as the whip cracks through the air.

"Did the scout say *why* the queen rejected our offering?" Cyan growls angrily, looking in the direction the scout flew in as if he could reach out and grab the tiny creature and demand the answers himself.

"She said it was because mortals and witches have misused their powers and created monsters." Eliana jerks her chin towards the mutant Kailadons. "That we have unbalanced the scales of nature, that..." She hesitantly looks at Cyan. "That you deserve to be punished for capturing and torturing their kind." Finally, she looks down at her feet. "*AndthatEdgarkilledme*," she sputters, and it takes me a moment to unjumble what she said.

Of course the Fae are pissed that Edgar killed her. They would have been angered at her existence or accepted her as part of their kind. And by how Fae came straight to her, it looks like the latter.

"What do we do now?" calls Chelsea. I look over at her. She's shit-scared.

They all are.

Except for Cyan, who looks like he is ready to die fighting. Which is typical Cyan. He's always looked at death like an old friend.

Eliana looks up at me longingly. "We fight," she says simply. I am so proud of her in this moment. "We fight to make things right. We're stronger together. We stand together, and we right the wrongs of the past." Cyan turns to look at her, and damn, is he smitten. Eliana meets his eyes briefly, and I swear they exchange something in that glance between them. A blood-curdling screech fills the air as the mutant Kailadons storm towards us. We huddle together, weapons drawn, ready to fight.

"We fight for justice," I say as I glance at Chelsea and Tyler on my left, then at Eliana and Cyan to my right. I take Eliana's hand in mine and give it a firm squeeze. "We fight for love!"

GLOSSARY

Achel–God of Life as worshiped by the people of Datura.

Aeimweriah–An elemental shrine to those who have been lost. Generally, aeimweriah are gardens but can also be bowls/vessels of water or an altar of candles.

Ashga–Seven-foot-tall, long pointed ears, boney fingers, glowing golden eyes. Generally friendly. "Doesn't usually enjoy the taste of flesh" -Mallrie.

Bottle-O–Liquor Store.

Camel Bite–When one person squeezes another person's thigh region hard, resembling the bite of an actual camel.

Enkanti Tree–Large Oak tree at the centre of the town of Datura. The Enkanti tree is named after the coven of witches that were the first owners of this land.

Hypreslep–Time elemental magic that allows one to go slip into a deep sleep quickly. The magic slows that person's body clock down, allowing them to become well rested (between 7 and 9 hours) within a few minutes. The spell for this can be quite tricky and if not done correctly, can have the opposite side effects. (i.e. sleeping for long periods of time and waking to only have the equivalent of 1 to 2 hours of sleep) When one is in Hypreslep, they are in their most vulnerable state.

Kailadon–A large nocturnal flesh-eating monster. The Kailadon is unnaturally tall and skinny, a thin layer of reddish-brown flesh stretching across its bones. The Kailadon is faceless save for two slits for a nose and a large mouth that stretches from where one ear would be to the other. This mouth peels open as if someone is slowly unzipping it revealing needle point teeth. The Kailadon's arms are long and pointed like two knives and deadly sharp, perfect for slicing off their prey's skin to consume.

Lorkreig–A species of elves that live deep within the Melsheim Forest, their magic is deeply connected with the earth. Their magic allows them to be able to manipulate the earth but also to summon it like the witches.

Meshlynk–A large and vicious creature that hunts for sport. Its body is covered in moss and shrubbery giving it the perfect camouflage within the Melsheim Forest. It has long claws that extend from its fingertips and stag antlers protrude from its head. The shrubbery that is growing from its body also acts as a hood protecting its skull. The Meshlynk will flip back this *hood* to expose its grey skull and glowing red eyes. If one looks into a Meshlynk's eyes too long the creature can dig into your mind and take control.

Misnac–A large magical cat that is now extinct (except for Winnifred.) The large cats are usually tanned with black spots, with large ears and claws. Micnac's are very loyal creatures, once serving those of royal blood. The large cats possess their own source of magic which was why they were hunted due to the witches jealousy.

Sure as eggs–You are very certain something will happen.

Taking the piss–Slang meaning to mock at the expense of others, or to be joking.

Vid–God of Death as worshiped by the people of Datura.
Vraska–The place between life and death. The Fae watch over Vraska and make sure the souls travel to the correct Afterlife.
Yeah, Nah–Slang meaning yes.

PRONUNCIATION GUIDE

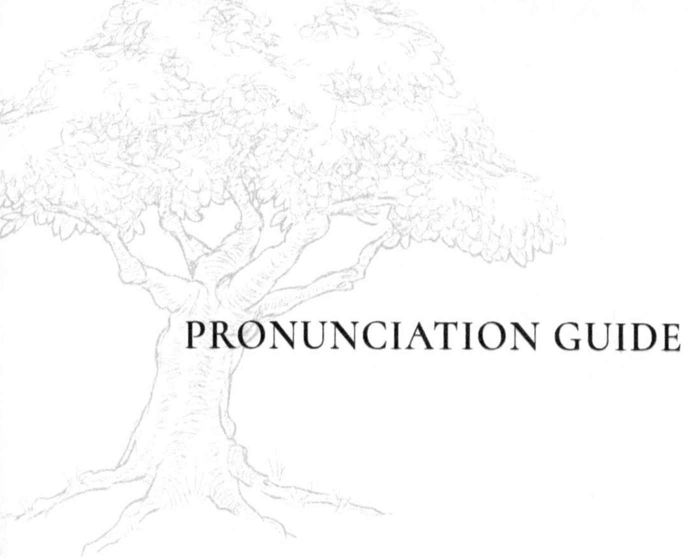

People

(Edgar) MacQuoid – mack-koid
Avark – a-v-arc
Cyan – ky-anne
Mallrie – mall-ree

Species

Ashga – ash-ga
Enkantian – en-can-tee-an
Kailadon – kai-la-don
Lorkreig – lor-kri-geg
Meshlynk – mesh-link
Misnac – mi-s-nac
Nechkrappe – ne-ssh-crap

Places

Datura – duh-chuor-ruh
Melsheim (Forest) – mel-shh-em
Vraska – v-ras-ka

ACKNOWLEDGMENTS

Where do I even begin? They say it takes a village to raise a child; I think the same can be said about writing books. When I started writing *Rise of the Witches*, the only person who knew was my husband, Alex. But a whole village of amazing people has helped transform *Rise of the Witches* from a thought and dream into what you're holding in your hands now, whether it's an eBook or a physical copy. So, let's dive into a quick-fire round of thank-yous and a round of applause for my little village.

First, Alex, thank you for your love, support, and unwavering belief that I could do this. Even when I was crying and ready to throw it all away, you were always there with gentle words and a shoulder to cry on. (And I think—or hope—that everyone reading this also thanks you for not letting me give up.) Thank you for taking on more work around the house so I could sneak away to write, edit, and edit some more.

To our beautiful children, Emily and Oskar, let this book be an example that you can do *anything*! (But don't read it until you're, like, 30!) Don't let anyone tell you that you can't pursue whatever your heart desires, because this book proves you can!

To Josh, thank you for your bravery in reading the first-ever draft of *Rise of the Witches* and for your encouragement. Your support was such an integral push for me to keep going.

To Briana, thank you for taking time out of your busy schedule to help me with that first round of edits.

To my parents, thank you for giving me the opportunity, as a child, to let my imagination run wild. For allowing my toys to spill into the lounge room and for giving me the freedom to create new worlds to dive into. A special thank you to my dad, Michael, for lending me his creative hand and drawing up these spooky monsters that now live rent-free in my head. They're genuinely terrifying, and I love them!

To all the amazing book babes I've met through Bookstagram and Booktok, thank you for letting me rant and rave about my budget zombies. And to my Writers Friday family—Lauren, Demi, Kaitlyn, Renee, Jen, Ashleigh, and Tom—thank you for all your love and support.

A massive thank you to the incredible team that supports me and ensures my books are the best they can be. To Brittany, my wonderful editor and cheerleader, thank you for your amazing work in polishing *ROTW* and making it shine. I've absolutely loved working with you again and can't wait to continue our collaboration. To Sarah (s.seidel.art), who is not only an insanely talented artist but also the sweetest and most supportive human being, thank you for bringing these characters and scenes to life. And finally, to Dom at 3 Crows Author Services for my stunning cover.

Lastly, to my readers, every single one of you, thank you! From the bottom of my heart, thank you for your love and support of this new author. Thank you for taking a chance on me and my book. I hope you enjoyed the ride as much as I enjoyed creating it.

ABOUT THE AUTHOR

Mel lives in Brisbane, Australia with her husband Alex and their two children, Emily and Oskar.

With an active imagination that can sometimes get her in trouble for imagining up unrealistic situations, and a joke made between Alex and Mel on a rare childless night out back in November 2021, Mel embarked on the journey of writing her own book.

Mel loves to spend time with her family but also enjoys curling up on the couch exploring new worlds as she reads a variety of books from different genres.

To stay up to date on new releases and bonus bookish content you can follow Mel on Instagram or sign up to her newsletter at https://www.mljewellauthor.com.au/

ALSO BY M.L JEWELL

Fall of the Witches

Signed paperbacks are available directly through M.L. Jewell's website:

www.mljewellauthor.com.au/shop/signedbooks

For a list of other stockists, visit:

www.mljewellauthor.com.au/stockists